Also by Laura Trentham

THE SWEET HOME ALABAMA SERIES

Slow and Steady Rush

Caught Up in the Touch

Melting Into You

THE COTTONBLOOM SERIES

Kiss Me That Way

Then He Kissed Me

Till I Kissed You

Candy Cane Christmas (novella)

Light Up the Night (novella)

Leave the Night On

When the Stars Come Out

Set the Night on Fire

The Military Wife

A Highlander Walks into a Bar

A Highland, Georgia, Novel

LAURA TRENTHAM

St. Martin's Paperbacks

This is a work of fiction. All of the characters, organizations, and events portrayed in this novel are either products of the author's imagination or are used fictitiously.

A HIGHLANDER WALKS INTO A BAR

Copyright © 2019 by Laura Trentham.

All rights reserved.

For information address St. Martin's Publishing Group, 120 Broadway, New York, NY 10271.

ISBN: 978-1-250-31501-4

Our books may be purchased in bulk for promotional, educational, or business use. Please contact your local bookseller or the Macmillan Corporate and Premium Sales Department at 1-800-221-7945, ext. 5442, or by email at MacmillanSpecialMarkets@macmillan.com.

Printed in the United States of America

St. Martin's Paperbacks edition / July 2019

St. Martin's Paperbacks are published by St. Martin's Press, 120 Broadway, New York, NY 10271.

8 7 6 5 4 3 2 1

Acknowledgments

It would have been impossible for me to write this book without my years-long obsession with British television. From the early days of watching Masterpiece Theater with my mom to *Top Gear* (and now the *Grand Tour*) with my husband and, of course, the *Great British Bake-off*. Honorary mention goes to *International House Hunters* which is always a fascinating peek into the homes of other countries. I hope I captured the flavor of the language difference between the UK and America even though we both speak English.

A special shout-out to Claire Scott, Scotswoman and avid reader, who provided feedback on the proposal for *A Highlander Walks into a Bar* to make sure Alasdair Blackmoor was authentic sounding.

A Highlander Walks into a Bar

Chapter One

"I brought home a surprise!" Rose Buchanan threw her arms out wide as if embracing the world. From the stories she told to the way she entered the room, Rose was exuberant and entertaining and enjoyed being the center of attention.

Isabel Buchanan, who was perfectly content on the fringes, pushed her wavy hair off her sticky forehead with hands that trembled from the nightmare drive through Atlanta to the airport to pick up her mom. Her mom's trip to Scotland had doubled as both research and vacation. The jammed stop-and-go traffic had left Izzy flustered and already dreading their exit from the airport.

Rolling her stiff shoulders, Izzy stepped around the bumper of the car, popping the trunk open on the way. Her mom had a beautiful plaid scarf of greens and browns and blues tossed over her shoulder and what appeared to be new earrings. Either purchase might inspire her mother to gush, and she would expect reciprocal gushing from Izzy.

Making an educated guess, Izzy asked, "Are those earrings your surprise?"

Without waiting for an answer, she hauled one of her mom's giant wheeled suitcases closer and prepared to heave it into the back. The sooner they got out of Atlanta, the sooner she could get back to work planning the Highland festival. Or she might pour an extra-large glass of wine and escape into a book. A guilty pleasure, considering how much she still had to get in order in three scant weeks.

"Allow me, please." A bearded man who had been rolling cases to the curb stepped forward with a grin and an accent Izzy couldn't place.

She checked her pockets and winced. No cash to tip the man, and no hope her mom had thought of something so inconsequential.

"Do you like them? They're hammered silver." Her mom flipped her bobbed matching silver hair to the side and displayed one earring with her fingers. "And as a matter of fact, I did buy them from a lovely shop in Edinburgh, but I brought something bigger home. Something more exciting."

"Your scarf? It's lovely." Izzy gave her mom limited attention while she watched the man load suitcase after suitcase into her trunk, fitting them together like a puzzle. More luggage than her mom had left with. She waved to catch the man's attention. "Hang on. That's not all my mom's stuff."

For the first time, Izzy really looked at the man. He was close to her mom in age, and good-looking in a bearlike way with a gleaming white smile highlighted by a salt-and-pepper beard. His full head of hair was a shade darker, but graying heavily at the temples. The expression on the man's face when he looked in her mom's direction—a mix of adoration and amusement—cleared the fog of confusion.

Lord have mercy, her mother had brought back a six-foot, two-hundred-pound-plus souvenir from Scotland.

Izzy stumbled backward, her heels catching on the curb.

She stumbled and was on her way to a bruised bottom—not to mention ego—when her mom's Scottish souvenir grabbed her arm and steadied her.

"Alright there, lassie?" His eyes were dark gray, not black but close, except for sparks of amber around the centers. He wore good-natured amusement like a comfortable sweater, and Izzy could imagine gathering around a fire and listening to him tell jokes and stories.

Izzy pulled out of his grasp and sidestepped toward her car. "Thanks for the save."

The man turned to her mom and held a hand out. She notched herself under his arm, the two of them facing Izzy as a united front. Instead of wilting from jet lag, her mom beamed at the man with all the energy of a college graduate on spring break. With his dark good looks and her mom being a certified silver vixen, they made a striking couple.

"Name's Gareth Connors." The man held out his free hand, and Izzy took it automatically in a shake. "Your mum has told me all about you, Isabel. I feel as if I already know you."

The burr in his voice was charming and attractive and friendly, yet Izzy couldn't get over the fact her mom had brought a man home. A man she'd known less than two weeks. It was impetuous and irresponsible and unreal.

Was Izzy dreaming? She swiped at her forehead again. Nope, not a dream unless the house had caught fire around her. The heat radiating off the concrete had hit inferno-like levels.

"I've invited Gareth to stay with us at Stonehaven. I'm going to show him around Highland. Everyone is going to adore you, darlin'." Her mom was too occupied straightening Gareth's collar to catch Izzy's pointed, panicked look.

A whistle blew and all three shifted to stare down the

sidewalk toward an airport security guard stalking toward them. They were taking too long in a loading zone.

Izzy froze. Was she actually going to bring a stranger home to Highland with them?

Gareth shut the trunk and nudged his chin toward the guard. "We'd best be going, Isabel, before the wee, angry man reaches us."

With one last glance at the security guard, Izzy made a decision she feared she'd regret in the dead of night with a strange man roaming the house with sharp cutlery laying around. "You might as well call me Izzy."

She slipped into the driver's seat, feeling like her sane, ordered—slightly boring?—world had skidded through an Enter at Your Own Risk sign. Even worse, her mom and Gareth had slipped into the back seat together.

"You should have warned her, Rosie," Gareth said. "We've shocked her."

"Don't be ridiculous. Izzy loves surprises, don't you, darlin'?" Her mother's singsong accent was Southern old-school genteel.

Rosie? Izzy shook her head to clear her shock. Even her daddy had never used a pet name for her mom. It was weird-sounding and spoke of an intimacy that seemed impossible after so short an acquaintance.

Izzy couldn't spare the attention needed to parse the new information coming fast and furious. She had to navigate out of the airport and back onto the interstate. Almost absentmindedly, she said, "*You're* the one who loves surprises, Mom. I hate them."

"Pish-posh. This is a *good* surprise though."

"Is it?"

Izzy glanced in the rearview mirror to catch an apologetic grimace reflected on Gareth's face. Her mom leaned close to whisper something in his ear, inspiring another of his merry-looking grins. If they started making out like teenagers, Izzy would pull over on the side of the road to separate them, life-endangering traffic be damned.

Cars and trucks weaved in and out of the lanes like in a video game. Her palms grew sticky on the steering wheel. The worst traffic jam in Highland, Georgia, had involved a standoff between old man Hicks and Mrs. Fortunato at the four-way stop in the middle of town.

As she exited the interstate for the two-lane road that weaved to Highland, her shoulders unscrunched and her fingers loosened on the steering wheel. The rolling green foothills of the Blue Ridge Mountains worked their usual magic.

Now she could keep an eye on the couple in the back seat without the danger of rear-ending another car. Her mom and Gareth were close, but not on top of each other, thank goodness.

Her mom was busy playing tour guide. She pointed out such scintillating roadside attractions like the "big rock" that teenagers spray-painted as a rite of passage and the boiled peanut wagon set up next to the pickup truck selling produce in a gravel pull off.

"Do stop, darlin'. Gareth must try the peanuts." Her mom touched Izzy's shoulder.

Izzy didn't say anything, but swung the car around on the two-lane road and pulled in next to the blue and white Ford truck with a bed piled high with summer produce. The farmer lounged on a metal foldout chair, fanning himself with a straw hat.

Izzy remained in the air-conditioning while Gareth and her mom took their time picking over what the farmer had to offer, coming back to the car with tomatoes, corn, and squash along with a steaming bag of peanuts.

"Izzy and I can whip up something delicious with the vegetables for dinner tonight, can't we, darlin'?"

She was to be their cook along with their chauffeur? "Sure, why not."

Her sullenness was a throwback to her awkward teenage years. Considering she still lived in the same town and in the same house—with her mother no less—the ghost of her doubt-riddled adolescent self took great pleasure in haunting her with regularity.

As the miles ticked down and while she had her mom and Gareth trapped in the car, she needed to ferret out what the heck was going on.

"Where are you from exactly, Gareth?"

"Cairndow. An estate in the Highlands. I'm the caretaker."

"It's simply gorgeous, Izzy. The views are to die for. Gareth lives in this quaint stone crofter's cottage, but he snuck me into the castle when the owner was away and showed me all the fun parts." Her giggle was shocking.

Shocking because her mom did not giggle. Or hadn't since her daddy had passed away a decade earlier. Izzy gripped the steering wheel tighter.

"How did the two of you meet?" she asked.

"We bumped into each other my first day in Edinburgh. Literally." Her mom tittered again, this time joined by Gareth's deep, resonant laugh. They already shared inside jokes. "I had stepped into a church to escape the drizzle as Gareth was coming out. We shared tea and biscuits and that was it."

"That was what?" Izzy asked.

"The beginning," her mom said cryptically, her smile directed at Gareth. "We spent every day together."

"When are you going home, Gareth?" Only after did her brusque tone register, and her face heated. Rudeness qualified as one of the deadly sins in her mom's eyes, alongside boasting and double-dipping chips. Injecting a practiced, albeit fake, politeness, she added. "It's a very busy time of year for us, and we need to be available to drive you back to the airport."

Her mom whispered, "Isabel," in the way she had when Izzy had disappointed her as a child. "We're taking things day by day, so who knows. Isn't that right, sweetie?"

Sweetie? Izzy stole another peek in the rearview mirror and tried to camouflage her dismay.

She slowed and pulled onto the narrow, winding drive that led to Stonehaven, their home. While Stonehaven might not be the biggest or grandest house in Highland anymore, it was certainly the most unusual. Built by her great-grandfather, who had emigrated with his parents from Scotland when he was a child, it payed homage to the castles of his homeland.

The stonework lent it a heavy, fortified feel from the outside with a turret in one corner, but it was only a façade. Inside, the house was warm and welcoming, and her parents had taken it upon themselves to modernize the electric, HVAC, and plumbing after they'd married.

From her first memories, her daddy had been the heart and energy behind the Highland festival hosted on the grounds of Stonehaven every summer. No one had expected him to die a week before his fiftieth birthday when she was only eighteen. Izzy had expected to have years—decades—before the weight of upholding the family traditions fell to her and her mom.

Instead, when she'd left Highland for college in Athens, Georgia, she'd carried with her the expectation of returning every summer to help and then moved home permanently upon graduation. She'd even given up the opportunity to study abroad one summer in order to come home, but had never laid her disappointment on her mom to bear.

The festival mimicked the traditional Highland games of Scotland. People from all over the southeast flocked to Highland to compete or watch men in kilts throw hammers and toss cabers. The traditional Scottish dancing, music, and foods were an even bigger draw.

This year's festival was on track to be the biggest yet and kicked off in less than three weeks. Izzy's job as a tax accountant slowed during the summer months, and she burned all of her vacation in order to plan and orchestrate the festival with her mom. It wasn't by luck. She'd put aside her dream of majoring in creative writing to pursue something practical. She hardly even thought about the might-have-beens anymore. The festival was her birthright, her burden, and her joy.

"What about the festival? You won't have time to take Gareth sightseeing, Mom." Izzy forced her voice to remain steady and adultlike when it began to dip into a childish whine. Pea gravel crunched under her tires as she pulled up to the front door of Stonehaven.

Her mom clapped once then linked her hands under her chin. "That's what makes this so perfect. Gareth can help with the festival."

"What?" Izzy performed an unintentional brake check.

"He'll bring a real authenticity to the games." Her mom was fairly batting her lashes at Gareth. It was like she'd been possessed by a debutante on the prowl.

"Wonderful. Excellent. Just peachy," Izzy muttered to hide her sarcasm. While not as egregious as rudeness, sarcasm and irony would earn her one of her mom's *looks*. The kind that still had the power to make her feel gauche.

"Your home is lovely, Rosie." Gareth's rumbly brogue was charming and warm, and fired mistrust in Izzy.

What was his angle? Izzy considered herself more worldly than her mother, whose last first date had been thirty-five-odd years earlier. As far as Izzy knew, her mom hadn't so much as looked at another man romantically since her daddy's death. Men like Gareth didn't leave their lives behind unless they wanted to . . . or *had* to.

Izzy glanced up to catch the reflection of him kissing the back of her mom's hand like a knight of yore. A blush pinkened her mom's cheeks, making her look younger and almost innocent. Izzy's insides performed a blue ribbon–winning jig, and her throat closed to nothing. Was this more than an extended vacation fling?

Darth Vader's theme song rang out from Alasdair Blackmoor's mobile. He whispered a prayer and gathered his strength before answering his mother's call.

"Hi, Mum." He kept his voice artificially chipper even though he was exhausted from a jam-packed workweek in New York City along with a banging case of jetlag.

"Don't 'Hi, Mum' me. Have you arrived at your destination yet?" The formality in her voice was nothing new. When he was four and home from his first day at pre-school, his mum hadn't asked him if he'd made friends or had fun. She'd asked him whether his day had been "satisfactory." He'd answered yes, even though he hadn't spoken to anyone except the teacher, and the conversation had been over.

"Not yet." He checked the navigation screen in his rental car. "Looks like another thirty miles."

"What could Gareth be thinking?" His mum's disappointment made him clutch the steering wheel tighter even though she was an ocean away and her disappointment wasn't directed at him. "Why isn't he answering his mobile?"

Gareth was probably thinking he was relieved to have escaped his sister-in-law's wrath by mere hours. Alasdair didn't say that aloud, of course. He'd learned from an early age not to actually express his anger or frustration or hurt. An Englishman's stiff upper lip dammed his Scotsman's passion.

"His mobile probably doesn't work on this side of the pond." Or he'd turned it off, which is what Alasdair had done more than once to escape his mum's well-intentioned meddling. He loved her dearly, but to label her as "high-maintanence" was an understatement.

"But why would he run off with an *American* tart?" His mum's derision gave the impression the American War for Independence had taken place in her lifetime. "What if she manipulates him into marriage, and she bears him a son?"

"Then we offer our sincere congratulations."

"Men can do that, you know."

"Do what?"

"Father a child in their dotage. Then, he would become the next Earl of Cairndow. When you see him, I want you to tell him that—"

"You're breaking up, Mum. I'll be in touch when I can." He hit the End button before she could get another word in and tossed his mobile onto the passenger seat.

He shifted and tapped his thumbs on the steering wheel. Driving on the wrong side of the road took concentration he was having trouble mustering.

His uncle's disappearing act worried Alasdair for different reasons than his mum. He didn't care if Gareth fathered a dozen sons as long as he was happy, but Alasdair refused to stand by and watch his uncle being taken advantage of. Despite the falling out they'd had a decade ago, Alasdair cared about Gareth more than he could put into thoughts, much less words.

For all of Alasdair's childhood, Gareth Blackmoor had been more than just his uncle. He had been a surrogate father and a friend and a general port in the storm. Alasdair had spent summers with Gareth while his parents traveled, and he'd chosen to retreat to Cairndow for many of his school holidays. Cairndow had been peaceful and grounding, and as much as Alasdair loved his parents, he'd hated navigating the chaotic mess his parents had created when they were together.

His parent's marriage had been tumultuous to put it mildly, ending when his father had lost control of his car on a curve and was killed on the road from Cairndow to Glasgow. Alasdair had been almost eighteen and headed to Cambridge, lacking the maturity to process the unearthing of his da's secrets and lies. Raw and shocked and overwhelmed, Alasdair had exchanged harsh words with Gareth. Words Alasdair had wished back a million times in the intervening years.

While they still talked sporadically—Alasdair was the heir to the title and the Blackmoor family estate—their once-easy relationship had acquired a patina of polite distance Alasdair hated but didn't know how to break.

How would Alasdair's sudden appearance to fetch his uncle back home like a wayward sheep be received? Would he be welcomed, or would their fractious family dynamic crumble? Would Gareth accuse him of only being interested in safeguarding his inheritance, or would he recognize that Alasdair cared about the man more than the title?

In fact, although he hadn't admitted as much to his mother, Alasdair didn't want the title anytime soon. Or at all, if he had the choice—which he didn't because of Britain's rule of primogeniture. The estate, however, could be willed to anyone, and Alasdair's mother was adamant Alasdair inherit it.

The estate, centered around the imposing Cairndow Castle, was striking and magical—and a money pit. Between repairs and modernizations, Gareth was forever brainstorming and implementing new strategies to bring in funds. Alasdair, on the other hand, lived in a no-maintenance flat in London and traveled monthly to New York for his work as an investment analyst. Even a houseplant had proved too much responsibility for him to handle.

Perhaps Alasdair should encourage Gareth's liaison with the "American tart," especially if he was happy.

Alasdair slowed, his mouth gaping as he took in the Welcome to Highland sign. It was a piece of art. Three to four meters square, the wood sign was hand-painted, the words in white calligraphy and set off with two men in Highland dress playing bagpipes while performing a jig (a near impossibility of lung capacity). Curlicues and scrollwork in greens and reds framed the picture. The detail was impressive, the colors vibrant, and he wondered at the time, energy, and cost it took to maintain the rustic masterpiece.

A horn tooted behind him, as polite and unassuming as a horn could be, and he pressed the accelerator, continuing into Highland, but slowing once more as he tried to take in the town. He sent a mental apology to the car behind him, but it pulled into a parking place in front of MacLean's Drug and Dime Store. Mimicking the look of the welcome sign, the Drug and Dime sign was wooden and old-fashioned, but not rundown. It was quaint, he supposed, if one appreciated such things. His flat in London embraced the black-and-white modernity of minimalism.

Baskets full of colorful flowers spilling over the sides hung from black wrought-iron light fixtures that sat at intervals on both sides of the street. Tartan ribbon circled the posts like a dozen maypoles, the tied off bows fluttering. The Scottish Lass restaurant graced one side of the street while the Dancing Jig pub caught his attention from the other. A placard out front announced live music on the weekends. A huge banner was strung from the top of a storefront to the opposite side of the street, announcing the upcoming Highland Games. Authentic Scottish food, dancing, music, and athletics were promised. The banner rippled in the slight breeze. The date listed was two weeks away. He'd be well gone before the fun started.

Tartan patterns of various hues were on signs and posters and used as bunting in most windows. Tartan was plastered on anything not moving—strike that. He spotted a man wearing tartan red trousers. It felt like a storybook street or perhaps even a movie set—he wondered for a moment if he was being filmed for an internet prank—but the people bustling along the sidewalks and ducking in and out of the businesses seemed real enough.

Highland was more Scottish than any village in Scotland.

Although it was a weekday, cars and trucks filled most of the slanted parking spots on both sides of the street. A coffee shop tucked into the row of shops called like the promised land. Alasdair wedged his rented sports coupe into a parking space between two massive four-by-four trucks.

The thick air made him feel like he was moving in slow motion, and a heat mirage wavered on the pavement like a portal to another land. He shook the fanciful thought away, stretched himself out of the car, and slipped off his suit jacket. The heat made it difficult to take a deep breath.

The air-con in the Brown Cow Coffee and Creamery veered toward arctic, giving him a shot of energy that he planned to boost with an espresso. Bagpipe music provided background noise, and the décor could best be described as Scottish kitsch.

With an obsession of all things Scottish on display, surely locating an actual Scotsman wouldn't be that difficult. Gareth would be a tourist attraction. The image of his uncle on a pedestal in the middle of town for all to admire plucked Alasdair's sense of humor. He would begin the search as soon as he had caffeinated himself.

The shop had a split personality. Along the left wall was the creamery, manned by a teenage boy bent over and scooping cones for a family of four, consisting of harried-looking parents, a young boy bouncing in anticipation, and a girl staring down at her phone and twirling her hair.

The coffee bar took up the right wall across from the ice cream. Hot and cold.

He veered toward the scent of freshly ground coffee, weaving through the round white tables dotting the middle of the shop. A half dozen were occupied by either pairs chatting or singles hunched over laptops.

A twentysomething woman with pink streaks in her hair sat behind the counter and eyed him around a customer she was helping, chewing gum with a slightly open mouth. He smiled and stepped forward when his turn came, rubbing his hands together. "Hullo, miss, I'm desperate for an espresso. Could you oblige me, please?"

"Well, butter my butt and call me a biscuit." Her words drawled out like stretched taffy.

"Pardon?"

Americans might speak a corrupted version of English, but it was still English even if her string of syllables didn't make sense. What did butter and butts and biscuits have to do with espresso?

She turned her head but never took her eyes off him. "Izzy! 'Nuther one of them foreigners has showed up."

A woman he hadn't noticed rose from a small table tucked to the side of the counter. An open laptop, papers, and a white coffee mug were strewn about. Her brown hair was twisted into a messy updo, tied back with a green and blue tartan scarf, wisps coming out in every direction in the back like a bird's nest. Finely arched brows framed eyes of indistinct color.

The woman approached, and the closer she got, the prettier she became, like a picture coming into focus. Her movements exuded a barely contained energy that reminded Alasdair of a brown wren.

"Are you acquainted with Gareth Connors?" the woman asked in a drawl that was more honeyed than the barista's but made about as much sense.

Alasdair uh'ed and ah'ed a few times to cover his confusion. *Connors*? Why had his uncle Gareth assumed the surname of the Cairndow groundskeeper? Presuming he had a good reason for the deception, Alasdair wouldn't rat him out to this stranger, but his hesitation at locating his uncle disappeared. Fair or foul, something was afoot.

"I do. He's . . . a mate of mine. I'm popping in for a visit actually. I don't suppose you'd be kind enough to give me his direction?" Alasdair deepened his brogue and smiled his most charming smile, reserved for receiving homemade jumpers from great aunts and his mum's surprise visits to his London flat. Americans usually ate it up. Especially American women.

The American woman in front of him looked not only unimpressed but as if she'd tasted something bitter. "Did he invite you?"

If he had to pinpoint her expression and tone, he would guess she suspected he was a thieving murderer. Not good. What was Gareth up to? "I'm in the States on business and heard he was here. Thought I'd look him up." Not a lie, although his loop from New York City to Atlanta to Highland was quite the detour to drop in on a "mate."

As the woman continued to stare at him as if he were the bearer of the bubonic plague, his smile faltered. He stuck out a hand. "I'm Alasdair Blackmoor."

Although he registered a split-second hesitation on her part, she took his hand. "Isabel Buchanan."

Her handshake was firm and no-nonsense, but her palm was soft and her hand small in his. On closer inspection, her eyes striated into all different shades of brown and amber, and freckles dusted her cheeks. He hung on to her hand for too long, but couldn't seem to pry himself away.

Breaking the spell, she wrested her hand from his, pulling it into a fist. Was she planning on throat-punching him? He rubbed his neck and took a step back, out of the radius of her magnetic energy, and her reach. On her approach, she'd seemed birdlike, insignificant even, but up close, he was having a hard time not staring like a first-class prat.

He was punch-drunk with exhaustion. It was the only logical explanation.

She stuck her hands into the back pockets of her jeans, stretching her red V-neck T-shirt tight. His gaze dipped instinctively and then stuck around to read the print on the pocket over the soft curve of her left breast: Highland. The Heart of Scotland in the Blue Ridge.

She cleared her throat. His gaze shot to hers, and he blinked to try to refocus his thoughts. "I was admiring . . . I mean, reading your shirt."

"It's not a novel."

His face heated. He couldn't remember the last time he'd blushed this hot and fierce. "Did Gareth secure a room at the local inn?"

"He secured a room at my house." There was a dry sarcasm in her voice that he might have found appealing in other circumstances. He'd always found women with a bite more challenging, and therefore more attractive.

As it was, Alasdair did his best to hide his consternation. While he couldn't fault his uncle's taste—Isabel was exceptionally pretty in a wholesome all-American way—imagining Gareth with her made his stomach stage a revolt. If his mum was correct, this woman was trying to seduce Gareth into proposing marriage.

"Are the two of you"—he made a leading hand gesture,—"serious?"

"Serious?" Isabel's confusion morphed to a combination of outrage and embarrassment. Pink rushed into her cheeks as she put a hand to her throat. "We're not *together*. Why would you think that?"

"He's staying with you."

"At my house. Not *with* me. Not like that. Actually . . ." Her eyes narrowed on him, but instead of finishing her thought, she said, "I can take you to see him. I don't think they've left yet."

He was only slightly chagrined at the relief coursing through him. The source couldn't be the fact that Isabel Buchanan wasn't exercising her considerable wiles on his uncle, but the fact that he'd found Gareth with very little trouble. "Thank you. I'd be most appreciative."

With her gaze constantly darting up to make sure he hadn't escaped—or maybe hoping he'd disappear?—Isabel retreated to her table to shove the papers and the laptop into a canvas bag.

"You still want that coffee, mister?" The woman behind the counter had watched their interaction as if they were starring in a reality show.

As Isabel didn't seem inclined to be sympathetic to his caffeine-deficient plight, he shook his head. "Unfortunately, I'll have to pass. Perhaps another time."

"Sure thing, handsome." The woman grinned around her gum. "You come on back and see me sometime."

Alasdair did a double take at her slightly salacious tone, but he didn't have time to worry over her intentions. With papers poking out of her satchel, Isabel swept by him on her way to the door. Something she'd said earlier gave his addled brain a kick in the hippocampus: *I don't think they've left yet.* Who was *they*?

He lengthened his stride to catch up with her, reaching the door the same time she did, their hands landing on the handle, his overlapping hers.

She pulled to open the door, but he held fast. The position put them close. He took a deep breath, the scent of honey and wildflowers distracting him from his questions. Did her morning routine include rolling around in sun-warmed flowers? If so, he'd like to watch.

"We're not going anywhere until you let go of the door, Mr. Blackmoor." In contrast to her sweet scent, her voice was tart.

He shoved his thoughts of flowers and fields and Isabel aside. Focus. Where was his legendary focus? "You said 'they.' Who is Gareth with?"

Her mouth thinned, her displeasure and disapproval radiating like shock waves. "My mother."

Chapter Two

Izzy took advantage of Alasdair Blackmoor's surprise and yanked the door open. The blast of heat and humidity was welcome after the chill of the coffee shop. Between the creamery and Mildred's preference for Siberian-like temperatures, Izzy normally avoided working in the shop, but her mom and Gareth's escalating PDA had driven her out of her own home.

Alasdair Blackmoor caught her wrist and forced her to a halt. He was overdressed for the weather, and for Highland, in a dress shirt with actual cuff links, a gray silk tie, and well-fitting, slim-cut blue slacks.

She tightened her hold on the strap of her bag and hoped he attributed her blush to the summer's heat. Lord help her, but the man was attractive—her gaze traveled up and over broad shoulders to meet a pair of gray eyes—and tall. His wavy dark hair was tousled in a way that might be contrived or natural. Tall, dark, and handsome. A walking cliché straight out of *Town & Country*, British bachelor edition. Was he a bachelor? Her brain got hung up on the question.

"I'm parked here." He thumbed over his shoulder. "I'll follow you."

For a hot second, she stared and knew she stared, but his ridiculously attractive accent had cast a spell over her as surely as Gareth had cast a spell over her mother. It was similar to yet different than Gareth's. Still Scottish, but less rough and more cultured to match his smooth shave and easy elegance.

Forcing a sharp edge into her voice to counteract her inappropriately gooey reaction, she pointed toward her daddy's old Ford truck—a relic of happier times and an advertisement for Highland. "I'm at the end in the truck."

Sometimes she drove the truck for the memories engrained in the worn leather seats. Sometimes she drove it because she needed to haul stuff. This morning she was glad to have the excuse of picking up card tables for the festival.

With her mother engrossed with all things Gareth, Izzy missed her daddy something fierce and wondered what he would say about the unexpected turn of events. The truck's AC hadn't worked in half a dozen years, and the engine had turned temperamental about catching in the last few months, but she refused to give her up. It would feel too much like moving on.

Alasdair Blackmoor's lips twitched. "That's something I've never seen in Scotland."

Her daddy had commissioned a special paint job when he'd spearheaded the start of the Highland festival twenty-odd years earlier. A red and black traditional tartan pattern decorated the hood, a swath down each side, and the tailgate. The rest of the truck was gunmetal gray. At one time, the tartan was shiny and bright, but time had dulled the color and left chips in the paint.

Tourists loved to honk in appreciation when she drove the truck to town, but she could imagine to an outsider like Alasdair, the truck looked garish and ridiculous. She was proud of Highland and what her family had helped build here, though, and a rare defensiveness rose.

"It's a one of a kind. People love it." She shifted her laptop bag and squared her shoulders. It didn't do much good. Alasdair was still a good six inches taller than she was. In a distinctly unhospitable voice, she said, "Well, come on if you're coming."

Planning the festival put her in contact with vendors and suppliers and the public. She was an expert at putting on a Southern smile of welcome and calm professionalism. Nothing about this situation made her feel welcoming or calm or professional. Agitation and unease were a potent cocktail that got her heart thumping too fast. What did Alasdair Blackmoor want?

She climbed into the truck, held her breath, and cranked the ignition, relaxing only when the noise under the hood settled into a low rumble. Alasdair had already pulled into the street and was waiting in his fancy silver sports car for her to lead the way.

Nerves had her goosing the gas pedal, and the truck streaked out of the parking space. With a yelp, she hit the brake with both feet. The truck rocked to a stop. She peeked in the rearview mirror. Alasdair Blackmoor's unhinged jaw was scarily close.

Shifting to drive, she led the way to Stonehaven, taking care to keep the truck between the lines and under the speed limit. What was wrong with her? It was like she'd never seen a good-looking man before.

She wasn't a total bumpkin. Holt Pierson was basically wearing a fluorescent sign flashing "ready and willing" to be more than friends. She could do worse, lots worse. Holt was good looking in salt-of-the-earth kind of way, but boring. Oh so, boring. But, then again, maybe that's because she'd known him since kindergarten, and he retained no mystery.

She'd even seen Holt's bare butt once (not half bad, if she was being honest) at a high school party on the river when enough alcohol had been imbibed to convince some of them to go skinny-dipping. Not her though. She'd stayed sober on the bank even though deep down, she'd wanted to jump in. She'd resigned herself to seeking adventure in her books instead.

Alasdair Blackmoor exuded sophistication and money and mystery. What was real and what was show? The threat level rose from moderate to high. She didn't trust Gareth, and a strange man showing up in out-of-the-way Highland, Georgia, looking for him didn't allay her suspicions.

Were they partners who planned to scam her mother out of money? While her mom didn't control a vast amount of liquid assets, she was land rich. The acreage alone was enough to make her attractive to schemers. Not that Izzy had ever worried about her whip-smart mother succumbing to a con artist. Until now.

She pondered her next move. She could lead him out into the woods where the low-slung sports car would get stuck in mud. Or she could hope Bigfoot was real and captured him. No, there was no use delaying the inevitable. At least this way she was in control. She wouldn't take her eyes off him. A devilish part of her chuckled and admitted that wouldn't be a hardship.

Turning onto the drive to Stonehaven, she glanced in her mirror, hoping he'd continue down the road past the Highland City Limit sign. He didn't. Bypassing the picturesque red barn where she would eventually unload the tables rattling in the truck bed, she joined him at the front of the house and approached him warily. He studied the house with his hands on his hips.

What did he see? A knockoff of a Scottish castle, or a house built with love and her family's history mortared between the stones? Would he laugh like he had at her truck?

He shifted toward her and took his sunglasses off, folding them and slipping them into his shirt pocket. "If the temperature wasn't registering somewhere around fiery pits of hell, I might think I was in Scotland. Brings back memories."

His smile knocked her suspicions off track. It was boyish and registered as sincere.

"Memories? Aren't you from Scotland?"

"I grew up in Glasgow, and only left when . . ." His gaze narrowed and looked beyond her until she wanted to glance over her shoulder. "I attended Cambridge and stayed in England afterward. I live in London now."

"That's why you talk like you do."

"What do you mean?"

"With a Scottish accent, but not like Gareth's."

His mouth pulled into a frown. "I never thought about it. Actually, my mum's English. My da was Scottish."

"Was?"

"He died in a car accident." His smile dimmed, his eyes squinting up at cloudless sky. The shot of intimacy left her off-balance, and she looked heavenward as well, as if both their fathers were beyond the great blue expanse.

"I'm sorry. My daddy died of a heart attack when I was eighteen. Sometimes it feels like longer, but then something will happen and my first thought is that I need to tell him, like my heart forgot he's gone."

At his silence, she dragged her gaze from the sky to find him studying her, his eyes serious and searching. Had her maudlin fancy revealed a vulnerability he planned to exploit? Until she figured out his game with Gareth, she had to remain alert and stoic.

She would do her best to quietly observe until conclusions could be drawn, logically and without emotion tainting the situation. Her mother certainly couldn't be counted on to be logical or unemotional. She was the definition of infatuated.

He loosened his tie and undid the top button of his shirt. The sun was brutal and the heat from the pea gravel could cook a potato. She cleared her throat and gestured at the front door. "Come on in before we roast."

She was uncommonly aware of him right behind her. The fringed rug tangled with the edge of her flip-flop and she staggered forward. He caught her around the waist, his grip even hotter than the sun outside. The near fall jolted her heart.

"Careful, now." A slight roughness in his voice hit her like a shot of Scottish whisky.

"I'm fine." She twisted her torso halfway around. This close, his height over her was emphasized and made her feel protected rather than intimidated. The golden circles around his irises sparked, lending warmth to his slate gray eyes. Familiarity panged distantly. She arched her back, but still he didn't let go.

Her blood quickened with something even scarier than fear. In a different time, she could picture him on horseback conquering a castle and claiming everything— and everyone—as his, and she wasn't sure she wouldn't willingly surrender.

"You can let go now." Her voice sounded like she'd sprinted a lap around the house.

"Of course. Pardon me." He stepped away and clasped his hands behind his back, his voice and veneer unruffled, whereas she felt as ruffly as her old Laura Ashley curtains.

Izzy led the way to the family area in the back of the house, taking care to keep her attention on where she put her feet. The hallway hooked a left, and they descended three steps to a sunken living area with an attached sunroom. Floor-to-ceiling windows showcased a stunning view of a flower-dotted field surrounded by tree-covered foothills.

Gareth and her mom shared a loveseat, their bodies angled toward each other, their heads close, talking softly. It was an old piece of furniture and had been her daddy's favorite. How many times had she seen her parents sitting just like her mom was sitting with Gareth? Izzy's heart sputtered along with her feet.

Alasdair's pace picked up, and he passed her. "Gareth?"

Gareth stood and took a step forward. Shock slackened his jaw before he shook his head as if clearing cobwebs. "Alasdair! Laddie, what in blazes are you doing here?"

"I'm, uh . . ." Alasdair glanced over his shoulder at Izzy. "I was in the States on business, heard you were here, and decided to look up an old friend."

Gareth's brogue was thicker than Alasdair's more refined version, but there could be no doubt as to their common birthplace. She sidled the periphery of the reunion to study the two men side by side. Their coloring was similar, but where Gareth was built like a bulldog, Alasdair had the lean grace of a panther.

A simple happiness at two friends reuniting did not materialize between them. In fact, an unspoken conversation seemed to pass between the two men encompassing complications and questions.

Gareth put his arm around her mom's shoulders and drew her forward. "Rosie, I want you to meet Alasdair Blackmoor. Alasdair, this is Rose Buchanan."

Her mom either didn't notice or was too polite to acknowledge the weird undercurrents and floated from under Gareth's arm to clasp Alasdair's hand in both of hers. "Lovely to meet a friend of Gareth's. Come and sit. Would you like some tea? Or would you prefer coffee?"

"Tea would be lovely, thank you. Jetlag caught up with me on the drive from Atlanta."

"Would you mind fetching tea for us, dear?" Her mom aimed a smile toward Izzy.

Normally, she wouldn't mind, but what if she missed an important, telling nuance between the men? Unable to produce a credible reason for not fulfilling her hostessing duties, she backed out of the den, only turning when her heels hit the first step.

In the kitchen, she rushed to get four iced teas poured and on a tray with a pitcher. She plopped the sugar bowl and slices of lemon in the middle and stuck a teaspoon in each glass. On the way back, she forced herself to take measured steps to avoid a mishap. It would be her luck to face-plant in front of Alasdair.

Her mom had maneuvered everyone into sitting around the coffee table. After setting the tray on the table with minimal spillage, she hesitated. Everyone had shifted as if a game of musical chairs had taken place in her absence. The only spot available in the conversational circle was next to Alasdair on the loveseat her mom and Gareth had occupied earlier.

She took the seat next to him, the old cushion dipping in the middle with Alasdair's weight. Her shoulder bumped his. She repositioned herself, but knocked her knee against his.

"Sorry," she muttered.

Her mom put lemon slices in two glasses and handed Gareth one before settling back into the chair to sip her own.

Izzy scooped several teaspoons of sugar into her glass and stirred, the tink of her spoon the only sound. Izzy turned to Alasdair. "I thought you were thirsty?"

"I am. Yes, of course. I'm sorry. It wasn't what I was expecting." He leaned forward, added a sparse teaspoon of sugar, and squeezed a lemon slice into his tea. His sip was less than enthusiastic. "I had a hot cuppa in mind, that's all."

Her mom half rose. "I can get you a mug of hot tea, Alasdair. It's no trouble at all."

"Certainly not." Alasdair waved her back to sitting. "When I'm in the States, I enjoy experiencing the local customs."

"Local customs" made them sound backward. Being a Southerner made her especially sensitive to jokes about no one wearing shoes or everyone using an outhouse or the lack of teeth. And absolutely no one of her acquaintance had married a cousin.

Izzy rocked slightly on the seat, trying to keep her agitation under control. "Southerners have been drinking tea this way since ice became available. It's refreshing during our hot summers."

"Iced tea is certainly refreshing, Miss Buchanan. It's just that hot tea has been Britain's drink since before your country even existed. The British empire was built on tea." His condescending politeness on top of him calling her Miss Buchanan like she was an old maid schoolmarm unleashed what her father had affectionately called her word salads.

"Fun fact: The British drank their tea hot, because of terrible water quality due to outdated sanitation practices. Basically, y'all had to boil your water or die of dysentery." Izzy had no idea why information popped into her head and straight out of her mouth without stopping for an edit. In the beats of silence that followed her fun fact, she dug the hole deeper. "Can you imagine having an intestinal infection with no bathroom available? The mess, the smell. I read that the Thames was basically a sewer for much of the nineteenth century."

"Isabel." Her mom shook her head and set her tea aside.

Gareth's booming laugh cut the rising tension. "Thank heaven for modern plumbing, eh? What do you think of Stonehaven, Alasdair? Doesn't it remind you of Cairndow?"

"Stonehaven is quaint and charming." Alasdair's word choice wiped out any good will he'd accrued outside.

"Quaint?" Izzy shifted on the seat, not sure why she felt the need to do battle when she wasn't sure what she was protecting, only that it felt in danger.

Her mom tinkled a laugh. "The Earl of Cairndow's estate is magnificent, Isabel. It makes Stonehaven look like a guesthouse. Do you work there too, Mr. Blackmoor?"

Alasdair and Gareth exchanged another pointed look before Alasdair said, "When I was younger, I did. Now I work in London with the occasional trip to the States."

"How excitin'." Her mother's Southern accent was lush yet delicate, her movements as graceful and captivating as a former ballet dancer's should be. She refilled Gareth's glass from the pitcher.

Although, her mom had tried to guide Izzy down the same path to glory, puberty had made clear that she'd inherited too much from her father, namely his spazzy energy and lack of anything resembling grace.

"When is your flight back to London?" Izzy swiveled her head toward Alasdair.

Her mom cleared her throat in a way that promised a talking-to later. "What my daughter means to say is that we hope you'll stay with us for as long as you're able. We have plenty of room, and I'm sure Gareth would love to have a friend from home here. He hasn't said, but I can tell he's homesick."

Her mom twined her arm in Gareth's and leaned into him as if she wasn't strong enough to hold herself up. Considering her mom had a hard-nosed instinct for business and was a feared negotiator with an honorary master's in manipulation, Izzy barely contained a hoot of laughter.

Gareth wore an adoring smile and stroked her hand. "You're too kind, Rosie." He transferred the warmth of his gaze to Alasdair. "You must stay, laddie. We have much to catch up on."

"That we do." The push-pull of another unspoken conversation had Izzy looking back and forth at them for a hint as to the topic. Finally, Alasdair said, "I would be delighted to stay a few days if it's not too much trouble."

"No trouble at all. Isabel will see that you're comfortable, won't you, darlin'?"

No trouble? Izzy sensed a heaping bushel of trouble—at least two hundred pounds worth—had landed square on their doorstep. She didn't know if Alasdair or Gareth were lying or not, but her instincts hollered for her to keep digging. If her mother was blind to the tension between the two men, then it was up to Izzy to discover the truth.

If looks could kill, Alasdair wouldn't have been surprised to find daggers protruding from various body parts. After grabbing his suitcase from the tiny boot of his rental coupe, he followed Isabel up a twisting flight of stairs. He'd half expected to be led down into a dungeon complete with shackles, but the room she gestured him into was warm and welcoming. A far cry from the musty, drafty, stone-walled room he'd occupied during his holidays spent at Cairndow Castle.

Touches of Scotland abounded. A green and blue tartan shot through with pink was folded at the foot of a four-poster bed covered in homey white eyelet pillows. A picture of windswept moors with Edinburgh Castle in the distance hung over a fireplace he couldn't imagine the temperature ever dropping cold enough to use. The modern hum of the air-con made the room feel like an oasis.

"I'm afraid we're sharing a bathroom. It's through that

door." Isabel pointed at a dark brown-stained door he'd taken for a walk-in wardrobe.

"I very much appreciate the hospitality, Miss Buchanan."

"Call me Izzy."

"But your mother called you Isabel."

"Yeah, but my friends . . . you're right. Call me Isabel."

He couldn't stop his lips from quirking up. Isabel's emotions were tattooed across her face. This one read "suspicious." Could Alasdair blame her? His uncle Gareth was certainly up to something. While the use of their longtime groundskeeper's surname had been surprising, Gareth's display of tender affection for Isabel's mother had been downright shocking.

He'd never seen Gareth show interest in a woman, much less be smitten by one, although he suspected he was viewing the present through a childish lens. Like most people, Gareth no doubt had a past—and present?—full of stolen kisses and crushes and broken hearts.

Alasdair nurtured his own suspicions about the Buchanans. Was Rose after Gareth's wealth or title? He'd run across his fair share of American women who were fascinated by British aristocracy even though the States had cast off such social mores two hundred years earlier. Rose was vibrant and charming and quite lovely for a woman of a certain age. But was his mum onto something? Was his uncle being manipulated?

Alasdair stowed his bag next to an ornate dresser and stepped to the window. It had the same view as the sitting room downstairs, but even more expansive from the higher floor. Covered with a lush green canopy of leaves and unbroken by development, hills extended to the horizon.

The beauty settled an ache in his chest. He glanced over his shoulder. "Does your family own all of this?"

Isabel stood in the doorway, her feet braced apart and

her arms crossed as if she were a medieval knight on guard. She softened at his question and joined him to peel one side of the curtains back, looking out the window alongside him.

"Stonehaven abuts a state park, so it's not all ours. You can't see it, but a river runs through the woods and marks our boundary." In a near whisper, she continued. "When I was a kid, I would sneak out onto the roof and dream about who and what might live out there. Fairies. Witches. Elves. I made up story after story. Daddy encouraged me to write them down."

With her hair wisping around her face and a tilt to her lips, he found himself staring at her instead of the view. Not only was she quite pretty, she was complicated. In the short time he'd known her, she'd displayed both a rigid loyalty and a propensity toward whimsical musings.

"And did you?" he whispered so as not to shatter the moment.

Her accompanying laugh was self-deprecating and attractive, but what struck him momentarily mute was her smile. A dimple creased her left cheek, lending her a charming asymmetry. Taken in concert with her sparkling eyes and the sprinkle of light freckles across her nose and cheeks, she magnetized his gaze.

Shaking her head, she turned away, and the loss of her smile made him want to reach for her. "They're stupid, childish stories. Not important."

He gave in to the impulse and caught her wrist, his thumb glancing over the delicate skin of her pulse point. Her heart was beating too fast. Or was that his?

"It's not stupid to dream." Even as the words left his mouth, it struck him that he was contradicting what he'd heard most of his life from his practical-minded mum.

His mum hadn't approved of his attachment to Gareth and Scotland and the old ways, and had encouraged his move to Cambridge and his rise at Wellington Financials. He had "excellent prospects," which was a phrase his mum batted around about many things in life—jobs, social standing, women.

How long had it been since he'd traveled from London to Cairndow to spend the weekend or even a night? Years. Somehow years had slipped by. Years he'd spent cultivating a career with excellent prospects that had left him exhausted and racing to a destination that seemed always just out of reach.

"I've outgrown make-believe." Her voice was brisk, but before she turned her back, the gaze she aimed out the window contradicted her statement.

"I won't be staying long, I promise." He felt the need to reassure her somehow.

She nodded briskly. "Good. Because we're busy getting ready for our Highland festival."

"Ah, I saw the banner in town."

"Yep. Mom and I plan and host it on the grounds at Stonehaven."

"That's generous of you."

She gave a half-shouldered shrug and fiddled with the hair at her nape. "We don't run it as a charity, although any profit we see is modest. It's a boon for the businesses in Highland though."

"Which came first, the festival or the name of the town?"

"The town came first. Founded in 1805. Scots settled all through the Blue Ridge Mountains. The festival didn't come about until the late 1980s, when the town needed revitalization." Her smile was polite, as if reciting facts for a tour. "I'll leave you to get settled and freshened up. Come on down when you're ready."

She pulled the door shut behind her. He stood there, debating his next move. He should give a minute for the hallway to clear, then find his uncle for a serious chat. Instead, he shuffled to the bed and toppled onto the mattress like a falling caber. Silence wrapped around him like the warmest blanket.

He let out a groan, toed his shoes off, and loosened his tie. After a week spent in airports and airplanes and hotel rooms with the noise of other travelers—strangers—around him, the serenity and welcome of the room was too much to deny.

His mobile vibrated in his pocket. The London office number flashed on top of a backlog of a dozen texts from his mum and coworkers. He tossed his mobile onto a chair in the corner, turned his back to the electronic appendage, and wallowed in the blankets. No honking horns or banging doors disturbed him. Birds sang and the breeze rustled the leaves of the trees outside his window.

He had things to take care of—namely uncovering the reasons behind Gareth's subterfuge—but putting a pause on his worries if only for a moment was blissful. He buried his nose in the pillow. It smelled fresh, like sunshine.

A soft knock on the door had him lifting his head. "Come in."

Gareth slipped inside and shut the door like James Bond on a scavenger hunt. "I was shocked to see you, laddie. How did you find me?" His voice was a gravelly whisper.

"Mrs. MacDonald ratted you out. Don't come down too hard on her though, it was Mum doing the interrogation." Alasdair propped himself up against the mass of pillows.

"That bloody infernal woman." Gareth's shoulders bowed up, emphasizing his bearlike physique.

Alasdair could hardly take offense of Gareth's opinion of his mum. After all, Alasdair had been dealing with the bloody infernal woman his entire life, but she did have her good traits—or at least, good for him. Devotion and a willingness to turn Machiavellian when it came to Alasdair were top of the list.

His mum, Fiona, and Gareth had been at odds for years, although early on they had maintained a truce. After the fracture of his parent's marriage and subsequent shocking death of his da, his mum and Gareth's relationship had devolved into a tense war with Alasdair as the prize. Alasdair had taken his mum's side, but now wondered what he'd surrendered because of it. His interactions with Gareth in recent years had been limited to updates about Cairndow.

"I was already in the States for work, and she sent me to round you up and fetch you home," Alasdair said.

"I'm not leaving. Not yet, anyway." Gareth moved to the window. "Dugan has things well in hand, and Iain is home giving him a hand."

"As a stopgap, Dugan is fine, but I thought Iain was deployed?" Dugan Connors was the actual groundskeeper at the castle and Iain his son. Dugan was a good, practical man, and Iain could fix anything, but neither had the patience or people skills to deal with tourists and tradesmen. Without Gareth's charisma and leadership abilities, the estate would suffer.

"He got out." A story lurked behind Gareth's simple statement, but Alasdair couldn't handle another family's complications when his was tangled beyond comprehension. "I'm having fun here in Highland."

"You are going home soon though, aren't you?" At the lengthening silence, Alasdair sat up and swung his legs off the bed. "Uncle Gareth?"

His uncle continued to stare out the window. Did he sense the same magic drawing Alasdair to the woods? Finally, Gareth turned with a smile, but his eyes didn't crinkle. "Of course I am. Although, I suppose it depends on your definition of 'soon.'"

"I thought we might fly out together in a couple of days."

Gareth crossed his arms over his chest as if preparing for an argument. "I'm staying at least through the festival. I promised to help bring an authentic Scottish flare. Why don't you stay too?"

Alasdair shook his head. "I have too much to do."

"Is that why you never come to Cairndow?" Gareth could have imbued the question with well-deserved disappointment, but he didn't. Only kindness lurked in his voice. Alasdair would have preferred the disappointment. Gareth's kindness inspired guilt and had Alasdair looking to his feet.

"After . . . everything that happened, it's complicated. You know that." They stood in silence for a few beats, and Alasdair knew they were both thinking about Rory, Alasdiar's da and Gareth's only brother. "Plus, my job at Wellington is demanding."

"I thought you bought up land like this"—he gestured out the window at the pristine forest—"bulldozed it, and plopped flats or shopping centers down."

"That's not—" He cut himself off. It essentially was what he did, along with other types of real estate developments around the world for his firm and its shareholders. He was paid well for it too. "I'm not here as a representative of Wellington," he added weakly.

"I would love for you to stay so we can catch up, and I'm sure Rosie would say the same." A pause hit before Gareth said softly, "It's been too long, Alasdair."

It had been too long, and standing shoulder to shoulder with his uncle made Alasdair wonder why he had allowed so much time slip to by, yet all he said was, "Isabel can't wait to see the back of me."

Gareth chuckled, but glanced toward the door as if Isabel might burst forth at any moment with an "A-ha!" and an accusing finger. "She's a funny one, she is. Watches me like I'm planning to pocket the silver."

"Speaking of deception, why are you masquerading as a bloody groundskeeper? Are you doing something underhanded?"

Gareth's smile fell. "Of course not. Rosie is a rare one, but I've been burned before by women only interested in the estate or my title. When Rosie and I met in Edinburgh, she assumed I was normal with no extraordinary burdens. I enjoyed the way she looked at me as a man and not a title. You know how it is."

Unfortunately, Alasdair did know. While he didn't advertise the fact he would someday be the tenth Earl of Cairndow, Debrett's listed him as heir and anyone enterprising enough to dig could uncover his lineage. Once a woman knew he was in line to inherit an earldom, including a picturesque castle on a cliff, he could never trust his instincts or her reactions. It had ruined relationships.

"Is that why you never married?"

Gareth stared off to the side, but Alasdair was sure he wasn't studying the wood details of the wardrobe. He was remembering someone, and it wasn't Alasdair's place to probe a tender memory. Protectiveness welled in Alasdair even though Gareth's hurt was in the past. He wanted to reach out to comfort his uncle, but the gap of distance and years seemed too vast in that moment to bridge.

"Any heartbreak is well behind me." Gareth shed the darkness like a cloak and everything about him lightened. This time his smile reached his eyes and lent a familiar twinkle. "The present is Rosie, and my promise to help with the festival."

"Where does the truth about who you are fit into your plans?"

His uncle had the grace to look chagrinned. "I never considered our dalliance would extend beyond the two weeks she was in Scotland. It was a lie that hurt no one, but then she invited me to Highland and I couldn't refuse. Didn't want to. I fear I've reached a point of no return, and she'll naught forgive me. I canna bear the thought. Will you keep my secret?"

The decision was made in a split second. All of Alasdair's best childhood memories centered around Gareth. Learning to ride and drive and fish. The peace and welcome and acceptance he'd experienced at Cairndow. The laughter and the tears and the triumphs they'd shared.

His uncle had more than earned Alasdair's love and loyalty and was more important than any new shopping center or housing development or promotion. An opportunity to heal the past was his to claim. Time and maturity had softened his memories.

Alasdair would stay, whether Isabel Buchanan wanted him around or not, to rediscover the connection he'd once shared with Gareth. And in the process, Alasdair would make certain his uncle wasn't hurt again.

Chapter Three

Izzy pressed her ear harder against the door separating Alasdair's room from their shared bathroom, but the duet of male voices rumbled indistinctly. Although perfectly mundane explanations presented themselves for the closeted reunion, suspicion lurked in the forefront of her mind.

The tension between the two men had been weird, and the age difference between the "old mates" even weirder. Not that it was impossible to have a friend thirty years older, but it was certainly unusual. What did they have in common? What did they talk about?

Did Alasdair suffer from bunions or hemorrhoids or gout? Did he worry about his retirement funds or like to yell at punk kids to get off his lawn? Not that Gareth seemed the type to worry about such things. He was young at heart, just like her mother.

Izzy absolutely, positively couldn't ask Alasdair whether he had hemorrhoids. Trouble was the thought was planted and the question likely to pop out in an awkward moment. She closed her eyes. Thinking about Alasdair and hemorrhoids brought forth a picture of his butt outlined in his slim-fitting pants. It was an incredibly nice butt. Firm looking and round, but not too round. And most likely hemorrhoid free.

Stop it, she mouthed as if that would have any effect on the whirl of her brain. She might have banged some sense into her head if it wouldn't have drawn attention to her snooping. Alasdair discombobulated her.

Even worse, she'd almost told him about her writing. Not about the silly stories she'd made up as a kid, but her years-long, so-far-unsuccessful quest to write a great Southern novel like Eudora Welty and Harper Lee and Flannery O'Conner. She glanced at the closed laptop on her nightstand. It was hard to find the time to tweak her current manuscript this time of year—which felt like a blessing at the moment.

While the constant stream of rejections hitting her in-box were depressing and discouraging, she had carried on until the email last week had her considering actually giving up once and for all. "Trite and amateurish." The words haunted her. It might not be stupid to dream, but it was feeling more and more like a waste of time.

She became aware of the silence on the other side of the door. Had they formulated their (possibly) evil plans? The door opened. With her weight still tilted into it, she head-butted Alasdair Blackmoor in the chest. His breath escaped in an *oof* and he took a step back, unbalancing her further. She grabbed hold of his tie with one hand, his shirt with the other.

She took a deep breath. His tie was loose and his shirt was unbuttoned, revealing the hollow between his collarbones. His scent was enticing yet subtle. Would he notice if she nosed the skin at his collar to capture the elusive spices? His shirt was soft and smooth, the muscles underneath firm. She imagined charting every ridge and dip like Lewis and Clark.

"Good grief. Sorry about that. I was . . ." She won the battle (barely) to keep her face out of his neck and lifted her gaze. Unfortunately, it got stuck on his mouth. Her mind blanked.

"You were . . . ?" His lips moved. They were well defined, the bottom curve lending an unexpected sensuality to his masculine features.

His jaw was strong, his nose patrician, and his cheekbones broad. Taken together, he was handsome, but not in the classic sense of a movie star. He was handsome in a more aggressive way that made her think that under his sophistication he knew how to get down and dirty between the sheets. Danger awaited her if she continued down that rabbit hole.

His thick, dark brows were lifted in expectation. What was he expecting from her? Oh yes. An answer to what she'd been doing pressed against the bathroom door. She searched her brain, but found an empty warehouse. "I was . . . stretching."

"Stretching?"

"Bathroom yoga. It's a thing." Was it? Weirder fads existed on the internet. "I'm just getting into it so I'm not very good yet." Her tongue seemed determined to further embarrass her.

"I enjoy yoga myself."

She made a humming sound. Of course he did. It was probably how he stayed so lean and hard. How flexible was he? Her hand opened and flattened round his torso as her imagination wallowed in the inappropriate thoughts.

"Maybe you could show me your moves." His brogue had roughened. No wonder generations of women had fallen at Sean Connery's feet.

"What moves?" She had a dearth of moves. Men were supposed to make the first move. At least, that's the lesson she'd learned from James McFarland when she'd asked him to the Sadie Hawkins dance in eighth grade, and he'd rejected her.

"Your yoga moves?" His voice dropped yet another octave. Something in her chest vibrated like a cat purring. He was close to laughter—at her expense, of course—yet, she couldn't locate any indignation.

"Ah, those moves. Yeah, they're pretty special."

The corners of his sharp eyes crinkled, and one side of his mouth rose higher than the other in a boyish smile. That was the only part of him that felt boyish. The rest was all man. The heat blazing a path through her threatened a five-alarm fire.

She forced her hands from his shirt and tie, thumbed over her shoulder, and shuffled backward. "I'll give you a lesson another time, I need to . . ." Now her thoughts were a desert, barren of coherent thought or logic.

"Wash your hair?" He propped a shoulder on the doorjamb and crossed his arms over his chest. The crazy thing was while he had every right to be annoyed, he didn't demonstrate anything other than amusement.

"Water my flowers, actually."

Another lopsided smile squirted lighter fluid on the blaze he was kindling inside of her. "Do you water that huge field of wild flowers?"

"Of course not. I have pots. With flowers in them. Obviously." She bit the inside of her mouth. This was going great. Real smooth.

"That makes more sense, although it's easy to imagine you . . ." This time it was Alasdair who seemed to lose track of his words. His smile disappeared, leaving behind the man with the steely eyes and aloof air.

"Imagine me what?"

"Not important. I'll be sure to knock next time. Please, take your time."

"I'm done. It's all yours." She closed the door on her side

of the bathroom, grabbed a magazine off her nightstand, and fanned herself, imagining him undoing his clothes button by button. With the noise of the running water masking her movements, she slipped out of her room. Not that Alasdair had his ear pressed against the door monitoring her movements like the fool she was.

She skipped down the stairs as if chased, only slowing when she stepped outside. Closing her eyes, she lifted her face to the sun. As far as she knew, the earth was still in rotation and hadn't spun off course. Nature exerted a grounding force on her suddenly topsy-turvy world.

This Scottish invasion couldn't have come at a worse time with the festival fast approaching. Alasdair's disruption had put her behind on her day's to-do list, yet she couldn't locate the concentration she needed to sit down and work.

The mindless task of watering her pots left her with time to dissect what she'd discovered, which was pathetically little. Gareth and Alasdair shared a secret, but whether it involved her mom or Stonehaven or (less likely) hemorrhoids was still in question. Searching his things would be crossing a line, and staging an inquisition would be too obvious.

The truth had a way of emerging like flowers pushing out of dark, cold soil in spring, but she was too impatient to allow events to unfold.

"And here I thought you were feeding me a load of codswallop." Alasdair's voice made her breath catch as she swung around. Water splashed onto his fancy brown shoes with the elaborate stitching. He high-stepped out of range, shaking his feet.

"Sorry! You startled me." Izzy dropped the hose and ran to turn the spigot off. "Is codswallop a Scottish delicacy? Highland might be billed as the Heart of Scotland, but our stomachs are pure Southern."

She got two nonplussed blinks from him before he erupted into laughter. "Codswallop is rubbish. Lies. Not something to eat."

The smile she tried to stifle broke free. It was hard to remain stoic and cold in the face of his good humor. "You can't blame me for thinking it's something you Scots might eat." She gave an exaggerated shudder then waved toward his shoes. "Leave your shoes out here. They'll dry in a jiffy in this heat. I hope they aren't ruined."

Alasdair shuffled backward into an all-weather lounge chair, toed his shoes off, and stripped his socks, water dripping. "They've survived countless London downpours. A Georgia drenching won't matter."

His comment was yet another reminder of their difference in geography. He rolled up the wet bottoms of his pant legs while she wound the hose back up and said absently, "You're going to mess up the crease in your britches."

He stretched his legs out, crossed his feet at the ankles, and linked his hands behind his head, tilting his face to the sun. With his sleeves rolled up to his forearms and barefooted, he was a far cry from the buttoned-up sophisticate she'd pegged him as in the Brown Cow.

"I suppose I'll survive without a perfect crease in my . . . what did you call them?"

"Your britches."

He smiled the charming crooked smile from earlier. "You talk funny."

The way Alasdair said it didn't make her think it was an insult. "So do you. I thought you came to New York on business all the time. I'm surely not the first American you've met."

"I'm in New York once a month." He tilted his head and squinted at her. "I've never met anyone like you up there."

His phone dinged from his pocket with an incoming

text. He ignored it, but she could see it cost him a certain effort. Another ding. Then, another. With a sigh, he pulled his phone out, glanced at the screen, then flipped a button on the side.

"Who are you blowing off?" She nudged his chin toward his pocket.

He hesitated, and she tensed. What if he said girlfriend or wife?

"My . . . mum among others."

"Your *mother*?" She couldn't stem the disbelief sailing her voice into the stratosphere.

"Did you think I sprang from moldy cheese or something equally as horrid?" His dry self-deprecation only made him more attractive—which was inconvenient considering he was a potential mortal enemy.

"I'm partial to a good gorgonzola," she sparred back playfully.

His laugh was a rumbling pleasant sound.

"Do you and your mother not get along?" she asked. "Is that why you're ignoring her?"

"Mum loves me. At least I'm pretty sure her exacting ways are born from love. She can be rather maddening."

It was yet another peek into his personal life. Or was it? She didn't have much experience reading liars. Old Mr. Brown, who spent his mornings in a rocking chair playing checkers out in front of the Drug and Dime, told anyone who would listen that his grandpappy had buried a fortune on his land, and he should be living in a big house instead of a trailer. Everyone knew he was lying to make himself feel bigger in town, but no one called him on the harmless delusion.

If Alasdair was a liar, he would be a talented one. She had a feeling he would be good at anything he put his mind to, even lying.

"Is your name really Alasdair Blackmoor?" she asked.

His eyebrows rose, but she couldn't detect any outrage, which was troublesome in itself. "Search my name on the internet if you don't believe me."

Dangit. That's what she should have been doing instead of listening at his door like a ten-year-old. Actually, these days a ten-year-old would have known to head straight to the internet for information. "Maybe I will."

"Fine." They stared at each other until he nudged with his chin. "Do it right now to settle your mind."

She slipped her phone from the back pocket of her jeans and typed his name in her browser, glancing up periodically to see if he was preparing to make a run for it. His expression remained bland. Several hits came up on her phone. Scanning the first page, she didn't see a police bulletin among them. She tapped the first link.

"You work for Wellington Financials?"

"As an acquisitions and development risk manager."

"Sounds interesting." Now it was her turn to lie, but it was a polite white one.

"I'm not exactly changing the world, but it's challenging." He didn't sound bitter as much as resigned. "I identify and determine whether an acquisition is worth the risk of investment. If it is, then we develop it for commercial use."

"Risk manager. Are you a risk-taker by nature?" She tried to read him, ready to Dr. Freud his answer.

"No." He switched his unblinking focus from her to the tree line off in the distance. "At least, not anymore."

Unable to gain insight from his answer, she huffed and followed his gaze to the expanse of virgin timber. "Are you counting all the houses and stores you could fit if you bulldozed the woods?"

More than one real estate developer had offered them a fortune for their land. Her daddy had chased one particularly persistent gentleman off with a shotgun. Izzy took a more sugared approach, taking their cards with promises to consider their offers but never returning their calls.

"Actually, I was wondering what sort of costs are associated with owning so much land in the states." His gaze was back on her and absent any sentiment. He looked ready to perform a risk analysis on her.

"The games help defray the costs." Without the games, they would have to sell off parcels to keep Stonehaven solvent until there would be nothing left. Her salary as an accountant was a pittance compared to their property taxes and upkeep, which made them vulnerable.

"Maybe I can help."

"What are you talking about?" Had this been the plan all along? Gareth would butter her mom up and gain her trust, then Alasdair would swoop in to make an offer for their land? His charm had breached her guard. She poked a finger into his chest. "We're not selling."

A flash of surprise crossed his face. "You misunderstand. I wasn't speaking as a Wellington employee, but a Scotsman. I've been to the real Highland games. I could help make yours more authentic."

"I don't need your help." Only after the words were out did her rude tone register. "Mom and I have been planning the games together for the last decade. We can handle it."

"I have no doubt you can, but Rose seems distracted by Gareth this year."

He was right. Her mom had already dropped the ball on confirming the food trucks, and Izzy had had to scramble to get commitments. Haggis and potato cakes would not satisfy the diverse crowd. "I have things under control."

She almost believed it. Before the stress and worry could transmit to him, she did an about-face and walked toward the field of flowers. Not picking up the elephant-sized hint, Alasdair fell into step with her. She clenched her jaw and looked the other way. If she ignored him, would he leave her alone?

"Gareth is a good man." His voice was thoughtful and lacked any defensiveness. She glanced his direction. He stared toward the horizon, his hands clasped behind his back.

"I never said he wasn't."

"You don't trust him with your mother."

"To be fair, I wouldn't trust anyone with Mom. Except Daddy." As it was clear she wasn't going to shake him, she halted. Wild tiger lilies swayed around them as if they were in a rolling sea of flowers. The beauty and tranquility did little to alleviate her low-key anxiety.

"He's been gone for a long time." His annoyingly calm voice annoyed her.

She tried to get a handle on her tongue and failed. "But not forgotten. By me, at any rate."

Wanting to kick herself at the admission, she crossed her arms over her chest. She'd given him insight to use against her. It was supposed to be the other way around.

"You're worried your mother has forgotten him."

He had laid her fears out in the starkest of terms. Betrayal twinged in her heart watching her mom and Gareth together. Her attitude made no sense, and she would never admit it aloud, but Alasdair was able to verbalize the ugly feelings she fought. Her gaze skittered down as if her shame were a physical ooze welling at their feet.

The scrunch of his toes in the grass cast her back to childhood when she'd spent her summers wandering the woods barefoot with only her imagination as companion. The grass and dirt would be cool, and for a moment, she wanted to kick her flip-flops off and run into the woods to discover what simple adventure awaited.

"It doesn't matter. You and Gareth will be gone soon

enough. Right?" Pushing her shame away, she hardened her gaze and tipped her chin up to meet his eyes.

Alasdair's expression was serious, but otherwise inscrutable. "Right you are."

She sensed an opening to redirect the questioning. "How did you and Gareth become such good friends?"

"We're both from Scotland." Alasdair rolled his shirt-sleeves higher, revealing a few more inches of taut skin.

"Everyone from Scotland is friends? How many million is that again?" She layered her sarcasm on thick.

"My da and Gareth grew up together."

"That doesn't explain how you and Gareth became such good friends."

"I spent my school holidays and summers at Cairndow with Gareth growing up. He never married. No kids. He taught me how to shoot and sail and swim. It was a treat to get out of Glasgow."

Their families must have been very close. Still, she couldn't imagine her parents sending her off for an entire summer. They'd been like the Three Musketeers. "So he's kind of like your godfather?"

"Something like that." It was clear the subject was a sore one and it wasn't her place to pick at the scab.

She cleared her throat to steady her voice. "Dinner will be around six. I have some festival business to handle. Feel free to borrow a book or watch TV in the living room."

"Thank you." He inclined his head, his tone formal and devoid of emotion.

She walked away and didn't look back or break stride until she entered the office she shared with her mom. The piles of papers on Izzy's desk looked chaotic, but they were segregated into logical piles. Stonehaven business was one pile—tax information and estate upkeep mostly. Another pile was work related to her accounting job. Her current manuscript was in a folder for her to edit with a red pencil. The tallest pile at the moment involved the festival.

In contrast, her mom's area was neat with only the bare essentials cluttering the desk. An unusual layer of dust marred the stained-glass panes of the lamp on her desk, and even stranger, her mom hadn't even noticed.

While her mom and Gareth had spent the week gallivanting around north Georgia, Izzy's to-do list had doubled. Things needed to shift back to the way they were that instant. Izzy was a big talker, but the truth was she couldn't do it alone.

She would put her foot down and force things to return to normal. She strode to the doorway and took a breath to holler for her mom. Before a sound escaped, the sight of her mom and Gareth ascending the stairs side by side, their heads close, squeezed her lungs like a vise. Her mom touched Gareth's beard with an undisguised tenderness.

Izzy closed herself behind the office door, slid to the floor, and buried her head in her arms.

Chapter Four

Isabel had retreated like a general at war, her stride long and her back straight. It was clear she didn't trust him one iota. Alasdair let out a long sigh, relieved her internet search hadn't delved deeper than his job at Wellington. If she'd scrolled further into the search results, she might have turned up his lineage and the direct bloodline connecting him to Gareth. Part of him almost wished she had discovered he truth. Lying didn't sit comfortably on his conscience. It made him feel squashed into a corner.

Yet, hiding poorly behind her suspicions was a sense of humor that had him smiling even now and a vulnerability that had made him want to take her in his arms. Or was the electricity that thrummed between them behind his wish to wrap his arms around her and bury his nose in her hair?

Alasdair let out a sigh and rubbed his jaw. His suspicions equaled Isabel's. She had been cagey with him, but he'd learned a few things. For one, Stonehaven's fortunes hinged on the festival.

Alasdair understood more than most how expensive maintaining a large estate could be. While Stonehaven didn't face the same issues as Cairndow, old houses and land devoured money at an alarming rate. Was it coincidence, fate, or intentional that Rose had found Gareth only weeks before the Highland, Georgia, festival?

Alasdair scrunched his toes in the grass and flowers. Bees flitted around him, darting from flower to flower. The scent was reminiscent of the hours he'd spent roaming the cliffs and moors around Cairndow. The best and most indelible memories from his childhood originated with Cairndow and Gareth. The Scottish games he'd attended with Gareth growing up had been the highlight of his summers.

Another memory inked the light with dark. It hadn't always been just the two of them. His da had been there one summer. The distant, shadowy figure on the edge of his memory resolved itself into flesh and blood.

His da had got smashed in one of the tent pubs. A fight erupted. Gareth had tucked Alasdair out of the way before striding into the melee like some ancient laird, his kilt swinging along with his fists to defend his kith and kin.

His pride for Gareth had equaled his embarrassment of his da. But like always, his da had brushed off the incident. It became a lark and it had been easier for Alasdair to forget. Except, he never actually forgot; he ignored it. He was like his mum in that way, he supposed. She had done too much ignoring over the course of her marriage to his da, and it had hardened her.

The sun inched toward the tree line, and Alasdair drew in a gusty breath. A sense of contentment blanketed him in spite of his worries. It was only when he named the feeling that he realized how long it had been since he'd experienced it. His work days were spent on the edge of spinning out of control. The first few years had been thrilling, like a roller coaster, but now he was exhausted.

The breeze sent a flower brushing against his hand, and his mind reeled back to Isabel. It was difficult to imagine her plotting and scheming unless she was protecting someone she loved. Or some*thing*. Stonehaven made a pretty picture against the deep blue, cloudless sky.

Was the estate in financial trouble? She'd certainly bristled when she thought he was probing too deeply. The resources to dig up and parse all of Stonehaven's financials were at his fingertips. He reached into his pocket for his mobile, ignored the unread messages, and fired off an email to one of the analysts who worked for him. By the time he woke in the morning, he would know how much the Buchanans spent on toilet paper.

He checked his watch. Dinner would be served soon. Showing up without a token of appreciation went against the rules of decorum his mum had drilled into him. He plucked a variety of flowers to form a bouquet of wild colors.

Unable to do anything at this point but wait for information, he ducked into the kitchen with his bouquet. Mother and daughter were side by side at the stove engaging in a whispered conversation. He cleared his throat.

Isabel cut a glance toward him before refocusing on the skillet of sliced squash she was tending. Whatever she and her mother had been discussing had left her emotional. His stomach lurched toward her, and he found his feet following.

Rose intercepted him, a lingering disquiet dimming her smile. "How lovely. Let me put them in water." The haphazard array looked incongruous in the heavy crystal vase.

He shifted and glanced at the stairs. Where was Gareth? "Can I do something? I'm a dab hand in the kitchen."

Rose was friendlier and less suspicious than Isabel, who was examining him with a worried crinkle between her eyes. "What's your specialty?"

"Sheperd's Pie."

"That's Izzy's favorite dish at the Dancing Jig, isn't it, darlin'?"

"Comfort food." Isabel shrugged. "I'm a fan."

"Me too." Alasdair and Isabel exchanged a glance of pure understanding, before she turned away.

"Twenty minutes until dinner. Would you rather freshen up or open a bottle of wine?" Rose asked.

If he went upstairs, he wouldn't be able to resist being sucked into a vortex of work and it would take hours to sort out his inbox. "Wine. Definitely wine."

As if the pop of the cork reverberated through the house like a dinner gong, Gareth joined them. The talk was small and inconsequential, yet Alasdair was more relaxed than he'd been in years. He watched Isabel watch her mother and Gareth flirt and exchange small touches.

Ovenlike temperatures kept them indoors for dinner. Alasdair was grateful, not having the wardrobe or the stamina for the heat. After finishing a tender, breaded pork chop and fried squash, he took a sip of wine. "And I thought New York was steamy this week."

Gareth pushed his plate away and folded his arms on the heavy wooden table that had no doubt seen countless family dinners at Stonehaven. "Even at the height of summer, Scotland can be downright chilly."

"Do you like our Southern climate?" Isabel asked, her gaze intensely focused on Gareth.

"Aye. While I love Cairndow, I've lived with the cold and damp all my life."

"Have you worked at Cairndow for a long time?" Isabel leaned forward, her hands flat on the table as if interrogating him.

"I was born on the property." Gareth's smile was faraway and melancholy, his gaze darting to meet Alasdair's for a blink before dropping. "Me and my brother both."

"Did your brother stay close to home?" she asked.

"He couldn't leave Cairndow fast enough. He's passed on now." Gareth shook his head. "As different as we were, I still miss him."

The loss of his da had left a hollowed-out place in Alasdair's life and history, but with a youthful selfishness, he'd never stopped to consider Gareth's loss. Gareth had lost a playmate, a friend and a brother—an incalculable vacuum left behind.

Rose tucked her hand inside Gareth's, and he raised it to kiss the back. Alasdair hadn't pegged his uncle for the romantic, demonstrative sort, but then again, he'd never seen Gareth woo a lady.

"Everyone has losses, don't they?" Isabel's rhetorical question was weighted with a sadness Alasdair carried himself.

Rose steered them to lighter topics with the deftness of an expert hostess. They discussed world events and politics. They laughed at the differences in customs and speech between Scotland and America.

With everyone's plates cleaned, the conversation stalled. Alasdair half rose. "Allow me to clear the dishes."

Isabel cut her gaze to him before focusing on Rose. "That'd be great. Mom and I could use some time to work on some details on the festival."

Rose's hand fluttered to land around her neck. "Oh dear. I promised Gareth an evening at the pub. The Lowlanders are scheduled to play."

"Mom! You're *killing* me. You've got to talk to Loretta about her deposit."

Rose patted Isabel's hand. "I will. I promise. First thing in the morning I'll drop by her shop and finagle the money out of her, okay? You should think about getting out and having some fun. The festival is practically running itself these days."

Gareth said, "Rosie, if you need to stay and—"

"I don't. Things are well in hand, aren't they, darlin'?" Not waiting for an answer, Rose swept out of the chair and put her hands on Gareth's shoulders, stooping to give him a kiss on the cheek. "Thanks for cleaning up, kids."

Isabel's sigh signaled her defeat. Not knowing what to say, Alasdair stacked plates and carried them into the kitchen. When he returned, she was sitting slumped with her chin propped on her palm, fingering the wildflowers. They already looked worn, and he regretted stealing their beauty.

A wilting purple flower dropped two petals and Isabel picked them up. "I love wildflowers, but they never last long once you pick them. They can't survive away from the land."

The fanciful bent to her tone captured his imagination. Before he could help himself, he asked, "Like you?"

"What's that supposed to mean?" Her cutting glance sheared away any softness.

He blinked and stumbled to find his footing. "Have you ever been to Scotland?"

"Not yet, but I'll go someday," she said defensively before her shoulders rounded once more. "I want to see Edinburgh and London and Paris. Someday."

"Why not now? Go book a ticket to Paris. It's lovely in autumn."

"My job has limited vacation, and I have to save it all for the festival." Although her voice was matter-of-fact, he could sense a trickle of frustration underneath.

In that moment, he understood her driving force. Understood it because he wrestled with it himself. Duty to tradition and family. Gareth and Alasdair's presence had thrown her off course.

"Are you sure I can't help in some way?" No doubt she'd turn him down flat again, but he couldn't stop himself from trying to ease her burdens even as he added to them.

Her brown eyes searched his. "You don't know me and I don't know you. Why offer to help?"

What she was really saying was that she didn't trust him, which was fair. "Consider it repayment for room and board."

"There's no need. You're our guest." She rose and with brisk movements wiped the crumbs off the table.

Obviously, Isabel didn't ask for or accept help often. He could relate. Lightly, he said, "Just a thought. I believe I'll retire to my room now."

She nodded. "Sleep well."

"I will." He wouldn't though. He hadn't had a good night's sleep in ages. Stress had become a constant companion whose nagging got worse at night when there was nothing to distract his brain.

He yawned, the long day of travel wearing him down. Maybe tonight would be different. He'd open his window to the cooling night, and sleep would slip inside and claim him. With any luck, he'd dream about a woman with brown hair and laughing eyes seducing him in the middle of a field of flowers.

The vibration of his mobile sloughed away hope of sleep. Tension pulled at the muscles of his neck and shoulders, and acid churned his stomach. Unable to ignore *his* duty any longer, he unlocked the screen and went to work.

Twenty missed calls. A hundred emails. Some from his mother. Most from various people in both the London and New York offices. He briefly considered stuffing the mobile under the mattress, but he opened his email and scanned for an answer to the inquiry he'd sent requesting information on Stonehaven. Nothing yet.

He tapped his mobile on his knee and then shot an unsatisfactory text to his mum, unable to let her know when he'd be home with Gareth. But then again, anything less than disclosing when he ate, shat, and slept would be too little detail for his mum.

He got ready for bed, pulling on athletic shorts and a faded Coldplay concert T-shirt from the days he had the time and energy to enjoy music. Sleep played hide-and-seek, never allowing itself to be caught. Finally at two o'clock, he scooped up his mobile and made his way downstairs, taking the steps slowly, the creaks loud in the silence.

It was seven in the morning in London, almost time for the office to fill with worker bees. Might as well put his insomnia to good use. He slipped into the office and closed the French doors. One wall was covered in corkboard and pictures were tacked up, some curling at the edges from age. There were so many, they blurred together.

Two desks were set up with laptops. One desk was neat with a pretty stained-glass lamp on top. The other was covered in piles of paper of varying heights and a rustic lamp of carved and polished driftwood. He didn't have to check whose was whose. The chaos on the desk matched the thoughts Alasdair could sense whirling in Isabel's mind at all times.

As he returned several calls to relay instructions on current projects, he stood and studied the closest snapshots. A history of past festivals was on display. Everyone was smiling and framed by mostly blue skies. Men in kilts, dancers caught mid-leap, children eating cotton candy with their arms thrown over one another's shoulders.

Many of the same faces made an appearance, aged slightly, from one year to the next. A sense of community emerged. It felt like the festival was more than a means to support Stonehaven. It was a way to connect. His mind wandered down Highland's streets, and he recognized the same sense of community there. The festival brought people together who might otherwise never cross paths.

"What do you say, Alasdair? Shall we move forward?" The disembodied voice on the other end of the line brought him out of his trance.

"Have the nnumbers worked up, and we can meet next week when I'm back." He signed off with a clipped good-bye and sat back down in Isabel's chair.

He eyed the nearest pile of papers, his heart picking up its pace. Surely a peek wouldn't constitute a crime. He opened the folder as if he expected a booby trap. He skimmed the first page of what appeared to be a manuscript with the heading "Chapter One." The page was littered with red pen marks. He read a few more pages, then thumbed through the rest. The material was dark and took itself very seriously, which wasn't the Isabel he was acquainted with. Fascinating.

He moved on to the next pile, opening the top folder with more confidence. A printed spreadsheet was on top. This was more his language. Adept at translating the columns of numbers into summaries, he scanned the sheet. It detailed yearly, recurring expenses for Stonehaven.

His eyes widened at the taxes—not as expensive as he'd thought—and at the yard maintenance, which was much more expensive. In a messy scrawl, Isabel had added a few items, like roof replacement. One-time, high-cost fees added up to an intimidating total at the bottom of the page circled in ominous red pen. Under the spreadsheet was a copy of an application for a loan, signed by Rose Buchanan.

He closed the folder, feeling icky, even though he'd learned something important and possibly damning for Buchanan's motivations. He didn't want to prove his mum correct; he wanted to find information that bolstered his uncle's faith Rose and Isabel.

He turned his attention to the one framed picture on the desk. A young girl with tangled brown hair and a big, open grin stared at the camera. She had an arm thrown around a man who sat in a wooden chair with his legs crossed. Although the man was looking at the girl and not the camera, the family resemblance was apparent in the shared strong line of their jaws and chins and uninhibited smiles. His legs were long like Isabel's, and Alasdair had a feeling Isabel had inherited her father's eyes as well.

The happy photo filled him with melancholy, and he set it down. A flash of metal caught his eye and he plucked a letter opener from its hiding place half under a manila file folder. He ran his finger down the blade to the wickedly sharp tip. The handle was an intricately molded puckish pixie under a toadstool. Made of silver, it was whimsical and polished to a shine with no hint of tarnish. He smiled thinking of Isabel wielding it.

"What are you doing?" As if Isabel had spirited herself into the office, she stood in the opened door, rubbing one eye with the heel of her hand.

He slipped the silver letter opener into the pocket of his shorts. The tip poked his thigh uncomfortably. The instinct to hide his snooping was like cramming pilfered cookies into his mouth as a child. Now, no matter how innocent his actions were, if he was caught with crumbs on his hands, so to speak, he'd never allay her suspicions.

"I couldn't sleep. Thought I'd get some work done."

She blinked. "It's two thirty in the morning."

"Not in London."

Her mouth formed an O of understanding. Her white tank top and pink short shorts emphasized curves and long legs. Her loose hair fell to her shoulders and was disheveled in a way that made him think of waking up next to her or taking her back to bed. She looked soft and sweet and sexy as hell.

He could almost see her mind spool up from sleep to perform an inventory of her desktop. He needed three seconds max to replace the letter opener.

"Are you almost done?" She took a step farther into the office.

"Yes, I'm headed back to bed." He stood.

The sharp tip of the letter opener shifted lower to a small tear in the pocket of his old athletic shorts. The fabric, weak after repeated washings, didn't stand a chance. It happened so quickly he could do nothing but register the slide of cool metal against his leg as the opener slipped out. Instead of a clatter against the wood floor, pain like a stubbed toe had him cursing in Gaelic.

"*Mhac na galla!*"

"What happened?" She was in front of him now, holding on to his arms.

Blood oozed from a cut along the outside of his foot. It could have been worse. The damn letter opener could have impaled his foot like a dagger. Instead, it lay with the sprite on the handle grinning up at him.

"It's nothing. Nothing." He pulled out several tissues from the box on her desk and slapped them over the cut.

She knelt in front of him, pulled the tissues away, and examined the cut. Taking more tissues, she folded them into a pad and pressed them against his foot. She looked up at him. "It's not terribly deep."

He stared down at her, their suggestive position firing synapses that hadn't been activated in a good long while. He could imagine tangling his fingers in her hair while her hands pulled at his shorts and—

"Is that my . . ." She picked up her letter opener and looked from it to him and back to it.

"I—" The vibrating buzz of his mobile saved him from bumbling out an explanation. The truth seemed silly enough. His waggled his mobile toward her as if needing to prove he wasn't making up an excuse to leave. "I have to get this call."

He answered with relief in his greeting. "Alasdair Blackmoor, here."

"Why in bloody hell haven't you returned my calls, Blackmoor?" The gruff impatience of his boss's voice had Alasdair tensing. Richard was intimidating and unlikable and impossible to please. He was generous with criticism, miserly with compliments, and made every decision with regards to promotions. And firings.

"I've been busy, sir."

"Yes, I got the report from George first thing."

"What report would that be, sir?"

"The one on the property in Georgia." The rustle of papers sounded on the desk. "Stonehaven, is it?"

The blood drained from his head, and he prayed it wasn't all gushing out of his foot. "One second, sir."

He pressed his mobile against his chest. "I'm going to take this outside so I don't bleed all over your floors. It's not a mortal injury. You can head back to bed."

Still kneeling, she shifted so he could brush by her, walking awkwardly on one heel. Once he'd slipped out into the darkness, he put the mobile back to his ear.

"That report wasn't ready, sir. It's preliminary." Alasdair grimaced and fisted a hand in his hair. It hadn't been meant for Richard at all.

"But interesting nonetheless. A certain Saudi I know would be very interested in investing in such a property. Work up the details and have it on my desk in a week."

Alasdair mouthed a curse, but tried not to let the agitation into his voice. "Actually, I'm attending to a personal matter, sir."

"Perfect. You can attend to this personal matter while you assemble a report on this place. Two birds and all that. Sound good?"

He was going to strangle George. No, strangling was

too good for the little git. He'd devise something positively medieval for the arse-kisser. The rack. Surely he could order one off the internet. "Actually, I'm busy and—"

A rustle on the other end of the line signaled Richard had taken him off speakerphone, never a good sign. A sharp pain in his stomach made him feel slightly nauseous. "Blackmoor. The next VP of acquisitions must display an unwavering commitment to the company."

"Yes sir."

"I thought you had such a commitment." Richard let the assessment hang with an unspoken question.

"I did—do, sir. It's just the personal matter I'm dealing with is more like a family emergency."

Richard was silent for a long, telling moment. "You're a smart lad. You can surely juggle a family emergency with a deal that could make your career. I'll expect the report next week." The clang of the receiver hitting the cradle reverberated like a gunshot.

Family was more an inconvenience than a priority for Richard. He was married with two daughters, yet beyond the requisite photo on the man's desk, Alasdair couldn't recall the man ever leaving early for a school function or to celebrate a birthday or anniversary. On the contrary, Richard had used work as an excuse to get out of going on holiday with his wife and daughters.

At one time, Alasdair had considered Richard's single-minded focus a strength, but the thought of betraying Gareth, not to mention the Buchanans, by spurring on Richard's single-minded interest buoyed by the strength of Wellington was unconscionable. While Richard wouldn't engage in anything illegal to obtain his goals, neither was he known for his politesse.

On the flipside, retreating to London with nothing to hand Richard made Alasdair feel weak and almost physically ill. His mobile vibrated in his hand. Richard's number again. He'd probably decided his threats were too subtle.

A pressure built in Alasdair's chest. An explosion ready to detonate. As if the mobile was a grenade with the pin pulled, he heaved it into the darkness with a bellow. As quickly as the mood came upon him, his vexation faded and he wanted his mobile back. Ghosting Richard wasn't going to solve his problem. Now that Richard knew about Stonehaven, he would send another minion and another until he got what he wanted. Alasdair leaned over and pressed the heels of his hands to his brows.

Gaelic and English curses strung themselves together until he ran out of breath. He'd retrieve his shoes and begin a search of the field. Straightening, he turned toward the house.

A light from inside illuminated Isabel in the glass door. Her hip was cocked and she had her chin propped on her hand. Had she heard him talking with Richard? He rewound the conversation and wondered what he'd given away, if anything.

Stepping gingerly on his injured foot, he made his way toward her. The door was cracked, and she pushed it fully open.

"Everything okay?" she asked. Before he could reply she added, "Of course it's not. Come over here and sit."

He took a seat at the table where an assortment of first aid supplies was laid out.

She sat in a chair across from him and without preamble, picked up his injured foot and set it in her lap. She dabbed the cut with an antiseptic that burned enough for him to jerk his foot away.

"Sorry." She massaged the arch of his foot in apology. He slumped in the chair, letting his head fall back and his eyes close. The drumbeat of a headache marched closer, and he rubbed his temples.

"Take these," she said.

He lifted his head and dry-swallowed the two pills she held out. If was only afterward that he thought to ask, "What were the pills?"

"Arsenic." Her face was so deadpan, it took a minute for him to recognize the teasing sparkle in her eyes.

"Putting me out of misery might not be such a bad thing." He groaned. "My mobile is somewhere in the middle of the field, and my boss is *not* going to be happy when he can't reach me."

"Judging by the entertaining litany of curses you unleashed, maybe the two of you need a break."

"Pardon me if I offended you. I assumed you had gone to bed and I was alone."

"I didn't want your cut to get infected or for you to bleed all over the floor."

She put an adhesive plaster over the cut. "There you go."

"Thank you, Isabel."

She smiled but didn't let go of his foot immediately. Her hands were warm and deft, and he couldn't remember the last time someone had taken care of him. He couldn't look away from her even though guilt and suspicion churned.

"Can I ask you something?" she asked softly as if she too was loathe to break the intimacy of the moment. At his brusque nod, she asked, "Why did Rupert fall out of your pants?"

Chapter Five

"Rupert?" Alasdair asked with a blank look on his face.

The letter opener was one of Izzy's favorite things despite the fact she rarely needed to use it. Everything was electronic these days, but even the act of polishing it made her smile. Because its silver molded face had been mischievous, she had named it Rupert and had made up an origin story that involved magic and quests and queens.

She picked up the letter opener and held it up. "Meet Rupert." Then, she addressed the opener. "Rupert, meet Alasdair. I'm sure there's a good reason he stuffed you in his pants, although I can imagine it was quite traumatic for you."

"I'm hurt that you think being in my pants would be a traumatic experience." Alasdair gave her a lopsided grin.

Her gaze dropped to the pants in question—a pair of worn athletic shorts that were thin and left little to the imagination. What popped into her head came straight out of her mouth. "I pictured you sleeping in a pair of fancy pinstriped button-up pajamas with cuffs and a collar."

"Actually, I usually sleep in the buff."

Great. Now her brain was going to have to contend with that image when she went back to bed. She was never going to get to sleep. Or worse, she would dream about him naked on the other side of the wall from her.

Her blush didn't contain itself to her face, but superheated her entire body. She stood and his foot thumped from her lap to the floor. "Do you want a snack?"

"A snack?"

"That's why I came down in the first place. I'm stressed out, which means I don't sleep well and the only thing that helps is comfort food. Are you in or out?"

"All in."

"Grilled cheese is my go-to." She bent over and pulled the electric griddle out of the bottom cabinet. When she turned, his gaze skittered away. Had he been staring at her butt? It made her very aware she was wearing a tank top and tiny shorts. She had an inkling that her nipples were up to no good, but was afraid to look down and draw even more attention to them.

"One or two?" she asked, holding the bread in front of her chest as camouflage. His stomach rumbled loud enough to make them both laugh awkwardly. "Two it is."

"Dinner this evening was delicious, by the way. I'm not sure why I'm so famished."

"It's the stress. I can relate." She gathered the cheese, mayonnaise, and butter from the fridge.

"How did the festival come about?" He sat on one of the barstools across the island from her, his stance casual, but his gaze following her every move.

"It was Daddy's passion project. A way to draw tourists when the economics of small towns became untenable. After Daddy died, Mom and I took over. We make a good team." Or had they *made* a good team? Was it ending?

Thoughts of beginnings and endings swirled in her head as she buttered bread and added cheese, not having to concentrate on the familiar task. The silence that gathered as she cooked was a surprisingly comfortable one. She flipped three grilled cheeses onto plates—two for him, one for her—poured two glasses of milk, and joined him on a neighboring stool. Her elbow jostled his and his knee bumped hers, but neither of them jerked away. His body heat was welcome in the cool of the air-conditioning.

He took a bite of his sandwich, let out a little moan, and closed his eyes. The first sandwich disappeared in seconds. "This beats room service at the best hotel in New York."

Pleasure at his pleasure suffused her. Attraction vibrated the air like staticky radio waves not quite dialed in to a song she could distinguish. Oh, this was dangerous. Especially since she'd caught him in her office. Her sleep-fuzzed brain hadn't moved fast enough at the time, but now she wondered and worried.

Before she could question him, he asked, "If the games are such a stressor, why not take a year or two off from hosting them? You could use your vacation traveling instead of working."

"It's not just Stonehaven that benefits from the festival. Most of the businesses in Highland count on the influx of visitors, and their money, to stay afloat. If we don't hold the games, it would cause real hurt to people I care about in Highland."

"You're like a feudal lord," he said.

She barked a laugh. "If only we could demand a tithe." Brushing her fingers together and pushing her plate away, she propped her elbow on the counter and shifted to look at him, her head in her head. "Are you going to tell me about Rupert?"

He did the same, facing her. "Rupert is a numpty who wouldn't stop talking about his mushroom, if you know what I mean. I told him if he didn't shut his geggie, he would get a close-up of my bollocks."

"Maybe you're the numpty." How could she not smile? "What is a numpty, anyway?"

"An idiot."

Still smiling, she asked, "You know I don't trust you, right?"

"I'm fully expecting to keel over from arsenic poisoning any minute. This may have been my last meal."

"Finding you at my desk in the middle of the night literally trying to steal the silver is disturbing." What if he'd done more than stuff Rupert in his pants? Her manuscript had been front and center. Plus, the folder detailing expenditures on Stonehaven. She couldn't say which discovery by him would be worse.

"I promise I was in your office because I couldn't sleep and had to return phone calls. That's it."

"And Rupert?"

"A misunderstanding. You startled me, and I stuck him in my pocket. It was reflex. Believe me, I don't want Rupert or his mushroom anywhere near my pants. Anyway, haven't I suffered enough?" He raised his large foot, the Snoopy Band-Aid incongruous yet charming.

"I suppose you have." It scared her how much she wanted to believe him.

He straightened, rubbed his hands down his thighs, and half rose. "I have to find my mobile now."

She dumped the plates in the sink and caught his arm halfway to the door. "No. We're going to bed."

His eyes widened and he leaned closer to her. So close, she could see the black of his pupils flare. It was only when he asked, "Are we, lass?" in a rumbly brogue that made her stomach flutter and her body scream an affirmative, did her bossy declaration register.

"Gah." She inhaled, her throat dry and her tongue working hard to form words. "Not together. Separately. In different beds. And rooms."

"Probably for the best." He cast a glance toward the

back door, worry shadowing his face. "But I need my mobile."

"Call it. We can follow the ringing," she said.

"It's on vibrate."

She retrieved a cordless phone. "Try it anyway. Maybe the screen will light up enough for us to find it."

He punched in numbers as they made their way outside, then stood at the edge of the patio with the phone to his ear. "It should be ringing."

She peered into the darkness, seeing nothing that resembled a phone lighting up and hearing nothing except for the call of crickets. "It'll be easier to find in the morning." When still he hesitated, she added. "Nothing will happen to it. A raccoon won't rack up a bunch of phone sex charges. Surely even your crazy boss understands time zones. You need sleep."

He heaved a sigh and handed her the cordless phone. "I am bone-tired and not in the mood to tramp through the field."

She led the way inside, throwing glances behind her to assure herself he followed. Despite the explanations he gave, she couldn't leave him downstairs on his own. It didn't matter that he made her laugh and attraction buzzed between them, she couldn't afford to trust him.

The "good nights" they exchanged were strangely formal considering the odd last half hour they'd spent together. She lay down on her bed, doing her best to stay awake in case Alasdair tried to slip out again, but sleep claimed her with a swiftness that was rare.

Izzy clutched Alasdair's phone and stood in front of the connecting bathroom door to his room. With rain imminent, she'd spent a half hour searching the field, underestimating how far he'd thrown it. She realized she should have added distance based on the unexpected brawn of his arms in the T-shirt last night. Finally, black and silver had glinted through the grass and flowers. Unfortunately, the screen was a web of cracks, the LCD glitchy when she'd surreptitiously checked to see if it was password-protected.

No sound emerged to indicate he was awake. He would want the phone back as soon as possible. That's the only reason she wasn't waiting downstairs for him. It had nothing to do with his admission about sleeping naked. In fact, she hoped he wasn't naked. Of course she did. She didn't need the embarrassment of walking in and seeing him lying on his bed as naked as the day he was born. But bigger. Way bigger and way sexier.

She knocked, but heard no reply. There was her answer. She would go downstairs and wait. She made it two steps before she turned back around. What if he was sick? The cut on his foot could have turned septic. Or he could have fallen out of bed and hit his head on the nightstand. He might even need help but be unable to call for her.

Her hand found its way to the knob and turned it before a dissenting argument could be lodged. The door creaked open, and she popped her head through. The man-sized lump under the covers jump-started her lungs. Not hurt or naked.

"Alasdair," she said softly. "Are you awake?"

She shuffled farther into the room until she stood next to the bed. He was curled on his side, hugging a pillow. His dark hair was mussed and stubble darkened his jaw. Parts of her body she'd thought had died had apparently only gone into hibernation and were now roaring to life. Why with him? A temporary guest who may or may not be in Georgia to bilk them.

The small smile tipping the corner of his lips made her wonder at his dreams. Dark smudged his eyes. Was sleep his only escape from the crushing pressure that had driven him to hurl his phone into a field?

Intending to leave his phone on the nightstand, she pulled it from her back pocket, moving slowly so as not to disturb him. Alasdair bolted upright as if he'd exited the Land of Nod on a bullet train. Surprise had her fumbling his phone like a piece of wet soap. It hit him on the bridge of his nose.

With a groan, he covered his face with one hand and sprawled backward. "What in blazes did you hit me for?"

"I didn't! At least, not intentionally." She patted the folds of the quilt in search for the phone, her right hand landing on his thigh. It twitched, and she yanked her hand away. His phone peeked out of a fold near his crotch.

"Did you request a wake-up call?" Her tattered self-control kept her from making an embarrassing grab for the phone. "I found your phone in the field this morning. It's right there near your . . ." She pointed.

Pinching the bridge of his nose, he propped himself up on his elbow, retrieved the phone, and stared at the spiderweb of cracks. "It's broken."

"Probably hit a rock. I hope your nose hasn't suffered the same fate." He took his hand away from his face, and Izzy gasped. "Oh my God, your face!"

"That god-awful ugly, is it?" His attempt at a smile turned into a wince.

Without answering, she pulled out several tissues and held them to his nose, sitting on the side of his bed. "Dizzy Izzy strikes again. Lean your head back."

He obeyed. "Dizzy Izzy? Have you been drinking already?"

"I wish I'd earned the nickname after a wild night out. Alas, it was from the seventh-graders who witnessed my cartwheels in gym class. I got off course and crashed into the wall. See, I still have the scar." She held up her elbow.

He wrapped his hand around her upper arm and pulled her elbow closer for an examination. Her torso shifted to hover over his. His hand could almost circle her entire arm, which meant either she was exceptionally puny (she wasn't) or his hand was unusually big. She swallowed hard trying not to do the math, equating his big hands with other body parts.

"It's a wee thing."

"It hurt like the dickens at the time."

He let her go, and for a second her torso swayed closer to his chest before she caught her balance and pulled away. "That's not all. Most of the town was in attendance when Mom made me dance in the festival when I was around eight. I fell off the stage."

His lips twitched and his eyes twinkled over the tissues she held to his nose. "Sounds charming."

"Uh-oh, you've got brain damage."

This time he laughed and pushed himself up on the pillows. "Thank you for finding my mobile. What time is it?"

"Ten thirty." The overcast skies had masked the sunrise. "A rainstorm blew through but it's all clear now."

His smile disappeared and he blinked. "Ten-thirty?"

She nodded. "I take it you don't normally sleep in."

"Never."

"Not even when you travel overseas?"

"I've disciplined myself to adjust immediately. Mind over matter."

"You were up in the middle of the night. You needed the sleep."

"You were up in the middle of the night too," he said almost accusingly.

"Yeah, but I know my terrible dreams and anxiety will end as soon as the festival is over. Yours seem constant. Why do you do it?"

"Do what?"

"Stay at a job you hate?"

"I don't *hate* it." He heaved a sigh. "I'm up for a promotion. More responsibility and more money."

Why did he sound as if he'd been tasked to drown puppies for a living? "Congrats?"

"My boss is a right bastard sometimes." He stared at something over her shoulder, but it felt like he wanted to say more. She waited, but nothing else came.

She rose. "I'll leave you to get dressed. I'm headed to town in a bit. If you want, I can drop you by Bubba's Fix-it shop."

"Can I trust a man named Bubba with my mobile?"

"If it settles your mind, his real name is Bocephus. His daddy was a big Hank Williams Jr fan. He can fix anything and everything."

"I think I prefer Bubba." He tossed the tissues in the can next to the bed. "How does it look?"

She propped her hands on her hips and examined him. His nose had stopped bleeding, but a red knot marred the bridge. With the dark stubble shading his jaw, he reminded her of a rakish highwayman. "You'll live."

His smile wasn't practiced or fake. It drew faint crinkles at the corners of his eyes and conveyed enough warmth to kindle a fire in her belly. Her cheeks ached and she laid her palm on one to find she was smiling back. "Come on down whenever you're ready."

She didn't stop to take the cold shower she needed, but made a beeline toward normalcy. Except, she came upon her mom and Gareth in the office canoodling in front of her mom's computer. She almost turned around.

"What if you included a stock show and utilize this area?" Gareth used a pen to point on the zoomed-in satellite map of Stonehaven.

"That's for parking," her mother said with nary a flirtatious giggle.

"You could move parking across the lane. Here and here." Gareth tapped his pen on the monitor.

Okay, not canoodling. They appeared to actually be working on the festival. Which was good, except it was supposed to be *Izzy* and her mom working together.

"What are you two discussing?" The defensiveness in Izzy's voice was peevish.

Her mom tossed Gareth a look Izzy had seen her parents exchange on occasion when she had been an adolescent. "Options for expansion next year, darlin'. That's all."

Gareth straightened and cleared his throat. "I was telling your mother that authentic Highland festivals include a stock show. Highland cows and sheep mostly, but the bairns show off their chickens and bunnies and such. Blue ribbons are awarded. It makes for a grand time."

"Having animals at the festival introduces a host of issues."

"What sort of issues, dear?" Her mom swiveled in the office chair with an effortless grace.

"The poopy kind."

"Excuse me?" Gareth looked confused.

"You know, feces. Excrement. Dung. Guano. Crap."

Alasdair made the turn into the office just as the last word landed in the middle of the room. "Morning. Sounds like I've interrupted something interesting."

Izzy closed her eyes. Of course, he would walk in when she was acting like a toddler forced to share a favorite toy. She needed to pull up her big-girl panties, not get them in a wad, and apply all other panty metaphors involving maturity as needed.

Izzy hoped her faked sunny smile saved the moment from descending into awkwardness. "Actually, a stock show might draw a new crowd. We've never tackled the logistics of animal trailers and runoff, but looking into what it would take is smart business planning."

"I agree. What a good idea." Her mom leaned over and planted a kiss on Gareth's cheek.

"Can I talk to you for a sec, Mom?" Izzy dipped her chin toward the entry and left Gareth and Alasdair in the office, but within sight. Just in case.

"It really is a good idea, isn't it, Izzy? A stock show?" Her mom was smiling and flushed with energy.

"Yeah, sure. Did you get Loretta's deposit?"

"Oh no." Her mom's forehead crinkled. "I forgot. Gareth and I were—"

Izzy held up a hand. "I don't need to know the specifics. Can you run by today?"

"Actually, Gareth and I have plans." Her mom put on the puppy dog eyes that lulled people into thinking she was demure and beseeching when behind them, she was a bulldog. She clasped her hands under her chin. "Will you handle Loretta?"

Her mom was an expert at finagling money from reluctant or tight-fisted vendors without causing any hard feelings. She was also good at getting her way. Izzy felt herself caving.

"You know I'm not good at this sort of thing. She'll probably withdraw from the festival entirely." When Izzy got nervous, she couldn't be held responsible for the things that came out of her mouth. Spreadsheets and budgets were easy for Izzy to manipulate and bend to her will—people were not.

"A couple of others have ignored my emails. Can I count on you to at least give them a follow-up call?" Izzy asked.

"Of course. As soon as Gareth and I get back from our hike. I'm taking him to Raven Cliff for a picnic."

"Fun times." For her mom and Gareth. Not for Izzy who felt like she was getting ready to take a test she hadn't studied for. Dropping her voice, she asked, "Have you heard from the bank about the loan yet?"

"Nothing, but I heard Sterling left town for a family emergency." Her mom expressed no worry about the loan they needed to replace the roof before winter. And, she was probably right. Stonehaven was a good investment for the bank. There was no reason to deny them. But, until she had the money in her account and the roofers booked, Izzy would worry. She trailed her mom back to the office.

Gareth said, "Alasdair has been to his share of Highland games and volunteered to brainstorm later."

"Wonderful!" Her mom tucked her hand into the crook of Gareth's arm. They only had eyes for each other, and a strange feeling of not belonging in her own home crept up Izzy's neck.

"We're headed to town then." When Izzy's announcement garnered nothing more than a slight wave and smile from her mom, she tucked a festival folder under her arm and turned to Alasdair. "Ready?"

He made a "ladies' first" gesture and followed her. She stopped at the front door and took inventory. Her striped cotton skirt, scooped neck T-shirt, and flipflops might be standard wear during Highland summers, but she wasn't exactly putting on a professional front to meet with Loretta.

"Should I change?" She tugged on the hem of her skirt.

"Why? You look fresh and summery."

"I sound like a dryer sheet." She bit the inside of her lip and looked up the stairs. "I have black pants and pumps I can change into."

"Stop it. You look lovely." He teetered toward laughter. The kind that was *at* her and not *with* her.

"I don't want to look lovely. I want to look like a professional ass-kicker like you." She outlined him with both hands.

Same fancy brown shoes. A different pair of slim-fitting pants that did amazing things for his legs and butt. A light blue dress shirt with the sleeves rolled up his forearms, revealing black hair over corded muscles. Granted, he hadn't shaved, but his finger-combed hair looked delightfully rumpled.

If anything, his rough-and-ready appearance made him even more intimidating. She could imagine him striding into a boardroom to wreak havoc on subordinates. One look at Alasdair, and Loretta would hand over her deposit lickety-split. Probably her underwear too.

He crossed his arms over his chest and narrowed his eyes. "Dare I ask what's going on in that head of yours?"

"You don't want to know," she muttered as Alasdair took her by the elbow and led her outside.

The morning rainstorm had left behind a sticky steam. She allowed him to guide her to his car, and he opened the car door and gestured her in.

She hesitated with one foot in and one out. "Are you offering to drive because I almost hit you the other day? I have an excellent driving record, minus the time I didn't see a speedbump and launched my car like the *Dukes of Hazard.*"

His lips twitched. "You don't have dukes in America."

"Oh, not fancy dukes; redneck ones. Can you imagine an actual duke or earl or whatever in Highland? That would be *hilarious*. The dude would think we were supreme bumpkins."

His amusement dimmed. "I doubt that. He'd think Highland was charming."

"Sure he would." In her imitation British accent that sounded like the queen had swallowed a cat, she said, "Iced tea? How vulgar!"

"Alright, your majesty. Get in the car."

"Seriously though, I should drive. I know where I'm going."

"The air-con in my rental is stellar."

She couldn't argue with that. The only time her truck

was a pleasure to drive was in the spring and fall when she could open the windows and let the cool mountain air flow through the cab. Also, she'd never been in a car as sophisticated and sleek and . . . sexy as his car.

She slid onto the buttery leather and wiggled, letting her head fall back in pleasure. She could get used to the finer things in life. He leaned over her in the open door, his forearm propped on the roof. "Comfortable?"

She grinned up at him. "Can you imagine how amazing it would feel to sit here naked?"

Alasdair's jaw went slack and his gaze skimmed down her body. Her knees clamped together. A combination of embarrassment and arousal ignited between them.

"I didn't mean . . . I wouldn't actually . . . It would be super unsanitary to be naked in a rental. I want you to know I would never violate your car like that." She swallowed to stem the tide of words.

"I wouldn't complain if—"

"Good, I caught you!" Her mom jogged down the front stairs. "Preacher Hopkins just called. The decorations are ready to be picked up at the church. He has a couple more tables as well. You don't mind taking the truck, do you?"

"Nope. We'll grab everything," she called out.

As soon as Alasdair stepped back, Izzy popped out of his car. On one hand, she was glad to be saved. On the other, she wanted Alasdair to finish his thought. What wouldn't he complain about? Did it have something to do with her clothing or lack of?

She shot Alasdair a glance on her way to the truck. "I'll try not to hit anyone or anything."

Alasdair slid onto the bench seat of the truck and rolled down the window as soon as she started the car. The hand of God hadn't healed the truck overnight. The vents still pumped out ambient air, which was only a few degrees cooler than the superheated cab.

"Is it always this blasted hot? You could steam a pudding in here," Alasdair said.

The truck jounced them over the gravel toward the main road. "Steamed pudding? Is that really a thing? Sounds disgusting."

"It's not like the pudding you serve in the states. You Americans gum more than eat pudding." His obvious dissatisfaction made her huff a laugh. Puddings did make regular appearances on hospital menus. "A Scottish pudding is hearty. It can be a meal in and of itself."

"But puddings are sweet."

"The Scottish variety can be sweet and bready or savory. Haggis is a pudding."

She made a gagging sound.

"Have you eaten haggis?" He set his back in the corner and draped his arm along the top of the seat, shifting to watch her.

The wind played in his hair and flipped his collar open to reveal the cut of one collarbone. Nearly breaking her promise and driving them into a gulley, she forced her focus back to the road.

"They sell haggis at the festival, but I've managed to avoid it." Incredulity lilted her voice. "Do you expect me to believe you actually like it?"

"It's delicious." His slow smile made the temperature rise a few more degrees. "How can I convince you to give it a try?"

"Uh, tie me down and force-feed me? Offering me an obscene amount of money would work too."

They shared a laugh. The fact she was comfortable around him made her uncomfortable. At best, Alasdair was a distraction. At worst, he and Gareth were plotting to take advantage of them in some way she hadn't figured out.

"I will never eat haggis. Just like I will never dance in

front of an audience." Her prim tone might have been put on, but she stood by the declaration.

"Not dance? Because of your mishap at age eight? That seems like an overreaction."

"Not just because of my humiliation at age eight. Although, developmentally speaking, eight is a pivotal year for the foundation of self-confidence in girls." She smiled and shot him a glance to gauge his reaction to her next bit of family lore. "Mom was a ballerina with the Atlanta Ballet before Daddy whisked her to Stonehaven. If I dance, I'm inevitably compared to her and come up way short. She opens the games at the whisky tasting with a dance and leaves everyone in awe."

"She is very graceful and serene," he said thoughtfully.

"Exactly. And I'm neither."

He didn't immediately contradict her, which pricked her feelings even though it shouldn't. "You certainly aren't serene," he finally said.

"Gee, thanks."

"You're better than serene."

"Better?"

He studied her from the corner of the truck for so long, she hunched over the steering wheel and fiddled with the hair tucked behind her ear. "You have an energy that's magnetic. You never slow down, do you?"

"I like to keep busy," she said weakly as she turned his assessment over in her head. Alasdair thought she was *magnetic*? Was that better than graceful or serene? She pictured two magnets drawn together by forces beyond their control.

"So you don't dance or eat. Do you have any fun at your own festival?"

She let out an exasperated huff. "The festival isn't about having fun for me. Too many people depend on me to do a good job to slack off eating and drinking and being merry."

She parked in a small lot at the end of the main drag of Highland, close to Bubba's Fix-it Shop. A giant sign with a hammer hitting a nail marked the entrance. "Bubba will be able to help you. I'm going to face the dragon in All Things Bright and Beautiful. Do you want to meet at the Brown Cow for a coffee?"

"Caffeine is a solid plan." He gave her a crisp salute and stepped through Bubba's door, the tinkle of the bell following her around the corner.

Normally, she loved strolling through town, window-shopping and watching the tourists be charmed by Highland. If the brick fronts and flower baskets and tartan ribbons weren't Technicolor bright, she could imagine the street as the setting for a black-and-white TV show. It was picturesque.

But this morning was different. Every step down the sidewalk built her sense of dread. Sweat dampened the back of her neck, and her hands turned clammy.

A banner stretched across the street advertised the festival, as did flyers stuck in every business window. The festival was as important for the town as it was for Stonehaven. This year was especially crucial because of the repairs Stonehaven required. Besides the new roof, the gutters and shutters needed to be replaced and a drainage issue at the barn had resulted in rotting boards.

The loan waiting for approval would help, but a profitable festival would go a long way to defraying the costs. And part of a successful festival was filling all the vendor booths.

She wouldn't go home until she had Loretta's deposit. If she couldn't manufacture real confidence, she'd have to fake some. Smile pasted on, check. Shoulders squared, check. Stride long, check.

"Izzy, dearheart!" A voice creaky with age stopped her on the sidewalk.

Izzy turned to see Mrs. Fortunato shuffling toward her and waving a hanky embroidered with her initials. She never left home without one.

"How is your arthritis faring this morning, Mrs. F?" Izzy leaned down to give her a gentle hug.

Mrs. Fortunato held up a hand with swollen knuckles. "Fair to middling. I was able to play the organ at church last Sunday. You should have been there." After a reproachful frown was aimed at Izzy, her face cleared. "Have you finished the next chapter?"

Mrs. Fortunato was not only a church organist, but Izzy's former English teacher and one of the only people she let read her work. "Not yet. The festival is keeping me hopping. Do you think I'm on the right track with this one?"

"You're getting closer every manuscript."

It wasn't exactly a ringing endorsement.

Mrs. Fortunato tapped her nose and fell back into her teacher pose as if she hadn't retired a decade earlier. "It's missing something. A bit of magic. I can't quite put my finger on it though."

Izzy wanted to pull at her hair and scream. It's the same vague statement she'd gotten in more than one rejection. No one could tell her what was missing from her writing, which meant she couldn't figure out how to fix it. The feedback veered from simply frustrating to totally disheartening.

"As soon as I have something ready, I'll send it over." Izzy tried to smile, but it was limp.

Mrs. Fortunato patted her hand. "You always were my favorite, Izzy."

"Ditto, Mrs. F."

After seeing Mrs. Fortunato into her car, Izzy pushed through the door of the All Things Bright and Beautiful shop, triggering an electronic tone.

Scents of potpourri and candles tussled for dominance, so strong she could almost taste dried rose and lavender. Bric-a-brac made in China jumbled with antiques on bookcases and shelving and tables around the store. The excitement of a treasure hunt imbued the atmosphere. In fact, Izzy had found Rupert hanging out on a shelf with a set of porcelain frogs a few years earlier.

Loretta floated from the back in a loose tunic that fluttered with her every movement. In her mid-fifties and still trim and attractive, Loretta projected a genteel Southerness that was fading from subsequent generations. Not that Izzy was fooled by the other woman's demure expression and small, folded hands. Loretta had a sharp business acumen and a will to survive.

"Nice to see you, Izzy." Her smile was wide and white but not warm in the least.

"I hope you're doing well." Izzy did her best to project professionalism, but her voice wavered.

"Just the usual aches and pains. What are you in the market for this fine morning?"

"I'm wrapping up some loose ends when it comes to tables and tents for the festival." Izzy tapped the folder she held to her chest like a shield.

"Oh really? How are vendor bookings coming along?"

"Swiftly. We've got new craft vendors coming from the Carolinas."

"Excellent news." Loretta moved away to rearrange a display of tartan scarves. "I've noticed your mother has been . . . distracted. I hope the festival doesn't suffer."

Even with the air-conditioning, Izzy fought the need to flap her shirt. Loretta had located Izzy's vulnerability in record time. "We have everything under control. In fact, I'm here because we haven't received your booth deposit."

"Your mother and I have known each other forever, Izzy. She's never had an issue giving me a little extra time." Loretta turned away as if the conversation was complete to her satisfaction. "If you'll excuse me, I have a delivery I must see to in the back. Toodle-oo, honey. Let me know if I can help with anything else."

Loretta disappeared through a hanging curtain to the storeroom, leaving Izzy at a loss. What would her mom do in the situation? The truth of the matter was that it would never have come to this point. Her mom would have gotten the money long before now.

Discarding the options of stalking through the curtain and demanding the money or staging a sit-in, Izzy chose to retreat and regroup outside. The bricks retained a hint of the night's chill, and she pressed her forehead against the rough wall.

"Things went that well, did they?" Although the voice came from behind her, Alasdair's brogue was unmistakable.

"I knew I should have changed into pants and a turtleneck."

His laugh echoed, and she turned her head, but didn't lift it off the brick wall. Alasdair propped his shoulder against the bricks and ducked his head to meet her eyes. Her gaze coasted down his body and back up to his face.

"What did you do?" She shifted until she faced him, mirroring his stance against the wall.

"It was either this or a tartan T-shirt that made my eyes cross. Plus, my shoes were still wet from the soaking you gave them yesterday. I didn't fancy contracting trench foot."

His blue button-down had been traded for a black T-shirt with the Scottish flag printed on the front that molded to every muscle of his chest and arms. While he still wore his dress pants, flip-flops had replaced his wingtips. The more casual look suited him as well if not better than Mr. *Town and Country*.

"They didn't have any shorts?"

"My choices were a pair that would fall to my ankles given the slightest tug or a pair that would rip along the seam the first time I bent over."

Thankful to have a wall for support, she blinked and stared at the zipper of his pants, wishing her imagination was a little less active.

"I look like a fool, don't I? You don't have to be nice." He tugged at the hem of the T-shirt. Was that a hint of self-consciousness reddening his cheeks or the start of heat-stroke?

"You look . . ." Hot. Sexy. Mouthwatering. ". . . like a Highlander. A native of Highland, Georgia, that is."

He nudged his chin toward the door of All Things Bright and Beautiful. "Did you slay the dragon?"

"No, I got singed."

"What can I do to help?" He raised an eyebrow, the gray of his eyes appearing slivery against the darkness of his stubble.

"Can you perform a personality transplant?"

"Even if I could, I wouldn't. Tell me what happened."

She beat back the blush his words incited. "She blew me off. I'll have to send Mom down to deal with her."

"Knowing how to handle confrontation takes practice. I promise you can do it with a little coaching."

"Who's going to coach me?"

He grabbed his heart like she'd delivered a mortal blow. "Ach, you wound me. Most of my job involves negotiation. The key is to be firm yet friendly."

"And if that doesn't work?"

"Then you have to be firm and not friendly, but let's go with step one for a start."

She didn't like asking for help or admitting a weakness, but she had a feeling Alasdair wouldn't hold it against her. "Alright, lay it on me."

They went over various scenarios and practiced with

Alasdair playing the part of Loretta. His ridiculous feminine Southern accent and playacting made it almost fun. He took her by the shoulders and turned her to face the door, his stubble grazing the shell of her ear as he rumbled. "You can do this, Isabel. Trust me."

She put her hand on top of his and looked over her shoulder at him. "Will you come in with me for moral support?"

He nodded, and she led the way into the shop. While she would never classify herself as confident, Alasdair had managed to instill some conviction. It might not be easy, but she could do this.

Loretta sat behind the counter on a stool and flipped through a magazine. Her urgent delivery had either been very small or an excuse. She glanced up, but flipped another page, her attention on her magazine. "Back so soon?"

Alasdair veered toward a display of Highland souvenir magnets.

Izzy took a deep breath and pasted on a smile. "I must get the vendor booths verified."

"You know I'll be there. I'm there every year."

"Yes, you are. And you know that a deposit is required every year. The festival has upfront costs that are defrayed by the vendor deposits."

"Honey, you're being unreasonable. Your mother has never had an issue letting me pay at my convenience." Loretta's voice edged toward annoyed, shedding its veil of politeness.

Was she being unreasonable? Should she back off? It was true Loretta had always paid. Eventually. Alasdair cleared his throat drawing her gaze. He gave her a subtle thumbs-up. His confidence had her shoulders unfurling from an inadvertent slump.

"Your delay is inconveniencing me, Loretta. Deposits were due two weeks ago. At this point, I can't guarantee your usual spot." Izzy consulted a sheet in her folder that was actually a diagram of where the portable potties would go. "I've got a very talented potter from the Carolinas that I'm sure will draw a crowd. He's planning a demonstration."

"I'm going to call Rose," Loretta said, dropping her smile and picking up her cell phone.

Loretta was her elder, and elders were meant to be deferred to and respected. Izzy fought feeling like a little kid in trouble. She had never made the transition to adult in Loretta's eyes. And whose fault was that? Not Loretta's, but Izzy's. She snapped her folder shut and tucked it under her arm.

"You do that. In the meantime, I can't guarantee your spot over a vendor who chooses to put down a deposit. Have a good day, Loretta."

She walked away on legs transformed into pudding—the Southern kind—fighting the urge to crawl back and apologize. A warm hand slipped to her lower back, offering support in more ways than one.

"Don't look back. You did well. Very well." His whisper held a smile.

They made it two steps down the sidewalk when Loretta pushed the door to her shop open, an envelope in hand. "Here. The deposit."

"Thank you." Izzy slipped it into the pocket of her folder without opening it.

"I expect my usual location."

"Of course." Izzy held Loretta's narrowed eyes and put her hand out. A peace offering and a sign of equality. After a moment's hesitation, Loretta took Izzy's hand in a firm shake, a new respect sprouting between them.

Half a block away, the adrenaline rushing Izzy's body exploded in a slightly hysterical laugh and fist pump. "I can't freaking believe I did it!"

"I knew you could."

"How could you possibly know? Loretta has railroaded me for years."

"You stood up to me and to Gareth."

"That's different."

"How so?"

"I was—*am*—protecting my mother." She put her finger in his face as a warning.

He grabbed her finger and pulled it away. "After seeing Gareth and your mother together, how can you possibly suspect their affection isn't genuine?"

She opened her mouth, then closed it. She feared her mother's affection for Gareth was one hundred and ten percent genuine. Now she was less concerned about Gareth stealing something than breaking it—namely her mother's heart.

Izzy stepped in front of Alasdair and forced him to a stop. "I assume you're aware of Gareth's circumstances back in Scotland?"

His expression went bland. "Somewhat."

"Would he ever leave Scotland? For good, I mean?"

Alasdair drew in a breath, but didn't answer beyond a small shake of his head that might have been an "I don't know" or a flat-out "no way." Either didn't bode well.

"My mother will never leave Highland."

"Are you certain about that?"

She *wasn't* certain. Unable to answer, she walked on.

Her mother was a romantic. A romantic who had given up a promising ballet career to move to the foothills of the Blue Ridge Mountains for love. Would she give up Stonehaven and move halfway around the world for Gareth?

"No use in worrying over something that will never come to pass, now is there?" she asked, not expecting or wanting an answer. The Brown Cow Coffee and Creamery beckoned them in with a bracing waft of fresh, strong coffee.

As she was most mornings, Mildred was behind the counter. Unlike most mornings when she acted like taking an order was a personal interruption, she popped off the stool with a smile aimed squarely at Alasdair.

"If it ain't one of our genuine Highlanders." She drawled out the word "gen-u-ine" to make it rhyme with swine. "I'm not sure I got around to introducing myself the other morning. I'm Mildred, but you can call me Millie."

"Nice to meet you, Millie. My name's Alasdair. Tea, if you please."

"Iced or hot?"

"Hot. I don't want dysentery." Alasdair winked at Izzy and a smile turned her lips before she could stop it. How could they already share private jokes?

"Sure thing, Alasdair." Millie said his name with satisfaction then poured hot water into a to-go cup and plopped a basket with an assortment of teas on the counter for him to choose from. "The honey ain't too bad if'n you're aiming to be healthy."

Alasdair chose a classic Earl Grey. While it was steeping, Millie stared at him with slowly blinking cow eyes and a grin so wide a strip of pink gum was visible at the top of her teeth. "Anything else I can get you? A cinnamon bun or a blueberry muffin?"

"No, thank you, lass." Alasdair's lips quirked.

When Millie didn't turn her brown cow eyes in Izzy's direction, she cleared her throat and stepped forward. "Could I have a to-go coffee, Millie?"

Millie pried her attention from Alasdair with obvious difficulty. "Sorry, Izzy. I kind of forgot you were there."

"We can't all be tall, hot as sin, and in possession of a sexy accent, I suppose," Izzy said dryly.

Alasdair swung around with wide eyes, and Izzy's snicker got stuck in her throat. Thinking it was bad enough, why had the opinion migrated to her mouth?

"I mean, if you're into that sort of thing. Which I'm not. At all. I prefer the complete opposite, in fact." Why was she still talking?

"Short, ugly, and with a terrible accent?" Alasdair tossed his tea bag and sipped from the steaming cup, his eyes dancing over the rim. He propped his hand on the counter and leaned closer to Millie. "Do you know a man who fits that description, Millie?"

"No shortage of short, ugly men around here." Millie handed Izzy her coffee. "Holt's not bad to look at though, eh Izzy?"

Alasdair's eyebrows hunched low with a scowl to match. "Who's Holt?

"Izzy's beau."

"He's not!" Izzy exclaimed.

"He'd sure like to be though, wouldn't he?" Millie elbowed Alasdair's arm. "He's been pining for our Izzy going on two years. Local farmer. Soybeans and pigs mostly. He's done well for himself even if he does trail eau de manure. But you'd never be short of barbecue or bacon, so that's a plus."

"A surplus of pork products is not a good enough reason to date someone," Izzy finally said.

"Or is it?" Millie asked as if she was prescient. "I sense something big happening soon, Izzy. Be on the lookout for a sign."

Old gossip about Millie's grandmother having the sight sent Izzy shuffling backward toward the door. Had Millie inherited the ability? "A sign like a plague of locusts? I think I'll pass. We'll catch you later. Alasdair and I have to pick up decorations over at the church."

Alasdair followed, albeit reluctantly and fighting laughter.

Millie called out, "You're going to sign up for the competitions, aren't you, Alasdair?"

He stopped at the door. "Competitions?"

"The athletic competitions. The caber. Hammer and stone throws. I'll bet you'd be great." Millie's cow eyes and gummy smile were back. "Izzy and her mom give the winners a trophy and a kiss. I'll bet Holt enters every single competition so he can get some of your sugar, Izzy." She waggled her eyebrows.

"I'm afraid I won't still be here for the festival," Alasdair said.

"That's a shame." Millie's smile had turned into a pout, and Izzy couldn't tamp down her own disappointment.

Alasdair gestured Izzy through the door. Once they were out of earshot, he asked, "What did she mean by getting your sugar?"

"Sugar is Southern-speak for a kiss. If you give someone sugar, you're kissing them."

"This Holt bloke is after your sugar and is willing to win it by engaging in the Highland games competitions? Sounds like something out of Robin Hood." The tease in his voice skated on the edge of laughter.

"It's not like I'm going to French the winner. It's a closed-mouth peck." Izzy chewed the inside of her cheek and shot him a side-eye glance. As nonchalantly as possible, she said, "You'll be missing a good time if you jet back to London before the festival."

"It can't be helped, I'm afraid. I've been gone too long as it is." His laughter morphed to something closer to longing. He stopped on the sidewalk and looked up and down the street. "I'll admit when I first drove up, Highland seemed like the punch line to a joke."

"And now?"

"It's growing on me."

"Like a fungus? Maybe I'll suggest that if we update our catchphrase." She tapped the writing on the pocket of his T-shirt. "Stay awhile. Let us grow on you like fungus."

All joking aside, she was proud of Highland. Maybe to outsiders Highland was a gimmick that provided a day or weekend of fun for tourists to laugh about later. Except, Izzy remembered what it had been like as a kid before the festival had taken hold. More storefronts had been empty and derelict than occupied. The gaily painted brick fronts had been blackened from time and inattention. Most young people left for college and never came back.

Izzy would never forget the wonder and excitement of attending her first festival as a seven-year-old. It started as a small county fair with a Scottish flair. The bagpipes and dancing had been magical, and that magic had breathed new life into the town. Now, they embraced and nurtured and protected Highland's small town charm at all costs.

Millie had stepped outside the Brown Cow and was leaning on a broom and talking to a couple of tourists who were taking selfies with their phones. Mrs. Younts, the librarian, was watering the red cascading flower baskets hanging on the iron light pole in front of the library.

A man in tartan britches tucked into black rubber boots bustled toward them. Dr. Jameson was a veterinarian, the mayor, and the leader of the Highland Pipe and Drum Corps. He took all his jobs seriously. He was a bachelor and an eccentric and was dedicated to all things Scottish. The perfect ambassador for their town.

"Izzy! Glad I ran into you before practice." His smile was a mile wide and all encompassing.

"Dr. Jameson. This is Alasdair Blackmoor, a friend of Gareth's." Izzy performed the requisite introductions with a true smile.

A small, wiry man with graying hair and boundless energy, Dr. Jameson took Alasdair's hand in an energetic shake, looking up and smiling into his face. "A real pleasure to meet yet another Scot. Believe it or not, we don't see many of the real thing around here." His old-fashioned drawl juxtaposed humorously with his all-Scottish all-the-time wardrobe.

"Nice to make your acquaintance as well." Alasdair chuffed a charming laugh. "To be fair, I'm only half Scottish, although I grew up in Glasgow."

"Half, whole, still a pleasure." Dr. Jameson looked back and forth between them. "Are you helping our Izzy with the festival?"

"She's got things well in hand and doesn't need my paltry help." Alasdair said it like he meant it.

"How are tickets to the opening night whisky tasting selling?" Izzy asked.

"Like hotcakes as usual. Preacher Hopkins left the storeroom door unlocked for one of us to pick up the table decorations. I've got practice then a foaling to attend. Would you mind running by and storing them in the barn?"

"I had already planned on it. Even better that I've got a pair of extra hands with me."

Dr. Jameson was off like a dervish, jogging into the street, almost getting clipped by the bumper of a truck, then stopping to have a laughing conversation with the driver.

"Did you just volunteer me for manual labor?"

"Hey, you're the one that keeps offering to help." They strolled down the sidewalk toward Bubba's Fix-it shop and her truck. "Is Bubba going to fix you up?"

"It will be ready before he closes up today."

"Is twelve hours of no contact killing you?"

She was teasing, but his voice was thoughtful when he answered. "It's been refreshing. Freeing even."

Mr. Timmerman poked his head out of the Dapper Highlander like a turtle. His attention to detail and his keen eye made him an excellent tailor and purveyor of men's clothes. "Excuse me, Izzy. I was wondering if you could take a tartan to Mr. Connors for his approval."

"Sure, no problem."

"Come in and cool down while I grab the sample." Mr. Timmerman slid back inside and disappeared into a back room.

Izzy ran her fingers over a traditional red and green tartan cloth that reminded her of Christmas. Alasdair fingered the hem of a kilt adorning a headless mannequin who also wore knee socks and fancy black shoes.

"Do you have a closetful?" Izzy came up next to him.

"I vaguely remember donning one for a school play when I was young, but I don't have one of my own." His smile didn't release into a frown, but she sensed a burgeoning tension around his mouth. "If my mum could have, I think she would have filtered my Scottish blood out."

She blinked up at Alasdair, his stare boring through the mannequin to a time and place beyond where they stood. She wanted to drag him back from the cliff's edge of sadness, but considering her track record of saying the wrong thing, she remained silent.

Still standing shoulder to shoulder, she brushed the back of his hand with her fingertips. His hand jerked, but instead of scuttling away like a crab, his fingers linked with hers, their palms pressed together.

Mr. Timmerman returned with a length of beautiful green and gray tartan fabric. A pair of reading glasses had scooched down his nose, held in place by the bulbous tip. His ruddy cheeks and barrel-like body meant he had been tapped as Highland's Santa in the Christmas parade for the last decade or more.

"Gareth asked me if I could obtain his family's tartan,

and I believe I managed it." Mr. Timmerman ran a hand over the folded sample as if it was shot with gold thread and precious.

Alasdair took the tartan out of his hands before Izzy could reach for it. He traced the lines of plaid with a finger. "It's lovely."

"It is rather. Not as vibrant as some, but I prefer the understated colors. I imagine the men wearing it would blend with the trees and grasses for successful hunts."

"What you're saying is this is the tartan version of our camouflage?" Izzy grinned, but both men ignored her. Mr. Timmerman had tilted his head to study Alasdair.

"Are you and Gareth kin?" Mr. Timmerman asked.

Alasdair pressed his lips together and bobbed his head in what could have been a yes or a no. "We're friends."

When it became clear Alasdair wasn't offering additional insights, Mr. Timmerman stepped back with a salesmanlike smile. "If you're in the market for a kilt for the games, come and see me."

With Alasdair still in possession of the fabric, Izzy led them back outside. He glanced over his shoulder. "How does a specialty store like that survive in such a small town?"

"Mr. Timmerman has orders come in from all over the United States and even other countries. He's the real deal when it comes to kitting out people for reunions or Highland games or simply because they love the look."

Alasdair made a sound of disbelief. "It boggles the mind that many people want to live in the past."

Izzy rolled her eyes. "You haven't spent enough time in the South. As a people, Southerners are obsessed with the past, no matter how problematic and complicated. But you should be proud of your Scottish roots."

As if the universe was trying to prove something, a single clear note from a bagpipe reverberated off the brick to settle in her chest. The Highland Pipe and Drum Corps had commenced their practice in the courtyard behind the Dancing Jig.

More bagpipes joined in, and the march they played made her heart ache with an emotion she couldn't categorize. Sometimes it was better to feel than understand. She and Alasdair locked eyes, and she grabbed his forearm to strengthen the connection.

"Do you feel it?" she whispered.

His lips parted but he didn't answer. He didn't need to. She could sense the effect the music had on him. They remained locked together on the sidewalk for the duration of the march. Izzy had a vague recognition of people walking past them, but it was like they were invisible to everyone but each other.

The note faded and clapping erupted from the tourists and locals alike. The noise broke the spell binding them. Alasdair pulled his arm from her grasp and rubbed the heel of his hand over his breastbone.

"I left Glasgow for Cambridge with conflicted feelings about Scotland. I even tried to shed my accent and adopt something more posh sounding, but I soon gave that up as impossible. Whenever I get upset or excited, my brogue intensifies."

"Why were you so conflicted?"

"Because my da was Scottish and I wanted no part of him after . . . after everything that happened."

All Izzy knew was that his father had died in a car accident. Whatever else had happened seemed equally as devastating as the loss. Not sure if he would welcome her prying, she bit her lip and worked to formulate a reply.

"Izzy!" A familiar deep baritone had her tensing and looking around like a hunted animal. Holt Pierson took ground-swallowing lopes across the street toward them. "I was going to ride out to Stonehaven this afternoon." Holt towered over her and had at least three inches on Alasdair, who he favored with a curious glance.

Whereas Alasdair moved with a feline, arresting grace, Holt was more like a bull. He was attractive in a good-old-boy way, his smile ready and wide, his blond hair sun-streaked, and his blue eyes crinkled in the corners from being outside. He was open and honest and uncomplicated. Because Izzy's mind never seemed to slow, his simple approach to life both attracted and repelled her.

Even though there was absolutely nothing going on with Alasdair—or Holt for that matter—Izzy's face went hot. Holt had been forthright about his interest in her. It had been refreshing and flattering and convenient. Except for the very inconvenient fact that she wasn't drawn to him.

She'd hoped she could cultivate an attraction, like tending a fragile green shoot in the garden. But that shoot withered and died right there on the sidewalk between them. Her instant attraction to Alasdair hadn't required tending; it grew like she had planted magic beans.

Forcing a polite smile, Izzy said, "I got your messages. I'm so sorry I didn't call you back, but I've been super busy with the festival. Are you entering the games this year?"

"Of course. I have to keep the streak alive." Holt curled his right arm and made his biceps strain at his T-shirt. He had won the Laird of the Games athletic prize three years running. It was given to the man who averaged the highest over all the events.

Holt turned his focus on Alasdair, his eyes narrowing as if was assessing how far he could toss the other man. Alasdair met the semi-civilized aggression with his own brand of belligerence, his arms crossed over his chest, his jaw set. The cloud of testosterone and posturing confused her.

Darting a glance back and forth between them, she said,

"Where are my manners? Alasdair Blackmoor, Holt Pierson."

"A pleasure to make your acquaintance." Alasdair stuck a hand out.

Holt stared at Alasdair's outstretched hand for a heartbeat too long before meeting him halfway for a perfunctory shake. The toothy smile that spread over Holt's face didn't lighten the contentious atmosphere. "Likewise. Sounds to me like you're kin to Ms. Rose's Scottish friend."

"Not kin, but a mate of Gareth's, yes."

"Will you be entering the games?" Holt asked.

"Unfortunately, I won't still be here."

"Oh well." Holt flicked his gaze up and down Alasdair. "You don't look like you've ever handled a caber anyhow."

"I can't say I make a habit of tossing around trees," Alasdair said as coolly as James Bond facing down a nemesis.

"Izzy and I went through school together." Holt's voice was oddly territorial. "We've been friends for years now."

"That's nice. How long have we known each other, Isabel?" Alasdair raised his eyebrows, the twinkle of amusement in his eyes surprising her.

"Two days?" How was that possible? Already Alasdair had planted roots in her head like kudzu.

"No one calls her Isabel." Holt snorted. "She hates it."

"Do you hate it?" Alasdair cocked his head and regarded her, waiting for her to confirm or deny.

She couldn't remember a time when she hadn't been called Izzy by almost everyone. It had been her daddy's nickname for her. "Isabel" belonged to a ballerina or a socialite who dressed to impress. Someone sophisticated. "Izzy" belonged to an awkward girl who fell off stages and too often said the wrong thing.

Except hearing her given name roll off Alasdair's tongue in his husky brogue made her insides tingle like she'd plugged into an electrical source. "I like it when *you* call me Isabel."

Alasdair and Izzy exchanged a smile that left Holt out.

"You mind if I borrow Izzy for a second?" Holt was an unwelcome insertion.

"Isabel isn't an umbrella to be loaned, but if you'd like a moment of privacy, by all means . . ." Alasdair linked his hands behind his back and strolled away.

"That was rude, don't you think?" Holt asked.

Izzy didn't give Holt the agreement he sought. She stared at Alasdair's broad back as he stopped to window-shop at Frannie's Antiques and Florist. With effort, she returned her focus to Holt. "What's up?"

A deep nervous rumble came from Holt's throat. "I was wondering if you want to get dinner with me this week. I had a great time the other night and . . . well, I'd like to see you again."

A second date. She hadn't even been sure their first dinner had been a date until he'd picked up the check at the end. She and Holt had known each other since kindergarten. Through playground antics and acne and prom (which they had attended with different people). The transition from old friends to a romantic couple had seemed a stretch a week ago. Now, it felt downright impossible.

When she didn't immediately answer, his voice took on a cajoling tone. "If not dinner, how about a drink at the Dancing Jig? I actually had an idea for the festival I wanted to run by you. Come on. No pressure. Please?"

Except, he was pressuring her. The Piersons were supportive of the festival and sponsored one of the food tents. She didn't want to jeopardize that relationship by hurting Holt's feelings, even if accepting left her with a squirmy feeling in her stomach. "Okay. A quick drink to discuss your idea. I'm slammed right now."

They firmed up the time. Izzy walked away feeling like

she'd made a bargain with the devil. After only two days, Alasdair knew more about her than Holt did, which was disturbing on multiple fronts. Why was she allowing herself to get close to a man who was leaving in days? Or was that exactly why she felt safe enough to share with him?

"What did your erstwhile suitor want?" Alasdair asked when she joined him in front of Frannie's, the explosive display of flowers and greenery beautiful.

The admission she'd agreed to meet Holt for drinks got stuck in her throat, though she couldn't say why. Alasdair wouldn't care, and she wasn't interested in Holt anyway. She and Alasdair might even share a laugh over it. Nonetheless, the not-date felt like a breach of a trust—a breach that was wholly in her imagination.

"The Piersons have been festival sponsors for years." Nervous heat flared at her non-answer.

"Isn't that nice," Alasdair said in not very nice voice.

Unable to read the situation and feeling uncomfortable, she shifted and restarted their stroll. It was times like this when her mouth ran away from her brain. Not this time though. She consciously steered them to a different topic. "You know, if you keep growing a beard, you and Gareth will look like father and son."

It took her two steps to realize he'd stopped in his tracks.

"Why would you say that?" The tension pulling his mouth into a frown gave her the impression of anger. But why?

"I don't know. Mr. Timmerman got me thinking about how much you favor Gareth."

"Gareth is not my da. My da is dead." His voice was flat and emotionless.

"I know. Sorry I brought it up." She waved toward the white steeple soaring behind them to stabilize the shaky ground she found herself on with him and gestured toward the truck. "Let's head over to the church and get the centerpieces and stuff."

The church sat behind the main thoroughfare on an oak-lined street. Built in the late 1800s, the church was a picturesque white clapboard building set with stain-glassed windows and a tall steeple. The deep red front doors were bright and welcoming against the white, but she bypassed them to circle around back to the bricked two-story extension added in the seventies to accommodate a growing congregation.

She parked close to the utilitarian doors of the entrance and let down the tailgate to make loading easier. As promised, the church was unlocked. The white concrete-block hallway was oppressively quiet and Izzy found herself tiptoeing.

The storeroom's dark gray metal door stood ajar at the end of a dim hallway. This part of the church smelled like crayons and cleaners. As a kid, she had spent every Sunday morning in one of the rooms learning Bible stories. Since she'd started writing, she skipped church in favor of working on her manuscript, showing up sporadically and only at her mom's prodding.

"I'll pull the stuff we need into the hall if you want to load it in the truck bed." She kept her tone brisk and brief. The mood between them had shifted and she didn't know how to get them back to their earlier ease.

With the door wedged three feet open with a wooden triangle, she slipped inside the crammed room, jamming her toe on the doorstop. She pulled the chain of a single light bulb swinging from the ceiling to reveal a catchall of items. Paper and pens and glass votives and silk flowers. Christmas decorations took up one corner and Easter another. An entire shelf was dedicated to the glory of tartan.

She squatted and pulled a cardboard box from under a

length of fake garland, opening it to verify the contents. Red and green tapers lined the box. A deepening shadow cut across the room and spun her around. Alasdair was fully inside, examining a figurine stashed on a shelf. The door was swinging shut, gaining momentum as it strived to make fools of the unsuspecting.

"Don't"—she barked the word and scrambled for the knob, finishing on a whisper of dread as the clang of it shutting faded into silence—"let the door close."

Chapter Six

"What's the matter?" Alasdair shifted away from a nativity scene made up of people and animals in tartan.

Izzy jiggled the knob and pushed, already knowing it was useless but needing to try. "The door is notorious for getting stuck closed. That's what the wedge was for." The one she had knocked cattywampus. Not that she planned to admit this was her fault.

"Here. Allow me." In his voice was a manly confidence she hoped he could back up with Herculean strength.

She stepped back and made a "be my guest" flourish with her hands. The top of her head knocked the dangling light bulb. It pulsed light as if gasping its last watts. Alasdair dueled with the door. He twisted the knob and set one shoulder into the door, grunting with the effort. His back muscles put on a show under his black T-shirt. Yet, the door didn't budge.

He braced both hands against the door and leaned all his weight into the push. The seams of his pants strained, and his T-shirt edged up exposing a strip of skin. The dip along his spine was flanked by muscles and absolutely no fat.

He straightened, shuffled his hands through his hair,

and linked them at his nape, giving the door a meaningless kick. She sidestepped around him and spent fruitless minutes banging and yelling. No one else had been parked in the lot. Preacher Hopkins had probably gone for food or to visit a sick parishioner. They were alone and stuck.

"Why did you follow me in? I said I would hand everything out to you." Misplaced or not, her frustration boiled over. The small space kept them within two feet of each other at all times.

"Oh, this is my fault? How was I to know the door was crafted by Satan's hand?" He leaned against the door, crossing his arms over his chest. The light cast harsh shadows over his face.

"It wasn't made by Satan; just installed by him." She rubbed her temples. "The door is a known menace. The choir director got stuck after practice one Wednesday night and her husband didn't notice until morning, which raised all sorts of questions as to how he spent his evening."

His lips twitched but a smile didn't crack through his irritation. "You might have warned me volunteering to help you would lead to my untimely death in a church cupboard."

"No one is going to die." The closet was getting stuffier by the minute. Either the air-conditioning didn't extend to the small room or the vents were being blocked by boxes. "Probably."

"Probably?" This time a hint of exasperated amusement was reflected in his raised brows. "Do you have service on your mobile?"

Izzy couldn't look him in the eye. "I sort of left my phone in the truck. Blame fashion designers."

"What does a bloody designer have to do with your mobile being in the truck?"

She patted her hips. "No pockets. Women need pockets as much if not more than men do."

He banged his head back against the door a few times.

"That's really not loud enough to get anyone's attention, Alasdair."

He pinned her with his gaze. "How long before someone finds us, do you think?"

"Lots of people know where we are. The preacher. Dr. Jameson. Mom. I think I even mentioned it to Millie, didn't I? Before dinner, for sure." As if on cue, her stomach rumbled. Her blackberry jam and toast for breakfast seemed a long time ago.

They stood in silence for a few minutes. Nervous energy invaded, and she turned in a slow circle. "There's got to be a couple of chairs stashed in here. We might as well get comfortable, right?"

"Right," he said unenthusiastically.

She pushed Christmas wreaths and garlands aside to search for folding chairs. Movement stilled her. A giant black smudge skittered up a piece of garland straight for her throat. Or at least it felt that way.

Her yelping scream echoed around her as she lurched backward. Her heel caught on the corner of a box and she windmilled to catch her balance. She hit a shelf with her hand and made a grab for stability, but her weight only popped it up and sent everything skidding off. Plastic forks scattered along with a pack of paper plates. A box of ribbons upended and covered everything like confetti at the end of a party.

Not that they had a chance to enjoy the colorful display. The back of her head smacked the light bulb. It popped, the sound electrical and physical, plunging them into darkness. The aftermath was silent. A sliver of light showed from under the door.

"Alright there, Isabel?"

She took an inventory, her finger catching on a piece of glass in her hair. She picked it out and tossed it away. "I've got some glass in my hair, but otherwise I'm okay."

"What's next, do you suppose? An invasion of rats? A flood? Or the plague of locusts Millie promised?" Unbelievably, she heard no anger in his voice. In fact, something that sounded like amusement rumbled under the surface.

"I don't know, but we're trapped with a giant man-eating spider. Let's hope it stays in the garland."

"Indeed." His warm hands grasped her shoulder, and he pulled her toward him. "Let's see about getting the glass out of your hair before you accidently open an artery with a shard."

"Har-har." She didn't protest when he skimmed his hands to her neck. His solidness was comforting in the dark.

Her breath caught. A shiver shot through her that had nothing to do with fear of giant spiders. He speared his fingers through her hair, his touch deft on her scalp. She sighed and tilted her head back, holding his waist. Pieces of glass plinked to the floor. He touched every inch of her scalp and finger-combed her hair. She could almost pretend his touch was meant for seduction and wasn't a mission of mercy.

A throaty hum of pleasure escaped, snapping her back to reality. "Um. Thanks. I'm good now."

"Of course." His jagged voice sounded like it too had been a casualty of her clumsiness.

They remained touching, her hands on his waist and his laying on her shoulders, his thumbs tracing her collarbones in a pseudo-caress. The darkness lent a dreamlike quality to the moment, but what happened here would have consequences.

She dropped her hands, but there was no retreat from

the warmth of his body. Her knees were wobbly and she fought the urge to lean into him. "Do you think it's safe to sit on the floor?"

"Let me check for glass." He squatted down. "Seems safe enough."

She lowered herself to the floor, tucking her skirt around her legs for protection as much as possible. "At least the concrete is cooler."

He didn't answer, but joined her, shoulder to shoulder, leaning against the door. He heaved a sigh.

"We'll be found soon," she said as much to reassure herself as him.

Time passed. It might have been five minutes or fifteen. As Alasdair shifted, the crinkle of cellophane broke the silence.

"It's not much, but I picked up a couple of peppermints at Bubba's. Want one?" he asked.

"Sure. Thanks."

Alasdair felt for her hand with both of his and laid the piece of candy in her palm.

The smell of their shared peppermints helped relax her. She closed her eyes since there was nothing to see anyway and let her mind wander.

She patted his thigh. "You can eat me, Alasdair."

He made a strangling sound, drawing his knees up, the strangle turning into a hacking cough. Izzy pounded his back until she heard him take a breath and relax back against the door.

"I swallowed my peppermint." After a beat of silence, he asked softly, "Did you offer to let me *eat* you?"

"Yeah, in case we're stuck in here for days or weeks. You'd be too tough." She poked his biceps.

His shoulder moved against hers. Was he choking again? Anxiety jolted her, and she put her arm around his shoulders, preparing to perform the Heimlich. Laughter rumbled from his chest. The kind that left him breathless and fighting snickers even after he got himself under control.

"What's so funny?" she asked, tightening her arm around his shoulders.

"*You*. You make me laugh." He slipped his arm around her shoulders, so she leaned against him more than the door. "Why would I be too tough?"

"Because of your muscles. You must maintain a serious workout schedule." She walked her fingers across his chest to squeeze his biceps. "See, too hard to be tender."

"Most women wouldn't complain about an appendage being too hard." More laughter vibrated his voice.

"I'm being serious, Alasdair. I would make a more pleasant meal."

"I have no doubt you would be delicious." His brogue had thickened with a sexy tease, and the conversation finally registered in a different context.

Her blush could have started a forest fire. "I wasn't talking about . . . *that* kind of eating."

Another laugh emerged from him. This one she could feel to her bones. When she tried to pull away, he resettled her so her back was tucked into the nook of his arm. He grounded her in the darkness, and she didn't pull away in spite of her embarrassment.

More silence took root. Their position would have been unthinkable an hour before, but trapped in the darkness, she felt strangely at ease. He wrapped his arm around her chest to hold her other arm, and she grabbed his forearm with both hands, letting her head loll back on his chest, tucked under his chin.

"Tell me something most people don't know about you," he said. "Something your alfalfa farmer doesn't know."

"Holt farms soybeans."

"Whatever. Tell me a secret," he commanded.

She could tell him about the time she'd shoplifted a book out of the used-book store, but that didn't seem deep or important enough for the mood.

"I want to be a writer. No, more than that, I want to write the next great Southern novel. Like *To Kill a Mockingbird*." She shrugged. "It's not going that great though."

"How can you judge how well it's going?"

"The growing number of rejections is a pretty good indication."

His hum was thoughtful. "What makes a novel Southern? Or great, for that matter?"

"Southern novels are full of angst and symbolism and a study of how our troubled past informs our present. As far as great . . . I want people to study it and debate on it."

"You want to write serious literature."

"Yeah, I guess so."

"But you're not serious; you're . . . whimsical."

She twisted around to send him a glare, but it didn't make an impact in the darkness, so she settled back against him. "That's a nice way of saying I'm weird, isn't it? I'm an accountant, for goodness sake. No one is more serious than an accountant during tax season."

"You're smart and I have no doubt, you are excellent at your job, but . . ."

"But what?"

"You named your letter opener Rupert."

She harrumphed.

"And introduced him to me."

"I was joking." She let a few beats of silence fall before she added, "Okay, so I used to make up stories about fairies and witches living in the woods, but just to entertain myself. And the kids at the library on occasion. And in the nursery at church in high school. But, they were mostly for Daddy. He thought they were funny. Since he died . . . I don't know."

"Death is sobering, and you turned to more serious subjects," Alasdair said.

"Exactly."

"I hope you write your great Southern novel. If that's what you really want." His tone made her think he was holding back thoughts and opinions she might not appreciate.

"It's want I want," she gritted out even though her doubts had grown heavier over the last year. "Your turn. Tell me a secret. A deep, dark one."

Alasdair took a breath as if gathering his nerve for a bloodletting. Was he actually going to confess all? The darkness whispered encouragements in his ear. The truth was a wound that needed excising, and Isabel would understand. He was sure of it. Sure of her.

"My parent's marriage broke up because Da had an affair with his assistant. She wasn't much older than me. Not the first woman he messed around with either, but she was the final straw for Mum. Da moved out and set up house with her."

"I didn't realize your parents divorced before he died."

"They weren't even legally separated at the time. It all happened so suddenly." He paused. It was only too easy to put himself back in his seventeen-year-old skin. The anger was still there, along with the regrets. "I was so blasted mad at Da for what he did to Mum and to me and our family. I stopped talking to him and to—" He'd almost given away a secret he didn't own.

He continued, not pausing long enough for her to question his near slip. "Da called me that morning. The morning he ran off the road."

"You couldn't know what was going to happen. It's not your fault." Izzy found his hand and clasped it. He hung on as if she were keeping him from falling off a precipice.

"Maybe not. I don't know anymore. But it happened, and it hurt that I was never going to be able to forgive him. That our relationship would remain stymied in all the bad. I left Glasgow for Cambridge a few months later and Mum followed soon after and never looked back. She didn't have any good memories of Scotland left."

"Neither of you ever went back?"

"I've been back. It's where my deep, dark secret lives."

Her hand tightened on his. "It's a person. Your father's mistress?"

He should have known she'd guess the gist. "And her son. My half-brother, Lewis. Kyla was pregnant when Da was killed. I think he would have married her eventually. At least, that's what she claimed, but after Da died, she was left alone and with nothing. Da hadn't changed his will and as he and Mum weren't even separated, everything went to Mum."

"Did your mother know Kyla was pregnant?"

"No. And I couldn't be the one to tell her. She was already devastated about the infidelity, the separation, and his death."

"But you said you've been back to Glasgow?"

"It took a few years to get over my anger and grief and guilt, but I finally ran Kyla to ground." It had been a shock to finally meet Lewis and recognize pieces of himself in the boy's watchful gray eyes. "Kyla married a nice man who owns a butcher shop and had two more kids."

"She doesn't resent you and your mother for everything that happened?"

"No, she's a decent lass and a good mother. Maybe Da would have been happy with her, I don't know." Might-have-beens were dangerous, and he put them out of his mind. "Lewis is eleven now. A fine lad."

He couldn't tell Isabel everything roiling around in his heart. Like how he wanted to take Lewis to Cairndow to teach him the joys of fishing and shooting and swimming in the loch. But to do so meant telling Gareth. Even in a place as isolated as Cairndow, thorny vines of gossip flourished and would carry the news to his Mum.

"It's been a long time. Maybe your mother would understand."

"Perhaps. But she'll never forgive and wouldn't approve of any relationship between me and Da's bastard child." He gave a gusty sigh. "Now you know my deepest, darkest secret."

"You'll figure out what to do about Lewis and your mother."

"How can you be so sure?"

"Because I can tell you care about them both. It'll all work out." She stroked his arm. Perhaps it was meant to comfort him, but it only made him more aware of her and all the places he wanted her hands. "Tell me about your mother."

Alasdair barked a laugh. "Her current obsession is getting me married to a woman of her choosing."

"What kind of girl earns her seal of approval?"

"English, of course. A lady, for certain. Actual title not required but appreciated." Every single one had been attractive and accomplished and interesting, but he'd been bored. Nothing like how he felt with . . .

He stopped before he finished the thought, but his arm tightened around her and he nuzzled his nose into the hair at her crown and took a deep breath. He would remember her scent long after he left Highland.

"Posh Spice."

He was getting used to not knowing how the words that popped out of her mouth connected to the subject at hand. "What is that?"

"You know, Posh Spice from the Spice Girls." When he

made a sound of puzzlement, she elbowed him in the ribs. "The gorgeous one married to David Beckham."

He smiled as the connection clicked into place. "Exactly who my mum would set me up with."

"But not who you would choose?"

"Not my type. At all."

"What is your type?" she asked innocently. Except she had grown rigid against him as if his answer was important.

What could he say? He'd dated but had never contemplated marriage. Even a weekend away with a woman had seemed too much of a commitment. But, if he had to choose a type . . .

"Someone who makes me laugh." Until Isabel he couldn't recall a single girl he'd been out with that met this one requirement.

"And?"

"And what?"

"Throw me a bone here. Blonde or brunette? Thin or curvy?"

"She has to smell good." *Like wildflowers*, he didn't add, afraid the truth would give too much of himself away.

"A funny girl who wears deodorant. You might want to set your standards a bit higher." Her voice lilted with her amusement, which made him feel lighter.

"I don't know. I've dated a string of woman and none of them have met my standards."

"A string, huh? I don't think my exes would even constitute a line fragment," she said on a self-depreciating laugh.

He smiled and rubbed his chin against her temple, her soft hair tickling him. Instead of shying away like he expected, she shifted toward him.

In the darkness, reality ceased to exist. The strange

cupboard in the middle of the Highland Baptist Church didn't abide by the laws of the universe. He and Isabel could have been trapped for minutes or hours or eons.

He cupped her cheek and stroked the silky skin of her jaw, his fingers guiding his lips in for a landing in the dark. He made contact with the corner of her mouth, but adjusted and caught her gasp. Their breath mingled, the moment achingly intimate.

He'd kissed other women before, of course, but all of a sudden, he couldn't recall when or whom. Her lips erased his memories or perhaps shoved them into a file labeled "insignificant." She took fistfuls of his shirt and pulled him closer. Her boldness jerked his heart into a gallop but she had surprised him at every turn, so why had he expected her kiss to be mundane?

"Alasdair." His name came on a wisp of her breath, turning stone to flesh inside of him. Hearing his name in her honeyed Southern accent sent blood rushing through his body.

He scooted down on the door and pulled her half on top of him, her leg notching between his. He nipped her bottom lip and when she opened, he touched his tongue lightly to hers. Little by little, the kiss deepened until their tongues twined, and their breathing grew rapid as if they were pacing each other in a race.

Her body molded against his, and he allowed his hands to wander down to chart the arch of her back, then through the curve of her waist to grasp her hips. She wiggled closer and his fingers glanced over bare skin where her shirt had ridden up. He took the invitation and slid his palm over her silken skin to the dip of her spine.

Even though he couldn't see her, he was aware of her every breath and movement. He'd never been so in tune with a woman both emotionally and physically. She wanted more as much as he did, but what would happen if they were discovered naked in a church cupboard? Would Isabel be run out of Highland by the townspeople with pitchforks?

Noise penetrated the isolation. Her tongue retreated, and his lips stilled. His heartbeat played a pagan rhythm in his ear, but that's not what had yanked him out of the carnal daze. Muffled male laughter. The *clomp* of feet. A fist pounded on the door, slicing them apart.

"You in there, Izzy?"

"It's Preacher Hopkins," Isabel whispered. "We should . . ."

He was gratified to hear the hint of reluctance in her voice. Once they were out, what would happen? "Yes, we should."

She scrambled to her feet, pounded her fist on the door, and called out, "Yes, it's me! Can you get the door open?"

"Wilt and I should be able to manage," the preacher called out.

While the men on the other side of the door discussed strategies, distance and dissonance grew between them. He hadn't felt as close to anyone as he had to Isabel in a long time, but had it only been a side effect of the darkness and confinement like a prisoner confessing all to his captor?

He didn't try to diffuse the rising tension between them, and for once, Isabel seemed at a loss for words.

Preacher Hopkins called out. "Are you ready to push from your side? We've oiled the hinges and levered up the door from the bottom."

"Allow me." Alasdair shifted over, bumping Isabel aside, and put his shoulder to the door.

"Ready!" Isabel called.

The men push-pulled on the door. Light blinded Alasdair

and he sucked in a lungful of cool air. Two men stood on the other side. One was wiry with a graying Afro; the other was younger with a thick neck and brown hair, his thumbs tucked into a pair of braces.

The older man glanced between Alasdair and Isabel as if there was a game of tennis being played. "Ah, you weren't alone, Izzy. I'm Elmer Hopkins."

Alasdair took his hand in a shake, introduced himself, then added, "It was my fault. I let the door close on us, sir."

"No, I feel responsible." The preacher clapped a hand on Alasdair's shoulder. "It's high time we change this door. Wilt, this door is next on your to-do list."

"Very good, Preacher." Wilt snapped his braces then pulled a measuring tape from a pouch in his tool belt. "I'll give it a measure right now."

"What time is it?" Isabel asked, still squinting against the light.

"Half past two," Wilt said.

They'd spent two hours in the closet together. Alasdair shook his head, trying to reconcile time. He'd emerged a changed person. How could that happen in a mere two hours? Days should have passed. Weeks even.

Then again, opinions could change in a second. Decisions debated in mere minutes. Whole new theories formulated in a half hour. Why couldn't their connection shift in two hours?

Preacher Hopkins helped them load the decorations and tables, all the while regaling them with stories of his afternoon spent visiting parishioners at the nursing home. Even the reverend's everyday voice held a cajoling, sonorous quality as if prepared to lead sinners back to Christ whether he ran into them at the grocery store or the petrol station.

With the extra set of hands, the truck was loaded with the decorations and tables in no time. The preacher retreated after inviting Alasdair to church. Then, he and Isabel were alone.

Isabel met his eyes over the truck bed for a blink before she looked anywhere but his direction. Was that anger, indifference, or regret radiating from her?

He was coward enough not to ask.

Chapter Seven

After a brief stop for Alasdair to pick up his repaired mobile, the ride back to Stonehaven was accomplished in silence. He gripped his mobile tightly in one hand and the plaid fabric for Gareth in the other. Two different worlds seemed to call to him.

Although, for all the attention Isabel paid him on the ride, he could have made his calls right then and she wouldn't have noticed. He felt invisible. From the corner of his eye, he studied her. Perhaps she wasn't as detached as he assumed. While her gaze was on the road ahead, her hands clenched the wheel so tightly her knuckles showed white.

In retrospect, kissing her had been ill advised. Yet the universe had asked too much if it had expected him to ignore her wildflower-scented hair and soft curves. He couldn't recall the last time he'd lost himself in a woman. And they hadn't even made it to any of the really good stuff.

The really good stuff would have involved them naked and breaking a commandment or two in a church cupboard. At the very least, his invitation to sit in the front pew at Sunday service would have been rescinded.

Isabel didn't seem the sort to indulge in an affair, and as an ocean separated their lives, it was all they could afford. She deserved more. Better. Perhaps Holt the turnip farmer could make her happy.

His lip curled even though Holt might be a veritable saint who treated his crops and livestock with respect and compassion. A shudder ripped through him imagining Isabel laughing and kissing and teasing Holt. For reasons he couldn't explain, he was angry. At her, at himself, at Holt, at Fate.

"I'm going to unload everything. You can go on in the house. I don't need your help." Isabel stopped the truck close to the red barn and hightailed into it with a box of candles before Alasdair could put in a gentlemanly protest.

She obviously needed space. Well, so did he. Or at least privacy to put out fires and soothe hurt feelings. Bypassing the front door, he made for the cover of a row of evergreens at the edge of the field, the trees providing privacy and shade.

The first call was to his mum. She answered before the first ring ended.

"Alasdair, darling, I've been worried." While she wasn't a warm, emotional mother, she actually did sound distressed.

"I cracked the screen of my mobile and had to get it fixed. Sorry. But everything is fine here." He almost barked a laugh at the understatement.

"And your uncle?"

"He's fine too." If he told his mum Gareth might be in love, she'd treat it as a deadly disease.

"You're a fount of information. When is he coming home to see to your inheritance?"

"Jesus, Mum. Could you sound any more cold-blooded?"

"I'm realistic. Have you met the woman yet?"

"Rose Buchanan is her name, and she's very nice and

charming, and the two of you would get along splendidly. Especially since you're around the same age."

"That is a relief." His mum's voice took on a less strident tone. "When are you leaving?"

"I don't know yet. Soon."

"I'll hold you to it," she said even though he hadn't specified when "soon" might be. "Ta-ta, then. Love you."

"Love you too." He disconnected and stared at the blank screen. His assurances would only satisfy her for so long, but he had bigger issues to tackle at the moment.

He skimmed his email, which didn't include the information on Stonehaven he'd requested. Not only did George hand the information off to Richard, it seemed he was screwing Alasdair altogether. It was evening in London, but Alasdair guessed George would still be at work. He punched his name and was rewarded by a clipped, very English, "Hullo. George Garrison."

"George, you little twit. Why did you hand the Stonehaven information off to Richard?"

"Alasdair. Having fun on your little retreat, are you?"

George came from an upper-middle-class family, had gone to Oxford, and made no bones about his ambition to climb at Wellington. His usual deference toward Alasdair had shifted to slight condescension, which could only mean, Alasdair was on Richard's "list of piss," which was a fearful place for any employee to end up.

His hand suddenly clammy, Alasdair adjusted his grip on his mobile. "Why did you hand it off without consulting with me first?"

"Because I keep my ears open and knew the Saudi was interested in just such a property in the States. Richard is salivating to acquire it, and your lack of cooperation has been noted."

If George had been within arm's length, he would have

earned himself a well-deserved punch. "Richard will have to focus his efforts elsewhere. Stonehaven is not for sale."

"*Everything* is for sale, Alasdair, if you know what leverage to apply. *You* taught me that."

And the pupil becomes the master, Alasdair thought sarcastically. "There is no leverage here. It's a family estate and not for sale."

"Lesson two: There is always leverage."

Alasdair closed his eyes and took a deep breath, feeling the muck he'd raked get deeper. "I would count it as a personal favor if you'd leave it alone, George."

"I might be persuaded to drop the matter, but Richard has the scent and he won't give up. You know how he is."

Richard was a bloodhound when he was after a property, tenacious and obsessed. Alasdair pinched the bridge of his nose, still sore from the knock it took that morning. "What are you after with this stunt?"

George gave a mirthless laugh. "A promotion, of course. At first I was hoping if you got promoted, I would get slotted into your job, but now I think I could leapfrog you for the VP position. Richard really likes me. Says I have untapped, raw potential."

"Go fuck yourself, George." Alasdair ended the call. That had been foolish. He should have soothed George and manipulated him into mitigating the damage, but Alasdair had lost patience with George and Richard and himself.

Alasdair needed to quit faffing around and get a commitment from Gareth on when he was returning to his duties at Cairndow. Then, Alasdair could return to London, squash George like the roach he was, secure his promotion, and resume his life. Such that it was.

He made his way to the back door, stopping when two figures came into focus through the glass. Rose and Gareth clasped hands, nose to nose, illuminated by the sun. He clutched the plaid in his hand and stepped to the edge of the patio, presenting his back to the couple, feeling as if he was intruding.

A soft breeze from the north eased the heat of the afternoon sun, and he tilted his head back and closed his eyes, breathing deeply. The door behind him creaked on its hinges, but Alasdair remained planted, unable to let go of the brief peace.

Gareth joined him and stared over the field toward the woods, his hands clasped behind his back, rocking on his feet.

"Everything alright, laddie?" Gareth's question called forth memories of coming in soaking wet or muddy from afternoons running wild at Cairndow. Gareth had never scolded him or restricted his explorations. Alasdair had been free at Cairndow. These days he felt weighted down by chains he didn't know how to escape.

Maybe a good start was to unburden himself. "No. I messed up, Uncle Gareth."

"How so?"

"I asked someone at Wellington to work up financials for Stonehaven. It was supposed to be for my information only, but the file got passed on to my boss."

Gareth ran a hand down his face. "Why did you ask in the first place?"

"To protect you. I was worried about you."

Gareth was quiet for a long moment and when he spoke, his voice was thick. "Ach, Alasdair. I appreciate the sentiment, but there's no need."

"I realize that now, but the damage is done. My boss wants Stonehaven for one of Wellington's biggest clients. A Saudi with unlimited capital."

"Rosie will never sell," Gareth said firmly.

"Wellington has a long reach and can make things difficult for Rose and Isabel."

"Can you stop it?"

"Maybe. I don't know, but I'll certainly try." Dealing with Richard as an adversary rather than an ally would be a challenge. A challenge that may upend more than his chance at a promotion no matter if he won or lost. He could very well lose his job entirely.

"Let's keep this development between the two of us for now," Gareth said. "It may fizzle into nothing. I don't want Rosie to fash herself over something she can't control with the festival approaching."

"Secrets aren't good."

"But sometimes necessary to keep those you love from heartache," Gareth said matter-of-factly.

Alasdair was keeping his half-brother secret from his Mum and Gareth for that very reason. But secrets weighed down the keeper and someday would crush him.

"I see Timmerman got the plaid in." Gareth took the fabric and shook out the sample into a large square.

The change of subject was welcome. "He said it was the family tartan. Does it belong to the Blackmoors?"

"You might not remember, but there's a portrait in the gallery of Roderick Blackmoor, your many-times great-grandfather wearing tartan in a pattern very much resembling this. It was painted sometime after 1746 while the Dress Act was being enforced. Quite a rebellious—some might say foolish—thing to do. He could have been arrested."

"Just for wearing a kilt?"

"After the Jacobite uprising, the English looked to squash any nativism of those who lived." The bitterness in Gareth's voice surprised Alasdair.

"Don't tell me you're a revolutionary?"

Gareth's grin gleamed white but there was still an air of defiance about him. "Blackmoors are born revolutionaries."

Alasdair let out a long breath. "I'm not, but then again, perhaps I'm not a proper Blackmoor."

"Now that's a load of codswallop if I ever heard it. You just don't know what you're rebelling against."

"I'm not rebelling against anything."

"Not yet, my lad." Gareth tapped the side of his nose. "But battle lines are being drawn inside of you."

A battle. That was a good way to describe the way his internal organs reorganized themselves on a regular basis since stepping foot in Highland.

"Tell me more about Roderick Blackmoor." Memories of Gareth sitting on the side of his bed in the turret room of Cairndow tread close enough to catch. Alasdair didn't remember the details, only the feeling of being caught up in an adventure that was all the more exciting because it had actually happened.

"Roderick was a scoundrel." Gareth's brogue settled into the rhythm of a master storyteller. Of course, he'd had plenty of practice while giving tours of Cairndow. "He was handsome and charming and had all his teeth, or so they say."

"What a catch," Alasdair said with good-natured mockery. "The lasses must have gone mad for him."

"It's said the woman he married used a love potion to gain his attention, but it must have been almighty powerful, because he loved her until his dying breath. Annie was her name. She bore him ten bairns."

"Obviously, he didn't die with Bonnie Prince Charlie."

"Ach, no, but his left hand was cleaved clean through by a saber at Culloden. It's said he wrapped it in his plaid and kept fighting, taking down another dozen Sassenach before he succumbed to blood loss. The story goes that Annie traversed the battlefield searching for her beloved Roderick, finally finding him half buried under the bodies of his kinsmen. She hauled him to Cairndow and nursed him back from the dead."

"Is there a portrait of Annie Blackmoor in the gallery? Sounds to me like she's the hero of this story."

"Aye, it does, doesn't it?" Gareth chuckled then added. "Unfortunately, her face is lost to history, but it's said all the Blackmoors take after her. I imagine her with silver eyes and hair as black as a raven's wing standing guard over Cairndow."

It was an unusually romantic thought coming from his usually practical uncle. But then again, what did Alasdair really know of Gareth's heart?

A sudden longing to set foot on the land that had belonged to the Blackmoors for hundreds of years welled up and filled the hollow places that London had carved like a stream eroding the bedrock of his history. He was homesick for a place that had never truly been his home.

Or had it? Cairndow had been his safe place. His favorite place. Riding beside Gareth as a boy along the two-lane road that wound through the moor had always lit sparklers of excitement in his chest. He'd learned to ride a horse and climb a tree. He'd had his first kiss and got foxed for the first time. He'd learned to drive in Gareth's old Land Rover. So many firsts. So many good memories he'd tried to bury after his da had died.

"After Da died, I shouldn't have . . ." The regret cut keenly into Alasdair's heart.

"No need to apologize, lad. Life is complicated and yours more than most." Gareth continued to stare into the woods and beyond, maybe all the way to Cairndow. "Your da made some foolish decisions, but he was my brother. I had to stand beside him, even in death."

"Mum was so hurt, and I was mad. So angry at what he'd done."

"I was too, but it didn't stop me from loving him."

"Didn't stop Mum either, which made things even harder for her." Alasdair hesitated. Gareth had the right to know about his nephew, and after speaking the truth to Isabel, Alasdair had found a new courage. "Speaking of secrets, I've been keeping a big one for a few years now."

"From me or your mum?"

"From everyone."

Gareth shifted toward him, tension pulled his mouth taut. "This sounds ominous."

Easing into the confession would only be more painful, like taking baby steps into the cold waters of the loch at Cairndow. Better to plunge straight into the deep waters. "Kyla was pregnant when Da died. You have an eleven-year-old nephew in Glasgow named Lewis."

Gareth's mouth gaped slightly, and he shook his head. Not sure whether he was in denial or merely processing the information, Alasdair went on. "I hired an investigator to track her down a few years ago. I wanted to connect with my half-brother."

"How did you know?" The question could have been applied to many of the facts.

"I confronted her after the funeral. I was furious she'd turned up and upset Mum. My outrage was immature and misplaced, but I was young. I was ready to blister her when she started crying and told me she was four months along and that Da had told her he was thrilled and they'd marry as soon as legally possible."

"Christ Almighty. What did you do?" Gareth murmured.

"I accused her of lying. Insulted her. Was generally a git. I ran home to tell Mum everything, but when I looked in her eyes, I knew it would break the last bit of her spirit. So, I said nothing." In a smaller voice, he added, "Did nothing."

"You're doing something now, though, aren't you?" Gareth's eyes held no judgment, only thoughtfulness.

"Nothing significant. Lewis and I text and video chat. I've been to Glasgow a few times to see him. Considering how badly we treated Kyla, she's supported our reconnection." Alasdair took the tartan fabric from Gareth and ran his hands over the soft weave. "I want to bring him to Cairndow. Would you allow it?"

"Allow it? I'll welcome you both with bagpipes and a feast." Gareth smiled but his eyes gleamed with sadness and his own regrets. "Does he favor your da?"

"He looks like all the Blackmoors. Dark hair and gray eyes." He and Gareth exchanged a telling glance. "Kyla married and has two other children, but she's never lied to Lewis about who his da was. The other kids though . . . they can be cruel about such things. Although, Lewis seems to bear up well with the teasing."

"Did Kyla give him the Blackmoor name?"

"No. His stepda is good to him and is Lewis's father for all intents." The revelation settled into knowledge and a new purpose. "Speaking of Cairndow, when do you expect to return?"

"After the festival, I promise," Gareth said. "I'll tell Rosie the truth and hope she can forgive me."

"I would think she'd be delighted to find out you're an earl in possession of a remote Scottish castle," Alasdair said dryly.

"Except, she is Highland royalty in possession of a remote American estate." Gareth's tart reply did little mask his worry. "Even if Rosie forgives my lying, she's bound to Stonehaven as surely as I'm bound to Cairndow."

A platitude wouldn't solve the very real conundrum.

Gareth squinted against the sun. "What about you?"

"What about me?"

"When are you leaving for home?"

It took Alasdair a heartbeat to realize home meant London. *My home is London*, he reminded himself. His flat was there. As was his mum. And his job—for the moment.

Nerves squirmed in his stomach. "I should have already left Highland."

Gareth shifted to regard him with fatherly eyes. "Yet, here you stand."

He'd done his familial duty. His uncle was of sound mind—his heart was another matter entirely—and wasn't being taken advantage of by Rose. In fact, Alasdair had never seen him so content and happy.

In addition, he could do more to protect Stonehaven from Richard's machinations in London than over the phone. There was every reason to book a flight, yet . . . here he stood.

Alasdair took a deep breath of pine-scented fresh air. Blue-green shrouded mountains stood sentinel in the distance, so different than the craggy, sparse peaks of the Highlands, but they offered the same escape and protection as Cairndow.

"I was due a vacation," Alasdair finally said.

"Is that what this is?" Gareth's gentle prodding was like picking at a newly formed scab. "Stay for the festival."

"I can't."

"Says who?"

It was a question Alasdair couldn't answer, even to himself.

Gareth's gaze softened with amusement and not a small amount of pity. He gave Alasdair's arm a squeeze. "Can I interest you in a trek through the woods to the river after it cools down a wee bit? It's quite lovely."

Getting lost in the woods sounded heavenly. "I'd love that. Maybe you can tell me more stories about our ancestors."

"Excellent. I'll let Rosie know our plan." Gareth retreated to the house.

Alasdair gave one last longing look toward the mountains and did the same, relieved not to see anyone. He stepped into his room and leaned against the door. It felt like a sanctuary.

His thoughts whirled as if his world had been knocked askew and was spinning into the great beyond. A shower might not help reorder things, but after spending his afternoon stuck in a stuffy closet and outside baking in the sun, he could at least be confused and clean.

All was quiet and the bathroom door wasn't locked when he turned the knob. A whoosh of steam clouded his vision for a slow blink. Isabel scrambled for a pink towel and held it over her front. His hungry gaze devoured her from head to toes despite a voice ordering him to retreat.

"The door was unlocked." He pointed as if she might not know what and where the door was, his voice sounding scrambled.

"My fault. I forgot to lock it." The noise that skittered out of her was a poor imitation of a laugh. "Nothing you haven't seen before considering the string of women you've dated."

He swallowed air, his mouth so dry he couldn't form words. The steam-clouded mirror was clearing from the bottom up with the burst of cool air from his room. Like an old-fashioned peepshow, the steamy mirror was revealing her bare bottom inch by glorious inch.

Now, not only was his mouth absent any moisture, but all blood flow was directed away from his head, depriving his noble impulses. Finally, he raised his gaze to the ceiling, knowing the slightly fuzzy reflection of her ass would forever haunt him.

"You've probably seen *many* naked women. Enough to

fill a dinner table." She paused as if expecting a response he was unable to formulate. "A van?" Another pause. "A school bus? A concert hall?"

A laugh hissed out of him like a teapot reaching a boil. "Not a school bus or concert hall. Unless you count digital women."

"Lord have mercy, that means you've seen a van's worth of women in the flesh?"

This time his laugh tamed the indecision that had plagued him since Gareth had asked about his departure from Highland. And Isabel. "And how many men have you seen? In the flesh and not online, that is."

"For your information, I don't peruse internet porn. I would die if I had to explain to Mom why my browser history was populated by man porn."

Unable to control gravity's pull on his gaze, he glanced down. She'd wrapped the towel around her like a toga, covered from chest to knees. A gentleman would close the door and allow her privacy. Instead, he forced her to make the move, backing to lean against the wall of his room. She didn't pull the door shut, but stepped forward until she was on the cusp of entering his room clad only in a towel.

He remained still, other than his hands, which clenched and unclenched. He was a patient spider, hoping she'd wander into his web. "Not a van load of men then?"

"A sedan maybe." The corners of her lips quirked into a crooked little smile, revealing a tiny dimple in her left cheek.

Only the left. Did other such anomalies exist elsewhere on her body? Were her freckles scattered evenly or did they cluster like constellations on her stomach or shoulder or hip? He should stop himself from wondering about things he wouldn't have a chance to discover.

Her gaze wandered to the floor and she fiddled with the

place where her towel was tucked. For one brief moment of heart-stopping rapture, he envisioned her tugging it loose and letting the towel puddle around her feet.

She tucked the edge in a little tighter and finally met his gaze. "Listen, about the closet situation . . ."

Referring to a kiss as a "situation" couldn't be good. "Situations" called for a response like a vaccine or a bombing campaign. "What about it? Should I apologize?"

"No, of course not. It wasn't anyone's *fault*. In fact, it—" She bit her bottom lip.

He wanted to grab her shoulders and shake her words loose. What was it? Thrilling? Arousing? Sexy?

"—shouldn't have happened."

"Of course not. After all, I'll be gone soon."

Emotions flashed like scattered snapshots. "Have you booked a flight home?"

"Home" was proving a difficult construct. No pets or houseplants livened up the sea of white and gray the expensive decorator had called masculine and classic and perfect for entertaining. He never entertained. "Not yet, but I have . . . things waiting for me in London."

"Including a van load of women?" she asked with maximum sarcasm.

Her interjection of light humor helped assuage his hurt feelings. Feelings he had no right to. "Indeed, but they won't all get dropped off at the same time. My flat would get crowded."

She took a step back—out of his web—and smiled, but it held a sadness of regrets. "Shower is all yours."

And then she was gone, the connecting door to her room closing with a soft click. He didn't bother to lock it. In fact, a not-so-small part of him would welcome her return, mistake or not, but breaching the divide of their lives would only lead to hurt.

Stepping under the warm spray, he closed his eyes and

let himself imagine a world where he could take his time and woo Isabel. A world where no secrets threatened. A world where he could lay her down on a tartan blanket in the middle of the field of wildflowers and fall under the spell of her laugh and her smile and her hands.

But the world—his world—was complicated.

Chapter Eight

Izzy slipped out of her room. The shower was running and all she could imagine was a wet, naked Alasdair. Part of her wanted to bust through the door like the Kool-Aid Man, but most of her wanted to curl up like a pillbug and hide under a rock.

Their kiss in the church closet had been a revelation. She'd never felt comfortable in her own skin. As a child, she'd been aware the grace her mom possessed hadn't made it into her DNA. Then, as she grew older, her imagination became a source of praise from teachers and ridicule from kids in school.

As a result, she hadn't dated until college, and even then, she'd never been a hundred percent sure what to do with her hands or her tongue or if she should talk less and do other stuff with her mouth.

But the darkness had stripped all her insecurities away. She'd given herself over to Alasdair's kiss and hadn't worried about anything. His kiss had even drowned out the humming anxiety over the festival.

The mood flipped as soon as the defective closet door had opened, and she hadn't been able to think of a single thing to say on their awkward ride back to Stonehaven. In fact, after she had taken refuge in the barn, she began to question herself. Had it even happened?

She touched her still tender lips. No, it had happened. Even now, her body buzzed in the aftermath as if she'd had a shot of good Scottish whisky. Yet, he'd asked if he needed to apologize like he'd bumped into a stranger on the street.

A glass of wine called. And food. It was almost dinner, and she still hadn't made up for her missed lunch. At least, she could count on her mom and Gareth acting as a buffer during dinner so she wouldn't have to pretend she hadn't enjoyed kissing Alasdair. Heck, without them around, she might be tempted to repeat the mistake until they made another, bigger mistake.

Gareth and her mom were in the kitchen talking in low voices in an embrace like they were slow dancing. Her mom's pink and white wraparound dress and heels complimented Gareth's dark gray slacks, white shirt with the sleeves rolled up, and blue and green tartan vest. They looked good together. More than good, they looked happy.

Izzy cleared her throat upon entering.

"Darlin', how did things go with Loretta? Let me apologize again for dropping that hot potato in your lap. I called the other delinquent vendors by the way." Her mom didn't step away from Gareth, only turned and leaned back against his chest. While her mom was comfortable charming men and women alike, this was the first time Izzy had seen her charmed in return.

"I squeezed the deposit out of Loretta and I hope she and I have reached a new understanding." A hamper stood on the kitchen island. "Aren't you two a tad overdressed for a romantic picnic?"

Her mom exchanged a glance with Gareth, a blush coming to her cheeks. "Actually, the hamper is for you and Alasdair."

"What?" She really hadn't meant to yell, but the word echoed back against the kitchen tile.

"Not romantic, of course. Just a friendly picnic. Gareth offered to take Alasdair to the river earlier, but I had already arranged for the two of us to meet Mike and Sally at Clarkson's for dinner. We were hoping you'd step in and take Alasdair down to the river. You know all the best spots anyway. Do you mind?"

Her heart thudded so hard and painfully, Izzy glanced down surprised not to see an arrow protruding from her chest. Mike and Sally had been her parents' best friends. They had hosted parties together and had gone to dinner as a foursome on a regular basis.

"Mike and Sally. Wow. A double date just like you and Daddy used to go on." Izzy had gotten used to seeing Gareth and her mom kiss and cuddle and whisper sweet nothings. Her mom deserved to be happy, and Gareth made her happy, but this date weaved Gareth into their lives in Highland like plucking old stitching out and remaking the fabric.

It was a shock, but Izzy would adjust. And until she did, she'd fake her pleasure at the turn of events. "I'd be happy to show Alasdair the river. You guys have fun. Make sure Gareth tries the catfish."

Her mom slipped from Gareth's arms, and after giving him a pointed look—which signaled his retreat—she took Izzy by the shoulders. "I know this is difficult."

Izzy pretended to misunderstand. "Entertaining Alasdair will be easy as long as you packed BLTs."

"Of course, I did, but that's not what I was referring to and you know it." Her mom tucked a piece of Izzy's still-damp hair behind her ear like she had when she was little.

"I know I should be used to it by now, but sometimes I miss Daddy so much." Izzy clenched her teeth like a dam keeping flood waters at bay.

A crease marred her mom's brow. "Me too, honey. I always will. Your dad was special and unique and we had a wonderful marriage."

Izzy filled in the word left hanging unsaid. "But?"

"But"—her mom shrugged—"I'm lonely. *Was* lonely. I didn't realize how much until I found Gareth."

"You have me." As soon as it was out of her mouth, Izzy recognized the naivete of her declaration.

"You'll understand someday." Her mom's smile hinted at a puzzle Izzy didn't have the key to decipher. "Perhaps even sooner than you think."

Heat flushed through Izzy like a wildfire sparked by memories of a dark closet and a hot half-Scot. "What are you talking about? Nothing happened."

"Not yet, but Holt won't give up. He's always liked you. Has he asked you out again?"

"No. Yes." Izzy ran a hand through her hair to attempt to reorder her jumbled thoughts, surprised Alasdair's kiss didn't have an outward manifestation everyone could see like a scarlet letter. "Holt and I are getting a drink together at the Dancing Jig, but only to discuss the festival. He's nice, but—"

"Give him a chance, darlin'. You might be surprised at what happens." Her mom leaned in to give her a hug, and Izzy nodded into her shoulder. Something niggled as being wrong. No, not wrong, just different. Her mom was wearing a new perfume.

"You smell nice," Izzy said when her mom pulled away. "And look amazing."

Her mom popped an exaggerated hip and slicked her bob down, patting the underside like an old-fashioned ingenue. "Gareth got me a new perfume, and I got the dress down at Emmy's shop."

"Have fun, and tell Mike and Sally hello," Izzy said with a smile she didn't have to fake this time.

Her mom backed away. "You try to have fun too."

Izzy opened her mouth then shut it so hard her teeth clicked. She remained in the kitchen after her mom and Gareth left. In the quiet, the creaks of Alasdair walking around in his room above her head was loud.

Now not only did she not have her mom and Gareth as a buffer, but they were headed into the woods together where anything could happen. Heat she couldn't blame on the weather or her recent shower rushed her body, and she leaned over the kitchen island and laid her cheek against the cool countertop.

The stairs signaled Alasdair's approach like a warning siren. Casual, she needed to look casual. Ending up with her elbow propped on the counter at an awkward height, her other hand on her hip, and her torso in an uncomfortable curl, she slapped on a smile.

Alasdair stopped in the doorway to the kitchen, his eyes narrowing. "Why do you look like you just killed someone and are about to ask me to help bury the body?"

Izzy harrumphed and straightened, fighting unexpected giggles. Any lingering awkwardness evaporated. "I was going for inviting and friendly."

"You might want to practice in the mirror before you unleash it on the tourists." He wore a pair of jeans and a white undershirt but no button-down or shoes. "I was looking for Gareth. He promised me a walk."

"Mom and Gareth left to have dinner in town with friends." His shoulders slumped, his disappointment palpable. Her offer came out sunnier than she'd planned. "I'm offering myself as a substitute. I know all the good places anyway. You'll have way more fun with me."

"Of that I have no doubt." Was that innuendo in his voice? She didn't have time to evaluate when he moved toward the hamper. "What's for dinner?"

"BLTs."

"Sounds delicious.

"It will be." She swung the basket to the crook of her arm. "Let's go."

"How's the festival coming along? I feel as if Gareth and I have been a distraction."

She had work to do assigning the booths to vendors and double-checking with the booking agents for the bands and verifying the porta-potties would be set up on time. A million little details awaited. While she hadn't played hooky from work in a long time, she used to escape to the woods on a regular basis to avoid homework.

"The calls will keep for tomorrow," she said simply.

The heat had broken and orange streaked the sky, promising a spectacular sunset. The river would be cool and refreshing, and the meadow overrun with flowers just like in the stories she'd used to make up. A frisson of anticipation electrified her nerves.

They both stuck their feet into flip-flops and set off side by side, stepping from the patio to cut across the field toward the line of trees. Taking the hamper from her, he said, "Allow me."

"Thanks." She didn't know what to do with her hands now, so she linked them behind her back. "It's been ages since I've been to the swimming hole."

"I don't have a suit."

"We can just put our feet in. The water will feel good." The grasses and flowers brushed against her jeans-clad legs.

"This field is a true wonder." The appreciation for something new and unusual was in his voice.

Izzy had grown up with the field outside of her back door. She had stared unseeing into the distance while she'd eaten her cereal before school every morning daydreaming of the woods beyond. Now, she took the time to appreciate what she had grown up with right outside her door.

"It really is beautiful. It's a shame we have to mow it down."

"Mow it down? Why?" He came to a stop surrounded by knee-high flowers.

"The bulk of the festival takes place in the field. The booths will be over there." She pointed east. "And the stage for the pipers and dancers and bands will be on the south side. The athletic events happen in the far corner."

He continued forward, but slower now as they entered the shadow of the woods. "When will the massacre take place?"

She snort-laughed. "Massacre is a strong word. Next summer, the flowers will be back and just as beautiful."

He hummed. "Rejuvenation. Rebirth."

"Exactly." Countless paths meandered through the woods, some leading to the river, others heading toward the hills. "When I was a kid I pretended the paths all shifted and every day might bring a new adventure. Which path shall we choose today?"

The calls of birds—a blue jay squawked over the softer song of a whippoorwill—blended with the evening symphony of the insects. It was her favorite time to be outside.

Alasdair pointed. "That one looks promising."

"Good choice. Let's be off, fellow wanderer." The path he chose meandered through the woods to the river. The trees grew dense overhead, filtering the sunlight into the premature dusk. As a child, she felt the woods had always been an otherworldly place full of a magic she might not be able to see but could surely feel in her innocent heart.

Many times she would turned at her head at shadows, expecting to catch sight of an elf or a wood sprite, but had always been too late. As she got older and wiser (some might say jaded), the magic faded until she accepted it had never existed.

"Was it solitary being an only child?" His voice was

soft and knowing and drew her gaze to his as if he'd read her thoughts.

A waver in her smile revealed her childhood loneliness. With no kids she could play with close by, she'd grown up relying on her own imagination. Maybe too much. "This may shock you, but I found it hard to talk to kids and make friends in school."

"Actually, that's not at all surprising." His voice was deadpan.

She punched his arm. "Hey, you could have feigned surprise."

He rubbed his arm like her puny punch had actually done him injurious harm, but with a smile on his face.

"The girls I knew were obsessed with Disney princesses." Even after the years gone by, disdain crept into her voice.

"And you weren't? With a field of flowers and magical woods to play in?" He made an expansive gesture.

"I prefer more gumption and derring-do from my princesses. I spent my free time making up my own stories and scribbling them in notebooks. The other kids thought I was strange." She rolled her eyes toward him. Even though she had friends now, the scars from those early days remained.

"It's not a bad thing to be different."

"Said by someone who, if I had to guess, was voted most popular by the boys and the girls. Especially the girls," she said dryly.

He sobered with a sigh. "Aye, I was popular, but only because I wasn't honest with any of them. I never told anyone about how watching my parents fight scared me so much I would hide under my covers. I never knew what kind of mood my da would be in when I walked in the door from school, so I went out for every sport—even cricket, which I absolutely loathed."

While she didn't have many friends growing up, what she did have were two parents who loved her unconditionally and provided not only a soft place to land, but were her bedrock. "That must have been so hard. It's not fair that kids suffer when parents can't keep it together."

"Mum tried, but she loved my da despite everything and she couldn't keep her hurt from coloring everything. Now that I'm older—I don't know about wiser—I can empathize with both of them."

"It's strange to realize our parents are human beings who fall in love and make mistakes and suffer heartbreak, isn't it?" she asked more to herself than expecting an answer.

"Do you ever resent the box you've been forced inside?" he asked.

"What do you mean?"

"Duty versus passion has been on my mind of late. What we want versus what's expected of us. Do you ever wish you didn't bear the responsibility of the festival?" He seemed truly interested.

"No." While the stark denial wasn't a lie, neither was it completely accurate. "Maybe? Sometimes? It's complicated. The festival is my birthright. I inherited it from my dad. I couldn't imagine Highland without it."

"The hard work is worth it?"

"You've seen the pictures in the office. Seeing how much everyone loves it makes all the hard work worth it."

"Even though you're sacrificing your dream to travel?"

"Not sacrificing. Postponing," she said firmly.

"Don't postpone it forever."

His warning resonated with the restless spirit inside of her she kept on a tight leash. "Honestly, the planning portion of the festival is the easy part, because I can control it. The hard part is dealing with what we can't control like the weather. Rain is bad; thunderstorms are worse. Starting around three weeks out, I have weather-related nightmares."

"So if I hear you screaming about being attacked by a rain cloud, I should run in and wake you up?" His tease shifted to sympathy.

The image of Alasdair distracting her from her nightmares in the middle of the night flashed. She had almost gotten him naked in her imagination when he said, "There's ancient magic all around us, isn't there ?"

She darted a sharp look at him. "Surely, *you* don't believe in such nonsense."

"Of course, I do. I'm Scottish. We come out of the womb believing. Whenever I misbehaved, my da claimed I was a changeling child. I'd wager, you're a believer as well."

"I'm a perfectly practical accountant," she said primly.

"Who has a letter opener named Rupert," he teased.

She pulled him to a stop. "Are you ever going to let that go?"

"It's too delightful not to bring up whenever possible."

She scuffed her flip-flops in the layer of dead leaves and pine needles on the path. "I used to believe in magic, but I grew up."

"Hence your desire to write a serious novel with no magic."

She stutter-stepped. "What made you say that just now?"

He shifted the picnic basket to his other arm and blocked the path forward. "You confessed you're writing a serious novel, aren't you?"

"Not that part. The bit about no magic. How did you know?"

"Know what?" His brow knitted together in what appeared to be genuine confusion.

"That's been the biggest knock against my work. While I'm proficient at putting words together, according to my many—*many*—rejections, I lack the secret sauce to make them sing. In short, my writing lacks magic." She air-quoted the last word.

His face cleared with a nod of understanding. "I see. I was actually referring to the real thing. Or at least, the kind of stories you made up as a kid."

"Who on earth would want to read those?" She stepped around him even though her heart had kicked her in the ribs. "If we don't keep moving, the mosquitos will feast on us."

The faint whoosh of water grew louder in the background and offered a welcome distraction. The opening in the trees was wreathed in the glow of the setting sun like a magical portal into another world, but the closer they got, the more mundane the scene became. It was simply a wood giving way to a meadow cut through by a stream.

Alasdair stepped all the way to the bank looking out at the wide bend that formed the swimming hole. He set down the hamper, took a deep breath, and whispered, "This is peaceful. It reminds me of Cairndow."

She opened the hamper and pulled out a blanket—red and black tartan, of course—and spread it over the grass. Flopping onto her back, she stared at the sky framed by the trees circling them. Alasdair lay down beside her, his shoulder nudging hers.

Colors streaked the sky like a finger painting, but at the edges was a deep orange giving the impression the tops of the trees were on fire. Summer sunsets were the most beautiful. If the festival didn't keep her so busy, she might stop to enjoy them more.

All around them lightning bugs flashed in the grass. If she squinted, she could imagine they were beacons from distant lighthouses. The woods made stories take root in her imagination, but she'd stopped nurturing them, afraid if she put them out into the world she'd look silly.

Alasdair shifted to his side and propped his head up on his hand, looking down on her and wreathed in magical light. He was going to kiss her. Expectation sent her tongue out to daub her suddenly dry lips.

His chest brushed hers, and her back arched ever so slightly. His face shifted closer, and she tilted toward him, closing the distance between points A and B. He stretched across her body and her blood sang a welcome.

In a sexy, husky brogue, he whispered, "I'm bloody starving."

He grabbed the handle of the hamper, lifted it over her body, and sat up, exclaiming in delight as he pulled out the food. She lay like a discarded rag doll. She was epically bad at reading signals. Confusing an imminent kiss with hunger was humiliating.

"Aren't you hungry?" Everything about him was annoyingly cheery.

"Please tell me there's alcohol." She pushed up on her elbows.

"A chilled Chardonnay." He pulled out the corkscrew and opened it with an efficient grace that made her wonder what those hands could do on skin.

He held out a red plastic cup with a generous amount of wine. Their fingers brushed on the handover, and she took several huge swallows to dull the edge of her arousal and embarrassment. God bless her dear sainted mother for not being a teetotaler.

They assembled BLTs and ate them on the blanket. There was no need to speak, because life teemed around them. Bullfrogs croaked and birds cawed. Crickets sang and squirrels rustled. The lightning bugs had risen into the brush, blinking their mating calls like Morse code.

"Did you know that lightning bugs can synchronize their blinks?" She kept her voice low.

"Really?" Either he was a good faker, or he was actually interested.

"Up in the Smokies, scientists study the flashes and

try to make sense of them. What if they hear their own music?" She smiled. "Can't you just picture a lightning bug orchestra in tuxedos?" Once upon a time, it was something she might have incorporated into one of her stories.

He cleared his throat and gave her an "I told you so look." She shrugged. "What?"

"You are proving my point for me."

She chose not to rise to his bait. "I'll bet there's nothing like this in London."

"No, but there's a glen with a crystal blue loch at Cairndow. My friend Iain and I would sneak off on moonlit nights." His stared toward the river, but he was seeing his past, a smile turning his lips. He refilled both of their cups, and she drank deeply.

A buzz hit her quick and hard, and for some reason, she decided to try a Scottish accent. "Did you and Iain find a wee spot of trouble in the loch?"

The sparkle in his eyes lit fireworks in her chest. He deepened his brogue until it was thicker than even Gareth's. "Ach, we'd drink and raise hell and use our silver tongues to lure bonny lasses into the water with us for some skinny-dipping."

She laughed, but breathlessly, her insides melted into goo. "That sounds naughty. And fun."

"Aye, it was." He resumed his usual accent. "Or would have been if the water hadn't been so blasted cold."

She did her best to stifle her wine-giggles with another sip. "I've never been skinny-dipping."

"That deficiency must be rectified immediately." He stood and held out a hand.

Her giggles trickled to a stop like a spigot being turning off. "No way. Uh-uh. Forget it."

"You can leave your knickers on if you want." He stepped to the bank and grabbed the back of his shirt to pull it off. The diffused light accentuated the shift of muscle and tendon across his back and shoulders. The waistband of his jeans loosened.

Izzy drew her knees to her chest and wrapped her arms around her legs and watched in wide-eyed amazement as if a magical creature had wandered into her woods. Or more accurately, she was witnessing an audition for Chippendales. He stepped out of his jeans with athletic grace. She tensed. Would his boxer briefs follow?

With them still on, he waded into the shallows of the river. "It's a mite warmer than the loch at Cairndow."

Farther still he went, the water rushing to his thighs until he reached the drop-off and disappeared. She popped to her feet, her eyes itchy from not blinking. He breached the water, and a flick of his head sent droplets scattering. He turned on his back and floated. Dusk had overtaken them fully and darkness crept closer on cat paws.

She shuffled to the bank and stalled, holding out the neck of her shirt and evaluating her bra. It wouldn't make the cut for the Victoria Secret fashion show, but it was lacy and white and newish. Her panties were plain pink cotton, no more revealing than bikini bottoms.

Did she take a chance or retreat?

"All I'm missing is a bonny lass." His voice came from the shadows in the brogue she had no willpower to resist.

Was she actually doing this? She shucked her shirt, dropped it on top of his clothes, and worked the button and zipper of her jeans open. With a shot of courage—or madness. Did madness run in her family? A question to consider later—she pushed her jeans to her ankles.

In her haste to kick them off and get into the cover of the river, she lost her balance and toppled like a cut pine tree. Her hip hit the ground hard enough to bruise, and pebbles scraped her knee. Kicking her legs free of her prison of denim, she hop-skipped into the river and dove under the water.

Her hand brushed smooth, taut flesh and she startled to the surface with a gasp. Alasdair treaded water, the white of his teeth showing in a grin. "Are you okay?"

Her hope that he had been distracted by a frog or a fish withered. "Now do you see why I was banned from dance school?"

His laugh raced over the water like the flight of a bird, and her stomach fluttered as if trying to keep up. She swam toward a sandbar in an eddy, her feet finding purchase on the bottom. Water lapped at her collarbones, trying to draw her into the current.

Joining her, he skimmed his hands over his face and hair. "The water's cooler than I expected, but nothing like the loch."

"The river flows from the mountains."

"What is winter like in Highland?"

"Changeable. A spate of warm days in the middle of January will see everyone in short sleeves. Then, a week later it might snow. We usually see flurries every year, and one significant snowfall. Even an inch will shut Highland down. Woe be it to you if you haven't stocked up on milk and bread beforehand."

"I got to spend a winter holiday with Gareth, and remember him driving us from the train station through a blinding snow in his old Land Rover. It was beautiful and scary and the best kind of exciting."

A sudden surge of undercurrent tugged her feet. Before she could be swept downstream, Alasdair caught her around the waist, and she grabbed his arms. Even after she regained her feet, neither of them let go.

"Where would the river take you?" he asked.

She tried to ignore the way his thumb brushed her hip bone. A shiver cascaded through her. No one had ever discovered the sensitive place.

"The current slows around the bend. The river isn't

dangerous." Except standing this close to Alasdair, it felt like the most dangerous place in the world.

"There are stories Gareth used to tell me about the ancient places in Scotland. Places that were traps set by beautiful, but deadly fairies. They lured young men to their doom in the moonlight. With one kiss they'd spirit the poor souls to the fae realm and they'd never be seen again." He spoke with the rhythm of a natural storyteller. She'd heard the same cadence in Gareth's voice. Maybe it was bred into Scottish men.

"How do you know they met their doom? Maybe the fae realm was so wondrous, those young men never wanted to leave."

"Perhaps you're right. I thought the fairies make-believe, but I'm beginning to wonder."

Even Izzy, as unsophisticated as she felt with him, cottoned on to his meaning. If this place housed old magic, then she must be the deadly faerie. Beautiful too though, he'd said. A flush warmed her.

"I wouldn't want to be a faerie in your story," she said softly.

"Why not?" His thumb traced the delicate curve of her hip bone once more.

"Leading men to their doom wouldn't be conducive to a second date," she said with a breathless tease.

He laughed. "I suppose not. What kind of faerie would you like to be?"

"A faerie who would save a hapless man from his doom in the mortal world only to become accidently bound to him." It popped into her head and out of her mouth as if the idea had been lurking for a long while. She poked his chest. "Don't say it."

His lips twitched, but stayed closed.

"You think I'm writing the wrong stories and have enslaved myself to Highland and the festival."

"A mite dramatic, but not altogether wrong, wouldn't you say?" With his hair slicked back, his sleek brows set off the strong bones of his face, masked by the growing stubble.

"You said earlier that passion versus duty had been on your mind. Why? Is it because of your half-brother?"

Humor leaked out of his face. "Not entirely."

"Is your job a duty or a passion?" She tilted her head and wiped at the water running into her eyes.

"Definitely not a passion."

"A duty, then. Does your boss inspire your loyalty?"

His laugh cracked and echoed off the water. "Hardly. Richard inspires fear, anxiety, competition. I looked up to him once. I think. Richard seemed strong where my da seemed weak, but everything has become twisted. Being here makes me forget why I'm killing myself to please him."

"That's good. Isn't it?" She wasn't sure if she should apologize or congratulate him on his enlightenment.

"Can we not talk about work?" Troubles ran deep under his outward stoicism, but she would respect his reluctance to delve deeper.

"What do you want to do then, Highlander?" The question came out suggestive.

He answered with an innuendo-laden smile. She scrunched her toes into the sand, anchoring herself in the expectation of having her world rocked. His lips brushed across her cheek, the rasp of his stubble sending chills through her. But, he didn't quite close the deal.

"Are you drunk, fairie-girl?"

"What if I am?" She could close the distance in a heart-beat.

"I don't want to take advantage of you."

She jerked back to meet his gaze. "Now is not the time for you to play the gentleman, Blackmoor. I want you in the part of the marauding Highlander."

"You'd better run then, before I catch you, lass."

She giggled and shoved his shoulder. She'd only meant to playfully free herself from his arms, but his feet shot out from underneath him and the current carried him away as if fairies had ahold of him. She cackled a laugh and set out in the other direction toward the bank. He would catch his footing and be right behind her.

Hardly slowing, she grabbed the mound of clothes and skip-ran down the path barefoot. Only when she stubbed her toe on an exposed root did she slow and question her sanity and, frankly, her maturity level, which had dipped into negative territory with the addition of too much wine.

Stopping, she pulled on her T-shirt and jeans. Her clammy underwear made it difficult to maneuver the damp denim over her hips. She was left holding Alasdair's jeans and T-shirt, which meant he was traipsing around in a pair of wet boxer briefs molded to . . . everything. Her heart kicked into a rhythm that would have raised alarms on an EKG.

She balled up Alasdair's clothes and returned to the river. Except, he wasn't there. She stood on the edge of the bank and called his name, hearing only her voice echoing back. Dire scenarios rampaged through her imagination.

The full moon illuminated the picnic basket and crushed grass. Crushed grass where the blanket had been. She fell to her knees and checked inside the basket. No blanket. She heaved a sigh. Alasdair had made it to the bank and was probably halfway back to the house by now.

Grabbing up the picnic basket, she ran as fast as the darkness would allow back to Stonehaven. Her mom and Gareth rocked on the patio swing with glasses of wine. Her mom was reclined on a pillow, her legs across Gareth's lap while he swung them as if she were a baby he was coaxing asleep.

"Is Alasdair back?" she asked breathlessly.

Her mom raised herself to an elbow. "I thought he was with you."

Izzy put the basket down and hugged his clothes to her chest. "I accidently lost him."

Her mom swung her legs off Gareth's lap. "He's not a hat or a pair of sunglasses. How could you lose him?"

"Um." She searched for an excuse that didn't involve playacting as an innocent lass running from a sexy, marauding Highlander. "He got swept downriver."

"And you didn't go after him? Should we call the authorities?" Her mom was up and pacing now.

"No, he's fine. Or at least, he didn't drown, but I have his clothes." She held up the bundle she clutched.

"Alasdair is lost in the woods . . . *naked*?"

"Not *completely* naked. He took the blanket and still has his underwear on. I . . . think." Her voice petered into silence as her mom looked at her like she'd lost her mind.

"Hang on," Gareth said. "I see the lad a'coming out of the woods."

The three of them lined up to stare into the moonlight-dappled night. Alasdair was indeed stalking through the field. Izzy's breath hitched and she shuffled to where the bricks gave way to grass.

He wore a plaid wrapped around his waist, the end thrown over his shoulder. The rest of him was beautifully bare. His hair was as black as the shadows that parted before him, his attitude positively primeval. Her knees wobbled. Not from fear but excitement fueled by the lowering of her inhibitions from the wine. Electricity like heat lightning arced between them.

He cleared the high grass. Closer now, she could see the clumsy way the tartan blanket hung around his waist, crudely tied with a vine. His feet were dirty in his flip-flops and his hair was still damp from his trip downriver. His exasperation was also evident.

"I can't believe you left me." He propped his hands low on his hips, pulling his muscles tight. So tight and hard she was having a hard time tearing her gaze from his chest to his face.

"I came back, but you had already taken the blanket and left. I thought you might have beat me home."

"I got lost on the millions of blasted trails in that god-forsaken wood."

"So no errant faeries lured you away to your doom?" She tried on a smile, but let it fall when he didn't return it. It appeared that they would not be resuming their little game.

He harrumphed and snatched his clothes from where she was hugging them. "I'm going to shower off the muck."

Once he was gone, her mom said in a chiding voice, "That wasn't very hospitable of you, Izzy."

Any explanations she offered would embarrass them both. "I'll apologize in the morning."

Her mom and Gareth retreated to the house, and Izzy took up their spot on the swing. Her mom had left a half glass of wine on the table. Izzy finished it off in two swallows, used one of the cushions as a pillow, and stared up at the night sky.

If her mom could have a fling with an attractive Scotsman, why couldn't Izzy? Just because she had never participated in a fling didn't mean she wouldn't be good at it. In fact, if she put her mind to it, there's nothing she couldn't excel at.

Even writing? Her gut begged her to listen to Alasdair's advice. What if she attempted one story of adventure and magic? What did she have to lose but time she would have spent churning out more "trite and amateurish" literature?

What's the worst that could happen? She could get her heart broken, her soul crushed, and experience utter humiliation. All three applied to writing *and* to initiating a fling with Alasdair. But if her mom was brave enough to put herself out there, couldn't Izzy give it a shot too? She sat up, holding her head, when the world spun around her.

She would try her hand at new things—writing and fling related—as soon as she sobered up.

Chapter Nine

The next morning, Alasdair found himself tiptoeing out of the house and into the middle of the field of wildflowers with his mobile clutched in his hand. Privacy was hard to come by, especially knowing Isabel was on the other side of his bedroom wall.

The urge to talk to his mum was odd, but the last few days in Highland had brought the past into sharper focus. He tapped her name.

"Alasdair, darling. Are you home?" Their connection was so clear, she might have been only a handful of kilometers away instead of thousands.

His throat tightened and he couldn't speak. Childhood memories rushed him and fought for his attention. It hadn't been all bad. Yes, his parents had had a volatile relationship that frightened him, but he remembered walking between them, holding their hands, for fresh scones on a Sunday.

"Is something wrong?" Her voice had pinched with worry. Worry and love went hand in hand.

"I'm fine. I'm still in Highland with Gareth. And the Buchanans," he added as a picture of Isabel, teasing him in the river last night popped into his head.

"What's the status of their relationship? Is it beginning to cool?"

"No. But he understands he can't leave Cairndow forever." An ache in his chest had him briefly closing his eyes. "I fear both of them will be hurt in the long run."

"She knows his situation."

But, Rose didn't know. He certainly wasn't going to betray Gareth to his mum.

"What is the daughter like?" his mum asked.

"She's . . ." He wondered if his mum could hear the smile he couldn't contain. ". . . special. Funny and smart."

"Pretty?" his mum asked with a sharpness that punctured his bubble of happiness.

How could he confess his confusion and guilt and want when it came to Isabel? If his mum didn't approve of Rose for Gareth, she certainly wouldn't appreciate his undeniable interest in Isabel.

"She's not bad to look at, I suppose. No hairy moles or crazy eyes." He bit his tongue to shut himself up and cleared his throat. "Anyway, how are you doing?"

She paused, then said suspiciously, "I'm fine. Why do you ask?"

With no small amount of shame, he realized how rare it was for him to ask. He was used to her high-handed coddling, and to never returning the favor. "Just wondering if you're, I don't know, dating anyone?"

"What's brought on this interrogation about my love life?"

"It's been a long time since Da died, and I thought maybe you were dating. I mean, you're still quite attractive."

Christ Almighty, could the conversation get any more awkward? He was ready to claim a case of virulent diarrhea to end the call when she said with unusual tentativeness, "Well, actually, there is someone."

"Bloody hell!"

"Why did you ask if you don't want to know?"

"No, I do. I'm glad for you. That's great. When can I meet him?" He cringed, thankful she couldn't see him.

"We can have dinner when you're back in London, if you really want to."

"Of course I do." No, this was good. His mum deserved another shot at happiness with a man. "How long have you been seeing him?"

"A little over a year."

"A year! When would you have mentioned him if I hadn't asked?" He was beginning to wonder what other secrets his mum was holding.

"I don't know." His mum paused. "I never plan on remarrying, and you're grown. Introducing you hasn't been a priority."

Alasdair scratched at the stubble along his jaw, his head whirling with the implications. "You could remarry. There's nothing stopping you."

When his mum didn't answer right away, he knew why. His da. Even with all the time gone by, his mum couldn't break the bonds. Alasdair didn't know whether love or hate was stronger.

Softer now, Alasdair said, "You deserve to be happy, Mum."

"I am perfectly happy, darling. I'll always have you, after all." His mum's voice was thick with emotion and she heaved a sigh. He could picture her patting her cheeks and stiffening her upper lip, and sure enough, when she spoke again, her voice was chipper. "When will I see you?"

"Soon. Probably." London was calling—literally as his mobile vibrated in his hand—but he couldn't summon any urgency to leave Highland. Had the place—or Isabel—cast a spell on him?

His mum made a worried little sound in her throat. "Ring me as soon as you land and I'll pop over with take-out so we can catch up."

"That sounds great actually." He bit his lip then added, "I miss you, Mum."

The silence was loud. "Call me again, Alasdair. Anytime."

They disconnected. Was he giving his mum short shrift when it came to her ability to handle the truth about Lewis with equanimity? For the first time, he second-guessed his decision to keep his half-brother a secret.

His mobile vibrated again in his hand. Richard calling for an update. Alasdair darkly considered whether "eff you" would be suitable.

"Richard. How are you?" Alasdair kept his voice level.

"What news do you have for me?" Papers shuffled, indicating Alasdair was on speaker.

"Stonehaven is not for sale. Move on to another property."

"No." Richard's brusque tone imbued the word with the feel of an expletive. "Make it happen, Blackmoor, or I'll find someone else who can."

"Who? George? He can't find his arse with both hands tied behind his back." Under Alasdair's bravado was desperation for Richard to shift his focus off Stonehaven as a project.

"I don't know, the little faffer has dug up some interesting information."

"What?"

"I'm inclined to let George take a crack at this nut, seeing as you don't seem motivated to close the deal. Ta-ta." Richard's jovialness was more worrying than a dressing-down would have been.

Alasdair muttered a string of curses. George was an

annoying arse-kisser, but not incompetent. How could he protect Stonehaven and Isabel when had no idea what attack Wellington might mount? George, wisely, had never sent Alasdair the file, so he didn't know what sort of leverage might be applied.

What the situation made abundantly clear was that his loyalties had shifted dramatically. He'd spent the last eight years of his life furthering Wellington and, in extension, Richard's interests around the world. Now, after mere days in Highland with the Buchanans, he was plotting to undermine Richard.

His time at Wellington was coming to a close. Whether he quit or was fired, the outcome would be the same, a bitter parting. He wasn't worried about money. With his experience, he could have another job at a firm like Wellington in a half hour. Was that what he wanted though? His orderly world had gone mad, and he was tired of the machinations.

He collapsed to the ground, closed his eyes, and enjoyed the pinpricks of light on his lids like a kaleidoscope. A simple pleasure he remembered from his childhood. The elemental scents of nature acted as a grounding force. Rustling had him blinking his eyes open. A halo of chestnut waves wreathed in light bent over him like an angel of mercy.

"Are you here to put me out of my misery?" He fought the urge to pull her down to him.

"I was watching from the window." Her voice matched her expression, a crinkle between her eyes. "Are you okay?"

He was feeling remarkably better with her there, but he couldn't tell her that. "My mum has a boyfriend."

"Join the club," she said with a quirking smile. "Don't worry. Once you get over the shock, it's not that bad.

At least, you don't have to watch them kissing and cuddling."

"Point taken. Although, she's invited me to meet him when I get back to London."

She sat crisscross next to him and angled to face him. "One thing I've learned is that our parents aren't just our parents; they're human beings with strengths and weaknesses and, heaven help us, sex lives."

He stuck his fingers in his ears. "Why did you have to put that thought in my head?"

"That was cruel." She looked off to the side, the sun firing lighter strands in her hair and casting shadows along her profile. "I need to apologize."

Unable to stop the compulsion, he reached out to rub a lock of soft hair between his fingers. "For what?"

"For running off with your clothes last night. You had every right to be mad." She tilted closer, but not close enough. He would only be satisfied with her body touching his.

"I wasn't mad; I was frustrated."

"With me," she said in a small voice.

He surrendered and wrapped her hair around his palm, tugging her down to him. She didn't resist, but lay her head on his shoulder. "With you, with me, with the situation. I wanted to kiss you."

"You did?"

How could she even ask him the question? "Who wouldn't want to kiss a fairie by moonlight?"

She tucked her head into his neck, her hair tickling his chin. "I was a little drunk last night."

Usually, such a statement was a precursor to make excuses. Tension roiled through him. "And?"

"I'm going to take your advice and write something literally magical." She propped her hand and chin on his chest. In her face, he could see the conflicting emotions. "It might be a total waste of time, but I'm excited about it, which I can't say about my great Southern epic."

"You seemed stuck. I have a good feeling about your new direction."

"Yeah, me too." She touched his stubbled jaw. "You seem stuck too."

He startled to hear his inertia verbalized by her. "Stuck in Highland?"

"No, silly. Stuck in your job."

Understatement at its finest. At the moment, he felt like he was in a hostage situation with Richard. "Even though I'd be giving up scads of money and throwing the middle finger at a promotion, I'm considering leaving Wellington. I'll probably have to start in a lower position at a different company and spend the next who knows how many years scrabbling my way back."

"Or you could do something completely different." Her simple statement realigned his confusion.

"What could I do?" He was asking himself as much as her.

"That's up to you." She shrugged and gave him a curious smile. "Where were you the happiest and what were you doing?"

He stared at her unblinking until she commanded, "Close your eyes and let your mind wander."

He did as she bade. The sun and the stroke of her hand across his forehead lulled him into a state between alert and dazed. "I loved my time at Cambridge."

"You could teach."

The suggestion didn't resonate. "No. I loved Cambridge because of the history steeped into the buildings and grounds."

"Yet you majored in business."

"I'm practical." He squinted up at the sky. "You of all people can't fault me there."

"Touché," she said with a smile in her voice. "When was another time you were happy?"

"At Cairndow."

"It all comes back to Cairndow. It's too bad your only connection is with the groundskeeper. I'd guess taking a job under Gareth would be too much of a pay cut."

He expelled a long breath. Isabel was correct. Cairndow was at his center. He was bound to the estate through duty, yes, but his love of Cairndow was at the center of who and what he was. He'd tried to bury the truth after his da had died, but Alasdair was a Blackmoor and Blackmoors belonged to Cairndow. It was an ancient bond Alasdair couldn't sever.

Isabel took his introspection in stride and continued. "I'll bet your financial wizardry could be put to good use."

"How so?"

"I watch PBS. I know how those old estates need money and work. You could consult with whoever owns them and help them stay afloat." Enthusiasm quivered her voice. "How much fun would it be to travel all over Great Britain to set all the historic houses to right?"

"I'm not sure such a job even exists." The practical side of him turned the idea over in his head and found holes.

"Even better. You can be the first and make it whatever you want. What do you think?"

He wasn't sure if other great houses in Great Britain needed him, but Gareth and Cairndow could use his help and expertise. Isabel's energy infected him and filled him with an optimism he hadn't realized he'd been missing until it reappeared.

"You might be on to something." He rolled them so she was the one on her back and he loomed over her, his shadow shielding her face from the sun. With her hair spread around her like a halo, she looked an angel, but he knew better. She was a tart-tongued, sexy dervish who had cast a spell over him. "Now, how much time do you have?"

"I made inroads on my to-do list this morning, so a break is justified. Why?"

"I'd very much like to play the marauding Highlander and kiss you."

A throaty sound that might have been surprise or acquiescence emerged. Her cheeks were pink and her eyes sparkled. The future was a long way off. He wanted to live in the present with Isabel.

Tangling her fingers in his hair, she said, "Is it still considered marauding if I'm willing and eager?"

His lips had almost made contact with hers when he whispered, "Promise you won't run off with my clothes?"

"I'd have to rip them off to do that." Her lashes threw spikey shadows on her cheeks, and her smile revealed the single dimple in her cheek.

"Let me rethink this. That plan does have merit."

She pressed her smiling lips against his, and he skimmed his hand out of her hair and down her side, delighting in the soft hint of her breast, stopping at the slope of her hip. He moved over her, notching his leg between hers, cursing the presence of his pants for many reasons, but mostly because he wasn't able to feel the skin of her calves and thighs against him. His chest pressed into her full breasts as her lips sweetly explored his.

The smell of wildflowers would forever be linked to Isabel. Halfway around the world at ninety years old, he could imagine taking a breath of blooming heather along the moors of Cairndow and rocketing back to this exact time and place with Isabel in his arms.

They were hemmed in by a wall of pink and orange and

white flowers, her hair tangled in the stems as if she was indeed fae and sprung from nature. He braced himself on his elbows, his nose close to hers, their breath mingling. While the moment had all the romantic hallmarks of a movie, a more primal urge rose between them.

He kissed her again, wanting to be gentle, but her hands pulled at his back, her nails biting through his shirt to skin, her impatience driving his own higher. He tilted his head to slip his tongue to spar with hers in much the same way they sparred with their words, give and take and with more than a little tease.

He shifted enough to glide his fingertips under the edge of her shirt and spread his palm flat along the smooth skin of her side. Her sharp intake of breath registered against the pads of his fingers.

His thoughts and worries had been wiped clean and replaced with one overriding goal—please Isabel. Her leg curled around his, and she pulled his weight more fully on top of her, the same time her hand wandered down to grab his arse. He muffled a groan as his pelvis ground into hers. It seemed her goal was opposite and equal to his.

He wanted to strip her down in the middle of the flowers and bury himself inside her. It was elemental and sexy and . . . Her hips bucked hard against him and her torso jerked like lightning had struck.

"I'm on fire," she said with a drawn-out moan that was more horror movie than porn flick.

"Uh, me too?"

"Get off." She shoved at his shoulders and he immediately shot to his hands and knees, giving her room.

"Did I scare you? I'm so sorry, Isabel." Confusion melded with horror. What had he done?

She rolled away from him as if desperate to put space between him, but instead of stalking away in disgust, she swatted at her ankle. "The little devils are eating me alive. Help!"

Peering closer, he could see the tiniest of insects crawling up her legs. She pinched one off and flicked it away. He scooted closer and slapped two off her calf. Finally, her frantic movements calmed, and she brushed her hands from thigh to foot.

It was then he noticed the angry welts on the tender skin around her ankles. He touched one. "Are you telling me that tiny little insect did that?"

"Fire ants. They earn their name. Nasty little things. These were just a few scouts. We'd both be in a world of hurt if we'd rolled over a mound." She leaned back on her hands, but kept her legs bent and out of contact with the ground. "Is it a sign?"

"Of an ant coup?"

"No, a sign we shouldn't be messing around."

While having sex in the middle of a field of flowers seemed romantic, apparently, the reality was far itchier and more painful. Yet he refused to believe the tiny ants were harbingers of disaster.

No, if disaster was going to befall them, it would be of his own making. There was still time to fix things. Alasdair would handle George and Richard and all of Wellington. Isabel and Rose never need know what he'd inadvertently set in motion. As for Gareth, his lie was white, or at least, beige.

"The ants were merely a sign to seek privacy before one of us was bitten somewhere far more intimate."

She gave an exaggerated shudder. "I can't even imagine an ant bite on my girly bits."

His laugh roared out as unstoppable as a rockslide, and a decision clicked into place. "I've decided to stay for the festival and escort Gareth back to Scotland afterward." He studied her reaction, hoping for a jump for joy. What he got was a worried draw of her brows. "If I'm welcome, that is," he added hastily.

"What if Gareth decides to stay in Highland? Forever, I mean."

Alasdair shook his head, knowing things Isabel did not. Gareth had to return home. Hundreds of years of tradition demanded it. "He has responsibilities at Cairndow."

"Surely, it's just a matter of hiring someone else."

Alasdair plucked grass from her hair. "You were ready to parade around town with his head on a pike after he arrived and now you're his champion?"

Her gaze darted like a bee searching for pollen. "As much as the thought of Mom with a sex life gives me the willies, I don't want her to be lonely. She deserves to be happy, and Gareth makes her happy. Ergo, I will do what I can to make it happen."

"You sound like you almost believe that." Alasdair wasn't sure what "the willies" were but he thought they might be the squirmy feeling assailing his stomach at the moment. He couldn't foresee a scenario where someone didn't get hurt.

"I almost do," she said softly, resting her chin on her knees.

A whistle startled Alasdair. From experience, he knew that whistle could cut through the wind and gorse and stone to call him home. "That'd be Gareth."

Isabel popped up faster than a jack-in-the-box, brushing at her shirt and shorts. Despite her attempt to degrass herself, she still looked as if she'd taken a roll in the hay. He was even worse off, but didn't care.

"See you later." She scampered toward the house, only slowing slightly to greet Gareth.

"Dare I ask what's put that smile on your face and the grass in your hair, laddie?" Gareth came up beside him to watch Isabel disappear into the house.

Alasdair touched his lips unaware he was even smiling. "What is it about the ladies of Stonehaven?"

"Perhaps the Blackmoors are genetically predisposed to love them," Gareth said with a wry smile.

"I don't . . ." Alasdair whirled on Gareth. "Ah, but you do love Rose."

"How could I not?" It was a philosophical question for the ages. In a brisker voice, Gareth asked, "And how does the Wellington saga proceed?"

"Badly. Richard is questioning my loyalty—rightly so—and is putting his new lapdog on the deal."

"What kind of bite does he have?"

"Not as ferocious as mine," Alasdair said darkly.

Alasdair smoothed a hand down his jaw and pulled at the hair on his chin. He'd shaved daily, even on weekends, since he was fifteen and had a standing appointment with a barber in London that he had missed because of his Southern detour. But letting himself go feral held its appeal.

"What will you do when you fly home?" Gareth asked.

Alasdair noted the singular, but didn't press Gareth further. "I've decided to stay through the festival."

"Your boss is okay with that?"

"One way or another, he won't be my boss for much longer." He'd already moved on from any regrets or grief over the loss. Throwing off the yoke seemed to satisfy the Blackmoor inclination to revolution.

"Ach, I'm sorry. Even more so if I bear the burden of causing the rift even unintentionally. I know how important Wellington is to you. It's your life."

"No paltry job is more important than you." Alasdair clapped Gareth's shoulder and gave him a bracing squeeze. If he'd still been a lad, he might have hugged him around the waist. In fact, he could almost smell the old tweed jacket his uncle favored in Scotland. Alasdair added thoughtfully,

"I want my life to be bigger than a soul-sucking job. I'm not sure what that looks like yet, but I'll figure it out."

After a long bout of silence, Gareth asked, "Might that life include Isabel?"

"I've known her mere days. How can I answer that?"

"With your heart. I knew Rosie was the one after our first pot of tea."

Even though they were grown men, Alasdair's throat dried and clogged with a wad of awkwardness. "Are the two of you . . . intimately involved?"

Gareth's cheeks turned ruddy. "Christ preserve me, are you attempting to have the sex talk with me?"

Alasdair couldn't help but chuckle. "Not the birds and bees portion, I assume you're well versed at your age, but responsible sex is important. I read in the *London Times* that the STD infection rate is actually highest amongst the elderly."

"Elderly?" Gareth's shoulders bowed up and reminded Alasdair of a bull shown a red cape. "I can still put you flat on your back, laddie."

Alasdair held his hands up in surrender. "I have no doubt you could. I just wanted to make sure you were being smart."

Gareth harrumphed. "Smarter than you."

"What's that supposed to mean?"

"Are you and Isabel—how did you so delicately phrase it—intimately involved? Or were you rolling around on the ground looking for a lost contact?"

Now the tables had turned, Alasdair searched for an escape route, because he wanted to become intimately involved with Isabel several times over but didn't want to answer to his uncle. "It was only a kiss."

"For you, perhaps. What did it mean for Isabel?"

Alasdair stared at back door as if he could conjure

Isabel. She soothed him and bolstered him and agitated him all at the same time. Like an addict, he wanted more. "What do you know of Holt Pierson, gentleman farmer?"

"Oh-ho! So that's the way the winds blow." Gareth mostly controlled the twitch of his lips. "Pierson is well liked and from a family who settled the land the same time as the Buchanans. According to Rosie, Holt and Isabel have been friends since they were in nappies. But recently, Holt's interest has veered romantic. I'll not lie, Rosie is partial to him. It would make sense, I suppose. Two scions of Highland marrying."

"You make it sound like olden times when two lairds would betroth their offspring."

"Some things never change."

"Should I quit the field? The man has been patiently waiting for his chance, and my life is across an ocean." Alasdair wanted Gareth to argue with him and encourage him to follow his . . . Actually, he wasn't sure which part of his anatomy was in charge of his life's sat-nav.

"As it was only a kiss, I'm sure it will be a simple matter to watch another man win Isabel."

Alasdair narrowed his eyes, but Gareth remained deadpan. Imagining driving his fist into Holt Pierson's blandly handsome face was strangely satisfying.

"A simple matter indeed." Alasdair couldn't keep a snarl from curling his lip.

Gareth rubbed his hands together. "Now that you're staying for the festival, we must kit you out."

"Kit me out in what?" Alasdair asked, grateful for a change in conversation.

"In Highland dress." He walked away and gestured Alasdair to follow, so he did. "You'll compete, of course."

"Holt the turnip farmer has more experience with

traditional Highland competitions than I do. I'll embarrass myself."

Gareth had an adventurous spring to his step that proved contagious. "Humiliation is likely, but you can at least look good while competing against the man after the fair Isabel's heart. And body."

Chapter Ten

Isabel pressed her hands against her cheeks, ducked inside of the house, and pressed her body against the cool wall. Spontaneous combustion was imminent.

One kiss while locked in a closet together could be attributed to the darkness or the solitude or to general stupidity. The river had been a near miss, but now their flirting had led to a second kiss in the light of day in the middle of a field of flowers. It had been deliberate and reckless and breathtaking.

Falling even an inch for the man was a horrible, terrible, very bad idea. And she was scrabbling by her fingernails on a cliff's edge. Still she did a little jig on the way to her expanding to-do list in the office, knowing she would at least have him until the festival. She would ignore the impending doom and live in the moment. If only she could figure out how.

It was times like these when a dose of motherly advice would be welcomed. And a pie, preferably peach. She took a detour and found her mom in the kitchen, humming a tune, and dipping chicken in beaten egg and then flour.

"What's the occasion?" Izzy asked, coming up behind her.

Her mother startled, and flour poofed up to dot her apron. "You scared the tarnation out of me, child. Must there be a special occasion for fried chicken?"

"There usually is." Izzy watched her mother work, taking comfort in the familiar.

"The festival is coming together nicely, the forecast is predicting blue skies, and I'm happy. That's plenty to celebrate."

When she was young, Izzy had never discussed boys with her mom and had certainly never broached the subject of men as she grew older. Izzy had assumed, wrongly as it turned out, that her mom wouldn't understand.

"Are you and Gareth in love?" The question popped out, and not for the first time Izzy wished she had a speedbump between her brain and her mouth.

Her mom's hands stilled in the flour for a moment before resuming their work. "What's brought this on?"

"Seeing the two of you together makes me wonder what's going to change."

Her mom's smile was knowing and a little sad. "Nothing. Everything. Who knows? Gareth and I haven't discussed anything beyond tomorrow."

"You're okay with that?"

"I'm content." The chicken went back into the egg for another round. "I assumed I'd used up all my good luck finding your father. I didn't expect to get another chance."

"Do you feel guilty?" Izzy wasn't asking to put the thought in her mom's head, but for guidance on how to handle her own mixed feelings watching Gareth take her daddy's place.

"When you love someone—and I mean really love them—their happiness will come to mean more than yours. Your father loved me beyond words, and he would want me to be happy. So, no, I don't feel guilty." Her mom looked up from the chicken and cocked her head. "You don't understand yet, but you will someday."

Her mom's words triggered an understanding deep in the marrow of her bones. Things might change, but she would never lose her mom, no matter what happened between her and Gareth.

Izzy forced her lips into what she hoped resembled a smile. "A cat seems more likely than a man."

An impish twinkle banished the shadows in her mom's eyes. "If that's what you want, then I'll support your feline endeavors, but I don't think you should buy a litter box just yet. I saw Holt in town and he's smitten with you, darlin'. Absolutely smitten."

"We're meeting for drinks tonight." Izzy's stomach took a detour to her feet.

Her mom narrowed her eyes on Izzy. "Why are you saying it like that?"

"Like what?"

"Like you've been sentenced to hang instead of enjoying a glass of wine with an eligible, interested man." Her mom shot her an exasperated glance. "Darlin', Holt is good looking, nice, and available. What the problem?"

"I don't know. Nothing." *He's not a dark-haired Scotsman with a crooked grin and sexy brogue.* "I'll keep an open mind where Holt is concerned."

"Good. You deserve to cut loose and have a little fun. I apologize for slacking off when I got home, but Gareth has been a wonder with new ideas. Working with him has turned what had become staid and mundane exciting again."

Diverting her scattered thoughts to the festival was welcome. "We need to make sure the booths don't arrive for setup before the field is mowed."

They both looked out the window to the flowers swaying in the slight breeze. Her mom said, "I wish we could leave them. Watching them get mowed down is a depressing sight."

Izzy waited until the last possible moment to schedule the mowers for the same reason, and this year the cut would be even deeper after the stolen moments in the middle of the flowers with Alasdair.

"I'll handle the mowers, the booths, *and* the vendors," her mom said. "Why don't you get your hair or nails done before you meet Holt?"

Izzy fingered the ends of her hair, her scalp tingling with the memory of Alasdair's hands. "I do need to run by the dance school. Anna wants to show me the costumes the girls will be wearing."

"I'm sure they'll all look just darling. Anna has such a good eye."

Not only did she have a good eye, but she had good ears to help Izzy parse her confusion.

Izzy exchanged polite greetings with the parents waiting in the front room for their children to finish their lessons. Instead of waiting with them, she slipped through the frosted double door and found Anna in the modern studio she'd refurbished after taking over the dance studio from her mother.

The sun diffused through the large oaks outside to bathe the studio in warm light and was reflected back from the wall of floor-to-ceiling mirrors. The light wood floor and cream walls added to the fresh and modern vibe.

Anna had a dozen pre-teen girls gathered around her, giving them a rundown of their upcoming events, including the parade and, of course, the games. With long, wavy red hair and a dancer's lean body, Anna could star on a travel poster for Scotland. It was easy to picture her standing in a tartan gown at the top of a castle turret with a wind-swept moor of heather in the background beating back invading Sassenach with her bow.

The illusion was broken the moment Anna opened her mouth and a thick honeyed Southern accent emerged. "The crowd might be intimidating, but I know the more experienced girls will help the young'uns manage their nerves."

A chorus of yesses accompanied hugs all around, and the chatter increased tenfold when Anna dismissed them.

Anna's mother, Clarice, had founded the dance studio thirty years earlier. She had been ecstatic when eight-year-old Izzy signed up for dance lessons. Ecstasy quickly flipped to disappointment when it became clear Izzy had not inherited Rose's balletic talent.

Anna had been a year behind Izzy in school, and Izzy had watched Anna shine on the cheerleading squad and dance team with awe and a small amount of envy. Anna had won the Highland games dance competition five years running.

With her arthritis worsening, Clarice had scaled back her time in the studio, finally retiring to travel with her church group. Anna had revamped the studio and the program, offering hip-hop dance in addition to the tradi-tional Celtic dancing the studio was known for.

"Izzy! Come on back and check this out." Anna was full of energy with a dark, sometimes biting, sense of humor. As a role model for her young charges, she was more P!nk than Mary Poppins.

After Izzy gave the requisite compliments on the dresses the girls would be donning for the festival, Anna held up an adult Celtic dancing dress in a mossy green with gold accents. Its flounced, almost childish skirt was offset by the tight bodice and low-scooped neck. She hummed a tune, swayed, and waggled her eyebrows.

"Have you taken it for a test drive? Did anything X-rated happen when you leapt?" Izzy's lips twitched. While Anna and Izzy hadn't hung out regularly in high school, they had become best friends over the last few years because of the festival.

"I'd for sure repeat as champion again if that happened."

"You forget that Miss Dunbar is one of the judges. Your boob buds might give her a stroke."

Anna and Izzy dissolved into giggles. Miss Dunbar had been their health and physical education teacher in middle school. A brief lesson on the changing female body had been riddled with euphemisms and outright dodging of reality. The word "nipple" had been deemed too scandalous to utter by Miss Dunbar. The replacement terminology of boob buds had imprinted on an entire generation of Highland's girls.

"If my boob buds accidently pop out, I might attract a brawny man competing in the athletic feats. Lord knows, I could use a giant caber in my life."

"You are terrible." Izzy guffawed and checked behind them for any eavesdropping parents or, even worse, kids.

"I don't have the chance to be terrible, but I'd like to." Anna hung her dancing costume back up and shot her a side-eye. "Speaking of available cabers to toss, I hear you have an honest-to-goodness Scotsman staying at Stonehaven."

"Two of them, actually."

"I've met Gareth—nice guy with massive googly eyes for Rose—but I was referring to the hotty-pants with the banging accent who's not eligible for AARP."

"Alasdair Blackmoor. Gareth's friend."

"Sexy name. What's the story?"

"He's some high-powered financial whiz. He spent school holidays with Gareth. Old family friends. He's flying home after the festival though."

"Have you slept with him?" Anna asked with no embarrassment whatsoever.

"What? No. Of course not. Geez." Izzy's face reached roasting temperatures. "I'm actually on my way to meet Holt for a drink."

Anna turned unusually serious. "Are you actually interested in Holt or are you settling because you're lonely?"

"It's just a drink." The same line had been on repeat since her acceptance, but now that Anna had caller her out, it felt weak and unfair.

"Holt wants more."

It was the "more" that set Izzy's stomach to dancing an award-winning jig. Words blurted out of her mouth. "I kissed him."

"Holt?" Anna's eyes bugged.

"Alasdair."

"Ah, the Hot Scot. How was it?"

"Good. Fine." When Anna made a "gimme more" gesture, Izzy continued. "Okay, it was frigging magnificent. We were laying in the field of wildflowers out back of the house."

Anna clutched her heart and took a step back. "In a field of flowers? Could that be any more romantic?"

"It was amazing until I got bit by fire ants."

"And?"

The fact Anna knew there was an "and" had her spilling the rest. "We got locked in that janky closet down at the Baptist church. The dark and the diminished oxygen levels impaired our judgment."

"Seven minutes in heaven in a church closet. That's classic!" Anna's laugh was infectious.

Izzy slapped her friend's arm. "I need serious help here. I kissed one man this morning and am meeting another for drinks in like"—she checked the wall clock—"fifteen minutes. You've dated more than I have. What do I do?"

"Having drinks with Holt does not mean you're engaged or anything, but don't lead him on. Keep it friendly and if you really want to send an 'I just want to be friends' signal, pay for your own drink."

"I can do that." It sounded simple enough.

"Try to get there before him and order at the bar, otherwise Holt will insist on paying, because that's the kind of guy he is. Avoid the tables in the back. It's dark and cozy and screams date. Keep your distance. Get the chair across from him and not right next to him. No flirting allowed."

"Pay for my drink. Stay in the light. Arm's-length away." Izzy parroted. "Keep the conversation centered on the festival."

Anna's brow knitted. "Poor Holt. He's a nice guy, but how could he possibly compete with your Scot?"

Izzy fiddled with the button of her shirt-dress. "He's not mine. He lives across an ocean."

"He doesn't have to be yours forever, but he can be yours for right now." Anna's wisdom was understanding and non-judgey.

Izzy swallowed. "You're talking about sex."

"Flirting and kissing and yes, maybe even sex with someone you're obviously attracted to. You work so hard on the festival, Izzy. Everyone has a great time. You deserve to have fun too."

"But the festival needs—"

"You need too! And even if Hotty MacScottypants is stellar in bed, it won't take more than an hour out of your schedule. At best. I think you can manage to pencil in an appointment." Anna air-quoted the last word with an impish smile.

"I don't even know if Alasdair wants to *go all the way*."

Anna's sniggered. "This is what living at home with your mother has done to you."

Izzy rolled her eyes. "Mom and Gareth are packing on the PDA. I wouldn't be surprised if they haven't already gone all the way."

Anna stuck her fingers in her ears and made a blech sound. "That's like imaging my mother with a dude. Thanks for putting that image in my head. Not cool."

"Mom and Gareth are actually kind of . . . I don't know, sweet together."

Anna cocked her head. "Are you good with that?"

"It's crazy, but yes. I'm totally good with it."

"Right." Anna's voice turned brisk and no-nonsense, and she rubbed her hands together. "What about protection?"

"Geez! How am I supposed to know if they're using protection? Mom and I aren't sharing our favorite sexual positions over cocktails or taking *Cosmo* quizzes together."

Anna poked her elbow in Izzy's side. "Not for your mom, you idiot. For you."

"For me? Oh, in case Alasdair and I . . . you know?"

"Yes, *I* know. I'm worried it's been so long you've forgotten." As if she were speaking to a certified idiot, complete with a framed certificate, Anna said succinctly, "Do you have condoms?"

"Even if I did have some, they probably would have expired."

"Disintegrated is more like. Ashes to ashes and dust to dust." Anna tossed a grin over her shoulder before she disappeared in her office. She returned with her hands full of an offering. "Here."

Like she was performing a magic trick, the package popped out of her hand like a triggered fake snake in a can, unfolding to cascade three feet toward the floor.

Izzy grabbed the condoms and worked to refold them, hiding them close to her body. Her heart raced like a drug deal was going down. "I don't need this many. One is fine."

"One is sad." Anna didn't bother to suppress her teasing amusement. "Take them. If you must know, I haven't needed them since Eddie moved."

Izzy had been glad to see Eddie's backside leave Highland. Anna had a strong personality and needed a man who could go toe-to-toe with her. Instead, she tended to pick easily manipulated men who drifted through life with little ambition. It was like Anna was only comfortable starting a relationship knowing it had an expiration date.

Izzy shoved the condom accordion into her purse. Anna glanced over Izzy's shoulder at the clock on the wall. "Ticktock. You'd better head on over if you want to beat Holt to your non-date."

A spate of nerves went off like a sparkler in Izzy's belly. She grabbed Anna's wrist. "Will you come with me?"

"I have no desire to be a third wheel or a crutch. Anyway, I have festival prep to do too."

Izzy put on her best puppy eyes and whimpered.

Anna sighed and made a throaty sound of disgust. "Okay. Fine. I'll head over in ten and grab a seat at the bar. If you really need an out, then signal me."

"What kind of signal?"

Anna cupped her hands around her mouth and made like a crow. "*Ca-caw. Ca-caw.*"

Through her nervous laughter, Izzy said, "How about I give you the stink eye?"

"Fine. We'll go with subtle." Anna gave her a push on the shoulder. "Pull up your big-girl panties and remember the plan."

Izzy trudged out of the door as if her sandals were made of concrete. Anna gave her a thumbs-up before flipping the sign to Closed and pulling the shade down. Izzy took comfort in the fact backup would be a mere stink eye away.

The Dancing Jig could have been picked up from a corner of Edinburgh and plopped down in Highland. The charming, old-world feel was both homey and foreign compared to the country bars that made up the rest of the Highland social scene on the edge of town. Wide, dark-stained planks on the ceiling, walls, and floors absorbed the light and cast long shadows.

A stage fanned out from one corner and hosted Celtic music on Friday and Saturday nights. Tonight it was empty, but most tables and booths were full and voices buzzed. She made her way toward the bar, which was a square in the middle of the pub. Step one of the "let's just be friends plan:" order and pay for a drink before Holt had a chance to offer.

Holt emerged from the shadows with a smile on his face and wearing khakis and a blue striped button-down. His blond-brown hair was still damp and a subtle waft of cologne enveloped her. "I grabbed a table in the back. What would you like to drink?"

She looked over her shoulder, but Anna hadn't arrived yet. "Gin and tonic, please."

Holt passed her request on to the bartender and with a hand on the small of her back, led her to the table he'd snagged in the most remote corner possible. Izzy wasn't sure Anna would even be able to see her stink eye from the deep shadows. She might have to resort to the crow call.

To make matters worse, the chair Holt held out would leave her back to the bar and the door. She hesitated, but perched on the edge, losing her balance and grabbing the table when he scooted the chair in for her unexpectedly. Along with the nice clothes and the cologne, his solicitous attitude was yet another sign this was a date. Not quite as fear inducing as the apocalypse, but close.

He took the chair not across from her but beside her so their elbows and knees brushed. Vonn, the bartender, bustled over and slid her gin and tonic onto the table. Holt smiled and said, "Put it on my tab."

The not-date was unfolding in the exact opposite way Izzy and Anna had planned. She took a sip of her drink just as Holt asked, "Did you have an enjoyable day?"

Enjoyable? Gin burned down her windpipe. Rolling around in the field with Alasdair definitely qualified as enjoyable.

Holt patted her back until she quit coughing. Except, even after she caught her breath, he didn't remove his hand, but draped his arm over the back of her chair. Her spine turned to steel and she made sure not to relax into his touch. Staring at the scarred tabletop, she said, "It was good. Normal. Nothing special. How was yours?"

"Great actually. Weather has been perfect for the soybeans. Apples are ripening for the picking. Hogs fetched a good price. Everyone loves bacon, right?"

Izzy did in fact love bacon, but not thinking about the journey from farm to skillet. She took another too-big sip of her drink. At this rate, she'd need another drink in seconds and would be drunk before Anna even made an appearance.

"Are you ready to compete in the games?" she asked, steering them into the conversational safety net of the festival.

With a teasing smile, he curled his arm and his biceps bulged against cotton. "I'm always ready to compete, and I plan to four-peat. I can't wait to claim my prize." His warm smile made her insides freeze as if a north wind had blown through.

She swallowed past a lump, unable to imagine kissing anyone besides Alasdair even if it was a mere peck on the cheek. This year, Izzy would claim halitosis or a cold sore or another horrible ailment and make her mom dole out kisses. She made a mental note to hit WebMD when she got home.

She glanced over her shoulder. Anna's red hair glinted under the bar lights, but she was turned sideways in conversation. Izzy relaxed marginally. Worst case, Izzy could excuse herself for the bathroom and grab Anna for a toilet stall strategy session. Another sip and she hit ice on her gin and tonic. Holt held up two fingers, and Vonn hustled over with another beer and a gin and tonic.

"How do you think the Dawgs will fare this fall?" she asked. Surely, football was a safe, innocuous subject. Highland was close enough to Athens to be a breeding ground of University of Georgia football fans. Even though Holt hadn't attended, he was rabid.

On ground not littered with emotional mines, her anxiety eased. She sipped her drink and interjected her opinions on the state of the team's coaching and recruiting.

Eventually though, they exhausted all things football. Holt leaned forward and took her hand. It was clammy from nerves and clutching her sweating drink glass, but mostly from nerves.

"I appreciate you meeting me for a drink," Holt said.

"No problem." Her voice had risen at least an octave, and she fought the urge to shoot a stink eye over her shoulder like the bat signal.

"I've always gone for what I wanted, no holds barred. I really like you, but I don't want to take a risk if I don't have a chance. So, tell me now; do I have a chance?"

Ca-caw.

Alasdair parked in front of the Dapper Highlander. Gareth unfolded himself from the low-slung coupe, stood on the sidewalk with his hands on his hips, and surveyed the street like he was the laird. "It's a corker of a village."

Alasdair joined him, taking in the quaint shops, metal

lampposts, and hanging baskets overflowing with colorful flowers. "It is picturesque, but you don't think it's over the top?"

"Highland is full of love for Scotland. To be honest, I've felt my ancestors more here than at Cairndow the last few years." He let out a sigh that spoke of contentment.

Alasdair swung his gaze to Gareth. "You're beholden to Cairndow. It needs you."

"If things were different, I could be happy here." Gareth's buoyant happiness deflated.

Alasdair hated the thought he'd done that to his uncle, but what could he do to ease his uncle's burden?

"Let's forget about Cairndow for now," Alasdair said with a forced lightness. "It's survived hundreds of years and will survive a few more weeks without you."

"Indeed. Let's get you a kitted out." Gareth opened the door to the Dapper Highlander for Alasdair.

Mr. Timmerman bustled from the back and gave Gareth a hearty handshake. "Good to see you, Gareth. And Mr. Blackmoor. Welcome."

"Call me Alasdair, please."

"Are you here for your kilt?" Mr. Timmerman asked Gareth.

"I was wondering if you could alter the kilt for my . . . for Alasdair. I have a kilt packed I can wear and he has nothing."

Alasdair turned to Gareth. "You had the fabric ordered especially. I can't."

"You can and will. I insist."

"As you're the same height, it should only require a tuck or two around the waist, I should think." Mr. Timmerman disappeared behind a curtain.

Gareth patted his belly. "His nice way of saying I've gone to fat."

"You're stout, not fat," Alasdair teased.

Mr. Timmerman returned with a kilt made from the beautiful green and gray Blackmoor tartan wool. "Slip it on so I can make my marks."

Alasdair followed Mr. Timmerman to a curtained-off room next to a floor-to-ceiling mirror. He took the proffered kilt and closed the curtain. Stripping down to his underwear, he slipped on the kilt and buckled the leather clasps. The wool was soft against his legs, the front flat, the back pleated. It hung slightly lower on his hips that it ought, but as he stared at himself a feeling of connection, not only to Gareth but to generations past, bound his chest so tightly he wasn't sure he could speak.

Gareth whipped the curtain back, tossed him a black T-shirt, and reclosed the curtain. Alasdair pulled on the tee, tucking it into the kilt. It gave the look a modern twist.

Voices conferred too low to hear on the other side of the curtain. Stepping out, Alasdair held his arms out and did a slow turn for Gareth and Mr. Timmerman. "Not too shabby, eh?"

"A better fit than I anticipated." Mr. Timmerman bustled over and tugged at the kilt, making marks with a fabric pencil he kept tucked behind his ear.

"You'll need boots. Timmerman and I were discussing whether you should go traditional or not." Gareth pointed to a display of shoes and boots along the wall. Traditional leather shoes took up a row. Next to them were a mix of brown and black knee-high riding boots and lace-up combat-style calf boots. "What do you prefer?"

Mr. Timmerman flanked his other side and tapped a pair of lace-up black leather combat boots. "As you'll be competing, may I suggest a functional pair with good tread and ankle support?"

"I never agreed to compete." Alasdair swung his gaze to Gareth with raised eyebrows.

"Fine. Let Holt steal the winner's kiss." Gareth's eyes

twinkled in a way that signaled a deep belly laugh was imminent.

"You sly fox," Alasdair murmured. Louder, he said, "I'll try them on."

Mr. Timmerman retrieved the appropriate size and handed him a pair of dark gray wool knee socks. Once Alasdair was kitted out in boots, kilt, and T-shirt, he stood in front of the mirror. He'd let his wavy hair have its way in the Southern heat and humidity, and hadn't shaved since he'd arrived in Georgia. His Wellington coworkers and clients wouldn't recognize him, but the man reflected back was an old friend he'd ignored for too long.

The bell over the door tinkled and in the reflection of the mirror, Alasdair met Rose Buchanan's wide eyes. A slow smile spread over her face. "My goodness, don't you look the part of a wild Scottish Highlander, Alasdair. In fact—" She looked at Gareth and then back at Alasdair, a smile still on her face, but a quizzical wrinkle squeezing her brow. "The two of you could be father and son."

"We're not," Gareth said sharply before modulating his voice to add, "although, if I had a son, I would be more than proud if he was like Alasdair."

Emotion clawed its way up his throat. How often had he pretended Gareth was his father? Enough times to cause a fair amount of guilt. Alasdair wanted to tell Gareth how much he meant to him and how much he regretted the fracture in their relationship but not in front of Rose and Mr. Timmerman. It was a conversation meant for a cliffside sunset at Cairndow.

Gareth laid a tender kiss on Rose's temple and she took his hand, her glow brightening. "What brought you by, Rosie?"

"I'm an interfering old biddy and wanted to peek in at the Dancing Jig. Izzy met Holt Pierson for drinks. I'm hoping it turns into dinner. Want to join me?"

Alasdair stalked to the front window and stared across the street at the pub entrance. The two kisses they'd shared weren't a commitment, yet a fever came over him knowing she was with another man, even if it was only for a drink.

A hand came down on his shoulder and squeezed. "What's your plan, lad?"

"What can I do?"

"Give her a decision to make."

Considering his career had been all about mitigating risk, Alasdair had forgotten what it felt like to take a risk in real life. It was scary. And exhilarating.

Without second-guessing himself, Alasdair stalked out of the Dapper Highlander. Alasdair would leave Gareth to take care of things with Mr. Timmerman. He had more important things to do. Like wooing a woman.

Chapter Eleven

An audible, simultaneous gasp brought Izzy's head around, hoping whatever it was provided her with an excuse to leave. Like the announcement of an imminent meteor strike or a zombie invasion.

It was something even more startling. Against a setting sun, a kilted figure was outlined in the doorway as if he'd stepped directly out of the Highlands of Scotland into Georgia. His stance was aggressive, and pity welled in Izzy for the object of his attention. The man took a step inside, and the door swung shut behind him.

It wasn't a ghost or a time-traveler but a sexy-as-all-get-out flesh-and-blood Alasdair. A form-fitting black T-shirt emphasized his broad shoulders and biceps. His kilt high-lighted muscular legs, and a pair of black leather boots amped up his sexy masculinity. Even in a town where all things Scottish reigned supreme, Alasdair's appearance at the pub was extraordinary.

Izzy's heart rate ramped up and heat flushed her body. She pressed on her chest as if she could turn off her reaction. The gin plus Alasdair made her feel light-headed, and she daubed her forehead with a flimsy bar napkin damp from condensation.

"You've gone as white as cotton," said Holt. "Are you feeling poorly or did you see a ghost?"

She hadn't seen a ghost; she'd seen a wild, marauding Highlander. *He's mine.* Or he could be if she was brave enough to take a chance. She clutched her purse closer and shifted around again to make sure she hadn't imagined him, but no, he stood in all his glory, scanning the shadowy recesses.

"Isn't that the guy staying with you? Albert or something?" Holt's voice came from miles away even as his hand touched her forearm, trying and failing to regain her focus.

Alasdair's gaze locked on her like a missile. Slow and steady, each of his steps sent seismic tremors through her even though logically there was no way she could feel them. The hairs on the back of her arms wavered.

"Alasdair." Her voice had taken on the qualities of a classic film seductress, throaty and sexy without a hint of levity. In fact, the moment veered darkly serious.

Alasdair stopped in front of her. The intensity of his gaze stripped her bare, the command unspoken yet clear. She stood as if he were her puppeteer. He held out his hand and without hesitation, she slid her palm over his, and their fingers knitted together.

Holt half rose. "Hang on a second. What's going on?"

A lump of regret and heartache grew in her throat choking back her words. Her mind had erased Holt as soon as she'd laid eyes on Alasdair. Holt was nice and kind and good looking in a wholesome Georgia country boy kind of way, and he deserved someone who appreciated all of his excellent qualities. The part of her who craved easy wished she could appreciate him. But it was too late.

Nothing besides friendship would exist between them,

even if Alasdair hopped a flight to London tomorrow never to be seen again.

Still holding Alasdair's hand, she turned to Holt. "I'm so sorry. I have to go."

"Have to go or *want* to go?" A belligerent frown was aimed squarely at Alasdair. Holt could have been a linebacker homing in on a quarterback with the football.

"Both, actually." She lightly touched Holt's biceps, tense and bulging with static tension. She wasn't sure if she offered comfort or a warning to stay away from Alasdair. Either way, she didn't have the words to make it right, because it wasn't fair to Holt.

Holt shook free of her touch and pointed at Alasdair. "Will I see you on the field or are you afraid of a little competition?"

"I'll be there, mate," Alasdair said with equal aggression. It was like the two of them had agreed to duel at dawn.

Holt stalked away without a backward glance at the two of them. The hum of conversation restarted with the pub's attention still focused on their dark corner, which meant they were the hot topic for the evening. Not that she could blame them.

"You look"—her gaze wandered down his body and back up—"ridiculous."

He tugged at one of the leather cinches at his hip. "I walked out of the Dapper Highlander like this. I'll change back into my clothes."

When he took a step back, she grabbed his T-shirt like a drowning woman. "Don't you dare. I meant ridiculous as in ridiculously hot and sexy and . . . and . . . lickable."

His eyebrows quirked along with the corners of his mouth. "Lickable?"

It might have been the two gin and tonics, but she

couldn't deny the truth. She wanted to run her lips and tongue all over his body—and she meant *everywhere*. Owning it, she raised her chin and said, "Yeah, I said it. You want to get outta here?"

His eyes flared, almost black in the shadows, and he gave her hand a tug. "Let's go."

She followed in his wake, enjoying the view, a smile on her face and laughter bubbling up from the sheer joy of surrendering to what she wanted. Anna spun around on her bar stool to follow their progress and made a thumbs-up, but there was a question in her eyes. If being dragged out of the Dancing Jig by a sexy Highlander wasn't what she wanted, Anna would jump in to save her.

Izzy returned a thumbs-up. The last thing Izzy saw was Anna giving her a slow clap on her way out the door.

He continued across the street toward his rented silver car, but then pulled up to a sudden stop, patting his hip. "My keys are in my pants."

As if summoning them, the door to the Dapper Highlander opened and Gareth stepped out, her mom peeking over his shoulder. "Here you go, laddie."

He tossed the keys. Alasdair caught them, gave Gareth a salute, and opened the car door for Izzy. She hesitated with a foot on the floorboard. "Hey, Mom."

"Hey, honey." It was clear by the way her mother's jaw worked that she wanted to say more and no doubt, Izzy would face an interrogation in the morning, but it was hard to care, considering what she had to look forward to with Alasdair.

"I'll see you back at the house." Izzy slipped onto the sleek leather and Alasdair closed the door, quick-stepping around the car to join her.

"Where can we go?" she asked more of herself than of him.

"What do you mean?"

"Mom and Gareth are right down the hall. Isn't that going to be awkward?"

The corner of his mouth ticked up. "You've never brought a bloke home before?"

"No." Nerves set roots in her belly but barely made a dent in her anticipation. "You think I'm a weirdo, don't you?"

He pressed a kiss on the back of her hand as he deftly steered with his free hand. "I think you're sweet."

"That's a nice way of saying pathetic." Words continued to spew out like from a shaken Coke can. "I'm not some innocent country bumpkin. I had fun in college, but living at home with my mom doesn't exactly boost my prospects in Highland. What guy wants to get it on with a girl's mom down the hall? Plus, I love her to pieces, but she's traditional—or so I thought before Gareth came along—and I fell back into old habits like I was still in high school."

He pulled the car over into a grassy area on the side of the gravel lane leading to Stonehaven and turned to face her. Had the deluge terrified him? Any sane, well-adjusted man would hightail it out of the country ASAP.

He leaned over the black leather console and kissed her. Their eyes were open and locked on each other. He pulled back slightly, but didn't make a move to keep driving.

"What was that for?" she asked softly.

"It was a reminder." At her questioning brow scrunch, he said, "A reminder of the funny, kickass, confident heroine who conquered the dragon Loretta and escaped the dungeon of the church and lured a hot, sexy, lickable traveler"—he ticked off her earlier compliments on his fingers with a barely suppressed laugh—"into her castle. The only question is what are you going to do next?"

She did what any self-respecting heroine of a fantasy would do and wrapped her arms around his shoulders, pulling his mouth to hers. He cupped her nape and deepened the kiss. When his tongue touched her, her eyes closed. The seclusion was welcome, but the lack of square footage grew her frustration with each brush of his lips. He was too far away. If they'd been in her truck, she could have climbed on top of him or he could have laid over her on the bench seat.

His reminder had hit home. She had never tried to hide herself from Alasdair. Whatever she was—dragon slayer or fool—she was enough for him.

"We'd have more privacy in the barn," she murmured against his jaw.

"I'm yours to command." After pressing one last kiss against her lips, he settled back into his seat and goosed the gas so hard the tires spun out on the gravel.

He pulled up to the side the barn, and she fumbled with the unfamiliar car door handle in the dark, finally finding the latch and pushing at the door with her weight behind her just as Alasdair made it around the side of the car to open it for her.

The lack of a counterbalance threw her off-balance. She teetered on the edge of the seat before tumbling out in the least graceful way possible. Her shoulder and one palm hit the combination of weeds and gravel. Her legs were twisted on the floorboard and instead of attempting to right herself, she let her body roll out, her legs in the air. Her purse, which she wore crosswise, got caught in the small of her back, the strap tight across her throat.

"Bloody hell, are you alright?" Alasdair squatted next to her and wrapped a steadying hand around her forearm. The position gave her an unimpeded view straight up his kilt. She blinked and forced herself to look away, too embarrassed to enjoy herself.

Her palm stung and her shoulder throbbed from the impact. Her pride was officially roadkill. "Run over me a couple of times and put me out of my misery."

"Come on, then, love." Laughter lightened his voice.

He'd called her "love," which was probably like an American calling someone "dude," but nevertheless an electric thrill quickened her blood and helped allay her embarrassment.

On a self-deprecating laugh, she said, "I can't be trusted in romantic situations, Alasdair. We got locked in a closet. I ran off with your clothes. I got bit by fire ants. And now I literally fall at your feet. I'm a joke."

He brushed her hair back from her forehead. "I've been serious all my life. Always doing what's expected of me. I want to have fun and laugh and take a risk. With you."

Somehow Alasdair knew the magic words needed to unlock her defenses. More than anything, she wanted to gift him with a heartfelt response. Instead what came out was, "You're wearing underwear. I thought Scots went commando under their kilts."

He threw his head back and laughed, a rumbly, pleasant sound, then tilted his head and regarded her with raised brows. "I notice you're wearing knickers too."

It took her a hot second to realize he was talking about her underwear and not a pair of short pants her great-grandfather might have worn. She lifted her head. Her position had left her shirt-dress riding high on her thighs. Her laugh joined his even as she pushed the hem down.

"Maybe we should do something about our pesky underwear." While she wasn't used to pre-sex banter, based on his wolfish smile, she was doing okay.

"Most assuredly."

He had her back on her feet in a blink, but instead of sweeping her into his arms and carrying her into the barn to do naughty, X-rated things to her, he examined the palm she'd fallen on.

"You've scraped yourself. A wash and antibiotic spray are next," he said.

"I'd rather do something about our respective underwear. Like shred them into confetti."

"I promise you can rip my underwear off and look under my kilt as soon as we see to your hand."

"I won't die from a scrape, but I might die if we don't . . . you know."

"If we don't what? Share a pot of tea before bed?" Although his face was tilted down examining the palm of her hand, good-natured teasing hummed in his voice.

"You aren't at all funny." Except she was smiling so widely her cheeks hurt.

"Five minutes of first aid and then you can have your wicked way with me."

She allowed him to guide her toward the house but stomped her way inside like she'd been deemed too short to ride the fastest, best roller coaster. Alasdair went straight to the cabinet holding their first aid supplies and rummaged through the assortment of medicines while she washed her hands with soap, biting her lip at the sting.

After he set out a box of Band-Aids and antiseptic spray, he put his hands at her waist. "Hop up."

Once she was sitting on the counter, he put his hands on her knees and pushed them apart, wedging his hips in between. The added height put them face-to-face, and the hem of her dress inched toward indecent. Her sugared pulse set a sensual rhythm through her body.

He blotted her scraped palm with a paper towel, handling her with the care and concentration of a man tasked with diffusing a bomb. His mouth was in a firm line and his brows drawn low. His dark hair waved over his forehead, and her free hand itched to feel the strands between her fingers.

The black T-shirt emphasized the taut planes and the bulge of muscle across his shoulders. Topography she wanted to chart in great detail. She would be the Lewis and Clark of Alasdair's body. "You work out a lot, huh?"

His gaze flicked up then returned to the task of cleaning her cut, but his mouth had relaxed into an almost smile. "Work and exercise kept me busy in London. And when I traveled, I usually found myself in the hotel gym when I couldn't sleep."

"That sounds bo-ring." She emphasized the last word in a singsong voice.

"I suppose it was," he said thoughtfully, any tease gone from his manner.

"You used past tense. Are you going change your ways when you go home?"

He didn't speak for a long moment, her hand taking more concentration than a little scrape merited. "I don't think I'll have a choice. I won't be returning the same man. Highland has changed me."

The moment seemed charged, and she kept silent rather than say the wrong thing. He sprayed her palm with the antiseptic and used two Snoopy Band-Aids to cover the deepest of the scrapes.

Giving up the fight to touch him, she shuffled her good hand through his hair and curled her fingers around his nape. "Will I survive?"

"In my expert opinion as a risk assessor, you will indeed survive." He brought her palm to his mouth and pressed a kiss over her boo-boo. He looked up at her through his lashes, his gray eyes gleaming. "Unless we don't . . .'you know' within the next ten minutes."

"Are we destined to keep hurting ourselves when we're

together?" The question was meant as a joke, but landed
with the weight of a ten-ton grenade.

His gaze searched her face, his mouth taut. "I don't
want to hurt you, Isabel."

"You won't," she said simply. "I know you're leaving.
It's okay. I want this for however long you're here."

Izzy finally understood why her mom had brought Gareth home and had grown closer with him even though it
was all temporary. A Highland fling. Knowing she and
Alasdair had an expiration date made things both easier
and harder, but Izzy would take what pleasure she could
with him both in bed and out and worry about the aftermath later.

Their lips met halfway. This kiss didn't begin with
a sweet prelude; it launched into a fugue of sparring
tongues and limbs. He grabbed her hips and pulled her into
him, then edged his hand under her skirt until his palm
branded her butt. More of her weight transferred to him
and she wiggled to get even closer, pulling his shirt from
his kilt.

Desperation drummed in her heart. The minutes it
would take to get to the barn and situated with a blanket in the loft seemed an eon. Too long. Her room, with
a mattress and pillows and clean sheets, was right above
them if only they could teleport.

"My room." She gasped the words between kisses.

"Are you sure?" He sucked her bottom lip between his
teeth, muffling her "Hell, yes" response.

He carried her clinging to him like a spider monkey
until he reached the stairs. Her feet touched down on
the first stair and instead of forging ahead to her room,
she worked his T-shirt up and off, tossing it over her
shoulder.

Magnificent. There was really no other word. He might

have stepped out of a book on ancient Scotland, bare chested with his kilt riding low on his hips. A warrior.

His skin beckoned and she ran her hands up the crisp dark hair on his chest, the Band Aids hampering her need to feel every inch of his skin. His shoulders were muscled and his back smooth. He put some space between them to work the buttons of her shirt-dress open. He looped her purse over her head and dropped it.

"I'm glad your back isn't hairy." The thought wiggled past her internal editor.

His smile gleamed in the dim stairway. "It probably won't stay that way. Have you seen Gareth without a shirt on?"

She tilted her head. "What does Gareth have to do with your hairless back?"

Alasdair's hands stilled on the third button down. "Just Scottish men in general."

Before she could reorder her thoughts, he scrambled them again with a kiss. Cool air hit her shoulders as he worked her shirt-dress down to her waist, her arms caught at the elbow. His big hands ran up and down her back, spreading warmth and leaving a trail of delicious sensation in their wake.

"I'm glad your back isn't hairy either." His breath was hot in her ear before he nipped her lobe between his teeth.

Unfiltered joy spread from her chest and through her body, her response coming on a breathless laugh. "Uh-oh. Have you seen my mom?"

His laugh rumbled alongside hers. They scrambled a few steps higher, closer to her room and her bed before another distraction stopped them on the landing. He pushed her against the paneled wall with his hips and pinned her wrists over her head with one hand. If she wanted to pull free, she could, but being captured by him only heightened the fantasy of a conquering Scottish Highlander.

"Your skin is so pale and soft." He dropped a kiss on the delicate skin on the inside of her elbow as the fingers of his other hand skittered up her torso.

She was exposed and at his mercy, but had no urge to cover herself. She arched her back, inviting more of his touch, almost as if the two of them had stepped from the mortal world into fae lands under a spell.

Finally, his hand cupped her breast. Not expecting the turn of events that had brought her to be pressed against a wall by a shirtless, kilt-wearing Alasdair, she hadn't chosen her underwear with any foresight. Her bra was white, utilitarian, and padded and covered more than it revealed.

"Sorry," she mumbled.

"What are you sorry for?"

"I didn't choose my underwear tonight for seduction purposes."

She could feel the laughter he kept confined to his chest. "I guess that means I'm not a poor substitute for Holt the squash farmer."

His voice was tinted unmistakably green? "Are you jealous of Holt?"

"Are you surprised?" He bit the soft juncture between neck and shoulder.

"Yes. Because you're . . . beautiful." It was only when he lifted his head to look at her that she realized how odd it sounded. Yet, it was true.

"No. You're the beautiful one, Isabel. Inside and out and everywhere in between."

She let herself believe him. Why not? The night was her adventure. Her fantasy.

Speaking of fantasies, she wanted to get back at it. She wiggled her hips against him. Was that his . . . ? She gasped. It was. And it felt as impressive as the rest of him.

She pulled out of his hold, grabbed his hand, and stumbled up the rest of the stairs into her room. He kicked her door closed and pressed her up against it. Searching to the side, she found the lock and snicked it into place. Finally, they were locked in a room with a bed, and Izzy planned to take full advantage. She fisted her non-injured hand in the soft cloth tartan of his kilt and pulled it higher.

"Are you tryin' to discover what's under my kilt, lassie?" His Scottish brogue was an octave lower and rough, sending a shiver through her.

"I could feel what was under it pressed against me on the stairs. I want more."

Alasdair muttered a curse tinged with awe. "I didn't peg you for a dirty talker."

"You think that's dirty? You'd be shocked to hear what kind of foolishness goes on in my head then."

"I can't wait be scandalized." His hand crawled up her back to fiddle with her industrial-strength bra strap. "Jesus. You're not wearing a chastity belt requiring a key too, are you?"

No embarrassment, only urgency surfaced. "No chastity belt. But I should warn you, it's been so long I might have re-virginized."

He dropped his head to her shoulder on a sputtering laugh. Needing reinforcements in his battle with her bra strap, his other hand snaked around her back. Finally, he vanquished the hooks and her bra loosened. A first rush of shyness had her closing her eyes as he slipped the straps down her arms and whisked her bra off.

An animalistic sound between a hum and growl emerged from him. She peeked. His expression settled her spate of nerves. She was a sheep to his wolf and couldn't wait to be devoured.

This time when he cupped her breast, nothing separated skin from skin. His thumb glanced over her nipple, budded and aching. She shimmied her hips and pushed her bunched dress to her ankles, leaving her in panties. While there was nothing lacy or particularly sexy about them, they were, thank all that was holy, not holey.

The hand not squeezing and molding and otherwise wreaking pleasure on her breasts dropped to skim along her hipbone to grab her buttock. "Based on your bra, I was expecting some ghastly knickers. These are hot."

"I have some thongs and some lacy see-through ones stashed in the back of my drawer—if they haven't been eaten by moths."

"Hmmm . . . sexy." Chesty laughter rumbled against her. She only had a moment to worry that making a soon-to-be lover laugh in the middle of foreplay wasn't sexy in the least.

He took her nipple between his lips and flicked it with his tongue before pulling it deep. She fisted his hair in one hand and slid the other underneath his kilt to tug the waistband of his boxer briefs down.

Highlanders should be naked under their kilts.

"Who am I to argue?" It was only at his teasing response that she realized she'd stated her opinion aloud. Moving his mouth to work over her other breast, he dispensed with his underwear. Her fingers skimmed a taut male bare bottom. The soft wool added an unexpected tactile pleasure.

He wrapped his arm around her waist, lifted her until her toes brushed the carpet, and whirled her away from the door. Her world spun and tilted into a new orbit, and she found herself on her back at the foot of her bed, Alasdair standing between her legs in all his half-naked kilted glory.

She propped herself up on an elbow and ran her hand down his chest, stopping at the top of his kilt. The tartan fabric tented toward her.

"I get now why men don't go commando underneath." She touched the end of his erection. "It makes quite the display."

His laugh was rueful. "I look silly."

"No, you look . . . lickable." She slipped a hand underneath the fabric and grasped him.

A primal sound vibrated from him, inciting her to squeeze him. "You're making me daft, woman."

"Is that good or bad?"

He put his knee on the bed and hovered partway over her. "Better than good. Exciting." Lowering himself to his elbows, his bare chest pressed on hers, inciting a sweet friction, he added in a whisper. "Scary."

Why was he scared? His departure for another country would simplify the ending of whatever this was. She made it clear downstairs that she expected nothing. Yet when his lips claimed hers in an all-consuming and arousing kiss, her toes curled and a swarm of butterflies attacked her stomach. Why was she scared too?

His mouth trailed across her jaw, and she arched her neck to offer a welcome he accepted, nipping and sucking and driving her into an ever-increasing frenzy of sensation. While he continued the assault by biting her earlobe, he glided his hand up her rib cage to cup her breast and give it a squeeze.

"How'd you get so good at this?" Warm breath wafted over her ear inciting another round of shivers. "Oh wait, I almost forgot about the double-decker busload of practice you've had."

His thumb glided over her nipple. Along with the undeniable pleasure was a signal growing in amplitude from between her legs that demanded more, and the faster the better. He must have possessed an antenna to receive her signals because his mouth moved south. But not far enough.

With his hand still playing with one breast, his tongue

and lips played with the other. Closing her eyes, she speared a hand through his hair and fisted the strands, her back arching and her hips undulating.

"I might die. Can someone die from pleasure?"

"We haven't even made it to the good stuff yet." His warm breath made her nipple pull even tighter.

She wasn't sure she would survive the "good stuff" with her wits intact. Her body felt ready to splinter into infinite pieces, never to be reassembled again. He moved farther south, his skin rasping along hers. She wanted him to slow down. No, she *needed* him to go faster.

He tugged her panties over her hips and any response was erased like a shaken Etch a Sketch. Urgency overrode modesty. She propped her heels on the edge of the bed and made room between her knees for his broad shoulders.

He scooped his hands under her butt and traced the most intimate part of her with his tongue. His touch was light but incredibly thorough. Not that she was surprised. He was a detail-orientated guy who strived for success.

Fisting her hands in his hair, she rotated her hips to encourage a firmer touch. He was kind enough to take the hint. His fingers teased her entrance as his tongue and lips worked magic. He pressed his finger inside of her, and an orgasm swamped her like a tsunami.

Bucking and squirming beneath him, she felt possessed. Words flew from her mouth, incomprehensible to her ears. Was she speaking in tongues? It certainly felt like a transcendent religious experience.

Finally, the tide ebbed and her heels slipped off the bed. Like a ragdoll, she lay there, fitting her fragmented thoughts back together. One overriding desire emerged. She wanted to drive him just as wild and crazy. Wanted to make him feel special and wanted.

He stood between her knees at the foot of the bed. She

sat up, slipped her right hand under his kilt and stroked the length of him.

His hips jerked and he grunted. Not in a "give me more" way but like he'd been stung by a wasp. "Ow. Your plasters pinched me."

She snatched her injured hand back and stuck her left hand under his kilt, fumbling to grasp him. "Sorry about that. Fair warning, not only am I out of practice, but I'm right-handed, so this might not be my best performance."

A gruff laugh had her tilting her head up to see him. He cupped her face and leaned down to kiss her, their smiling lips meeting and sending a shock through her. Not because it was the sweetest or the sexiest kiss, they'd shared, but because it was . . . fun. Being with him, in bed and out, was fun.

Nuzzling his nose next to hers, he said, "While I appreciate the effort, it won't be necessary tonight. In fact, I'm so blasted eager to be inside of you, I can't stand it another minute."

With little effort expended on his part, he scooted her up the bed, the soft wool of his kilt doing nothing to disguise his erection. He sat back on his heels, his hands going to the leather clasps of the kilt. "Let me—"

"No. Leave it on." She propped herself up on her elbows, hit by a bolt of insecurity. "Is that weird? You'd think living in Highland would give me immunity to men in kilts, but this is different."

"Different is good?"

"The best."

"After this I'll have to buy it, huh?"

A laugh stuttered out of her, but she didn't look away from where he stroked himself, the kilt hiked up. "If you don't buy it, I will."

He shifted closer and she tilted her pelvis toward him,

reaching over her head to clutch the bedspread. He paused, and she wanted to cry. Or yell.

"We need protection. Do you have any?"

"I don't keep condoms around for all the imaginary men I bring home." She popped to her elbows. "Wait. Actually, I do have condoms in my purse."

"Where's your purse?"

"Bottom of the stairs. Should we rock-paper-scissors to figure out who should retrieve it?"

"Never accuse me of not being a gentleman." He dropped a kiss on her nose and levered himself off the bed.

She held out a hand and said in a falsely dramatic, breathless voice, "You're my hero, Alasdair Blackmoor."

In the short time he was gone, Izzy tried to find the sexiest position and ended up with one leg bent and the opposite arm thrown over her head. He walked through the door and halted a few feet from the bed, his gazed fixed on her.

"Ach, you're driving me mad, Isabel."

She shivered, craving his warmth over her, under her, between her legs. "Grab one. Hurry." She sat up, dropping the affectation of trying to be sexy, and made a "gimme more" gesture with her hands.

He unzipped her purse and pulled out one, but the rest followed like her purse was a condom clown car. "I'm impressed."

"My friend Anna had a feeling we might need them."

"'We' as in you and me or you and Holt?"

"You and me. Only you and me."

He stood at the side of the bed and tossed the condoms between them like throwing a gauntlet. "Do you think we can use them all?"

"Tonight?" her voice had gone squeaky.

"Shall we try to demolish them before the games?"

She rolled to her stomach, tore one square from the rest,

and removed the rolled-up latex. While she had never been directly involved in the application process, the mechanics didn't require an engineering degree.

Propping herself up on her elbow, face to penis, she wrapped her good left hand around the base of his erection. The condom was forgotten in the desire to prove to him how lickable he was. She closed her eyes and twirled her tongue around the flanged head before sucking him into her mouth.

"You're turning me into a dobber, lass." He plucked the condom from her fingers and made quick work of rolling it on. "Are you ready?"

"I was born ready." She lay back and pulled him down with her. "Actually, that would be super icky and strange. Forget I said that." The last words ended on a moan as he positioned himself at her entrance and pushed inside of her without a preamble.

He made her forget everyone who'd come before. No one had lit her on fire like a sparkler, crackling with pleasure. His slow slide seemed neverending, filling and stretching her until he was buried.

"'S good, Isabel?" His words sounded like they'd been sent through a shredder, and it took her a second too long to reconstruct the meaning. He started to withdraw on a groan.

"No." She sank her nails into one of his buttocks. "I mean, yes. You feel absolutely glorious."

His sigh left his body curved over hers, his weight on his forearms. Like he couldn't bear to lose contact with her, he withdrew only an inch before pushing deep again. But with each thrust, his hips gained in speed and amplitude and demanded an answer. Her body responded by kindling another orgasm.

She touched every part of him she could reach. While the kilt hampered her explorations, the feel of the fabric pooled against her skin aroused her in its own special way. Sensations streaked through her body and she clung to his back, the only solid, real thing in her universe.

She wasn't sure which of them fell apart first, but as her inner muscles clenched with another climax, he buried his face in her neck and shuddered his release. Dreamy and satiated, she made a slow return to reality and wondered when they could deploy condom number two.

Chapter Twelve

Alasdair lay beside Isabel in the aftermath. They'd crossed a line. No, they'd leapt across. Or maybe sped across in a Porsche. The line was so far behind them, they could never get back within sight of it. Yet, he didn't regret taking her to bed.

What he did regret was the looming crisis he'd accidently set in motion at Wellington. But he'd fix it. As soon as he figured out how. Isabel and Rose need never know. The more immediate dilemma was whether he stayed at her side or sidled through the connecting bathroom into his room.

He very much wanted to stay, but didn't want to overstep his welcome. Indecision kept him on edge but unmoving.

Isabel heaved a sigh and flopped to her back, one arm thrown up over her head. She had maneuvered her way under the sheet, much to his disappointment. Returning after retrieving her purse to the sight of her laid out naked on the bed like a personal sensual buffet had been startling in the best, most arousing way. He flipped his kilt down to cover his nakedness.

"I'm glad we didn't end up in the loft of the barn," she said on a yawn. "It's secluded, but I don't think it would have been all that comfortable. Forget ants. Can you imagine coming face to face with the beady eyes of a possum in the middle of the good stuff? It might have put me off sex for the rest of my life."

His body relaxed the longer she talked. "That would be a shame because you're so good at it."

She turned to punch his arm playfully then resumed her position. "You did all the hard work. In fact, if I had one, I'd give you a gold star."

"Where would you put it?" He propped his head up on his hand and grinned down at her.

The moon had risen over the horizon and shone through the window, turning her pale skin luminescent. Skin he had caressed and kissed mere moments ago. Her hair was tousled from his hands and her thrashing while she'd been in the throes of her orgasm. He did feel rather proud of himself.

"I'd put it on your very talented mouth." She ran her finger over his bottom lip, her eyes shadowed and mysterious. The corner of her mouth quirked. "Or maybe right on the tip of your magnificent erection."

His gasp morphed into a laugh.

She covered her eyes. "I swear, I usually don't say what I'm actually thinking. Just around you."

"I love it." The L-word hovered in the air like an interloper.

To cover his discomfiture, he kissed her. What was meant to provide cover for his slip of the tongue turned into a kiss so sweet and sexy, his growing erection longed to earn a second gold star. Their lips parted, their quickened breathing mingling. He couldn't seem to get close enough.

"I wasn't sure I even liked you when you showed up," she said. "I was convinced you and Gareth were here to scam us like *Dirty Rotten Scoundrels*."

Although, neither he nor Gareth were attempting to bilk the Buchanans of money or possessions, the morass of what he was hiding shadowed the moment. He attempted a light tone. "I was sure your mother was using Gareth."

"For what? Mom said even his cottage is owned by the earl." Isabel misread his disquiet, stroking his cheek and adding. "Don't worry. Mom doesn't care if he doesn't even have two cents to rub together. I think she might even be in love with him."

As if on cue, footsteps and whispers echoed from the foyer. "They're back," Isabel said in her best horror move voiceover imitation. She added in a normal voice. "Do you think they know?"

"They would have known if they'd been in the house. We weren't playing quiet mouse, still mouse, that's for certain."

"I think I lost consciousness for a hot second when I . . . Am I loud? Oh my God, am I a screamer?"

"You're a talker, not a screamer."

Laughter sparkled in her eyes. "Don't even think about repeating anything I said. My bed is like Vegas."

"A slot machine?"

"No, you crazy man. The slogan. What happens in bed, stays in bed." Their combined laughter faded into silence, which Isabel broke in a casual voice. "Speaking of what happens . . . What happens now?"

He linked his hands on his chest. "My bed is too far away. I hope you'll let me stay tonight. Tomorrow, how about I use my not-inconsiderable skills to help you with the festival?"

"What are your specialties?" Her smile was magic and moonlight.

He ticked off on his fingers. "Moral support. Brute strength. Stress relief."

"What kind of stress relief?"

He slipped his hand under the sheet to her bare hip. "I have the next hour available for a job interview."

"Wow, an hour seems pretty optimistic."

"That sounds like a challenge if I ever heard one." He stripped the sheet away from her body to the accompaniment of her breathless giggles.

A crash from downstairs cracked their cocoon. Ears straining, Alasdair froze. Quick footsteps passed down the hallway followed by the slam of a door.

Isabel sat up, grabbed the sheet, and whispered, "Oh, dear."

"A lover's spat, do you think?" He wanted nothing more than to ignore the brewing trouble and remain in her bed. Isabel's hair fell over one shoulder, her back luring him closer. Without being able to help himself, he trailed his fingers down her spine and dropped a kiss on her shoulder.

She shoved his shoulder. "Go check on your friend."

He sighed, but rolled off the bed. His shirt was nowhere to be found. Padding through the bathroom, he retrieved another and pulled it on, exchanging the kilt with worn athletic shorts. He could hear Isabel rustling for clothes in her wardrobe as well, but when he returned to her room and stopped short, she was still in bed.

"Aren't you going to check on your mother?"

"Are you crazy? If I ask Mom about her and Gareth, she'll ask me about you, and I'd rather maintain a don't ask, don't tell policy where s-e-x is concerned." Her voice dropped to a near whisper at the end.

"Are you embarrassed we had s-e-x?" If he had to quantify the emotion roiling him, it would be something akin to hurt feelings. He was self-aware enough to see the irony of not wanting to be her secret when he was keeping secrets from her.

"Super embarrassed to talk to my mom about it, yes."

At his silence, she rose to her knees. The sheet fell away and left her in a tank top and short-shorts. Blast and damn. If he could keep her naked in bed twenty-four hours a day, he'd be a happy man. She crooked her finger. "Come here, Alasdair."

Alasdair obeyed. When the heat of her body pressed into his, his hands automatically found her bottom. "What?"

"Sex"—she said the word as if it was a forbidden curse, but at least she hadn't spelled it again—"is complicated when you live with your mom in the middle of the Bible Belt."

"Bible Belt?"

"You can't throw a rock and not hit a church in Highland and along a stretch of Southern states, hence Bible Belt." The hands she ran over his chest and back and through his hair ramped up anticipation for the sin they'd wreck in her bed later.

"I'll report back." He gave her butt a slap and kissed the tip of her nose. "Don't go to sleep."

"I'll try not to." She flopped backward on the bed and yawned.

He descended the stairs and found Gareth sitting in the dark morning room overlooking the moon-touched field of flowers, drinking whisky. Alasdair joined him with a drink of his own and waited.

"I thought you were otherwise occupied," Gareth said.

"I was about to be occupied a second time when a crash and a slamming door killed the mood. Do you need to talk?"

Gareth took a large swallow from his glass. "Rose asked me to stay in Highland."

"Until when?"

"Until . . . forever."

Alasdair drank from his glass and sat forward, resting his forearms on his knees. "Did you tell her?"

"No. I . . . I tried, but the truth got stuck. She took my bumbling non-answer as a rejection."

"If you told her the truth, she might understand the reason you can't stay has nothing to do with her."

Gareth's reluctance was palpable, but Alasdair couldn't pinpoint what his uncle's internal struggle involved. "I've promised I'll come clean after the festival and I will."

Alasdair's stomach rocked, and he took a sip of whisky. Instead of a confession, he hoped to neutralize the threat he'd unleashed. If he failed, Isabel would never forgive him for setting Wellington on Stonehaven.

"What got broken?" Alasdair asked, wanting a subject change.

"Nearly my head. I tripped over the end table." He paused, then with a smile in his voice, said, "Ah, but Rosie is a bonnie thing when she's angry."

"Gareth, it isn't funny."

"No, it's ironic I fell for an American who is tied to her life and land as surely as I am tied to mine." Resignation weighed Gareth's voice.

"Couldn't you work something out? Like she stays with you part of the year and the two of you come back here for the festival." Even as he suggested it, he wondered where that would leave Isabel. More responsibility would fall on Isabel's shoulders, and she wouldn't have the time to travel to London for a visit, or anywhere else for that matter.

"Perhaps, there are options," Gareth said with a glimmer of hope.

"Or, I don't know, I could take care of Cairndow, so you could stay here." The suggestion popped out as a way to keep Isabel from being tied too tightly to Stonehaven, but it would leave him tied to Scotland, unable to restart his career or pursue a relationship with her. It seemed Alasdair and Gareth couldn't both achieve happiness.

Gareth shifted on his seat and swirled the whisky in his glass. Light sparked on the surface of the thick crystal. "Is that a serious offer?"

"I'm not sure, to be honest." In a desperate move to gather his wits, he drained his glass of whisky, the burn only clouding his thoughts further. But the offer had come from somewhere. Had his subconscious been mulling the idea since Isabel planted it in the field?

Gareth patted his shoulder. "Your life has been turned on its head. You don't have to upend it further, even though I appreciate the offer."

Alasdair took both glasses, refilled them, and returned, dropping heavily into the chair. "A week ago, I knew exactly where I was headed and what I'd be doing for the next decade."

"Did the future you envision bring joy?"

Alasdair considered the question as he sipped on the whisky. "Not joy, but satisfaction. Success. Money."

"And that would have been enough?"

Alasdair slumped over his knees, clutching the glass in both hands. The past year had seen him neither happy nor fulfilled. With a promotion being dangled like a carrot, his job had turned from challenge to crucible.

"Once upon a time, it's all I wanted." Alasdair ran a hand down his stubbly chin. "I would have been the youngest VP at Wellington. Mum would have been proud."

Gareth regarded him with eyes so like the ones that stared back at Alasdair in the mirror every morning, it was uncanny. Although Gareth's reflected years of wisdom Alasdair had yet to earn.

"My brother was a spoiled younger son. Intemperate, unreliable, but bloody good fun." Gareth smiled into his whisky before turning serious once more. "Your mum deserved a better man. She worked hard to salvage a life for the two of you."

"What are you talking about?"

"I'm talking about state of your da's finances after he went and got himself killed. Do you not know?" At the brusque shake of Alasdair's head, Gareth took a sip. Alasdair gained the impression Gareth was suppressing his surprise and gathering his thoughts. "Your da left her destitute. Actually worse than destitute. Because they never filed separation or divorce papers, she assumed his debts and treated them as her penance."

Alasdair riffled through a catalogue of memories. Soon after he left for Cambridge, his mum had started work at a real estate office, eventually buying in and becoming a majority owner. She'd worked long hours during those early years, but Alasdair had assumed she'd wanted to, not had to.

"I tried to help her, but she's prideful and refused." Admiration warmed Gareth's voice. "She did allow me to help you with your expenses at school."

"Gareth," Alasdair whispered. "Why didn't you tell me? Why did you even help me after I acted like such a little git after the funeral?"

"Because you're my nephew and I love you, no matter our falling out. Now that I know about Kyla and the lad, I understand why you were upset with Rory and me and your Blackmoor heritage."

Alasdair slumped back in the chair, considering the past through clearer eyes. "I thought I knew everything back then. I thought I was so right. I didn't know shite."

"Ah, the vagaries of youth. It's a universal truth that anyone under twenty thinks they understand the world until they hit thirty. At some point, you'll realize none of us really know what we're doing. Even the old codgers like me muddle through."

"I'm not sure if that's depressing or comforting." Alasdair killed the rest of his drink feeling pleasantly warm and buzzy but still confused. "What are we going to do?"

Gareth stretched himself out of the chair and set his empty glass on an end table. "A good place to start is to figure out what will make you truly happy; not what will make me or your mum or anyone else happy."

"But what about you and Rose?"

"I suppose I need to take my own advice." Gareth's smile flickered like a bulb on its last watts. He stood and laid a hand on Alasdair's shoulder, giving him a strong squeeze. "By the way, you might want to collect your shirt from the banister."

The creak of the stairs signaled his uncle's retreat. Alasdair stayed where he was, considering his future, but seeing only brambles and no path through. His uncle was still hale and vibrant and deserved to experience life outside his indenture to Cairndow. Yet, was Alasdair ready to assume the responsibility?

A week ago the answer would have been an emphatic no, but he waffled on the precipice of change. The idea didn't seem as preposterous as it would have a week ago.

He gathered his shirt from the banister and slipped into Isabel's room, the house and its occupants at rest if not at peace. She was sprawled on her back in the middle of the bed, an arm over her head, snuffling a little in her sleep. The abandon she exhibited when kissing or making love and now sleeping was at odds with the reserved, suspicious woman he'd met that first morning in the coffee shop. How many people got to see this side of her? Not many, he'd wager.

He slipped under the covers, shifted Isabel like a doll onto her side, and spooned her from behind. She mewed a little protest and elbowed him in the stomach, but didn't wake. This was as quiet as she'd been all night. Never had he been with a woman who teased and said anything and everything on her mind before, during, and after sex. He smiled and kissed the top of her head.

Her musings had not only made him laugh but they'd turned what had always been a purely physical endeavor into one that charmed him body and soul and made his release all the more intense.

Even though it felt like a beginning, the end loomed in the distance like a hurricane he was approaching at warp speed in a teeny plane with no parachute. He would ignore the warnings and live in the moment while the skies were still cloudless and blue. Sleep finally caught him, although his dreams were fitful and saw him chasing Isabel along the cliffs of Cairndow.

Chapter Thirteen

The next morning and weighed down with super-sized trepidation, Izzy approached her mom on leaden feet. Pensive looking, her mom stood in front of the double doors to the porch with a mug of coffee, seeming to be in a different time and place. Her fight with Gareth hung over the house like a pall.

Adding to the tight feeling in her chest was the fact her mom knew something had happened between her and Alasdair. Izzy prayed to Bacchus the subject wouldn't come up, which sure to bring a lightning strike upon her next time she went to church.

"Good morning?" Izzy hadn't meant for it to sound so much like a question than a statement. The sun was shining, there wasn't a cloud in the sky, and even the weather reports were favorable. Although things could change without warning.

Her mom glanced over her shoulder with a half smile and raised brows. "I would think so. You and Alasdair have fun?"

Izzy's face heated like the surface of the sun. "Yeah, it was okay."

"Only okay? That's a shame."

"It was good. Great. Amazing." Izzy poured herself a mug of coffee even though she didn't need the jump-start. Her body was already buzzing. She'd left Alasdair in the shower to finish washing after he'd joined her halfway through shampooing her hair. It had been a new and invigorating experience she most definitely didn't want to discuss with her mom. "Can we not talk about it? It's too embarrassing."

Her mom's expression morphed from teasing to contemplative. "It never occurred to me how difficult it must be for you to be living at home. You're an adult with adult needs and are more than welcome to bring gentlemen callers home with you."

"Mom! I don't want to talk about gentlemen callers." Izzy flapped her shirt to keep from conflagrating.

The clang of machinery drew Izzy's attention to the backyard. The mowers were here. The decapitation of the wildflowers was a process Izzy couldn't bear to witness even as she was grateful for the distraction.

"If Stonehaven and the festival weren't ours, what would you want to do?" Her mom stared out at the field with an expression Izzy could only quantify as pensive.

"It doesn't bear contemplation. Stonehaven is ours and we're going to keep it in the family. Yes, it needs some work, but Sterling should be calling any day now for you to sign for the loan."

Her mom dismissed the practicality with a wave of her hand. "Use your imagination, Izzy. What would you be doing right now if it weren't for Stonehaven?"

"I love Stonehaven." The conversation made Izzy nervous and she wasn't sure why.

"Just because you love something—or someone—doesn't mean they can't become a burden."

"Stonehaven is not a burden, Mom."

Dark circles made her mom appear older and less vibrant than usual even as she gave Izzy a small smile. "Would you quit your job to travel and write?"

"No, but . . . I would like to travel and see the places I read about." It felt treasonous to admit as much to her mom. "What about you? What would you do if it wasn't for Stonehaven?"

With the tables turned, her mom shook her head, her silver bob swinging like strands of silk. "I made my choice when I married your father. I understood what Stonehaven meant to him and agreed to become its caretaker. But you haven't had the same choice."

"I *want* to be here. Promise." Feeling like she had stepped into a bog of quicksand, Izzy was desperate to get back on solid, familiar ground.

Her mom patted her hand. "I have a favor to ask."

"Sure. Anything." Izzy grasped eagerly for the branch her mom offered.

"I want you and Alasdair to act as hosts at the whisky tasting and dance."

Izzy's chest squeezed. Her mom had always been the face of the games while Izzy handled the behind-the-scenes details like portable potties and parking. "I'm not getting up in front of half the town and humiliating myself by dancing. Remember what happened last time?"

"For goodness sake." Her mom tucked a piece of Izzy's wavy hair behind her ear. "You were eight. You've grown into a confident, beautiful young woman that I couldn't be more proud of. You need to let go of all these old hang-ups."

Her mom strolled toward their office, leaving Izzy to sort through the warm, fuzzy feelings her mom's praise had stirred up. Izzy followed and found her already ensconced at her computer with bright blue reading glasses on.

"I appreciate the confidence, but I was born with two left feet, and it's short notice for a foot transplant."

"Don't be silly. You are wonderfully graceful." Her

mom ignored Izzy's derisive snort. "Anyway, Alasdair seems more than a capable partner."

Izzy threw her hands up. "How do you even know Alasdair is willing?"

"Willing to do what?" Alasdair's deep voice echoed in the foyer as he descended the stairs.

"Dance with me. It's this ridiculous custom that opens the games at the whisky tasting Friday night."

"I would be honored to dance with you, Isabel." He performed a bow, handsome in his charcoal gray slacks and white pinstriped button-down. The cuffs were rolled up to reveal his hairy, sinewy forearms. His stubble toyed with being a beard and gave him a dangerous edge. If he'd been wearing the kilt, she might have actually swooned. As it was, her knees went wonky.

"You've been warned already that I'm a terrible dancer. Like 'I might maim you' terrible."

"Bollocks. I'd wager you've never had the right partner."

He's not talking about sex, she reminded herself even as her thighs clamped together. Or was he? The way his eyes sparkled made her think about long nights and tangled sheets.

Her mouth opened and closed a few times, but nothing emerged. Her mother clapped her hands together once and rubbed them together. "I'm glad that's settled. I'll leave the two of you to arrange a time to practice. You should enlist Anna's help, Izzy."

When it was obvious her mother was done on the subject, Izzy grabbed Alasdair's hand and tugged him into the kitchen. "How could you?"

Alasdair poured himself a coffee—black—leaned casually on the counter, and shrugged. "It's only a dance."

"The genesis of my greatest childhood humiliation."

His lips twitched around the rim. "All you have to do

is relax and trust me. I guarantee you'll enjoy the experience."

"Hang on." Her eyes narrowed. "Are you talking about sex or dancing?"

He sputtered on a sip and set the mug aside, pulling her between his legs. "Dancing, but I suppose the advice works for both. By the way, last night was . . ." His expression turned more guarded.

"If you say 'a mistake,' you'd better be wearing an athletic cup."

Any distance—real or imagined—vanished as he dropped a kiss on her lips. "Last night was incredible. As was the shower this morning."

She let out a pent-up breath, her heart performing its own clumsy dance in her chest. "I concur a thousand percent."

A silence full of portent was broken by the mowers as they fired up in the backyard. She kept her eyes averted. "I know it has to be done, but I can't watch the carnage. If we're going to dance, we'd better figure how much of a miracle we need to pray for. Let's take your fancy car with air-conditioning to town."

Gareth stopped them at the door. "When are we going to practice, laddie?"

Izzy cocked her head. "Are you and Gareth going to take a turn around the floor together too?"

Alasdair gave a rueful chuckle. "Gareth is going to train me for the athletic events. Believe it or not, I've never thrown a hammer or a stone."

Izzy didn't have the heart to tell him it would take more than a few days training to beat someone like Holt. "We shouldn't be more than an hour or so."

Alasdair made plans to meet Gareth in the field that afternoon after the mowing. Ten minutes later, she and

Alasdair pulled behind the dance studio and parked next to Anna's small sedan.

"Is the situation so dire we need professional help?" Alasdair asked with a laugh in his voice.

"Yes, it is. I don't think you understand what you've volunteered for. We can't step onto the dance floor and shake our booty to some random song. The same waltz has opened the games since the first year." Izzy took a bracing breath. "This is worse than a dentist appointment."

The back door was unlocked and Izzy walked in, calling Anna's name. The studio was empty, and their footsteps echoed. Anna sashayed out of her office wearing a black leotard and a diaphanous wraparound pink skirt tied with a ribbon. If only Izzy could borrow a measly percent of her friend's grace.

Anna's grin grew to blinding proportions when she spotted Alasdair. She brushed Izzy aside and stuck a hand out toward Alasdair. "Well, hello there, Highlander. I'm Anna."

"A pleasure to make your acquaintance. Alasdair Blackmoor." He took her hand and instead of shaking it, clasped it in both of his.

A blush lit Anna's cheeks. "I just love your accent, Alasdair."

Izzy plucked Anna's hand from Alasdair's. "Hands off. The Highlander is mine."

Anna's fake pout was ruined by her smile. "Yeah, I noticed the way the two of you eye-fucked your way out of the pub last night. I assume you advanced the cause afterward."

"Anna!" Izzy covered her eyes out of embarrassment but also because Anna would see the truth in her eyes.

"She's so fun to tease, isn't she, Alasdair?" Anna asked. "What can I help you folks with?"

"Isabel seems to think we need professional help."

Anna held up her hands in mock surrender. "I talk a big game, but I'm no sexpert."

Izzy fought the urge to strangle her friend. "Dance help, you nut. Mom has decided that Alasdair and I should open the festival at the whisky tasting."

"I see." A serious frown and furrowed brow replaced Anna's tease. "We don't have much time."

"Is there any hope?"

Anna turned to Alasdair. "Do you know the 'St. Bernard's Waltz'?"

"I can stumble my through a traditional waltz. I'm better with the Latin dances like the salsa and tango, but I can manage a credible foxtrot given enough alcohol."

Izzy looked heavenward and cursed softly. "Are you serious?"

"Mum insisted I take ballroom. She thought every"—he stumbled over his words—"young man of a certain station should know how to conduct himself on the dancefloor."

"Traditionally, the hostess"—Anna gestured toward Izzy—"opens the festival with the St. Bernard's Waltz. It's a bit more complicated than a Viennese waltz, but eminently doable with your solid dance background."

"I was afraid you were going to suggest the *Dirty Dancing* lift," Alasdair said.

"We want to avoid a medical emergency." Anna waggled her eyebrows.

"Har-har," Izzy said.

"While I would love to use more modern music, Dr. Jameson will insist on accompanying you with the pipes." Anna threw an apologetic glance toward Alasdair.

Izzy avoided making eye contact with herself in the mirrors lining the room. A panicky sweat spread from the back of her neck to her armpits. A pair of strong hands took hold of her shoulders and massaged the tension away.

"You're taking this much too seriously. You're not being asked to perform brain surgery in front of an audience." The tease in his voice did nothing for her nerves.

"I think I would do better with the surgery."

Bagpipe music came over the speakers that hung in the four corners of the room as Anna rejoined them.

"Okay, Highlander, let's see what I'm working with here. I'll show you the steps and we'll take a spin around the room." Anna snapped her fingers at Izzy as if dealing with one of her preteen pupils. "Pay attention, Izzy."

Anna walked Alasdair through the basics. Izzy tried to pay attention to Anna's feet and count steps, but Alasdair kept distracting her with his hotness. After a mere fifteen minutes, Alasdair was able to lead Anna around the room. It wasn't flashy but no one's toes were mashed and no one tripped and fell.

Anna laughed after Alasdair twirled her to a stop. "Excellent. You're a strong partner. We can make this work. Come on, Izzy. Your turn."

The song looped on repeat as Anna positioned Izzy in Alasdair's pseudo-embrace. The feel of him made her step even closer. A flash of him standing in the shower with water sluicing down his naked body replaced a portion of her nerves with arousal.

Anna lowered her arm between them like a crossing guard. "Back that ass up, girl. St. Bernard's waltz isn't sexy like the tango."

"Did you know that when the waltz was introduced in England during the Regency, it was scandalous? Unmarried men and women had never been able to get so close." Izzy barked a laugh. "Actually, that must not be totally true because it's estimated at least thirty percent of women were already pregnant when they married. So, they were able to get super close, if you know what I mean."

Alasdair had a bemused smile on his face while Anna shook her head and asked, "How do you know that?"

"I read a lot."

Anna thumbed toward Izzy. "This girl was either reading a book or scribbling in a notebook in school. You remember, Izzy?"

"Of course I do." She dropped her gaze to stare at a button on Alasdair's shirt.

The books and the stories she wrote were her lifeline out of the petty social interactions of a small-town high school. Back then, Anna wouldn't have given her the time of day. Izzy's friends had all been girls like her—not pretty or talented enough to cheer or play sports.

Anna continued, shooting Izzy a warm smile. "Izzy was valedictorian and got a scholarship to UGA. She was so smart and nice and pretty. What I didn't realize until we got to know each other after college was how funny she is. I'm lucky she's my best friend now."

Although it wasn't how Izzy remembered herself, Anna's words were a bear hug to the shy, awkward girl still taking up space in Izzy's psyche. Unable to put into words what Anna's friendship meant to her, Izzy gave her an actual hug.

"Enough of the mushy stuff. Get in position, you two." Anna stepped back as Izzy swung her focus to their feet.

Anna spent the next ten minutes drilling Izzy on which foot to move where and when to twirl. "Don't look at your feet, Izzy, look into Alasdair's eyes."

As soon as her gaze melded with his, she forgot the steps and stomped on his foot. "Ugh. Sorry. This would be easier if you were uglier."

Alasdair shook his beleaguered foot and rubbed his jaw. "I'm working on it. I've never been this long without a proper shave or haircut."

"If you think not shaving is making you less attractive, then you don't understand women." Izzy turned toward Anna with sigh. "I'm hopeless, aren't I?"

"Don't give up on yourself," Anna said breezily while going over the steps yet again; and once more, Izzy smashed Alasdair's foot within the first ten seconds.

"Can we take a five-minute break?" Alasdair asked.

At Alasdair's pointed look, Anna nodded briskly and retreated to her office. The music cut off.

"Are you about to give me a pep talk?" Izzy crossed her arms.

"I know what's wrong," he said.

"Really? Okay, hit me Dr. Phil."

Confusion had him scrunching his eyes. "Who?"

She waved both hands. "Never mind. Go ahead and analyze me."

"Your mind leaps and spins from thought to thought too fast and furious—and I love that about you—but to dance you must get out of your head and slow your thoughts to just one. Do you know how to do that?"

Far from leaping and spinning, her mind was stuck on one word. "Love." Just like the first time it had come out of his mouth, hearing the word in relation to anything about her was startling in an interesting, but good way. Not that he meant romantic love, more like how a person loved bacon or pizza.

Her scattered thoughts only reinforced his opinion, and she refocused on his question. How could she slow her mind? "Drugs? Alcohol?"

A slow smile spread across his face and his voice was low and smooth and seductive. "No. You need to concentrate on me. Stare into my eyes and don't let yourself think about anyone else watching."

Hypnotized, she tilted toward him, her face upturned, her unblinking gaze on his face. She half expected him to sweep her into the steps of the dance. Instead, he kissed her in the middle of the studio.

Not an innocent brush of the lips, but a sexy, dirty kiss, including sparring tongues, love bites, and a firm squeeze of her bottom. When they broke apart, he assumed the position of the dance, and through some secret signal to Anna, music filled the room.

She surrendered herself to him and didn't miss a step. The last notes petered out and she shuffled to a stop after a final twirl, her body twanging like a tuning fork resonating sweetly. His hand pressed her closer until her chest almost brushed his. Tension, both physical and emotional, held her in its grip.

Anna's whoop shattered the intimacy. "That was so awesome! You were as graceful as your mom, and that's saying something. All you had to do was give yourself over to the music."

Izzy smiled but her lips quivered. It wasn't the music she had given herself over to but the man.

"You two need to practice whenever you can so you won't forget the steps. Let's discuss clothes. I assume you'll be wearing the traditional kilt from the other night, Alasdair?" At his nod, Anna faced Izzy and ran her gaze up and down her body. "What about you?"

Still feeling like she was in the middle of an out-of-body experience, she said, "I've got a pleated tartan skirt I could wear."

"Not that old thing you've worn for the last five years?"

"What's wrong with it?"

"Nothing if you want to fuel inappropriate Catholic schoolgirl fantasies for Highland's male population, but no way am I letting you wear that to the opening dance." Anna tapped her lips. "I might have something we can alter. Hang on."

She disappeared into a storage area and Izzy rocked

on her feet, shooting a glance toward Alasdair. He looked composed and calm even while she stirred her own chaotic internal stew. "You're going to book it out of Highland in the middle of the night, aren't you?"

Alasdair narrowed his eyes at her as if disappointed. "Will you put a little faith in me, lass?"

The slowing of her thoughts during the dance had been temporary and as if making up for lost time, his question entered a particle accelerator and gained in weight and meaning. How could she put her faith in a man she barely knew?

But was that really true? She hadn't known him long, true, but she understood him. Much like he understood her. Could that be enough for the time they had left? Banishing her doubts, she pasted on a "fake it until you make it" smile. "I suppose I can spare a teeny-tiny amount of faith."

Taking her hands in his, he rubbed his thumbs along the backs. "I've never *not* had a plan, but I don't want to think about what will happen after the festival. Or tomorrow, for that matter."

"I've never winged it either, but this feels good. Healthy even. We'll have fun and enjoy the time we have left. Fun, fun, fun." She sounded like a clown on speed and cleared her throat to bring her voice down an octave.

"We're obviously compatible in bed, but I want you know that it isn't just about sex for me." Why did he come off sounding so mature when she was an overflowing basket of awkwardness?

"If you're into Catholic schoolgirls, I could—" *What was she saying?* She bit the inside of her cheek in an old habit to stop the flow of words. "That came out sounding really weird."

Anna saved her with an armful of gauzy mossy green

fabric. "Why don't you grab some tea or coffee at the Brown Cow while I fit Izzy, Alasdair?"

"Sounds lovely. I'll be waiting." Alasdair inclined his head toward them and strolled out.

Izzy stared at the door he'd disappeared through until Anna slapped her arm and brought her out of her daze with a muttered, "Ow."

"You are a goner, woman. I never thought I'd bear witness to your fall." Anna smiled but it was tinged with melancholy.

"He's leaving right after the festival. Before you walked up, we were discussing how we are going to have fun and have sex and not think about tomorrow." The twinge at the thought of him gone wasn't fun at all, but painful.

"Are you okay with that plan?" Anna cocked her head.

"Why wouldn't I be?"

Anna hummed as if censoring her opinion, shook the dress out, and held it up to Izzy. "I don't think it will need drastic alterations. Come on back and slip it on."

Izzy followed her, picking at the conversation like a loose string. "We aren't serious. We can't get serious. He's leaving."

"Yeah, you said that already. Has he bought his plane ticket yet?" Anna asked.

"I don't think so."

"Why not ask him to stay?" Anna asked.

"No way!" It would be the Sadie Hawkins dance all over again except exponentially worse.

"Oh no. Was the sex not any good?"

Izzy sputtered a string of inanities before admitting, "It was amazing. The way he moves on the dance floor is nothing compared to what he can do in bed. And in the shower."

Anna grabbed her throat in a classic pearl clutch and

gasped. Inside, Izzy was gratified she'd managed to shock Anna.

"Girl! I'm super happy for you." Anna's surprise faded into a frowning concern. "But, I know you. You wouldn't have slept with Alasdair if it wasn't more than a fling. You like him."

Anna took her forearm in a comforting grip that somehow squeezed tears into Izzy's eyes. Her vision blurry, she looked toward the ceiling and blinked. "His life is in London and mine is here. That's the way it is."

"Maybe so, but things can change. Keep an open mind—and heart—about the matter." Anna grabbed the hem of Izzy's T-shirt and tugged it up. Anna's time in dance had left her with no sense of personal modesty and no understanding of other people's body hang-ups. "Off with your clothes."

Anna dressed her like a doll, bestowing compliments like candy. "I wish I had your boobs and your curves and your hair."

Izzy swung her head around. "What? Your hair is amazing. Unique."

"It's too red." Confidence was Anna's hallmark, but a hint of self-consciousness had revealed itself. "I was thinking about dying it."

"What color?"

"I don't know. Something normal."

"But you're not normal." Izzy met Anna's eyes in the mirror. "And I mean that in the best possible way. You are gorgeous."

"Fine, fine." Anna laughed and held up her hands, but before her gaze dropped, a glimmer of deep emotion punched Izzy in the gut. Anna seemed more vulnerable than usual, and Izzy didn't know why.

"What do you think?" Anna shifted to stand behind her and pinched each side seam, pulling the bodice taut to

Izzy's body. It molded to her curves and highlighted the best parts of her. The bodice of the dress scooped to reveal the tops of her breasts and was made from a stretchy fabric, overlaid with the same gauze in the skirt. It was tea length, but had a split to make movement easier and add a dash of sexiness. The green would be a good match for Alasdair's tartan.

"Wow. I look great," Izzy said as if she'd stolen and assimilated Anna's confidence.

While Anna retrieved pins, Izzy swayed and swished the skirts, imagining herself in Alasdair's arms, losing herself in his eyes, as the town oohed and ahhed over their combined grace.

"Hold still," Anna said around a mouthful of pins.

Izzy did as she was told. "I want to pay you for the dress and time. You're as busy as I am with preparations for the gremlins."

The nickname for the kids Anna taught didn't make her smile. She huffed and glared at Izzy through the mirror, her words garbled around the pins. "Not a chance. You deserve to be Cinderella."

Izzy had never connected with the light and frothy Disney fairytales, preferring their dark counterparts by the Brothers Grimm or the ones she made up. "I'm not Cinderella and Alasdair is not Prince Charming. And I wouldn't want him to be. I mean, seriously, what did Cinderella know about the man other than he had a foot fetish? That was not the basis for a strong marriage."

Anna's guffaw spilled the pins from her mouth. The front door jangled and high-pitched voices carried through the studio. "Speaking of gremlins, my five-year-olds class is here."

After unzipping her, Anna left Izzy to get change back into her clothes. With a little wave, Izzy slipped out the front door. The Brown Cow beckoned with the smell of freshly roasted coffee. Coming out as she was entering was Sterling Smith, one of the managers at the bank, and the man Izzy had been trying to track down for a week. They stepped to the side of the door on the sidewalk.

"Sterling! I was so sorry to read about your aunt in the paper." She touched his hand.

"Sad times, but the funeral turned into a family reunion. We even managed to squeeze in a trip to Disney World while we were in Florida for the funeral. It's terrible to admit we had fun, isn't it?" His smile was sheepish.

"I'll bet your aunt would have approved." She smiled in absolution before asking, "Is everything in order for the loan? Are you ready for Mom to sign?"

Sterling ran a hand over his balding pate, a sheen of sweat popping out. He was in a baggy suit and held a cup of coffee. Two years older than Izzy, they had had only a passing acquaintance in high school, but they'd been thrown together during Highland events many times since Izzy had come home from college.

"Actually, I checked the system this morning and it's still listed as pending. I'm going to call corporate as soon as I dig myself out of the work that piled up on my desk. I'll call you to set up a time in a couple of days." Sterling waved over his head and hustled across the street at an awkward jog, his former athletic prowess diminished by his desk job.

"Appreciate you!" Izzy called out. She'd wanted the issue settled and the roofers lined up to start right after the festival, but there was nothing to do but wait.

Inside the Brown Cow, Alasdair held court at a table with Dr. Jameson and Mr. Timmerman, with Millie hovering.

Millie spotted her first and jogged back behind the counter. "You want the usual?"

Her usual was regular coffee with a dash of cream

and sugar. On the cusp of saying yes, Izzy changed her mind. She was going to live in the moment and take some chances. "Actually, I'll try the vanilla chai latte."

Izzy thanked Millie when she handed the cup over and took a sip. The richness of the flavors made her close her eyes and take a deep breath. Alasdair retrieved a chair from a neighboring table and gestured for her to sit. Their thighs touched in the close space. Alasdair wrapped both hands around his mug of tea while the other two men had coffees.

"Alasdair was telling us about a real Highland games he attended," Dr. Jameson said. "It's been a decade since my last trip to Scotland. I'm due another, but I have another year in my tenure as mayor."

"You must plan on staying with Gareth at Cairndow," Alasdair said.

"I thought he lived in a small stone cottage?" Izzy cast him a curious glance over the rim of her cup.

"He does, aye." Alasdair seemed to be gathering his thoughts. "It's a good-sized cottage with an extra bedroom. I can testify that it's cozy and charming. I'm sure Gareth would welcome the company."

"I'd be absolutely tickled." Dr. Jameson seemed to already be planning his trip, a dreamy smile on his face.

"Where in Scotland did you grow up?" Mr. Timmerman asked Alasdair.

Something of Alasdair's body language turned defensive even though his voice remained level and friendly. "Glasgow until I left for Cambridge, but I spent summers at Cairndow. My da and Gareth were very close, and Da didn't want me to be a city lad who didn't know a sheep's backside from its head."

"My hobby is genealogy. I'd love to trace your tree, Mr. Blackmoor," Mr. Timmerman said.

"No," Alasdair said forcefully, then modulated his

voice. "You're busy getting ready for the festival. I wouldn't dare impose."

Izzy watched the exchange with a sense of missing a vital piece of information. The brief beat of awkward silence was broken by Dr. Jameson. "How do you think the land compares to ours?"

"The actual Highlands are harsher. More barren. Less green. For all that or maybe because of it, it's breathtaking. When the heather blooms, you've never seen anything so beautiful. The mountains of Scotland couldn't be any more different than your Blue Ridge, but there is one way they're the same."

"What's that?" Izzy had scooted forward on her chair, mesmerized by his voice and forgetting all about his earlier odd behavior.

He held her gaze and spoke softly, "Ancient magic infuses both places."

She wanted nothing more than to take him into her woods and explore for hours, days, weeks. Then, she wanted him to show her all the places in Scotland he held dear to his heart. They didn't have enough time. There would never be enough.

Anna was right; Izzy was a goner.

Chapter Fourteen

The week leading up to parade—the official kickoff of the festival—passed in a blur of checking and double-checking nothing was headed off track. Like approaching the finish line of a marathon (or so she'd heard as she'd never tackled one herself), Izzy was equally exhausted and euphoric. Her nights were spent in bed with Alasdair where they made a good-size dent in the stash of condoms.

The weather forecast was partly cloudy, which meant a drop in temperature from scorching to mere roasting. Having Gareth and Alasdair had made a difference in the workload and morale. Dinners were spent going over last-minute details while sharing bottles of wine and plenty of laughter. The four of them fell into a familial ease that both comforted and set Izzy on edge.

Because even though she was unbelievably happy, she couldn't stop herself from wondering what would happen after the festival. Afraid of the answer, she never asked, but she'd caught Alasdair watching her in the same fearful, perplexed way. As the days ticked down, their relationship careened toward a cliff and certain death.

The day of the parade and the whisky tasting and the

dance found Izzy lying in bed watching the slow creep of dawn light into her room. Soon the field would be full of contractors and volunteers setting up booths and preparing for the influx of people the first full day of the festival would bring.

But for now, only the faint calls of waking birds sounded on the breeze. Alasdair was curled around her back, his body slack and his arm heavy over her waist. Three days more. A weekend. The end was nigh.

Not the apocalypse, but the aftermath would be a test of survival. Hard questions asked and answered. The temporary halt Alasdair had put on his life and career would lift, and forward motion would resume. She would go back to her nine-to-five accounting job and start writing again in her free time. Everything would revert to the way it was *before*. Before Alasdair.

Except, some things had changed. She was going to try writing something new and exciting and (hopefully) magical. She was more confident, not only in her own skin, but in dealing with vendors and townspeople who tended to still view her as a kid. And, her relationship with her mom had shifted toward equality and a deeper friendship.

"What are you thinking about?" His voice rumbled close to her ear. He'd woken up without her realizing it.

"Nothing." It was a kneejerk response and so obviously untrue, she couldn't leave it hanging between them. "The whirlwind begins as soon as we get out of bed. Three days of nonstop motion and then . . ."

He didn't try to fill in the blank with a platitude or false promises, and she appreciated the honesty. The hard brutal truth was sure to break something fragile inside of her. Not her heart. It was too soon for that. Maybe a valve though. Or a ventricle. Could she live with a broken ventricle?

Gently, he turned her to her back and settled over her.

Neither of them spoke the questions swirling and threatening to drown them. They made love tossed in the battling currents of urgency and melancholy. She was loathe to let him go, yet aware he was already slipping away.

Afterward, Izzy took a quick shower and pulled on shorts and a tank top and secured her hair into a ponytail. Alasdair dressed in his single pair of athletic shorts and his Scotland flag T-shirt.

"Should we practice the dance one more time?" he asked.

"I'm not sure I'll have time. The marathon officially turns into a sprint to the finish today. The parade starts at two, then the whisky tasting at six. Until then, we'll be slammed here."

As soon as their feet hit the first floor of Stonehaven, preparations swamped Izzy. She'd been through enough festivals now to accept the panic. Even though it didn't feel like it at the moment, everything would get done.

Her mom thrived on the stress and excitement. She fairly glowed as she directed the workers. It was like a hive of bees had moved into their field, buzzing with energy and purpose as they constructed the vendor booths and performance stage like honeycomb.

Izzy headed down the lane to make sure the portable potties were delivered and stocked. Less exciting than the dancing and piping and caber throwing, but even more important. All of their contractors had worked the festival before, and except for any last-minute hiccups, they knew where to set up.

Alasdair and Gareth organized the sport section of the field and got in a little more practice before the events kicked off the next day. Izzy shot glances in their direction, but they seemed to have things well in hand. It was lunch when her mom hip-bumped her.

Swiping the screen of an e-tablet, her mom said, "We're

ahead of schedule. Are we that good or is it the extra hands?"

"Some of both."

Her mom shot her a side-eyed glance. "Are you going to the parade?"

"I thought it'd be nice to take Alasdair down so he could watch. Is that okay?"

"Yep. Gareth and I will keep things moving along here." Her mom gave her cheek an air kiss and hustled off to her next task.

Izzy freshened up in the bathroom and changed into a lightweight skirt in a pink and green tartan print and a matching pink T-shirt. She ceded the bathroom to a sweaty Alasdair after laughingly pushing him away when he'd tried to claim a kiss.

Izzy kept up a stream of chatter on their way to town. Main Street was closed off, and the closest parking spot was several blocks behind the church on a residential tree-lined street with bricked two-story homes.

"This is lovely." Alasdair slotted his rented car into a space next to the curb.

Live oaks crossed arms overhead and dappled the ground with shadows offering shelter from the sun. The lush green yards were meticulously maintained, the walkways lined with flowers. She preferred the chaos of their wildflower field, but she couldn't argue with his assessment. "This street is referred to as banker's row. Although it houses a fair share of lawyers and doctors these days."

Alasdair took her hand and linked their fingers as they strolled toward Main Street. The occasional bleat of bagpipes cut through the thick air of the afternoon. It wasn't long before they joined up with others headed toward the parade.

Some she knew, most she didn't. Tourists with cameras stepped lively as they herded kids along. The parade would feature various businesses and floats from the high school clubs, churches, and various organizations around town. Anna would be marching with her pint-sized dancing gremlins in tow. All of them would be throwing candy to the crowd. But the main draw would be the Pipe and Drum Corps led by Dr. Jameson.

As they grew closer, they were carried along on all sides, buffeted by the current of people. The hum of conversation was like the swell of a river, and even after seeing the parade countless years, Izzy's pace quickened with her excitement, and she pulled Alasdair along.

"I can't believe it." His eyes were wide, taking in the packed sidewalks.

"It'll be like this all weekend." She led him around the line that snaked out of the Brown Cow for both ice cream and liquid refreshment. She stopped a few feet from the Dapper Highlander to claim a spot behind a vertically challenged family with two already-wilting kids.

The firetruck's siren pierced the air, and a cheer went up. The firetruck always led off the parade. Floats passed by with smiling, waving people. Alasdair caught several pieces of candy and passed them over to the kids.

"Could I have a moment of your time, Mr. Blackmoor?" Mr. Timmerman had sidled up next to them.

"Make sure you're back for the pipers. It's the highlight of the parade." Izzy shot Alasdair a smile, but did a double take of Mr. Timmerman.

A tape measure hung around his neck and a fabric pencil perched behind his ear. All perfectly normal, but instead of his usual jolly Santa-like smile, his brow was crinkled and his lips were pinched.

Alasdair disappeared inside the store, and a niggling itch in her brain grew more insistent. It had been bothering her off and on since their shared coffee in the Brown

Cow a week before, but she couldn't quite figure out what it meant. She turned back to the parade, but her enjoyment had dimmed.

Alasdair followed Mr. Timmerman into his shop with the gait of the condemned. Still, Alasdair tried to put on a bland smile. "Do I owe you for the alterations?"

"No, no." Mr. Timmerman waved him off, but didn't meet his eyes or smile in return. "It's another matter. I realize it was overstepping, but I was so curious, you see. I traced the Blackmoor name."

"You connected the branch between me and Gareth." It wasn't a question, yet Mr. Timmerman continued.

"At first, I assumed Gareth Connors was a different man than Gareth Blackmoor, but . . ." Mr. Timmerman glanced up for a sign of confirmation.

"They are one and the same."

"He's your uncle." At Alasdair's brusque nod, Mr. Timmerman whispered, "And an earl."

"Yes." Alasdair didn't add anything about being his heir. He had a feeling Mr. Timmerman's thorough research had uncovered that as well.

"But, why—?" Mr. Timmerman made a sweeping gesture that encompassed the lies told.

"It's quite innocent, I assure you, Mr. Timmerman. Gareth didn't want anyone, especially Rose, to treat him differently because of his title. I agreed to go along with deception."

"Rose and Isabel don't know?"

"Not yet, but Gareth plans to confess all after the festival. He didn't want to be a distraction." Alasdair leaned closer. "Can I ask you to remain mum until he can tell Rose?"

"If for some reason, she asks me, I won't lie, but I won't seek her out. I'm not a gossip." Mr. Timmerman took his glasses off and cleaned the lenses in a fussy manner that spoke of his uneasiness with the situation.

Alasdair was equally as uneasy now that Mr. Timmerman had been drawn into the morass. Not that Alasdair's situation with Richard and Wellington was resolved yet. His most recent conversation with Richard had been less than satisfying, but Richard's interest in Stonehaven seemed to have cooled.

A bullet dodged. Maybe. Richard was unpredictable, which made him dangerous. Until he was sure Stonehaven and Isabel were safe from his machinations, Alasdair would remain on guard.

The note of a single bagpipe lilted through the town, then a dozen joined in playing "Scotland the Brave." Alasdair's heart stirred into a rhythm that tightened his chest in a good way. After murmuring a thanks to Mr. Timmerman, he hurried out the door and rejoined Isabel. The family had left, clearing a spot in the front.

The music scythed through him, cutting away the hurt and pain he'd carried with him when his da had died. None of that mattered anymore. The notes of the pipes gave him courage, and he understood how they roused men in battle. The battle he fought now was with himself.

It was time to forgive. It was time to go home.

The pipers came into view. In deference to the weather, they didn't wear full regalia but T-shirts with their swinging kilts. White spats flashed smartly as they marched by. The notes echoed off the buildings until he was sure his ears would ring afterward. He loved every second of it and wished Gareth was at his side.

In a blink, he descended from the highest of highs into hell. As the last line of drummers passed him, he spotted George on the opposite side of the street. He dropped his gaze, trying to recalibrate his brain, and looked again. Unfortunately, George wasn't a figment of his imagination.

A welling of anger had him straining to keep from stalking across the street and launching himself at the smaller man.

Isabel whirled, her eyes alive with the same energy and gusto he'd felt not thirty seconds earlier. "What'd you think?"

"It was entertaining." The smile he grit out didn't fool her.

Fiddling with hair at her nape, her gaze focused over her shoulder. "It doesn't compare to Edinburgh or Glasgow, I suppose."

Alasdair gripped her wrist and pulled her hand to lay it over his heart. "It stirred my heart."

"That's how I feel too." Her tense expression eased into an almost smile. "There are a couple of people I need to talk to. Will you be alright for a few minutes?"

"Take your time. Do you want meet in front of the Brown Cow?"

She patted his chest and plunged into the crowd. Alasdair waited until her brown hair was swallowed in the swell of people and crossed the street. George had disappeared. Alasdair turned right and worked his way through the milling crowd like a salmon heading upstream. He was rewarded when he spotted George's thinning blond hair and white dress shirt, the sleeves rolled up to his elbows.

With his quarry in sight, Alasdair quickened his pace, murmuring excuse me's, until he was close enough to nab the shoulder of George's shirt, yanking him to a halt.

"Here now, what's this?" George's huff was one of annoyance. He turned and stared at Alasdair as if he were a stranger, but as recognition registered, his lips quivered into an unpleasant moue. "Oh, it's you."

"What are you doing here?" Alasdair asked through clenched teeth.

"Finishing your job. Then taking your promotion." The casualness of George's announcement was meant to demean and rub Alasdair's face in the fact he'd been usurped in Richard's eyes.

What George failed to understand was that Alasdair's loyalties had shifted. Alasdair swept his gaze to either side without moving his head or releasing George. Too many people around to do what he really wanted to do, which was to tear George limb from limb.

Instead, Alasdair manhandled him into a bricked alcove with a mural of the mountains providing a backdrop. It afforded them a small amount of privacy. "Let me make something perfectly clear to you, George. You are not to approach either of the Buchanans with an offer. Stonehaven is off the table. And if you cross me, I'll pull your arsehole through your throat."

Perspiration dotted George's forehead and at Alasdair's threat, a rivulet ran down the side of his face, emphasizing his pastiness. "I told Richard months ago he couldn't trust you. You can't keep your cool during negotiations, and now you've gone positively primal. You don't scare me."

Alasdair barred and snapped his teeth. George flinched. Alasdair whispered, "You're a liar and a sneak for going behind my back in the first place. But I don't think you understand the situation. I no longer owe my allegiance to Richard or to Wellington. Any action you undertake against the Buchanans will be met by direct opposition from me."

George tried to break the hold Alasdair had on his shirt, but the effort was puny. "You don't have any authority here."

Alasdair pushed George against the wall and leaned in to whisper, "Try me," before letting him go.

George straightened and smoothed his hands down the

front of his shirt, revealing underarm stains that hadn't been there before. Whatever else happened Alasdair had at least given George a humiliating scare. He deserved worse.

Alasdair left him and jogged across the street, finding Isabel already waiting on the sidewalk of the Brown Cow. Her eyes were narrowed on him, and he tamped down any lingering ferocity.

"Who was that man you were talking to? I didn't recognize him," she said.

"A bloke needing directions." It was weak, but the first excuse that popped into his head.

"And he asked you?"

"I guess he thought I looked like a local." Alasdair took her hand. "Shouldn't we be heading back to Stonehaven to prepare for the evening?"

With questions still shadowing her eyes, she nodded. Alasdair was anxious to put as many miles between Isabel and the trouble he'd brought to her doorstep as possible, but feared it wouldn't be enough.

Chapter Fifteen

As soon as Isabel stepped through the front door, her mom swept her away from Alasdair, and the questions circling in her head remained unasked. The truth was she feared the answers.

"I can't wait to see you in the dress Anna altered. It will be even lovelier on you than it is on the hanger. Are you nervous about the dance?" her mom asked, her face alight with all the fizzing nerves and excitement of the day before the festival. Usually Isabel battled the same feelings, but unease had sidled into her psyche this year.

Perhaps her strange mood was due to her imminent date with humiliation. She had tried—mostly successfully—to put the dance out of her head all day. A wave of nausea had her grimacing. "Ugh. I wasn't until you brought it up."

"What could possibly go wrong?"

"A multitude of things including but not limited to a fall, a wardrobe malfunction, a maiming."

Her mom's laugh was one of delight. "You are so funny. All you have to do is trust Alasdair."

Her mom made it sound easy. Izzy gazed toward the far end of the field and easily picked Alasdair out where he'd gone to talk to Gareth. The warm goo rushing her chest muffled the dread hollowing her stomach. Her body was fighting a battle between her heart and her gut instincts, and her brain didn't know which to name as champion.

"Go shower and take your time getting ready." Her mom shooed Izzy toward the stairs. "I want you to enjoy tonight. I've got everything under control here. Go on."

Izzy rolled her eyes all the way to her mom, but once they locked gazes, the understanding reflected back killed the quip on her tongue. Without saying it, her mom was telling her to live in the moment because happiness was fleeting.

Once in the solitude of her room and under the warm spray of the shower, she put away her worries about Alasdair and promised to enjoy herself. She closed her eyes to visualize the dance steps, but all she could see was Alasdair's smile and laugh and the way he looked at her like she was a puzzle he was trying to fit together.

An hour and a half later, she swayed at the window in the beautiful green dress Anna had altered for her, waiting for Alasdair. Bumps from the other room signaled he was getting ready. The moment loomed like the first step down the plank toward a drop into the sea.

The beginning of the end.

A soft knock sounded on the connecting door. She smoothed her skirts and turned. "Come in."

Alasdair entered in his kilt and boots, wool socks pulled to under his knees. A new black button-down shirt dressed up the look, but with his dark beard and unruly hair, a sexy, animalistic vibe radiated off him—and if she wasn't an integral part of the evening, she'd fake sickness and make him play doctor with her.

His gaze was as busy as hers. "You look lovely."

"Thank you." Izzy touched the back of her neck. She'd spent an inordinate amount of time intricately braiding her hair and twisting it into an updo, wisps framing her face.

"I can't even take how hot you are right now. I might melt in your arms tonight."

"I was worried—okay, hoping actually—my kilt might make you lose control and take scandalous advantage of me." He waggled his eyebrows.

Her laugh erased the nerves and tension and dread to a shadow that might trail her but wouldn't overtake her like a dark cloud. She was going to dance—and possibly humiliate herself, but Alasdair would be there to help her laugh about it—and drink whisky and have fun with her friends and neighbors and Alasdair.

"Don't worry, Highlander, I'll bring you to your knees later." She sashayed toward him, her pantherlike intent ruined when her ankle wobbled in her heels and she grabbed his arm.

He dropped a kiss on her nose, repositioned her hand into the crook of his arm, and escorted her down the stairs. Her mom and Gareth were waiting in the kitchen with glasses of champagne, the activity outside left to a handful of workers.

Her mom lifted Izzy arms and examined her head to foot. "Anna is a wonder. You look gorgeous."

"Thanks. So do you."

Her mom's emerald green jumpsuit and strappy heels emphasized her lithe grace. Gareth was dressed in a traditional dress kilt with knee socks, blazer, and sporran.

"I'm so happy you decided to stay with us through the festival, Alasdair. You look very handsome." Her mom bestowed a maternal smile on him and turned to a chair with a dark green blazer hanging off the back. "I thought you might want to borrow a jacket for the evening."

Izzy's heart crimped. It was one of her daddy's. Her mom helped slip it up Alasdair's arms to settle on his shoulders as if it had been tailored for him. Did it retain a hint of her daddy's aftershave or did it smell of cedar?

Izzy prepared for resentment or melancholy to invade, but there was only a feeling of rightness and the world spinning and the laws of nature being proved true. She brushed her hands down his shoulders and arms and took his hands in hers. "Now you're ready to open the festival with me."

Gareth handed them two glasses of champagne before retrieving his own and clearing his throat. "I need to say something."

Izzy smiled and glanced toward Alasdair. He wasn't smiling. In fact, he was so still and tense, Izzy wouldn't have been surprised to reach out and find him turned to stone.

Gareth continued. "These last weeks have been the happiest of my life. Meeting you, Rosie, wasn't luck; it was fate. I bless the day I found you, because only then did I realize I had been looking for you all my life."

Emotion drew tears into her mom's eyes, and she tucked herself into Gareth's side and wrapped her arms around him.

Gareth wasn't done. "Getting to know you, Isabel, has been a joy and to have my . . . to have Alasdair here as well really is a dream come true." Gareth grabbed Alasdair's shoulder. Like a modified man-hug, Alasdair returned the gesture.

Her mom laughed and flapped her hand. "I'll not forgive you if you make me bawl and mess up my mascara, you big bear."

"*Sláinte.*" Alasdair raised his glass. They all repeated the toast and drank.

Izzy blamed the burn of tears in her eyes to the sharp tang of the champagne. While uncertainty still lurked in the not-too-distant future, optimism bubbled up like a newly discovered natural spring.

In high spirits, they made their way to the whisky tasting in separate vehicles, Alasdair and Izzy in his rented car. She ran her hands over the leather. "I'm going to miss your car."

"I'm going to miss it, too." His smile didn't reach his eyes, and she had the feeling the car wasn't on his mind. She looked out the window and blinked back the sting of tears. She didn't have the time or energy for sorrow.

"What do you drive in London?" she asked.

"I don't keep a car. My flat's close to the tube and trains."

"Is this what you'd want if you could have anything?"

"It's been fun, but it's not practical. I've always been partial to four-by-fours."

"Like Daddy's truck." She grinned.

"Exactly like your truck except with functional air-con, heat, cushioned seats, sat-nav. You know, anything a vehicle would have standard in the last decade." He linked their fingers and kissed the back of her hand. "Gareth had an old Range Rover that I loved. I would probably buy a newer model."

Alasdair parked and helped her out of the car. The room was already packed. Dr. Jameson greeted them at the door, his color high from excitement or perhaps from sampling the wares.

"An excellent crowd has gathered." Dr. Jameson grasped her hand and nodded at Alasdair. "Rose tells me the three of us are going to open the festival this year."

Izzy tamped down on the nerves that sprouted like kudzu around her stomach. "Yep. Do I have time for a drink?"

"Two if you double-fist them." Dr. Jameson's lopsided grin made him look a decade younger. "Seriously though, you have fifteen minutes."

Self-proclaimed whisky aficionados came from all over the Southeast and paid for premium tickets to sample a variety of whiskies from Scotland in a back room. Those with general tickets milled in the main area and were made up mostly of Highland residents. A dark wood bar took up a corner of the room to prepare full-sized drinks for cash. Profits went to the local animal shelter and for beautification projects in Highland.

A spotlight shined in the middle of the room and the guests scooted around the bright light like insects. She and Alasdair would dance under that light for all the world— her world of Highland, anyway—to see.

"I need a drink stat," Izzy said.

"What would you like?" he murmured in her ear.

"I know it's sacrilege but a whisky and Coke, please."

Alasdair shouldered his way through the crowd toward the bar. This was the weekend the men and women of Highland wore their finest Scottish fashions. Alasdair was far from the only man in a kilt, but she didn't spot anyone who wore one better.

As soon as the drink made contact with her hand, she drank half in one go. The cascading warmth helped lubricate her stiff joints. She focused on Alasdair like he was a buoy ready to save her from drowning in her own fears.

Looking disgustingly unruffled, Alasdair sipped on a whisky neat. "I've never seen this much tartan in my life. It's really quite something."

"That's a polite way of saying that we're crazy, isn't it?"

"I'd go with enthusiastic." His genuine smile turned into a pensive one. "Believe it not, being in Highland, farther away from Scotland than my London flat, has made me feel more connected with my heritage. It's time to face my past."

"Will you tell your mother about Lewis?" Although the room was buzzing with the noise of a hundred people, they were easy to ignore with Alasdair so close.

"I should have told her a long time ago. I'm bone-tired

of keeping secrets." His chest expanded on an inhale and his lips parted.

Izzy tensed, instinct telling her what he said next was sure to upend everything.

The crackle of the sound system as it fired up was like a lightning strike to dry brush in her belly. She was grateful and exasperated and terrified by the interruption. After downing the remainder of her drink and depositing it on a tray, she rubbed her shaky, clammy hands together.

"Is this thing on? Can y'all hear me?" The spotlight moved to cast its terrifying circle on Dr. Jameson. Standing on a dais next to the DJ station, he held a microphone in one hand and cradled his bagpipes in the other. An explanation about the sampling room and the events of the evening followed.

"I'm not sure I can do this," Izzy said through dry, numb lips. How could her mouth be so dry and her hands so sweaty? It defied nature.

"Of course you can." Alasdair took her hand in his and led them toward the dance floor.

"What if I permanently disfigure you?"

"I'll wear any scars you inflict upon me with pride."

As if she'd entered a long tunnel, she heard Dr. Jameson's voice echo. "And now, to open the Highland games, welcome Isabel Buchanan of Stonehaven and her escort, Alasdair Blackmoor."

Her escort. It made it sound like she had paid Alasdair for services rendered. A hysterical-tinged laugh clawed its way up her throat. Keeping her gaze focused on Alasdair and not the wall of people surrounding the floor, she clenched her jaw and grimaced out a smile to keep it in check.

Alasdair led her to the middle of the dance floor and whispered like a ventriloquist, "Quit looking at me like I'm planning to sacrifice you to the gods."

"They wouldn't accept me; I'm not a virgin." The quip popped out. Alasdair's shoulders shook with suppressed laughter. Her pent-up nerves emerged on slightly hysterical giggles.

Her mom and Gareth beamed like proud parents at the two of them. Anna gave her a wink and thumbs-up. Even Holt was there in a kilt, although absent an encouraging smile. She let out a breath and rotated her jaw.

The spotlight caught them. Blinded, she blinked up at Alasdair, his head rimmed in starbursts of light. An expectant hush lengthened and stretched until she thought she might snap in two.

"Steady now," Alasdair murmured. "Focus on me. Only me."

The first strains of Dr. Jameson's bagpipes brought a rush of relief. Something familiar in the entirely unfamiliar situation of being the center of attention. With a count of three, Alasdair led her into the dance.

She didn't get lost in his eyes or in the moment like the romantic books she'd read, and no one would think she'd missed her calling by not following her mom into professional dance, but she didn't embarrass herself, even finding a genuine smile for Alasdair.

She didn't know why he had confidence in her, but she was grateful.

Except, he didn't return her smile. In fact, contrary to his frequent admonishments, he wasn't staring into her eyes as he twirled her to the left. Someone over her shoulder had caught his attention. The urge to steal a glance made the hairs on the back of her neck waver, but she didn't want to risk her grasp on the beat and the steps.

Alasdair took a misstep and trod on her left foot. She stumbled. He stumbled. Doing her best to reinsert herself into the dance, she stepped forward the same time Alasdair did. Her forehead hit his nose hard enough to make her head ring.

He dropped her hand and pinched the bridge of his nose, muttering a curse involving bollocks and blood. The blood appeared more metaphorical than literal. Somehow, their feet realigned with the music and moved them around the floor.

Her mom and Gareth had joined them and so had Holt and Anna. Other couples who knew the St. Bernard's waltz and even some couples who didn't filled the floor. The spotlight moved away from them. They shuffled back and forth like they were at a middle-school dance.

"Are you alright?" Izzy peered at his nose. It was red across the bridge, but wasn't bleeding. The rush of relief at having completed the dance bordered on euphoria. "It's not as bad as when I bonked you with your phone. I would like to point out, it was you who messed up and not me. This time."

Her tease didn't garner a returning smile. Again, his focus was elsewhere. Without having to worry over the complexities of the dance steps, Izzy looked over her shoulder.

It was difficult to parse the wall of people surrounding them. Someone had rattled Alasdair to the point of immobility. Izzy grabbed Alasdair's hand and cut through a gap in the wall of people, a smile pasted on her face as she nodded at friends and acquaintances and strangers.

Once they achieved the relative seclusion of an alcove against the far wall, Izzy stopped and pulled Alasdair around to face her.

"You okay?" she asked.

"My nose will be fine." The words were sharp.

"I'm not asking about your nose."

His full attention transferred to her. His body language

spoke of anxiety. They hadn't crashed and burned on the dance floor. Why was he still distressed?

Anna swished up and linked her arm through Izzy's. "Y'all did great, and you look fabulous. I'm so proud."

"Thanks," said Izzy. "We couldn't have done it without you."

When Alasdair didn't speak, Anna widened her eyes at Izzy. "Let's go to the bathroom and freshen up."

Anna didn't let go until they reached the bathroom. "What's up with the tension between you two? Did something happen?"

"No." As Izzy considered the day, she wasn't sure she spoke the truth. "I don't know. Things have been weird since the parade. I saw Alasdair talking to some dude that I didn't know."

"Did you ask him about it?" Anna touched up her red lipstick, popped her lips, and met Izzy's eyes in the mirror.

"He claimed he was giving the man directions, but that's not what it looked like."

"What'd it look like?"

Izzy hesitated, but her suspicions emerged. "Like Alasdair was threatening him."

Anna was quiet while an older lady washed her hands. When they were alone once more, she said, "What are you going to do?"

"Honestly, I don't have the energy to expend on unearthing the story. The festival will become all-consuming tomorrow." In fact, Izzy planned to be on the way home to Stonehaven within in the hour. She couldn't afford to be tired or hungover in the morning.

Izzy stepped out of the brightly lit bathroom into the dim main room, blinking to locate Alasdair. Sterling eased up beside her with a loud clearing of his throat.

"Hey, Sterling." She spared him a quick smile before resuming her search for Alasdair.

"Do you have a second to talk business?" he asked.

The seriousness of his tone garnered her full attention. "Our loan?"

"I'd rather be doing this in the office, but I know how busy y'all are, and it can't wait."

"You're scaring me. Are we not approved?"

"You are but it's . . . complicated."

Her relief was tempered by his qualification. "Spit it out, Sterling."

"I talked to an old frat buddy in the corporate loan department, and he said your loan had been flagged. It was to be approved, but as soon as Rose signed, the loan was to be sold. Our bank would no longer hold the lien."

"Who would?"

"A British company called Wellington."

Visceral emotion speared through her to pierce her heart. Pain radiated, yet she stood, pride and anger and grief stiffening her spine and holding her upright.

She refocused on Sterling and what he was saying, "—no idea why."

"I know why." She wanted to rewind her life five minutes. To before she understood how badly she'd been used by Alasdair.

Sterling leaned closer. "I've sent your loan application to Mindy at Farmer's Credit Union. She's going to set you up, and there's no chance of interference from big shots."

She took Sterling's forearm and gave him a grateful squeeze. "Thank you. You deserve a raise."

"Not sure the corporate yahoos would agree, but you're more than welcome." Sterling strolled toward the bar.

Izzy turned in a slow circle and scanned the crowd.

Alasdair was in a heated conversation with a woman. Not bothering with a polite smile, she cut a warpath in his direction.

The woman's back was to Izzy. She was trim and wore

a black, tailored pantsuit with an easy sophistication. Her blonde hair was swept into an elegant chignon. While her chronological age was a mystery, she had a timeless air about her.

Alasdair glanced up and caught sight of Izzy. His gaze widened and darted between her and the woman he was talking to as if debating whether to make a run for it. She hoped he did so she could kick off her heels, hunt him down, and tackle him to the ground like a wild banshee.

She flanked him, not sparing the woman a moment's attention, and met Alasdair eyes with an unflinching gaze. "I have a good mind to dump you naked in the mountains without a blanket to hide behind this time."

Chapter Sixteen

Alasdair struggled for words. Isabel's honeyed accent held a new bitterness. Obviously, Isabel had discovered something, but what? He would have to stall until he could get her alone and feel out the situation.

"Mum, this is Isabel Buchanan. Isabel, I want you to meet my mum, Fiona." The polite introduction seemed to take Isabel aback. Or maybe his mum appearing in Highland attributed to the shock. He had certainly been gobsmacked to see her standing on the edge of the crowd during their dance.

"I take it my son has somehow earned your ire?" His mum's accent was posh and British compared to his brogue. Neither did they look alike. He was dark where she was fair, but there was something in her strength of expression that he'd noted in the mirror.

"He's earned a good kick in the pants." Her gaze shifted back to him. "When were you going to tell me the truth?"

Which truth was she referring to? He took an educated guess. Plus, it was easier to throw Gareth under the huge double-decker bus bearing down on him. "Gareth being my uncle changes nothing. Except for the fact he's not Cairndow's caretaker, but its owner."

Isabel's jaw slackened. "Gareth's your uncle?"

Bloody hell. He'd chosen poorly, but backtracking wasn't an option, especially with his mum staring back and forth between them, her face a mask of fascinated horror. "His name is actually Gareth Blackmoor, the ninth Earl of Cairndow."

"He's been lying to my mom since the day they met?" Isabel said more to herself than him.

While true, Alasdair couldn't let the harsh statement stand. "Yes, but only because he wanted your mother to see the man and not the title. I don't think he expected to . . ." He didn't want to lay his uncle's heart out for examination.

"Expected to what?" his mum asked.

Both women's gazes bored into him, and a nervous sweat broke across his neck. "Only Gareth can answer that. Isabel, I swear he was planning to tell your mother after the festival."

"And I'm supposed to believe anything you promise after you've been plotting behind my back to leverage Stonehaven for your corporate overseers?" Isabel was righteous in her fury, her eyes stormy with lightning meant to strike him dead on the spot.

His life was falling apart like a sand castle being wiped clean by a wave he should have anticipated, but had caught him by surprise. He thought he'd have time to fix everything, but his time was up.

Had George gotten to her? Alasdair had half expected him to make an appearance, but hadn't seen him since the parade. "That was a misunderstanding."

She made an unbelieving guffaw. "So Wellington wanted to assume control over our loan for altruistic reasons?"

He mouthed a curse, earning him a pointed look from his mum, which he ignored. Upsetting his mum with choice language was the least of his worries. He should have guessed. Assuming loans was a common enough method of persuasion, if not a little devious.

"How did you find out?" he asked.

"Sterling, the bank's loan officer, is a friend. He doesn't want to see me or Mom hurt. Not that you would understand the novel concept." Sarcasm dripped like acid from her voice.

"I swear I didn't know Wellington was trying to acquire your loan."

"You knew there was a plan afoot." It wasn't a question.

Alasdair was losing her. His lips were dry, so was his mouth and throat. His body was numb. Had all the blood drained out of heart to puddle at their feet?

"I didn't intend to lie to you. I never thought we would"—he glanced toward his mother—"connect the way that we did. I assumed getting Gareth home would be a simple matter of bundling him back to the airport. When it wasn't, I decided it would be prudent to discover as much as I could about your circumstances."

"And that meant gathering information on our financial situation?"

"Something like that. It was intended for my information only, but the man I asked to handle the research took it to my superior instead of sending it to me." The anger festered in his voice.

"You feel betrayed too? Good." Isabel pushed past him, scanning the crowd.

Alasdair did the same, in a race to find Gareth and Rose before Isabel, but it was too late. She nimbly dodged through the crowd whereas he was left to bulldoze a path. He didn't notice his mum on his heels until he halted, and she bumped into him.

"Sorry, Mum." He was apologizing for a myriad of things but mostly because he had disappointed her.

"For what?" She stopped him with a hand on his arm, her expression unreadable.

"I've made a hash of things. If you haven't caught on yet, my job at Wellington is over. I plan to quit if Richard hasn't already left a message firing me. Even though I thought I was doing the right thing, I've hurt people. People I care about a great deal. You came all this way to see me fail."

Her mouth softened into an almost smile. "Darling, I came all this way because you obviously needed me."

He took a breath. "How . . . ?"

"Your recent calls have been rather enlightening as was your text informing me you were staying through the games. I did some research and booked a flight. If everything turned out to be fine, I decided I could use a fun weekend away from London."

He'd never thought of his mum as an emotionally intuitive person, but he was discovering he'd been wrong about a lot. "I care about Isabel. More than I can fathom. I told myself it was only a fling, but I knew it wasn't even from the beginning."

His mum's smile reflected the same melancholy in her eyes. While it held notes of sadness, there was a solace to be found there too. "You remind me of Rory in the best possible ways, Alasdair."

It had been a long time since his mum had spoken his da's name aloud to him. "I thought you hated Da."

"I did." She arched her brows with a familiar haughtiness. "But, I loved him too."

He glanced over at where Isabel was holding forth with Gareth and Rose. Gareth's face had blanched behind his beard. "Uncle Gareth requires reinforcements. Can we maybe talk more about Da later?"

His mum nodded. "Of course."

Alasdair shouldered his way to Gareth's side, his mum

hovering in the background. Rose's body was stiff as she shuffled to stand next to Isabel, facing them. They had assumed their battle lines.

"I don't know what to say." Rose ran a trembling hand over her forehead.

Assuming Isabel had launched all her accusations, Alasdair accepted his kamikaze mission. "Rose, please don't blame Gareth for my misstep. My sole purpose in soliciting information about Stonehaven was to protect my uncle. This was before I got to know the two of you and realized . . ."

His brain went numb as he processed what'd he'd learned about Isabel and himself over the last two weeks.

"And realized we were easy marks? Too trusting? Simple and unsophisticated?" Isabel's anger was fed by hurt. Knowing he was the cause clawed at him, leaving wounds that might never heal.

"I realized how special you are. Please know that I tried to stop what I'd put into motion." He wanted to touch Isabel and comfort her. If he tried, he had the feeling he'd end up curled up in physical pain on the floor.

"After everything we shared, why didn't you tell me your real name, Gareth?" Rose's pale-faced disappointment was somehow worse than Isabel's fury.

Gareth stumbled on his words before find his voice. "I . . . You . . . It was nice not to be the ninth Earl of Cairndow for a little while. I planned to tell you after the festival. I promise you I did."

"How can I believe you now?" she asked.

"By remembering everything else that I've said to you. You know in your heart I didn't lie about anything else."

At Rose's contemplative silence, Gareth lifted a hand, but Rose took a step back from him, reaching blindly for Izzy's arm. "The festival kicks off in the morning. Izzy and I can't deal with this right now. If you'll excuse us."

Gareth, Alasdair, and Fiona followed the Buchanans out the door and into the still-humid night. Gareth gave it one last try. "Rosie, please."

"Perhaps after the festival we can discuss the matter, but not now. I don't have the time nor energy." Rose glided away with the bearing of a queen, and Izzy followed with the barely veiled aggression of a bloodthirsty knight.

Alasdair stared until Rose and Isabel disappeared into the shadows. He'd known the literal moment of truth was coming. He had tried to prepare for it. Had tried to mitigate the fallout. But nothing had prepared him for the pain and hurt and betrayal he'd caused Isabel.

"You lads need a drink," his mum announced as she herded them back through the door. "Come on then. My treat."

Wearing his years heavily, Gareth slumped his way to the bar. Similarly shell-shocked, Alasdair let his mum take charge. She handed them each a whisky neat. The three of them raised their glasses in a silent toast and knocked them back. His mum signaled for three more.

"After Rose has a chance to cool down and consider the situation, you can reason with her and throw yourself on her mercy." Alasdair slipped an arm around Gareth's shoulders for a bracing shake. "I don't think Isabel will ever forgive me and rightly so."

His mum made an unladylike noise and tapped her empty glass on the bar top. "Women will forgive worse sins than the two of you have committed if they love you. I know from experience."

Gareth cleared his throat. "Fiona. I'm—"

His mum held up a hand. "No. I'm not here to ruminate over past misdeeds committed by either one of us. Or by your brother."

"Then, excuse my bluntness, Fiona, but why are you here?" While a truce tempered the air between then, Alasdair could remember the anger on both sides after his da's death.

"I was worried about the two of you, of course," she said.

"Worried I'd make the mistake of marrying an American?" Gareth asked bitterly. "There seems little chance of that."

His mum studied Gareth for a moment before turning the intensity of her blue eyes on Alasdair. "For goodness sake, I've never seen such glum faces as the two of you are wearing. The battle may be lost, but not the war. Not while you have me on your side."

"Isabel hates me, Mum. I've lost her."

"You're not a quitter." None of his mum's confidence was wearing off on him.

"Except, I informed you not ten minutes ago that I'm quitting my job."

"Pish-posh." His mum waved off his evidence based-argument.

"After all your talk about American tarts, I don't understand why you aren't thrilled about the outcome and bustling both of us on a plane back to London." Alasdair thunked his glass onto the bar and threw his hands up.

"I might have overreacted a smidge to Gareth's abdication." His mum had the grace to look chagrinned. "It's just that you've lost so much, Alasdair, I didn't want you to lose the one thing your da left you."

"Are you saying if I marry Rose, you'd be content with an American countess?" Gareth's incredulity was fair, considering his mum's first reaction to his flight from Cairndow.

"Of course. I was only concerned you were being taken advantage of."

Alasdair had doubts as to the virtue of her concern, but he'd let the matter lay. "What about Isabel?"

Warmth flared in his mum's eyes. "When you told me she was funny and smart and mole-free, I knew you cared for her more than you would ever admit to me. Maybe even yourself. All I want is for you to be happy, Alasdair."

In that moment, he forgave her for all the times her overbearing protectiveness had chafed. She had done what she could to keep him from being hurt in the only way she knew how.

"Rosie's not answering my calls or texts." Gareth slipped his mobile back into his jacket pocket and slumped over the bar, his chin propped up on his hand.

"Give them time," his mum said with a wisdom Alasdair wanted to buy. "Another round of whisky?"

Alasdair hesitated. "I'm competing tomorrow for Laird of the Games."

"Feats of strength to impress Isabel is not the worst idea I've heard." His mum patted his arm. "But not the best either. We'll think of something, but right now, we need a place to stay the night. I'll be back."

Alasdair wouldn't be spending the night in Isabel's bed. He might never feel her cuddled next to him or kicking him or have her hand flop his face in the middle of the night ever again.

Before Alasdair could curl up on the floor in a fetal position, Holt, the eggplant farmer, sidled up to Alasdair's elbow, his fair skin ruddy from his own alcoholic indulgences. "Is it true what they're saying?"

"What are they saying?" Alasdair asked.

"You two are royalty." Holt gestured between Alasdair and Gareth with a hand holding a glass, whisky sloshing up the sides.

Gareth barked a laugh. "Not hardly. The Blackmoors were a thorn to the English for centuries. We hung onto our land and title through schemes and a bit of luck. It didn't hurt that Cairndow is impregnatable. Never been breached by any enemy. Except mold."

"Gareth is the ninth Earl of Cairndow. I suppose someday—not anytime in the near future, mind you—that I'll be the tenth," Alasdair added.

"The Buchanan ladies seemed a mite upset over the glad tidings," Holt said with a sarcasm Alasdair hadn't realized he possessed.

Gareth dropped his head into his hands with a groan at Holt's pronouncement, and Alasdair didn't see any reason to give Holt further ammunition by admitting his misdeeds went even further.

"I'm sure you're thrilled. You can swoop in and console Isabel." Alasdair took Gareth's unfinished drink and emptied it in one swallow followed by a chaser of bitterness at the image of Holt wooing Isabel.

Holt raised a shoulder in a gesture that struck Alasdair as strangely Continental for a bean farmer. "Izzy is pretty and nice and close to my age. Those are few and far between in a small town like Highland. I thought, why not give it a shot? But after seeing the way she looked at you at the pub, I realized Izzy and I would only ever be friends. And that's okay."

A rush of empathy flooded Alasdair. Loneliness radiated off Holt. It might have been the whisky talking—no, it was definitely the whisky talking—but he found himself patting Holt on the shoulder and saying, "You're a good-looking bloke, Holt. You'll find the perfect lass someday. What about Anna?"

"Anna?" A laugh burst out of Holt. "She's pretty and all, but she'd make a terrible farmer's wife."

"I couldn't imagine leaving London until I came here and met Isabel."

Holt made a throaty sound between humor and disbelief

and sipped at his own drink. "Are you saying love conquers all? Please."

Another whisky miraculously appeared in front of Alasdair. Who was he to turn his back on a miracle? He drank deeply. "Love? No, of course not. Ridiculous. I've known Isabel mere weeks."

"My dad said he knew the first time he met my mom that she was the one. *The one*." Holt's snort was squarely in the camp of disgust this time. "Luck is more like."

Alasdair's mum returned from wherever she'd been—maybe consulting with her boss in the Underworld?—and clapped her hands to get their attention. "Every room in town is booked, but I met a nice gentleman who has offered us accommodations." She pointed, and everyone turned to see Dr. Jameson waving merrily to them.

"Why should we bother sticking around? Isabel will refuse to see me tomorrow," Alasdair said glumly.

"You could win her back," Holt said from over Alasdair's shoulder.

Gareth stood and threw his arm across Holt's shoulders for support more than comradery if Alasdair had to guess. "Yes! Win her back, laddie."

"And how would I accomplish that?" Alasdair asked.

"Feats of strength, o' course." Holt's Southern accent had grown thick with whisky and honey.

Alasdair made a gesture toward Holt and addressed his mum. "See, he thinks it's a good idea too."

"Yes, but all three of you are sozzled." His mum sounded more exasperated than angry.

The laugh that rumbled out of Alasdair only confirmed his mum's assessment. Holt tapped him on the arm with a vigor that veered painful.

"All you have to do is win tomorrow and receive your prize from Izzy," Holt said as if it were as simple as showing up. "She'll have no choice but to talk to you."

"Great plan," Alasdair said dryly. "Except, I have no chance of winning the games. You'll beat me handily."

The three men were quiet for a moment considering the problem of Alasdair's lack of experience at Highland games.

His mum made a scoffing noise. "It's obvious, isn't it, darling? You'll have to cheat."

"Mum!" Had his mother been taken over by aliens?

But Holt nodded and wagged his finger at Alasdair's mum. "Yep. She's right. I know what I can do: lose on purpose."

"Why would you do that for me?"

"I don't know." Holt rubbed his chin and rolled his eyes toward the ceiling like any good philosopher before favoring him with a boyish, lopsided smile. "Prolly cuz I'm drunk."

"You'll not be feeling quite so mag-magnanimous in the morning, I'd guess."

Holt just shook his head and gave Alasdair a once-over. "I don't know what that means, but I do know you're going to need lots of help to win. *Lots*."

Alasdair wasn't sure whether he should be insulted or grateful. With Gareth still hanging around his shoulders like a barnacle, Holt pointed to the back room and shuffled away.

Alasdair turned to his mum, but she only gestured for him to proceed. "Your farmer friend is correct. Let's see what kind of pull he's got."

The classy whisky tasting had devolved into a party. A dozen or so men gathered in the back room. A couple were beefy enough to break Alasdair in two. Holt deposited Gareth in a chair with a group of three kilted men, returning to clap Alasdair on the back. "Here's your competition tomorrow."

"This is impossible." Alasdair had practiced all the

events except the caber toss. He'd become proficient, but something spectacular would have to happen to give him a shot at being named Laird of the Games.

"'Course it isn't. Lemme just . . ." Holt stuck two fingers in his mouth and blew a gust of air. Muttering a curse, he tried again and this time a shrill whistle emerged and a quiet cascaded over the men. "This here is Alasdair. He's competing tomorrow for the first time."

A call of welcome went up around the room. Holt waved them back to silence. "There's more. For extremely personal reasons, he must win."

A chorus of good-natured, whisky-soaked boos rang out.

"I know. I know. It's a crazy notion, but I'll let him explain. Go on, Alasdair." Holt stepped back and waved Alasdair forward.

Fighting the urge to strangle Holt, Alasdair pasted on a smile and attempted to sound sober. "Gentlemen. Ish my great honor . . . That is to say, *it's* my great honor to be standing here with you this evening." He gave a small bow, which upset his equilibrium enough to make him have to step forward to keep upright.

Laughter rolled through the room. Undeterred, Holt yelled, "Shut yer yaps!"

Alasdair panicked. Gareth, his cheeks ruddy and his eyes bright, nodded at him in encouragement. His mum stood near the doorway with Dr. Jameson, her expression one of fascination as she watched him "uh" and "ah." His English sensibility stumbled for words while his Scottish heart was branded with a torrent of emotion.

"I have been a monumental idiot when it comes to women." Several of the men nodded and clinked their glasses together in agreement. At least, he wasn't the only one. "One woman, in particular, I should say."

"And who would that be?" one of the men called out.

"Isabel Buchanan."

Another chorus of voices rose to a din. "She's a pretty one."

"So is her mother." A wolf whistle sounded from the middle of the group.

"Does she like you back?" one of men hollered above the rest.

"She did until I did something dumb," Alasdair yelled back.

"And winning tomorrow will win Izzy back?" another man asked.

Alasdair ran a hand through his hair and shook his head. "I don't know, but I'm desperate. If I don't try, I'll regret it the rest of my days."

Someone took pity on him and shoved a drink in his hand.

After that, the events of the evening ran together like a watercolor painting left in the rain. There was singing involved with his arms thrown around the shoulders of two men whose names never registered, but were his best friends in the world in that instant.

Then George ruined the feeling of brotherhood. He stood in the door of the backroom with his thin top lip curled and his nose scrunched like he had trod in manure. Alasdair strode over, grabbed a handful of George's shirt, and shoved him up against the wall.

"You little git!" Alasdair yelled into the sudden quiet. "You thought to leverage a loan against Isabel? You're begging for my fist in your face."

George pushed ineffectually at Alasdair's wrist. "I suppose you warned her. Is that why the application was pulled?"

Alasdair's laugh was mean-spirited and felt good. "You and Richard didn't count on one thing."

"What's that?"

"Highland is a small town, and Isabel has friends everywhere. Even the bank. Not everyone is willing to sell their soul for a promotion."

"You certainly won't need to worry about getting a promotion." George's sneer was an invitation for Alasdair's fist. He drew his arm back and—

Gareth caught his elbow. "Ach, the little whelp isn't worth the trouble he could cause you, laddie. Let him run back to London like a lapdog."

Gareth was right. With a teeth-rattling shake, Alasdair tossed George toward the door. "Get out of Highland. Tonight."

George straightened his shirt. "You are an uncouth, uncivilized Scot. If you come near me, I'll contact the authorities."

Alasdair growled and stomped his foot in George's direction. The man fled like hellhounds were on his heels, and Alasdair let a wild laugh loose. With his bravado dialed to maximum, he called Richard.

The minutiae of the conversation didn't stick in his memory, but the broad brushstrokes involved several Gaelic curses and the intimate location where Richard could shove Alasdair's job. In short, he quit in spectacular fashion.

At what felt like the wee hours of the morning, he stumbled into the night air, cool enough to be refreshing, and found himself shoved into the back seat of a four-by-four that smelled of dog next to Gareth.

Dr. Jameson drove and Alasdair's mum was in the front at his side. A fear formulated in his whisky-soaked mind and he stuck his head between the seats. "You're not taking me to the airport."

His mum shifted to give him a shake of her head that somehow conveyed both amusement and disappointment.

"As if they'd let you on a plane in your state. Now, sit back and try not to sick up on the drive."

Alasdair did as he was told because the motion was indeed nauseating. He let his head loll back on the support and patted Gareth's knee. "Alright there, old man?"

"I'll survive." Gareth was leaned against the window.

Alasdair's thoughts drifted. He would survive too. After all, that's what he'd been doing the last few years in London. Surviving. But more was within his reach. He'd done his best to mitigate risk in his love life and work life, but if he wanted to be happy, he'd have to risk something fundamental to his survival. He'd have to risk his heart.

Chapter Seventeen

Sleep never came easy the night before the festival began, but Izzy had only dozed for what felt like minutes when the rising sun woke her. A quick, cool shower helped wash the grit from her eyes, and she dressed in a kilt-like skirt, a Highland-branded T-shirt, and blue Converse tennis shoes. Comfort was key.

Her mom was already up, sipping a mug of coffee and flipping through her notes and to-do lists for the day. Dark smudges under her mom's eyes were a testament to her own battle during the night, but her hair was neatly twisted and pinned up, and she was dressed in black flats, slim-fitting red ankle-length slacks, and a sleeveless white blouse.

In a half hour, the whirl would begin and wouldn't stop until they fell into bed that night. This was Izzy's only chance to explore the crater last night's bombshell had left.

"Have you talked to Gareth?" Izzy asked.

"Not yet. He called and texted a dozen times last night, but I needed to gather my thoughts." Her mom sounded shockingly calm.

"And have you? Gathered your thoughts, I mean?" Izzy had planned to follow her mom's lead, which she assumed would mean cutting the Blackmoor men out of their lives. Yes, it was painful, but necessary. Like wart removal.

"Gareth and I need to talk. Yes, he lied about his name, but he loves me. I believe that. Unfortunately, it won't be enough."

"What do you mean?"

"I have Stonehaven and he has Cairndow. We are geographically incompatible," her mom said simply yet with an underlying sadness.

It was too big a problem for Izzy to tackle at the moment, so she pivoted to Alasdair's betrayal. "What do you think about Alasdair having his company dig around our finances?"

"He was protecting his uncle. Alasdair didn't know anything about us yet, but don't forget, he was aware Gareth had a title and an estate. It sounded like Alasdair very much regretted the events put in motion, and no harm was done. Sterling mitigated any damage." Her mom's attitude shocked Izzy.

"Don't you worry he'll lie to you again? Hurt you again?" Izzy couldn't hide her exasperation.

Her mom huffed a sigh, put her to-do list aside, and took both of Izzy's hands in hers. "Will you allow your mother to give you some love-life advice?"

"If I must." Izzy girded herself to stave off embarrassment.

"None of us are perfect, darling, and no relationship is either. It's easier to tally who is right and wrong and hang onto your resentment and turn your back, because forgiveness and understanding are difficult. What you should tally are laughs and kisses and how many times you are made a better person because of your connection.

I don't know if Alasdair is that person for you, but I've never seen you this happy. Isn't it worth exploring to find out?"

As usual, her mom was like a human Pez dispenser filled with nuggets of wisdom. "For all I know, Alasdair is on a plane with his mother on their way home." Even imagining him gone hurt.

"I wouldn't worry about that. He doesn't want to leave you." Her mom gave Izzy's hands a squeeze before turning brisk and no-nonsense. "We have important work to do. The Blackmoor gentlemen will have to wait until we have time for their groveling, yes?"

Izzy found her first smile of the day even if it was bittersweet.

The next hours were filled with festival details large and small. Izzy directed vendors to their booths with an ingrained Southern hospitality. Most knew one another from years past and greeted one another like the festival was a family reunion. Small hiccups erupted that she smoothed—a dance troop showing up late for their performance, a vendor forgetting their credit-card reader, a fender bender in the parking area.

She didn't have time to obsess over Alasdair even as her gaze narrowed on the gathering contestants for the athletic events. Where was he? Contrary to her mom's confidence, she could picture Alasdair's mother spiriting him away during the night.

The skies were blue, the puffy white clouds gifting them with temporary shade, but the temperature rose steadily and the crowd grew by the minute. Troops of young dancers competed for ribbons accompanied by traditional Celtic music. The call of the pipes overlay the hum of the people strolling around the festival. The smell of fried food hung heavy in the humid air.

Izzy moved toward the stage to watch Anna's girls

weave and high kick a complicated routine. The crowd whooped and clapped their appreciation. Anna would compete in the adult division the next day along with the pipers.

The loudspeakers set up around the field crackled with an announcement urging spectators to the athletic field for the start of the competitions. Like a school of fish, the crowd moved in that direction, the buzz of excitement buoying them along.

The athletic events were the highlight of the first day, the ribbons awarded before the evening concert. She picked her way through the crowd to where her mom stood making notes on her tablet in a cordoned-off area where the judges, including Dr. Jameson, conferred. Men in kilts gathered at the far end in preparation for the hammer throw.

None of them were Alasdair. An embarrassing sting invaded her sinuses that had nothing to do with allergies. But then, miraculously, the scrum parted and there he was. Relief weakened her knees and made her feel slightly nauseous.

"Alasdair's still here," Izzy said.

Her mom didn't look up, but smiled. "Yep. Five of the competitors dropped out and all the boys looked a little green when they registered. I heard from Dr. Jameson the party got raucous last night. Apparently, Alasdair and Gareth were right in the middle of it."

"Glad they had fun after stomping all over our feelings last night."

Her mom glanced up to acknowledge the rampant sarcasm in Izzy's voice with arched brows. "Dr. Jameson won't tell me, but something is astir with the competition."

"In a good or bad way?" While Izzy was partly asking because the success of the athletic events was a measure of how well the day went, she was mostly worried about

Alasdair. Despite his Scottish heritage, he was a beginner, and she'd seen experienced competitors get hurt.

"The twinkle in Dr. Jameson's eyes makes me think good. Or at least, entertaining."

Izzy stared at Alasdair and huffed. She wasn't close enough to judge the color of his complexion but the rest of him looked as hale and hearty as ever. He was wearing the black T-shirt with the Scottish flag emblazoned on the front, his new kilt, and his boots.

"Why does he have to look so good in a kilt?" she asked.

Her mom laughed. "I asked myself the same thing about Gareth."

"You've seen him, then?"

"From a distance." She chucked her chin toward the other side of the field. "He's with Alasdair's mother watching the competition. Looks like they're getting started."

The first man stepped up to the line holding the hammer, which wasn't a hammer at all. It was a twenty-two pound iron ball fitted to a rattan handle the length of a broomstick and was thrown for distance. The competitor's feet had to stay planted, and it required a huge windup before it was released. The hammer could easily fly astray in inexperienced hands.

The first two men threw their hammers respectable distances, but nothing close to where the top competitors like Holt would reach.

Alasdair stepped up and gripped the hammer's handle. Her mom clasped her tablet to her chest and shielded her eyes from the sun. Izzy fought nerves even though she wasn't the one competing.

She put a hand over her eyes, but peeked through her fingers. "I don't want to watch."

Alasdair wound the hammer up and let go. It bested the distance of the first two men. Holt was next and, having seen him compete before, Izzy was sure he would beat Alasdair's distance easily. Except, he only matched Alasdair's effort.

A call about a defective potty had her retreating before the next event. It was a half hour before she made her way back to the athletic field and found her mom in almost the same spot.

"I missed the stone toss?" Izzy asked. The stone toss was like the Olympic shotput except the stones varied in size and weight from sixteen to twenty pounds.

"Yes and Alasdair is in the top three." Her mom shook her head, but was smiling.

"That's impossible. Is he a prodigy? Or is it genetic or something?"

"Honestly, Holt should have bested his distance based on his performance last year. All I can figure is the boys are hungover," her mom said thoughtfully. "I'll make the rounds so you can stay a watch. I'll call you if I need backup."

Izzy gave her mom an absentminded wave, her focus on the field. Being hungover didn't explain the surprising standings, but she knew who could explain it. Dr. Jameson, clad in a Christmassy red and green kilt, white button-down, and sporran, was the official stat keeper. His jaunty red bow tie added a Southern touch to his ensemble.

The competition progressed to the weight toss, which involved throwing a sixteen- to twenty-five-pound weight dangling from a chain attached to a metal handle. She could easily imagine a group of bored Scots standing in a field hundreds of years ago challenging one another to throw various objects. The simplicity of the events and playground quality of the smack talk lent a fun vibe that carried through the crowd.

Again, Alasdair overperformed. After the last man took

his turn, Izzy met Dr. Jameson at the table he'd set up on the edge of the field. "What are the standings?" she asked.

"MacGregor was in the lead, but he tripped on the weight toss. Not quite sure what happened. That leaves Alasdair Blackmoor as the current leader with Holt a close second." Dr. Jameson didn't meet her eyes.

"I don't believe it." She snatched the e-tablet Dr. Jameson used to track the scores and scrolled through. "Alasdair isn't embarrassing himself, but he should be in the middle of the pack at best. The distances the other men are putting up are frankly pathetic. What happened last night?"

Dr. Jameson's gaze dropped to his feet, skidded toward the woods, and finally settled on something over her shoulder. "The boys had a bit too much fun last night."

"The boys always have too much fun at the whisky tasting, and they always pull it together to compete the next day. I want the truth."

"I know nothing." Dr. Jameson's denial was weak at best. "Sheaf toss is next. I need to confirm the height."

Dr. Jameson scurried to the far end where rigging was being set up to lift an adjustable bar. After the caber toss, the sheaf toss was the most archaic of the events. Competitors would use an actual "storm the castle" pitchfork to toss a sixteen- to twenty-pound bag of hay or straw over the bar.

Performing a quick turn around the festival grounds to identify potential fires and put them out, Izzy circled to flank the competitor section of the field, hoping to catch Holt by himself.

He was busy giving Alasdair tips in tossing a sheaf. How could the two have become so chummy overnight? She waited, making sure to stay out of their line of sight until she caught Holt's eye and gestured him over.

In spite of his good-natured grin, he looked like he'd

been hung out to dry. His eyes were shadowed and blood-shot, and he retained the faint aroma of whisky. "Hey, Dizzy Izzy."

The hated nickname had stopped bothering her. Was that a result of tougher skin or the shedding her adolescence skin? "Can you tell me what in Hades is going on?"

"Can I? Yes. Will I? Absolutely not."

"How come you and Alasdair are all of a sudden besties?"

"We bonded over hair-care products." Holt rubbed a hand over his short blond hair and winked.

"You look like crap, by the way. How much did you guys drink last night?"

"Enough to bury the hatchet. And not in anyone's back either." His grin slipped into a quizzical quirk of the lips. "Listen, whatever happens, I hope you know that I'll always be your friend. Just a friend, I promise. But, if you need to talk or whatever, I'm here."

While she couldn't imagine laying out her confusion and heartache for Holt Pierson to clumsily pick through like bolls of cotton, the sentiment touched her. "Thanks, Holt. I appreciate that. I have a favor to ask."

"Anything."

"Make sure Alasdair doesn't get injured in the caber toss, will you? It's the one event he wasn't able to practice."

"I'll do my best, but it's man against tree out there when the time comes." The wrinkle of worry between his brows in turn worried her. He gave her a two-fingered wave over his head as he jogged back to the milling men.

Izzy could only throw up her hands and wonder at men and their machinations. She wasn't an idiot. It was clear now that Alasdair was going for Laird of the Games, and Holt was helping him and even cheering him on. Was Alasdair trying to prove something to himself or to her?

Alasdair's muscles screamed. *Why are you doing this to me?* lamented his biceps. *What have I ever done to you?* cried his quads. He lay spread-eagle in the grass, too sore and hungover and exhausted to even scratch his sweaty, itchy beard.

Holt blocked the sun, and Alasdair was grateful for small favors. "Do you want to practice the sheaf toss a couple more times?"

"My head says yes; my arms have mutinied."

"Save your strength for one good toss then." Holt lay down and propped himself up on his elbows, his ankles crossed. "Izzy cornered me."

Alasdair squinted. "Obviously, she wanted to know how I am anywhere near the lead."

"Among other things." The sun glinted off of Holt's hair and the stubble along his jaw. He was so quintessentially all-American he should be handing out baseballs and apple pies to foreigners as they alighted from airplanes.

"Did you mention how my amazing athletic prowess burgeoned overnight?" Alasdair asked.

"She's no dummy. She didn't ask outright, but she suspects you're getting some inside help. I don't think she understands why though."

"Isn't it obvious it's for her?"

"It's not exactly a straight-line correlation between winning Laird of the Games and a declaration of your intentions."

"A grand gesture made sense last night."

Holt chuckled. "Everything makes sense after that much whisky. Hell, Andrew thought he'd cracked the mysteries of time travel."

The amount of whisky he'd pickled himself in last

night had been an embarrassment, but the other men had matched him drink for drink. It was no surprise when the number of competitors had shrunk the next morning. Alasdair had woken up feeling like his mouth had been stuffed with decaying cotton balls.

"If I was sticking around, no doubt, we'd all become mates," Alasdair said.

Holt pushed up and waved a hand around. "I thought the point of this farce was for you and Izzy to live happily ever after in Highland."

Alasdair hadn't thought beyond getting Isabel to forgive him. The future loomed indistinct, but it was starting to come into focus. Unfortunately, it was Cairndow's towers taking shape and not the woods or flowers of Stonehaven. He didn't know what that meant for him and Isabel.

"Blackmoor! You're up!" Dr. Jameson's stood at the ready.

Saved from having to answer Holt, but sentenced to compete, Alasdair staggered to his feet. His shirt was sweat-stained and ripped at the shoulder seam. His knees had dirt and grass stuck to them and one of his socks had lost its elastic and refused to stay up. He eyed the caber laying to the side of the field and dread squat in his stomach.

Even if he managed to fork the sheaf over the bar, he wasn't sure whether he could even lift the caber at this point. But, dammit, he would try. Not only for Isabel, but because a connection to his ancestors grew like roots in fertile ground, and he wanted more.

Alasdair took up a pitchfork and rammed it into the burlap-wrapped sheaf of hay. He had three tries to get the blasted thing over the bar. While it was only twenty pounds, it registered twice that by his sore back and arms.

Swinging the fork for momentum, he released too soon and the sheaf went straight up with a good height, but not over the bar. His next attempt was better but still missed the mark. If he didn't make the toss, then he would get a zero for the event and his chances of winning the overall title would be nil.

Holt watched him along with two of the other men who had promised to help the night before. Alasdair rammed the forks home again.

"You've got the forks too deep. Get it more on top." One of the men said in a Southern accent so thick, Alasdair had a difficult time deciphering his instructions.

Alasdair glanced over at them and saw Holt nod. He worked the forks out and slid the forks higher and gripped the shaft.

The other man said, "Take a wider grip on the handle."

Alasdair slid one hand close to the forks and the other near the end. "Better?"

"That'll do. Now swing at least half a dozen times and fling her over. You can do it."

Alasdair couldn't help but smile a little at their encouragement. He did as he was told, building up an explosive energy in his body, and flung the sheaf with a guttural yell. It sailed up and over the bar with inches to spare.

Alasdair heaved in a breath of the thick, humid air and made his way over to Holt and the other men for pats on the back and congratulations.

Holt was last to compete and he put very little effort in his failure to reach the bar. When he returned to Alasdair's side, he said, "Caber is next."

"I appreciate your help. You've been a good friend." He offered Holt his hand.

Holt barked a laugh, but took Alasdair's hand in a shake. "That's what I am: a good friend. It's what I've always been. Especially to women. Friend-zoned. Why is that, do you think?"

Alasdair shook his head at a loss. "Familiarity maybe? You and Isabel have known each other since kindergarten, right? Maybe you need to meet someone new."

"Easier said than done in Highland."

An announcement came over a loudspeaker encouraging everyone to gather for the caber toss. Alasdair would have preferred no witnesses, but a sea of humanity gathered behind the ropes.

"You're on your own for the caber toss." Holt slapped him on the back. "As long as you manage to turn it, you should lock up Laird of the Games."

The contestants gathered around Dr. Jameson, who explained the rules. Alasdair would have to lift the caber, make a run, and flip it end over end. The goal was to keep the caber in the straight twelve-o'clock position. Points were deducted accordingly the farther away from twelve it landed.

A slightly hysterical laugh snuck out of Alasdair. They would have to run—bloody well *run*—whilst balancing the trunk of a tree in their arms. It was wild and dangerous and crazy. In other words, the perfect sport to represent Scotland.

Even knowing failure was probable, Alasdair studied the technique of the men who went before him. Faces turned red and sweaty with effort. Arm and leg muscles bulged. Four men didn't successfully turn the caber. One limped off the field holding his hamstring. Another sprained his ankle and had to be helped off by Dr. Jameson.

Had anyone died due to caber impalement? Alasdair mused all the ways he could get hurt and came up with twenty on the long walk onto the field for his attempt. Was the effort worth it?

The nerve endings on the back of his neck tingled. Was that impending doom he sensed? His gaze darted to the sideline. Isabel watched him. She looked adorable in blue trainers and a skirt, her hair pulled back with wisps escaping to frame her face. No matter how hot it was or how hard she'd been working, she looked fresh and alluring. It took a tremendous amount of willpower not to crawl to her and beg forgiveness.

Two helpers stood the ready, balancing the caber with the heavy end resting on the ground. He knew what to do, but didn't know if he could do it. Alasdair didn't care where it landed. He would be happy if it turned at all.

He shook out his arms in an attempt to shed his nerves. Taking several huffing breaths to get himself pumped up, he hugged the caber and linked his hands, ratcheting himself downward until he cupped the end and lifted.

The muscles of his back and arms screamed even louder, but somehow he straightened with the weight of the caber resting on his right shoulder. Like a pendulum, he was driven back two steps. A collective gasp went through the crowd. He dug his boots in and reversed the momentum. To keep balance, he shuffled forward in mincing steps that grew into strides and finally an awkward jog.

Letting out a great guttural sound, he heaved the caber. Something in his left shoulder wrenched and white-hot agony speared through his arm and upper back. He went to his knees and grabbed his upper arm.

The caber wobbled on its end, its destination in question. It might fall back toward him, in which case, he should probably move, but pain held him immobile. The caber knocking him senseless might be a blessing.

A breeze ruffled his hair, cooling the sweat on his neck. As if nature had given the caber a push, it toppled and landed like the hand of a clock at noon. The crowd erupted in cheers. A sense of relief and accomplishment did little to dull the pain in his shoulder. Now that he had no adrenaline left, exhaustion swamped him. He fell to the grass and closed his eyes against the sun, pinpricks of light dotting his vision behind his eyelids.

His mission wasn't yet complete. He had to talk to Isabel. Desperation and futility battled. He should have trusted her long before now, just as Gareth should have trusted Rose.

"I'm a fool," he muttered to himself.

"Not a fool. Just foolish." A shadow loomed over him and a sugared feminine voice coaxed his eyes open. Isabel was on her knees at his side, her face hovering over his, her expression equal parts worried and mad. "Why did you put yourself through this?"

"Because if I won Laird of the Games, you would at least have to award me the prize and I could throw myself at your feet and beg your forgiveness. That moment will make all of this worth it."

Her lips compressed before she asked in a gentler voice, "How badly are you hurt?"

"Not as bad as I hurt you last night." He thread the fingers from his uninjured arm through the fine hairs that had escaped at her nape. "I'm sorry, Isabel. You can't understand how much. Gareth is family, and I was ready to do whatever it took to protect him. I had no idea how special you would become to me or what was going to happen between us. If I had, I would—"

She kissed him. Not a sexy, sensual kiss, but a shut-up kiss with maybe even a hint of forgiveness.

"I'm not going to sugarcoat it; I was pissed last night. Punch-you-in-the-face, kick-you-in-the-nuts pissed." Anger had left its mark like a barely healed cut in her voice.

"Unless this is some kind of weird foreplay, I assume you're not going to kick me while I'm already down." He tried for a smile, but everything around his shoulder, including his heart, ached.

"You were torn between loyalty to a beloved uncle and

me," she whispered, her lips brushing his, this time with a definite flavor of forgiveness. "Honestly, if I'd had the resources, I would have done the same thing to protect Mom."

He wanted to pull her down with him and lay in the field together until the sun went down and the crickets serenaded them. A woman's voice called out, "Get it, girl!" A few whoops followed.

Color exploded in her cheeks like a sunburst. "Can you get up or should I call Dr. Jameson over?"

"I can walk." His voice reflected more confidence than he actually felt. He sat up, his head swimming. Tentatively, he rotated his shoulder. The stabbing pain had dissipated to a throb. "Give me a hand?"

They clasped hands and she hauled him to his feet. He staggered into her, draping his arm across her shoulders, more from the need to feel her close than for support.

Dr. Jameson set his tablet down and met them at the sideline. "A perfect caber toss, my boy. Sit and let me look at that shoulder."

Alasdair sat. "I thought you were a veterinarian."

"And what is man but a social animal?" Dr. Jameson adjusted his glasses. "That was a butchered quote by Aristotle, by the way. Alright, tell me where it hurts."

Alasdair communicated in ouches as Dr. Jameson probed his shoulder.

Finally, Dr. Jameson squeezed his arm and smiled. "I don't think you've torn anything. My suggestion is ice, rest, and ibuprofen. It looks like you've locked up Laird of the Games with that caber toss, by the way."

Alasdair laughed sheepishly. "I had a little help from my . . . well, friends."

The tentative bonds he'd made over the course of the last decade seemed gossamer while over his short stint in Highland, he'd formed attachments with Kevlar-like strength.

Isabel thread her fingers through his. Their connection was the only one that mattered. "Come on, Highlander. I'll get you fixed up."

He followed her like a sheep over a cliff, but she bypassed the first-aid tent set up by the side of the vendors and led him to Stonehaven's front door. Unlocking it, they stepped into cool air and blessed silence. An oasis from the chaos.

While she readied an ice pack and retrieved the medicine, he was afraid to blink in case she disappeared. What if he had passed out in the field and was dreaming this. "You've forgiven me so easily?"

"Mom and I talked this morning. You're lucky she's mature and wise. Unlike me." She tossed him an inscrutable look over her shoulder. "You didn't lie about the important stuff, did you?"

"Never about how I felt. Feel." He swallowed the pills she pressed into his hand with a sip of the iced tea. "Gareth was going to confess the truth to your mother about his lineage and responsibilities as soon as the festival ended, which meant I could tell you."

"And Wellington?"

"I truly thought I could neutralize the situation before it affected you and Rose and Stonehaven." He paused. "I quit last night. Rather epically if my memory can be trusted."

She fiddled with the lid of the medicine bottle, her gaze down. "What happens now? Are you going home after the festival like you planned?"

"That depends."

"On what?" She darted a look under her lashes at him.

"On you. On what Rose and Gareth decide."

She heaved a sigh and when she finally met his gaze straight on, tears glistening. "Mom said they are geographically challenged and nothing can change that."

"What if I told you I had an idea? A wild and crazy idea."

A spark of hope had her leaning closer to him. "I'd say, bring it on, Highlander."

Chapter Eighteen

Izzy thrummed with nerves and excitement at Alasdair's wild and crazy idea. While it might solve their geographic problems, it was a huge step and one she wasn't sure any of them were ready for. An announcement of the ribbons being awarded for the athletic events came over the loudspeaker.

"Come on, we've got to get out there." While she wanted nothing more than to lead him upstairs, build a pillow fort, and hide inside—preferably naked—she was in the thick of the festival and had responsibilities.

Hand in hand they approached the stage where the athletes and the crowd had gathered. Her mom stood behind a small table covered in ribbons and welcomed everyone, her voice distorted by the sound system. Usually, Izzy announced and her mom bestowed, but her mom made no move to relinquish the microphone.

When it came time to award Alasdair the ribbon for Laird of the Games, whistles and yells erupted from other competitors. Pats on the back and handshakes slowed Alasdair's progress to the stage. He and Holt even exchanged a bro hug.

Alasdair dropped his chin in an "aw shucks" way, but

his slight smile was puckish. He stepped close and spoke as if in a confessional. "I never would have made it up here without the blokes' help, especially Holt."

"I knew as soon as Mom said you were at the top, something shady was going on." She pressed the prize to his chest. It was round and blue and trailed a dozen or more ribbons which fluttered in the slight breeze.

"My whisky-impaired brain thought winning your favor through feats of strength would be a good idea. If I had known it would only take hurting myself, I would have dropped the weight on my head this morning."

"You are silly." She tilted her face toward his. "Are you ready for your kiss?"

He obligingly presented his cheek, but Izzy took his face between her hands, and kissed him square on the mouth. The crowd faded into white noise. It wasn't a sexy or intimate kiss, but it was firm and punctuated the promise knitting itself together between them. They broke apart. Only a second had passed, but everything was different.

He retreated to stand at the foot of the stage, and she understood he was waiting for her. He would always wait for her.

The last event of the evening was a performance by the Scunners, a Scottish band that fused traditional Scottish music with rock beats. The lead singer, a petite woman with short hair dyed platinum, bounded onto the stage. Her mom looped her arm through Izzy's and pulled her to a relatively secluded area at the back of the stage.

"You and Alasdair have made nice." Her mom's tone and expression were a study in contrasts; happy and sad, scared and content.

"Have you talked to Gareth yet?"

Her gaze darted over Izzy's shoulder and sharpened. "Not yet, but he's been trailing me all afternoon, waiting to pounce."

"Waiting to throw himself at your feet and beg forgiveness, you mean?"

Her mom spoke so softly Izzy had to lean closer. "The sooner we talk, the sooner it will all be over."

"You don't know that. In fact, before you and Gareth talk, the four of us have something to discuss. Come on." Izzy shushed the argument her mom tried to launch.

She pulled her mom out of the shadows and to the stairs leading off the stage. As she knew he would be, Alasdair was at the bottom and smiled up at her. Gareth was at his side, looking worried and uncomfortable.

"Let's go to the house for a few minutes of privacy," Izzy said.

"We can't leave, Izzy. What if something happens?" Her mom looked anywhere but at Gareth, who had fixed a stare of longing on her mom that was both pathetic and sweet.

"The festival is not going to descend into chaos in fifteen minutes, but to put your mind at ease, I'll call Dr. Jameson to let him know we'll be occupied for a bit and ask him to cover for us."

Off-duty policemen were hired to keep the festival attendees corralled and to make sure none misbehaved in the woods or in the shadows of the house. The concert brought out a wilder set than attended the earlier events, but it would be over before full darkness fell. She waved at the officers they crossed paths with and continued on.

The tense silence that greeted them in the house was like the seconds between when the pin on a grenade is pulled and the explosion. Izzy slipped her hand into Alasdair's and faced her mom and Gareth. "You two need to talk—alone—but before you do, Alasdair has an idea that affects all of us."

"Well, speak up, laddie?" Gareth asked after it was clear Alasdair didn't know how to begin.

"Cairndow," Alasdair said simply.

"What about it?"

"It was my favorite place in the world. You were—*are*—very important to me, Uncle Gareth." Alasdair took a deep breath. "And I want you to be happy."

"I'll settle in again when I get home." The starkness in Gareth's voice wasn't lost on anyone.

"You and Rose care for each other. A pile of stones, neither here nor in Scotland, should come between you. If you had no responsibilities in Scotland, would you choose to leave or stay in Highland with Rose?"

Gareth sucked in a deep breath and turned to her mom, reaching for her hands. "I would choose Rosie in a heartbeat."

Alasdair stood as a preacher did during a wedding, and Izzy supposed her mom and Gareth were making a sort of vow to each other. "And would you, Rose, leave Highland to be with Gareth if you had no responsibilities to Stonehaven?"

When her mom cut a glance in Izzy's direction, Izzy said, "Don't make me part of your choice, Mom."

Her mom heaved a sigh that was more resigned than happy. "I would choose Gareth."

"As you all know, I'm out of a job." Alasdair's smile helped diffuse some of the tension. "And, someday, hopefully many, many years from now, I'll inherit the title and Cairndow from Gareth. I propose that I take over the management of Cairndow now."

Gareth muttered a string of Gaelic before shaking his head. "Are you mad?"

"Quite possibly. But there's more." Alasdair tugged Izzy and tucked her under his good shoulder.

Izzy lifted her chin and smiled at her mom. "Alasdair has invited me to Cairndow."

"For how long?" Confusion and shock ran rampant over her mom's face.

Izzy forced herself not to glance uncertainly at Alasdair. "Hopefully, for a long, long time, but we'll see what happens. I can maybe find the magic I've been missing and write my masterpiece there. Plus, my accounting background and experience running the festival will be put to good use at Cairndow."

Touching her mom's arm, she added, "Even if things work out, I'll come back every summer to help with the festival. Although . . ." She cast a meaningful glance at Gareth.

Gareth straightened his kilt and his spine. "If Alasdair is manning Cairndow, I would be free to offer my assistance to you, Rosie. My heart too, if you'll have it."

"You'd be free," her mom said with wonder in her voice.

"I'd be free." Gareth's grin made his eyes twinkle.

Her mom's expression lost its joy as she turned to Izzy. "Is this truly what you want? Scotland is a long way."

A pang that felt suspiciously like homesickness made Izzy feel light-headed. How was it possible to miss something she hadn't left yet?

"I'll miss Stonehaven and Highland and you terribly, but I'll be back to visit. Alasdair has been the greatest adventure of my life, and I'm not ready for it to end."

"It's exactly what I always wanted for you." Her mom's eyes sparkled with tears even as she smiled and swept Izzy into a hug that smelled of cotton candy and cut grass. She smelled like the Highland festival. Izzy closed her eyes and took a deep breath, tucking away the memory for later when she was far away and missing home.

When her mom pulled away, both of them were wiping tears away with laughter. Sending a look under her lashes in Gareth's direction, her mom said, "If you two will excuse us, Gareth *Blackmoor* and I have a few more issues to hash out."

Gareth turned the color of a July tomato. "Rosie, I'm so incredibly sorry I misrepresented myself, but all the important bits were true, I swear."

Alasdair and Izzy retreated while her mom made an insinuating comment about Gareth's *important bits*.

They slipped out the front door, but when Izzy would have made her way back toward the music, Alasdair pulled her into the shadows of the evergreens at the side of the house. The sharp scent was comforting and fresh.

"I need to make sure havoc is not being wreaked." Izzy's protest was weak at best and she wrapped her arms around his neck.

"How are you feeling?" He nuzzled her nose.

How well he understood her second-guessing, doubting nature. "I'm ecstatic for Mom and Gareth."

"What about your decision to accompany me back to Cairndow? You can remain at Stonehaven with your mom and Gareth, you know."

She leaned back a little but didn't release her grip on him. "Are you trying to talk me out of coming home with you?"

"I want to make sure you're coming for you—for us—and not just to give your mom and Gareth space." Tension thrummed through him, waiting for her answer.

Alasdair had invested his heart in her decision. His vulnerability took her out by the knees, and she pitched into him, kissing him with all the wildness and passion she'd kept at bay on the stage earlier.

"Hey there now! Break it up!" A booming voice cut them apart. "Terribly sorry, Izzy. I thought you were a couple of teenagers sneaking off."

Izzy's laugh was carefree. She grabbed Alasdair's hand and skirted the periphery of the mass of people enjoying the concert. The air was cooling, and while her feet hurt and she couldn't wait to take a shower and climb in bed, she was happy and excited.

Her gaze kept darting to Alasdair as if he might disappear.

"Have I grown two noses?" he asked.

"Nope. Still have the one that's been bonked twice in as many weeks. You might as well resign yourself to getting it broken before year's end." Her tease turned a bit more serious. "How's your shoulder?"

He rotated it. "Sore, but better."

A woman stood alone at the edge of the field, her blonde hair appearing white in the setting sun. "Isn't that your mom?"

"Yes, and you need a proper introduction." He changed their direction.

Izzy wanted to dig her heels in. She had made a terrible impression the night before, and Alasdair's mom seemed the type to value appearances. With her free hand, she smoothed her frazzled hair back and tugged at her T-shirt.

"She probably thinks I'm a harridan after last night," Izzy said.

"Mum can be intimidating, but she wants what's best for me. You are best for me. Therefore, she will welcome you with open arms." His reassuring words were working until he added the caveat, "Eventually."

Izzy muttered some choice words that made Alasdair smile.

"Mum," Alasdair said as they drew closer. Izzy dropped his hand and stood to the side.

Fiona turned with a gasp and took Alasdair's arms, looking him up and down. "Are you alright? I looked everywhere for you, then you disappeared after you received your ribbon."

"Dr. Jameson doesn't think I did any permanent damage."

"Dr. Jameson is a veterinarian, and you are not a dog," Fiona said slowly as if Alasdair had taken a knock on the head.

Alasdair turned and drew Izzy forward. "Last night was a bit of a mess, but Isabel and I have hashed things out."

Fiona transferred her cutting blue gaze to Izzy. "Lovely to meet you once more under more promising circumstances, dear."

Izzy pasted on a smile and held a hand out for a shake, hoping it wasn't sweaty with nerves. "Nice to see you again too, Mrs. Blackmoor."

"Call me Fiona, please." While her voice was aloof, it wasn't antagonistic, which Izzy counted as a win.

"Mum, we've made tentative plans." Alasdair spoke as if he expected an argument.

"Are you staying in Highland?" Lines bracketed Fiona's mouth.

"Actually, Isabel and I are going to manage Cairndow while Uncle Gareth remains in Highland with Isabel's mother." Alasdair's body grew taut against hers.

"Well." Fiona narrowed her eyes and looked toward the stage where the plaintive notes of a bagpipe faded into an eruption of applause and whistles. When she turned back to them, she'd composed her face into the facsimile of a smile. "That seems a neat solution. You always did love Cairndow."

"It's strange but since I've been in Highland, I feel like Cairndow is calling me home," Alasdair said.

Fiona's smiled eased into warmth and she patted his cheek. "You're a Blackmoor. How could it be any other way? You've already got the look of a wild Scot. Is that why you grew the beard?"

Alasdair rubbed his hand over his jaw. "No. Maybe? Perhaps it was my subconscious giving me a shove in the right direction."

"I haven't been to Cairndow since . . ." Fiona shook her head, but shadows remained in her eyes.

"You'll come visit once Alasdair and I are settled in, won't you?" Izzy wasn't sure what prompted the urgency of the invitation. Perhaps the tentativeness Fiona projected when it came to Alasdair and Cairndow.

Fiona took one of Alasdair's hands and one of Izzy's. "While I wouldn't have paired Alasdair with an American, you seem entirely capable of handling my son and Cairndow and the expectations that will fall to you as Countess of Cairndow if you are married."

The shock of hearing the M-word along with a title attached to her made her heart beat like it had been kicked. "Countess? Are you kidding me?"

Fiona's laugh was amused and incredulous. "Alasdair will one day be the tenth Earl of Cairndow. Did it never cross your mind you would be a countess?"

"Not for a second." Izzy couldn't wrap her head around the notion. "I mean, we haven't discussed marriage. It's too soon. We're still getting to know each other. Even though we're compatible in—"

One of Fiona's perfect brows twitched higher, and Izzy covered her mouth to keep from embarrassing herself further in front of this elegant, proper creature who was Alasdair's mother.

Izzy's phone buzzed with a text. Dr. Jameson needed help closing out the ticket counter. She waggled her phone. "I've been neglecting my duties. Please plan on staying with us at Stonehaven, Fiona. You guys go relax with some wine."

She exchanged a brief kiss with Alasdair then ran as if escaping a chain gang toward the crowd of people.

Even though she was tired, her senses had sharpened, taking in the sights and smells and sounds of the festival. If things with Alasdair didn't work out the way she hoped or even if they did, she would be a different person by next year's festival. She was excited and scared and ready to leap into the unknown.

It was after midnight when Isabel crawled into bed after a quick shower and heaved a sigh. Alasdair had fought his own exhaustion to wait for her. "Everything okay?"

"A successful first day in the books, and we're well prepared for tomorrow. Did your mom settle in?" she asked with a yawn.

"She's next door in my old room, so no funny business," Alasdair teased.

"As if I have the energy to do more than just lie here. Although, if you're still in your kilt . . ." She raised her head and checked under the covers. "How disappointing."

"My entire wardrobe will be made of kilts as soon as we get home." Alasdair smiled in the dark.

"Home." The seriousness of Isabel's tone shifted the mood. "It's strange to think Stonehaven will no longer be my home."

"Stonehaven will always be your home, Isabel." He groped for her hand and raised it to his lips. "But I hope you'll come to appreciate Cairndow."

"As long as you're there, I have no doubt I will. I want to invite everyone for a visit. Our mothers, of course, but also Dr. Jameson and Anna and even Holt."

"That sounds wonderful." He measured his next words. "I told Mum about Lewis. I'm tired of keeping secrets."

Isabel turned to her side to face him. "What did she say?"

"She was hurt, but not devastated. I don't know if she'll ever want to meet Lewis, but she understands why I want to have a relationship with my half-brother."

"I'm sad for her. She went through so much with your father."

"I think—hope—she's past it all now. After all, she's got a boyfriend." It was still hard to say the word in connection with his mum. "And, while I'm not sure she'll ever stop meddling in my life, she seems content with my choices of late. You, included."

"She actually said that?"

He chuckled. "Not in so many words, but it's inferred by the fact she's still here."

"Great," Isabel said sarcastically before snuggling into his side. "Will you tell me about Cairndow?"

He did, and as he spoke of the cliffs and moors and the castle, a feeling of surety settled over him like the warmest of blankets. He'd found his path and person he wanted to share it with. He wasn't sure when she fell asleep, but a snuffle interrupted him.

Kissing her temple, he nosed into her hair and wondered how his fate and fortunes had tangled with hers so completely in such a short amount of time. He fell asleep and dreamed he chased Isabel along the cliffs of Cairndow under blue skies, but this time, he caught her and would never let her go.

Epilogue

SIX MONTHS LATER

Iain Connors parked his old Land Rover in front of the main entrance of Cairndow. January was colder than a sheep's teat on the moors, and he pulled the collar of his wool-lined jacket tighter around his neck, but the chill wind found a way to invade every crack and crevice left unprotected.

Blustery snow stuck to his eyelashes on the short walk around to the kitchens. It was habit to bypass the formal entrance for the warmth pumped out by the AGA cooker kept busy baking bread to sell in the village.

Since Alasdair and Isabel had taken over the management from Gareth, changes were afoot. Changes Iain found both refreshing and disturbing. Even though he had no formal claim on Cairndow, Iain had been raised in the shadow of the castle. The grounds and moors had been his home through all the seasons, not just summers and the occasional school holiday like Alasdair.

His da, Dugan, was content as the Cairndow grounds-keeper, and it was understood Iain would take over after his da retired, which would never happen voluntarily. Iain expected his da would signal his retirement by keeling over one day in the flower beds.

Iain wasn't even sure he wanted the job. Yes, the stark beauty of the moors and cliffs and ocean fed his soul, but there was more to heaven and earth than Cairndow. As a second lieutenent in the 19th Regiment Royal Artillery, Iain had seen more than he'd ever dreamed of as a boy at Cairndow. He'd seen great beauty and extreme ugliness in people and places, and struggled to resolve the existence of both in the world.

After his discharge, he'd spent the autumn in Glasgow working construction. The physically exhausting job helped defuse the thoughts and memories that plagued him, but the echo of Cairndow had called him home. The serenity and peace he searched for remained elusive. Nothing ever happened in the middle of winter at Cairndow, yet a sense of anticipation had kept him wired. The quiet chafed instead of calmed.

It was this restlessness he fought as he entered the castle and stole a scone from the cooling rack, scooting out of the way of Mrs. MacDonald's flapping hands with a wicked laugh.

"Och, you're a fair delight in the kitchen, Mrs. Mac." He gave her a wink.

"Get on with yourself, boy. Flattery will get you no-where with me." Except, she grinned, pleased as punch and tossed him another scone.

Mrs. Mac was as close to a mother as Iain had ever had, and he dropped a kiss on her papery, flour-dusted cheek on his way to meet with Alasdair in the castle's library.

Taking the stone steps two at a time, he emerged into a tunnel-like hallway. The thick rug underfoot had been worn down the middle by years of footsteps. He ducked his head under the low doorframe to enter the library. At six foot four, Iain had been made bigger and wider than whatever earl had built the castle.

The library was a large room with walls lined with

books both ancient and modern. A fire burned in the fireplace, but the heat didn't reach him, and he chose to keep his jacket on. A desk was positioned away from the drafty windows and had been commandeered by Isabel. Not only was she a dab hand at keeping the books, but she was a writer. And quite an entertaining one based on the pages she'd allowed him to read.

Usually sunny and funny, Isabel slumped in one of the cushy armchairs, clutching a tissue while Alasdair knelt on the floor at her feet, rubbing her arms and whispering. Obviously something had happened that required Alasdair's deft touch at encouragement or commiseration.

Alasdair had had to learn to navigate tricky emotional waters at a young age, and Iain had always admired his ability to smooth feathers and charm his way into good graces. Iain had been raised among men, minus Mrs. Mac, and didn't possess the faintest inkling on how to translate a woman's body language. He'd been told he was a right large son of a bitch more than once by the fairer sex.

And forget about a woman's tears. If they were real and not the manipulative sort (which again he had problems telling apart), they had the power to bring him to his knees, which is why he avoided crying women at all cost.

Alasdair looked up and crossed gazes with Iain. With every day that passed, Alasdair reminded Iain more and more of Gareth from the shaggy black hair to the trimmed beard he maintained.

"I'll come back this evening, Alasdair, and let you . . ." Iain cleared his throat and made a vague gesture with his hand.

Alasdair stood and Isabel turned in her chair, her eyes red-rimmed. Surprisingly, it was Isabel who spoke. "Now is perfect, Iain."

"But you're upset and I . . ." *have no idea what to do or where to look*, he wanted to say.

Isabel blew her nose, the sound like the call of the geese in the fall, and stood, offering him a smile. "I probably look like a giant chigger, don't I?"

He had no clue what a chigger was but assumed it would not do to agree. "No, of course, you don't."

Her smile grew wider, which seemed all wrong with her tear-swollen eyes. "You don't even know what a chigger is, I bet."

Had Isabel decided she couldn't survive a Scottish winter? She wouldn't be the first to abandon Cairndow. Iain's own mum had taken off the winter after he had been born and had never come back. Iain often wondered if it had been him or the weather that had driven her daft.

Iain had never seen Alasdair so enamored of a woman before, and they'd pursued many a village girl during their youth. It would break his friend's heart if Isabel deserted him.

"Winter can be a mite harsh, but spring will knock your knickers off it's so lovely, you can be sure of that." Iain stole a glance at Alasdair to try to determine the right path forward to soothe Isabel.

"Alasdair's told me how lovely it is and I can't wait to see the heather bloom." Emotion got the better of her once more and she pulled another tissue from the box on the side table, pressing it to her nose.

While Iain was relieved to hear she would still be around come spring, he was confused as to his presence in so obviously a trying moment. While he and Isabel got on well, their talks had centered on books and innovations planned for the grounds and gardens of Cairndow.

Alasdair and Isabel exchanged a long glance. Alasdair cleared his throat, obviously uncomfortable.

A suspicion sprouted. While he considered Cairndow his home and Gareth had made him feel as welcome as family, perhaps things were different with Alasdair and Isabel. "Are you working up the courage to fire me? I realize my return to Cairndow was impetuous, but—"

"No!" Alasdair barked on a laugh that contained no mirth. He ran a hand through his hair and said, "Quite the opposite. We're in need of a favor. A rather large one, I'm afraid."

The tension that had drawn Iain's shoulders toward his ears dissipated. While he might not want to stay at Cairndow forever, he had no desire to head back to Glasgow to find mindless work in the middle of winter either.

"Name it." Although, their friendship had been of childhood, those summer months had brought Iain a brother in Alasdair, and he wasn't wont to forget such loyalties, no matter how many years had passed.

"I'm pregnant." The news burst out of Isabel accompanied by a tear-marred smile.

"Congratulations?" Iain lilted, not sure whether the news was welcome or not.

"I'm not quite sure how it happened," Alasdair said with an air of bemusement.

"If you need it explained to you, mate, then I'd say that's your problem." Iain raised his brows, but didn't smile.

"Very funny. I meant that it wasn't planned. Mum is going to flip out."

Iain gave a soft whistle. "That she will. You two might want to marry over the old anvil before she catches wind of your happy news."

"I'm not sure what will be worse for her; not being able to plan a big wedding or seeing her future daughter-in-law walk down the aisle pregnant." Alasdair huffed a small laugh.

"Ach. Who cares what she thinks as long as the two

of you are happy about it. Although, based on the tears, I can't tell myself."

Isabel's familiar, lighthearted laugh settled Iain's nerves. "We are happy. And shocked. And scared. Don't mind the waterworks. It's the hormones. Brace yourself, because according to the internet, it gets worse."

"It'll be good to see children running around the castle again. Alasdair and I had good fun playing chase and hide-and-seek."

Alasdair's smile was broad and full of memories. "We were hellions according to Mrs. Mac."

"No fun in acting like angels, now is there?" Iain and Alasdair exchanged grins full of fond memories.

"I'm sure the castle is going to be a wonderful place for a child. Minus the stone stairs and the priceless paintings and frigid drafts, but I digress." Isabel paced in between Iain and Alasdair. "I did the math."

"Well, you are an accountant," Iain said with a touch of dry humor.

"If my calculations are right, I'm due in July." She stopped and faced him, emotion wobbling her chin.

Iain had no idea why she was so upset. "Excellent timing, I'd say. You wouldn't want to be snowed inside Cairndow when the time came. Da is the only one with any birthing experience and that's with ewes."

"The timing couldn't be worse, Iain. We had planned to return to Highland in July to help Uncle Gareth and Rose with the festival," Alasdair said.

Understanding dawned as to Isabel's emotional state. He supposed a lass would want her mother around at such a time. "You won't be able to travel to the States."

"And Mom will be in the throes of planning and won't be able to come here." A tear made an escape from the corner of Isabel's eye. She didn't wipe it away, and Iain found himself staring at the track with a longing to scuttle out the door. "Unless . . ." Isabel fluttered her tear-spiked lashes at him.

"Unless?" Iain was ready to donate an organ to stop Isabel's tears.

"Unless we send someone we can trust to Highland to help plan the festival so Rose and Gareth can be here for the birth," Alasdair said with a pointed look at Iain.

"Me." Now it was Iain's turn to be shocked.

"You." Alasdair held up his hands in supplication. "I realize it's a big ask and will upend your plans, but—"

"I'll go." Though Iain wasn't one to overthink things or second-guess himself, he surprised himself with his decisive answer.

"Are you sure?" Alasdair asked.

"I'm sure. Never been to the States. Highland is in the southern bit, isn't it?"

"Yes. Georgia." Alasdair smoothed a hand down his beard in a gesture Iain had seen Gareth perform a thousand times. "I'll warn you, it's quite a change from Scotland. For one thing, it's as hot as the blazes of hell in July."

Isabel choked a laugh out and slapped Alasdair's arm. "It's not that bad. Highland is close to the mountains. Granted, not mountains like Scotland. Okay, if I'm being totally honest, it's hot in summer. Take lots of shorts. Or kilts. Or whatever gets you the best air circulation."

Alasdair's smile cracked the worry plastering his brow into furrows. "You don't know what a load off this is, mate."

Isabel did not wear the same relief. "Mostly likely, the timing will work out where Mom can be in Cairndow for the birth and in Highland for the festival. But if not . . . Mom and Gareth will have everything planned, and I have a friend in Highland who will help as well. Anna Maitland has been part of the festival since she could walk."

Iain shrugged. "I don't need help. I've run events on

the grounds here, and I was in charge of men in the regiment."

"This is an order of magnitude bigger than anything Cairndow has hosted. And dealing with the vendors and performers takes some finesse." Alasdair clapped him on the shoulder. "You'll be grateful for the help if it comes down to it."

Iain didn't argue, but he wouldn't require the services of Anna Maitland or anyone else. Not only was he Scottish and had grown up attending the traditional games in the actual Highlands, not a tourist destination putting on a show, but he was a solider used to organization and the chain of command. He was good at giving orders and expected them to be followed.

"We can count on you?" Alasdair asked.

Iain extended his hand for a shake. His da had taught him many things; how to fix anything, how to build whatever he could envision from wood, how to coax plants and flowers to grow in harsh terrain, how to appreciate a sunrise and sunset, but mostly loyalty and honor and strength.

"Always."